WHAT SARA SAW

WHAT SARA SAW

Stephen Geez

Roanoke

WHAT SARA SAW

Fresh Ink Group
An Imprint of:
The Fresh Ink Group, LLC
PO Box 525
Roanoke, TX 76262
Email: info@FreshInkGroup.com
www.FreshInkGroup.com

Edition 1.1	1999
Edition 2.0	2004
Edition 3.0	2011
Edition 3.1	2016

Book design by Ann E. Stewart

Cover design by Stephen Geez

Cover art by Anik

Cataloging-in-Publication Recommendations: General Fiction;
Literary Fiction; Art Studies (Fiction); Religion (Fiction);
Buddhism (Fiction); Relationships (Fiction);
Childhood (Fiction); Trauma Recovery (Fiction);
San Francisco, CA (Fiction); Coon Rapids, Iowa (Fiction);
Laurel, Mississippi (Fiction)

Library of Congress Control Number: 2011922300

ISBN-13: 978-1-936442-03-4

For Karen Carrino,
Her too-brief life and enduring art
And to Deborah Carrino,
For sharing her sister's legacy in
The Spirit of Children
This story is not about them,
But rather how they inspired me to imagine another

Acknowledgements

Thanks to the following visionary souls:

Team Leader: Ann E. Stewart, Managing Director, The Fresh Ink Group, LLC

Production Team: Anik

Research Team: Susan Stewart

Content Team: Lucas Cale, Beem Weeks, Mark Allen North

Support Team: Kent D. Casey, Lucas Cale, Todd Tessin, Marshall Shearer MD, Jean Buchanan, Lendia Buchanan, Dillard Greenwell

Member Team: All of *you* who discover Geez books and shorts, then subscribe to the newsletter for updates and free stories at www.FreshInkGroup.com. It keeps us going when you buy our books and spread the good word.

CHAPTER 1

The boy looked back.

Of all the artwork in this gallery, the paintings and drawings reflecting absent artists' vicarious pleas for recognition, only one had the audacity to look back at Geoffrey Drousseau:

The pencil sketch of a small boy.

Geoffrey paused to study the image, but its subject persisted with the annoying characteristic of appearing to watch its own audience.

Distracted and even somewhat aggravated by such blatant provocation, Geoffrey glanced away, then turned to consider other pieces in this collection, many the products of considerable talent, most doomed to be treated as decorative commodities judged primarily by how well they might match new furniture from some home-furnishings mega-warehouse clearance sale, choice of vibrating recliner included free. Geoffrey's eyes roved quickly, his fleeting attentions focused largely on nebulous points just beyond the canvases, for to linger too long before any particular piece would acknowledge that an artist had somehow affected him, tacit admission he could even be bothered with such irrelevance.

Then the boy called to him, a simple song amid the silence.

And Geoffrey decided to give the sketch one last look before moving on once and for all, lest the very effort of ignoring it require more attention than a mere pencil drawing deserved.

The boy appeared to be five or six years old. His eyes, admittedly disarming, impressed Geoffrey as somehow animated and quite expressive. His silky hair hung in jagged bangs and feathered down over his ears, a look the artist succeeded in depicting as blond, though rendered in graphite and charcoal. Given the appearance of being nude, he stood in water at the edge of a country pond, pausing amid tall cattails and bent reeds strategically drawn for modesty. Glancing up from studying a doodlebug, the subject appeared to have just noticed someone watching him, yet he registered neither surprise nor alarm, seeming pleased by the attention, maybe even somehow reassured. His face looked serene, his eyes glinting with a hint of carefree mischief, the overall image one of innocence.

"He knows what you're thinking," she said. The young woman tending the gallery had eased up from behind.

"He couldn't possibly," Geoffrey returned without looking at her.

"It's true. That's why you came back to him. I've been watching as you wandered around staring at everything and looking at nothing. You're avoiding this boy because you sense his presence, and I think he even annoys you. Now you must discover what he sees when he looks back at you."

Turning to study her, Geoffrey found himself impressed by her elegant, lyrical face and hazel eyes that hinted at Asian ancestry, and by her long exquisite hair in hues of shaved cinnamon. Draped in a long, floral-print dress, she looked like one of those Korean-American valley girls.

"I am Phrekka," she offered, bowing slightly. "Phrekka Churán."

He sighed, now an unwitting participant in what he had most hoped to avoid: inane conversation. "I'm Geoffrey Drousseau," he traded. "You're full of crap, you know."

She allowed a knowing smile, tilting her head toward the sketch. "He does it to *me*, too."

"Does what?"

"Notices you. Pays attention. He's curious, and he can tell what you're thinking. He wants you to be happy, but when you're troubled—like you are today—that just makes him sad. He tries not to show it, though."

"You're reading way too much into this. It's just a drawing."

"Sometimes, when nobody else is here—" She leaned closer, her revelations too personal for the phantoms of this cavernous gallery to overhear. "He calls me over so we can ponder my worries; then he shows me how to see beyond them, to remember how it is to feel like he does." She nodded in confirmation, the truth revealed. Amen.

Geoffrey smirked, glancing back and forth between her and the image of this child. "Yeah, like *you* have any real worries," he scoffed. "You probably have a perfect life."

"That's not true—"

"Oh, come on, let me guess: you live rent-free with your parents, go to school on scholarship, work here part-time, have a rich boyfriend—"

"You're wrong," she asserted, "but that doesn't matter right now—you're the one who's frustrated, the one this boy is watching. Why are you—?"

"How am I wrong?" he persisted. "Look, I'll tell you why I'm upset if *you'll* be honest with *me*."

She took a deep breath, her eyes avoiding the sketch, maybe embarrassed but determined to accept his challenge. She fixed him with her gaze, then answered, "I *was* living with my mother, attending Pepperdine University at Malibu to pursue a degree in fine arts, hoping for a career that would allow me creative expression and opportunities to immerse myself in the noblest ideas and images from great minds;

but then Grandmamá grew increasingly ill, and I moved here to Sausalito to help care for her. She started getting better, but that changed and there was nothing either of us could do, and I lost her." She hesitated, her voice faltering, then looked down at her hands, instruments rendered ineffectual in her time of greatest need.

"I'm sorry," he offered, his sentiments suddenly sincere. "So why don't you move back home and return to school?"

"I can't. Mother is married to a parasite, a drunkard who thinks whatever's mine is his, one who decided he could also have me, and who made it clear that what I might not freely give, he would be forced to take. I can't even visit anymore. Pepperdine is lost to the past. Forward is the direction I move. I live here now, on my own." She looked at him, an expression not unlike the boy's in the drawing, quiet resolution in her eyes. "Now tell me *your* frustrations," she urged softly. "You may think they're secret, and you may hide them from yourself, but he already knows—" She tilted her head toward the sketch without looking away from Geoffrey's face, promising, "And I won't tell a soul."

Geoffrey wanted to turn and walk away, but she had called his bluff, rising to his challenge, leaving him no honorable way to back out. Fixing his gaze on the drawing, he snapped, "Okay, here's how it is: my girlfriend's packing up and moving out right now so she can be gone before I get home from work, but I don't work anymore because I just got fired, which is why I'm standing here killing time. I got fed up with my boss and blew off the job I moved to California for in the first place." He mimicked her bow. So there.

She disarmed him with a gentle smile. "No wonder he was so curious about you. He senses a kind of perplexity he's never felt."

"It's nothing more than a very good drawing," Geoffrey said quietly, a deliberate attempt to bring an element of reality back to this conversation.

"He looks just like you."

"I don't think so."

"You have the same face, the same silky blond hair, the same eyes."

The boy in the sketch did look rather prime-time hit-show cute. Geoffrey liked to consider himself fairly handsome, too, and maybe he did sort of favor a grown-up version of this child standing amid cattails and reeds, the background a glass pond reflecting wildflowers and trees and birds . . . "Who's the artist?"

"Her name is Sara, and that's all we know about her," she answered, showing him where the name appeared hidden among stones and leaves in the lower corner. "This piece came to the gallery from a woman who bought it many years ago at a tag sale. Did you know any Saras when you were growing up?"

"I lived in dirt-farm Iowa, nowhere near any ponds like this, and I could name ev-erybody within twenty-five miles. Never knew any Saras."

She looked disappointed. "How old are you?"

"Twenty."

"Same as me," she said, sounding pleased. "This boy looks about six, I think."

"That's not what I used to look like," Geoffrey pronounced, case closed.

She tilted her head, regarding him for a moment, then shrugged. "You need to buy him, take him home," she said hopefully.

He chuckled. "How much is it?" He didn't want to buy this picture; he was just curious.

"Twelve-hundred."

"For a tag-sale drawing?!"

"I'm sorry if his price exceeds your means." She looked sad.

"I could afford it," he said defensively, "if I wanted to—but twelve-hundred for a pencil sketch?"

"For the pencil sketch of a boy who made you surrender your own troubles long enough to notice him, of a boy who knows what you're thinking—even if you don't . . . Of this boy who looked back."

"So you want me to take it home," he scoffed, "and put it on my wall—just so it can stare at me all day? It's nothing more than a simple drawing of an arrogant little smart aleck."

"But that's not him you're describing. Maybe it's what you insist on seeing; maybe it's what you're afraid he's seen in you."

Geoffrey snorted rudely. "I could hang it up *facing* the wall. That would teach this brat not to stare at people."

"Yes! I like that idea," she sparred, her eyes twinkling. "And you could wait until you're ready, until that very moment when you're willing to see what he sees, then take a chance, be the big brave man, and finally turn him around, this simple drawing of a boy who makes you so angry."

Geoffrey made another noise and shook his head, exasperated not by the sketch, but by her patronizing attitude. He'd admitted frustration over the losses of his girlfriend and job, yet she persisted in playing these mind games, amusing herself at his expense, plying him with mystical platitudes both silly and insulting. Still, though, he regarded her as quite beautiful, very sensual, her delicate features mysteriously alluring, the fragrance of her shimmering hair rather inviting. "You mean when I'm willing to tell him my problems," he said, now playing the game her way, this dance of the minds a necessary prelude, hopefully, to increasingly intimate conversation—especially the wordless kind.

"No," she said sadly. "You don't get it—and you must not want to. This boy is too innocent to understand such complex issues. Don't you see?—he simply knows how they make you *feel*, your essence revealed, your layers of self-protection stripped away."

"It sees all that, huh?"

"Look at him," she challenged, "even if all you catch is a fleeting glimpse." She touched his hand. "Just look," she urged quietly.

He stared at the image, but found himself distracted by an awareness of her watching him. Then she looked toward the drawing, too, and Geoffrey felt free for the moment, floating unfettered before this two-dimensional vision from some artist who spied an innocent child playing naked among his cattails, portrayed by a woman named Sara who wanted to share with others what she'd seen, what she'd felt. Why did it seem like the boy looked back? Why did Phrekka believe this depiction could possibly have any sentient interest in some strange man who stomped blindly through a gallery while his lover abandoned him, an agonizing interlude before drifting home to wrap himself in the familiar walls of his apartment.

The drawing's eyes sparkled. This boy had never known loneliness, had never worried, had cherished all things unashamedly . . .

Geoffrey's shoulders tensed, then relaxed again as he took a deep breath. It seemed like he'd captured a glimmer of something, but it disappeared, and he couldn't be sure what it was, if anything. "You just want to make a sale," he said quietly, taking the offense in his own defense, "—to make a commission."

"I'd rather sell you anything else in the gallery." She spoke the truth; that much he believed. "I don't want to see him go, but I think you need him more. Maybe he needs you—I don't know, but you'll never leave him behind, whether you buy him, whether you consign him to face the wall, he's yours, own him or not."

"Then if I buy this sketch, will you come to my place to see it again sometime?"

She smiled, bowing gracefully. "Thank you for such a generous invitation, but I'm not sure if I should."

"You can trust me," he said earnestly, trying not to sound like it mattered—though it did, much to his surprise. He wanted her to come and see for herself, to discover the real Geoffrey, not just what she thought this drawing could tell her about him. "You can trust me," he repeated softly, also speaking the truth.

She shook her head. "You're too frustrated, too anxious right now. I'm not comfortable, and you're too—" She fell silent, the potential for offense best left unoffensive.

"You think I'm too hard-headed to read something surreal into this kid," he shot back, suddenly angry at himself for acting as if it mattered.

"But you did see something. Only, you kept it to yourself. Share it with me, if you can. Take your time and look again. Don't try to see it all, just something, anything. Then tell me what that is."

Geoffrey took a deep breath. He could still play along, no risk in that. She did look incredibly beautiful, and his girlfriend was moving out, and he hated to spend nights alone . . .

And the boy looked back.

Geoffrey could sense the child's serenity, if only for an instant. "He loves somebody," he said quietly. It reflected in the boy's eyes—that much he could admit. He'd given the easy answer.

"With all his heart," she whispered, now touching Geoffrey's arm. "Someone who embodies his whole world."

"He feels, I don't know . . . safe," he added, also whispering now.

"Everybody wants that feeling, but most forget what it's like."

Geoffrey studied the setting, the cattails, the wildflowers and trees and birds reflecting in the water, poignant counterpoint to this innocent lad communing *au naturel.* Then he noticed more detail, a delicate butterfly, the caterpillar grazing a curled leaf, a fuzzy bumblebee, the tiniest birds' nest swaying in the branches . . . "He really likes where he is."

"It's wonderful," she agreed.

"And he thinks he already has everything he could ever possibly want."

"I believe I might have felt like that once," she said wistfully. "It's difficult to remember."

"There's something about his eyes," Geoffrey said, studying the boy's face carefully.

"Yes, and it's more than how he looks right at you. There's something else, too, but I haven't figured it out."

"If you'll come over tonight, maybe we could try together."

"Come visit me here again first. Now that I've made a sale, I can afford to stay at least a few more weeks." Her hazel eyes sparkled delightfully.

"I will," he promised.

They looked upon the sketch for several minutes, the silky-blond boy watching from amid his cattails at the edge of an idyllic pond, his sanctuary replete with everything a child of innocence could possibly want, an enchanted world where he feels safe and content.

Geoffrey sighed. "I wonder who it is he loves."

* * *

"Thanks for covering, Miss Churán," Marva gushed, hurrying into the gallery. A heavyset, middle-aged woman in chiffon, she had accented her ensemble with bracelets and brooch, her silver-brunette hair swept into a swirl, casual yet elegant. "Where is he?! You sold him?"

Phrekka nodded absently as she entered the credit-card transaction into the sales log.

"Did you actually get four-thousand dollars?"

Phrekka smiled knowingly. "No, I quoted only twelve-hundred." She jotted the customer's name and address on a separate slip of paper, folding it into her pocket.

"But you had me tell that woman—"

"I didn't want *her* to have him. He needed to go to the right person."

Marva accepted the log, carefully arranging it in the desk drawer. "Just between you and me, even twelve-hundred's probably a lot more than its market worth."

"I would've given it for free, if need be. I just wanted to make sure the buyer appreciated its value, and would treat our boy with the respect he deserves."

"Sometimes the true value of a work of art far exceeds the highest buyer's bid," Marva mused, straightening items on the desk.

"And oftentimes our expectations are shaped by the price we hear, thus influencing our own assessment of what we see."

"And then the price goes up even more," Marva concluded, a gleam in her eye.

Phrekka lingered a moment, glancing around the gallery at her remarkable collection, some pieces more extraordinary than others, all divulging stories of deception or truth. "By the way, he thinks I work here, and he'll probably come back to see me. Watch for a handsome young guy with silky blond hair who looks a lot like the boy in the sketch. If he shows up, say I'm on a break, then call me discreetly, if you would." She turned to leave.

"I will, Miss Churán. I'm curious, though—I assumed you were keeping that piece for yourself."

Phrekka smiled, one hand on the door, the glass dancing with reflections of luminous late-afternoon sunshine dappling the waters of Golden Gate's Richardson Bay. "I was—until I discovered its rightful owner. Geoffrey and that boy have a lot in common. They both want—they both need—the same things."

"The same what?"

Phrekka opened the door and found her world transformed to a mosaic of translucent shimmers in the blinding glare. "I'm not sure," she answered, "and neither is Geoffrey . . . but the boy knows."

CHAPTER 2

Geoffrey was nine years old the winter he built a birdhouse. Everybody knew him as Geoffrey Calhoun back then, the Calhoun boy, only child of Ernest B. and Marjorie Calhoun of Coon Rapids, Iowa.

Diminutive and frail, taciturn by choice, timorous by default, little Geoffrey tended to sneak off by himself to read stories of adventure and heroics, out of sight and out of mind to avoid his stern father, a sturdy and righteous Christian who farmed corn by day and toiled at the Des Moines River Concrete Works by night. Geoffrey eventually gave up trying to earn his father's approval, realizing that to attract any attention risked punishment, for nothing about this boy ever seemed to be regarded as acceptable. He most feared the "lessons," those grotesque displays of correction and discipline meted out by Ernest, the wayward child as protégé, his Father as preceptor and spiritual protector whose primary commandment was that every waking moment shall be devoted to precisely what God expects of us, nothing more, nothing less.

The idea of a birdhouse came from Billy Marloney, a schoolmate Geoffrey's age who lived a half-mile closer to town. Billy and his father had built one the year before and, mounting it on a light pole adjacent to their silo, succeeded in enticing a pair of bluebirds to nest. Geoffrey grew excited at the idea of attracting some for himself, of watching how they would protect their eggs and nurture their hatchlings and teach their precious offspring to fly, a devoted family grateful for his creation. Maybe they would understand his affection for them and become his friends, returning every year with their children and grandchildren and great-grandchildren, and Geoffrey would build even more birdhouses and protect and care for them all.

Of course Ernest disapproved, those pesky birds a nuisance, Geoffrey's frivolous scheme an idle waste of time and otherwise useful materials. But Marjorie Calhoun finally interceded, pausing from her romance novel du jour just long enough to sip tepid coffee and argue his case between stubbing out one cigarette and lighting the next. "Leave the boy be. He'll use his own money and work on it after his chores. Maybe we'll get to see some baby birds." And with that she returned to her book, transported again to a world where the young and beautiful Charlotte, consumed by the ache of loneliness, dreamed of a day when Lance would sweep her off to a villa on the Mediterranean to run naked in the surf and make love under the moonlit sky, where surrendering to unbridled passion is the expected thing to do, nothing more, nothing less.

After much scrounging, a trip to the hardware, and countless painstaking hours in the tool shed each evening after Ernest left for work, Geoffrey managed to create a flawed but serviceable birdhouse featuring an ornate cornice along the roofline and stout perch in the front, painted light blue and coated liberally with varnish. He carried it out by the silo that night, enshrouded by wisps of fog skulking across the muddy slush-patterned fields, moist and clammy air portending the arrival of spring and giving notice for the birds to begin considering their nesting sites; then he carefully climbed the extension ladder and proudly attached it with baling wire high atop the pole. Over the coming days he settled in to watch and wait, ignored by his mother, admonished by his father, but otherwise undaunted and resolute, eagerly anticipating some bluebirds or maybe a family of swallows or thrushes.

As the weeks passed, with Billy Marloney often bragging about his bluebirds returning to their nest, the mother now sitting her eggs, none seemed willing to establish residence in Geoffrey's birdhouse. He grew increasingly despondent, angry at his failure, frustrated over the flaw in design or execution that rendered his effort worthless, his father victorious. Geoffrey had wasted his time and his money with idle pursuits, all to no avail.

But then it happened. He spied some wrens flying in and out. Soon they started bringing bits of twig and grass and debris scavenged from around the farm. Thrilled and proud, Geoffrey boasted to the Marloney boy, then to his own mother who, pausing to sip her coffee and light another cigarette, glanced from her romance novel long enough to wonder, "Of course, what did you expect?"

But as suddenly as Geoffrey's new friends started to move in, they abandoned their home with its cornice and perch, leaving their nest unfinished, their plans for a future on the Calhoun farm unfulfilled. Geoffrey continued his vigil until finally he spied a blue jay flying sorties to steal the abandoned nesting material. Distraught over this blatant theft and symbol of still further rejection, he dragged the ladder from the shed, propped it against the pole, and climbed with a hammer hooked in the waistband of his faded jeans. Only the very last sprigs remained inside the deserted house, scant evidence that any had ever considered moving into this home created by Geoffrey Calhoun with his own hands. The blue jay perched on the eaves of the silo, cawing a warning for the intruder to move away, mocking the boy's incompetence. His frustration unbearable, half-blinded by tears, Geoffrey hammered and smashed at the house, slamming again and again until it fell to the ground in splinters and shards, only the baling wire remaining as proof he had ever been foolish enough to try.

The birds obviously had never needed or wanted any part of Geoffrey . . .

Nor did he need those ungrateful birds.

Geoffrey Drousseau climbed the stairs to his apartment, gingerly maneuvering his framed sketch wrapped in brown paper and tied with stout twine. Returning early, he hoped to intercept Melanie before she could finish moving her belongings out, his last chance to convince her to stay. Palpable silence greeted him, the rooms sounding hollow and deserted, punctuated only by the *tick-tick* of his clock and the hum of his freezer's ice-maker. Several of Melanie's boxes stood before him, neatly stacked by the entranceway, these last sprigs the only remaining evidence of her brief dalliance and subsequent desertion of the home that Geoffrey built.

He set the covered drawing on his dining-area table, propping it against the wall, then opened the blinds to reveal his balcony overlooking the rolling hills east of Mill Valley, his narrow slice of view showcasing the cerulean waters of Richardson Bay. He'd carefully chosen this unit for the prestige of its vista, and for its comfortable spaciousness, two full bathrooms, walk-in closets, substantial kitchen, the kind of open and airy place a young woman would like to share. Soon after furnishing his new home, he'd started dating Melanie, the auburn-haired waitress at a seafood restaurant near his new job in Sausalito. Now, only three increasingly tumultuous weeks after moving in, she was leaving.

He heard the sound of a key; then Melanie entered, her friend Donna right behind. The women stopped, surprised to find him there.

"Melanie, can we talk about this?"

She shook her head, sadness in her eyes, gently massaging the back of her neck as she looked away.

Donna hefted a box and retreated down the steps.

"Look," he assuaged, "I've decided it's okay if you want to keep working. I mean it—if it's that important to you." He moved closer, but she stiffened, the barriers he'd sensed these past few weeks now fortified by new resolve, by an alternative option, by yet another potential route of escape.

"You wouldn't be satisfied." She studied him. "You don't want to share me with other people."

"It's not that—it's just that I don't understand why you wear that demeaning uniform and let yourself be ogled all day. I can support us. I have enough money—"

"*Your* money. I need money of my own, too. I have to be able to support *myself.* I moved in here so I could have more freedom, but you don't want me to have *any.*" Angry now, she shook her head again, then reached for the last box.

He pulled it away from her. "I just worry about you—"

"No, you don't trust me. You don't trust anybody. Just give me my things and let me go," she demanded, reaching again, her composure dissolving.

He stepped back. "But there's a lot of dangerous people—"

"I can take care of myself!" she fairly shouted. "See? You always have to be in charge—just like my father."

"I was trying too hard," he explained, but she snatched the parcel away from him, turning to leave. "I'm sorry. Please forgive me—"

But she was gone, his extra set of door keys—the set he'd made for the lover who would share his home—dropped unceremoniously to the floor at his feet . . .

Scant proof anyone had ever considered moving into Geoffrey's life, the last sprigs.

"Who is responsible for this?!" Ernest B. Calhoun had demanded, fury in his eyes, brows arched in rage. Clutching pieces of the broken birdhouse, he shook them at the sky.

The skinny blond boy cowered from the towering man, his head bowed, his eyes brimming with tears. "I broke it," little Geoffrey answered meekly.

"Why is this? Why is this?"

"The birds didn't want to live in it." Geoffrey breathed hard, his heart pounding, trying not to tremble. He must not appear guilty or ashamed.

"I warned you against such foolishness, did I not? Did I not?"

"It was my money. I built it," he protested, mustering all his courage. "It was mine."

"If you did not want to keep this birdhouse, you could have sold it at Stockmoore's. Instead, now it is waste. God would not approve." The big man stepped closer. "Do you hear me? God would *not* approve!"

"It was mine!" he blurted out as Ernest grabbed him by the arm and shook him.

"Your senseless tantrum has offended our Lord!" He forced the whimpering boy to the floor. "On your knees! You will pray for his forgiveness. What we make with our hands, what we grow from the soil, it is all for the glory of our Savior. It is not ours to waste."

"Please, God," little Geoffrey sobbed, "I'm sorry. Please forgive me!"

Geoffrey watched from the balcony as Melanie and her friend drove away. He stomped around the apartment, fighting the urge to destroy something, anything, whatever she had left behind . . . But no, he couldn't allow that release, wouldn't dare lose control. There was nobody present who might condemn such an outburst, but Geoffrey would disapprove, and so much failure in the face of his convictions might scare him, rendering him afraid even of himself. Nobody could take charge of him anymore, not even his ex-boss at the graphics-design firm, because Geoffrey controlled his own destiny, and he would conduct himself with the respect he deserved.

The apartment fell quiet again, the clock ticking, the ice-maker humming. Geoffrey sat on the couch and collected his thoughts. He turned on the television, fixing his gaze at some point just beyond the screen, seeing faces that couldn't or wouldn't look back. He felt lonesome, but sensed that perhaps he was not entirely alone. That two-by-three-foot framed sketch, wrapped in brown paper and tied with stout twine, sat quietly waiting.

Geoffrey rummaged through the stack of newspapers he'd purchased, sorting through want ads. He circled a dozen or more, then reconsidered and highlighted a select few before losing interest so quickly he left the marker uncapped.

Tomorrow. Tomorrow he would seek employment in earnest. Tonight nothing seemed right, and he had nobody with whom to commiserate. He would try to put aside his feelings for now, thus avoiding futile self-confrontation in favor of sublime escape.

He climbed into bed, reclined against pillows and cushions, and tried to read the latest installment of his favorite novel series, yet another tale about that shy young gazillionaire who seeks out people in need of help, accompanied by a mystical lady-friend on quests to understand and unleash his mysterious powers, a man loved by his friends as much as he loves them.

But Geoffrey couldn't concentrate, couldn't focus his attention or muster his comprehension, and the funny parts didn't seem very funny, and the sad parts were too sad, and he couldn't feel good about what the hero and his friends might accomplish or learn . . .

Because it felt like somebody lingered in the other room, silently waiting.

Confused by this odd sensation, frustrated with his uneasiness, Geoffrey found himself drawn to the dining area, a tableau eerily lit by the glow of his clock, prisms of neighborhood light refracting through the balcony doors. He gently unwrapped the picture of a boy pausing among his cattails and reeds, gingerly propping it back against the wall. He eased himself into one of the chairs, careful not to disturb those very same phantoms who eavesdropped while Phrekka whispered her secrets, and sat gazing at the sketch. He sighed, shook his head, and even half-smiled at himself, looking at this boy who looked back, this child who had invited himself into Geoffrey's home and brought with him a pond and some flowers and a bird's nest swaying in the limbs, steadfastly refusing even to dress for the occasion.

It was just a drawing, and Geoffrey even considered turning it to the wall, but that seemed somehow disrespectful. This child never deserved such harsh treatment. This child wouldn't understand the rage of a grown man directed at a helpless soul who wants only to be accepted, to be loved, to earn approval for simply being himself.

After some time, Geoffrey grew weary, then very sleepy, so he left the boy there and returned to his bed, lying in the darkness and feeling not so much alone anymore.

He wondered if somebody used to tuck that boy into his bed each night, if they hugged him, maybe reading him stories until he drifted into a dreamworld of wonder and bliss.

Geoffrey had yearned for that feeling all his life, but so far it eluded him. He tried to achieve a sense of contentment with Melanie, but he never understood how, and she never seemed willing to help him learn. He made room for her in his life, but she had no room for him in hers.

If nothing else, he had offered her a spacious and comfortable home, the kind of place a young woman should want to share.

The design seemed perfect, so the flaw must have been his execution.

Little Geoffrey had been banished to his room. He hated his father, this man who loved God but not his own son.

Ernest finally left for his job at the concrete works, so it would be safe for Geoffrey to creep out of his room. He dressed in pajamas, then found his mother curled on the couch in a cloud of blue-gray smoke, reading yet another romance novel, swilling her tepid coffee, the long ashes of her cigarette crooked and ready to drop.

"What was that about?" she asked absently, getting up to rinse and refill her mug.

"I smashed my birdhouse," little Geoffrey answered.

She ignored him, adding sugar and powdered cream to the brew before returning to take up her place on the couch, lighting another cigarette.

"I'm ready for bed," Geoffrey said.

"I guess you shouldn't have done that," she said, referring to the birdhouse, her fleet attention catching up, if only for an instant.

"But it was mine," he protested. "It was *my* money, and I built it for *me*."

She looked across the top of her book, studying him for a second, puzzled. "But I thought you built it for the birds."

CHAPTER 3

Phrekka Churán was nine years old the first time they permitted her to summer with Grandmamá. Her mother had finally coaxed a suitably prominent man to the altar, trading in the role of well-to-do widow to become the socialite wife of a wealthy industrialist.

Phrekka feigned disappointment at being sent away, but she secretly found relief in escaping this man who always ignored her, pleased for the opportunity to learn more about her mysterious grandmother with the beautiful hazel eyes.

Grandmamá had settled into the Sausalito house after Grandpapá died, a beautiful mansion at the top of a long zigzag drive protected by an ornate iron gate, an enchanted castle wrapped in decks and balconies overlooking Richardson Bay and the Golden Gate, across Alcatraz to the San Francisco peninsula, even boasting a partial view of the mist-shrouded majestic bridge. The interior exemplified distinctive elegance, appointed with the finest furnishings, decorated in classical European and Asian styles enhanced by an astounding art collection that overflowed to Grandmamá's gallery down at the waterfront, her window to kindred souls who shared her appreciation for creative beauty.

Phrekka divided her spare time between visiting the gallery, exploring the shops along surrounding avenues, and conducting expeditions through the mansion's many rooms, thrilling at the discovery of Grandmamá's exquisite treasures, each with its own story of deception or truth. At these moments she could glimpse into the soul of this gentle woman who had given the gifts of life and love to Phrekka's father, the man whose legacy would be a little girl he never lived to know.

During one such exploration, Phrekka discovered her father's room just as a teenage boy would have left it, clothing and collections, books and magazines and cassette tapes . . . She tried to envision him living there, reconciling the photos she'd studied so many times with the tangible, physical world around her, imagining for a moment she could sense him, gather in his scent, hear him breathing softly as he slept, feel his strong arms and pretend he was rocking her to sleep . . .

But that could never be. That boy, that man, he seemed no more real for once having lived in this room than he appeared in those photos that stared blankly from the album tucked in the bottom of her mother's drawer.

Even by age nine, Phrekka sensed that her mother had married him for his money and social standing, and she began to resist the woman's every effort to pass along her shallow values: that learning is but a means to glib conversation, that etiquette exists merely for impressing others, that material wealth confers respect and prestige. Even after Grandmamá's passing left Phrekka remarkably affluent, with more money and houses and cars than anyone could ever enjoy, she most cherished her gallery and the ongoing metamorphosis of its collection as a means to discover everyday people who truly appreciate art. Studiously avoiding any association with the beau monde, she affected a public image pointedly more austere, a mask from those who would judge her for what she owns rather than who she is.

Instead, she would devote her attentions to introspection, to seeking self-understanding and inner peace; and to exploring the rhythms of her physical embodiment, buffeted as much by the forces of the moon and the stars as are the tides and the winds and the rains; and to expanding her mind, discovering her unique awareness and lovingly embracing her own spark in the great conflagration that is humanity; and to enhancing her spiritual self, to achieving a sense of the eternal, conjoining with the fabric of life in its every manifestation; and to forging even the most tenuous bond with the man she never knew, the boy who had lived in this room. Now she dwelled here, waiting for the father who would never come, enveloped by sadness and a sense of loss, realizing that what she wanted was a connection she would never feel.

Standing there among her father's things, she found herself drawn to the strangest sort of painting displayed over his desk, an abstract with patches of brown and green and yellow surrounding and partially obscuring a blocky, burnt-orange shape at the center; plus three squares in faint yellow, some odd circles and bars in faded blue, and several exuberant brush strokes in shades of gray near the lower corner.

"You have discovered your father's favorite, my sweet child," Grandmamá said quietly. Phrekka turned to see she'd been caught, the older woman's eyes glistening.

"What does it mean?"

"This was private for him, a secret he never shared. We would find him gazing upon it, sometimes for hours. If he felt sad, these colors and shapes could tease his smile, yet they might also reduce him to tears, at least once making him weep sadly for a very long time. At those times, he would close the door, and I would leave him be. Whatever my son was able to see, it remained a part of him—a part of your father."

Phrekka studied the painting, wondering what could evoke such passion, what power it must wield. Then, just for an instant, it seemed she could feel it, and she could feel her father. She discovered a glimmer of recognition, the possibility she might come to know him after all. She turned to her Grandmamá, but the older woman had left, maybe to be alone with her thoughts and to mourn the loss of her child, or maybe so Phrekka could discover what she may without distraction or translation.

She closed the door and sat on the bed, her eyes searching the mysterious image that seemed to have been waiting for her all these many years. She felt anxious, maybe a little scared, but inexorably drawn in. Then without effort or intent, those bold strokes of gray down by the lower corner inexplicably transformed into a lonely puppy, overwhelming Phrekka with the most profound melancholy, and she allowed herself to weep. She wondered if her father had seen that puppy, and if he loved it even as she did now. She reached out for his touch, this man she could never see. Then, for the first time in her young life, she realized the power of circumstance beyond choice or control, and that her father had never left her, but had been taken from her. She longed for assurance he had loved his baby girl, and in this enigmatic painting there existed a suggestion of hope that she might finally find it. This moment, this connection, this became her opportunity to believe, to strengthen her faith, and to love him back, no matter how far away he had gone.

And she could almost feel his strong arms around her, holding her tenderly, gently rocking her to sleep.

As she drifted into a dreamworld of wonder and bliss, she glanced one more time at the painting on the wall and whispered, "Daddy, what else did you see?"

"Oh, there you are, Miss Churán." The houselady found her sitting on the bed in her father's room. "It is the telephone—for you."

"Thank you, Miss Cilla." She nodded affectionately toward the older Korean woman who had been managing Grandmamá's house as long as Phrekka could remember.

"Not for some time have I seen you come in here. Shall I take a message?"

Phrekka allowed the hint of a smile. "Maybe it's been too long—no, I'll take the call."

Marva greeted her from the phone. "He was here—Geoffrey Drousseau. I informed him you would be away for thirty minutes. He indicated he would return."

Phrekka quickly dressed in one of her more austere outfits, brushed her hair, then hugged Miss Cilla before driving an electric golf cart through the twisted, sloping streets down toward the waterfront, entering from the rear in case Geoffrey loitered somewhere out front. She preceded him by scant seconds, positioning herself in time to admire the sunlight dancing highlights into his blond hair as he came through the door.

"Good morning, Mr. Drousseau." She bowed demurely, surprised at herself, maybe happier to see him than she had expected.

He smiled shyly. "If I apologize for yesterday, and request to further engage your expertise, will you agree to call me Goeffrey?"

"I will accept your apology if you'll tell me what you did wrong and likewise agree to call me Phrekka."

"I said you must come to my home in order to see the sketch of our boy in the pond, Phrekka. I've changed my mind."

"Oh?"

"I'm willing to bring him here to visit you."

From his smile, Phrekka knew his humor revealed the truth, that he really would bring the sketch if she so desired. "And of my expertise?"

"I would like you to help me find another Sara, hopefully of the same boy, but any Sara."

"I will make inquiries—discreetly, so as not to drive up the price."

"So when should I bring him by?" he teased.

"I *would* like to see our boy again," she said with a hint of tease in her voice, "but do you expect just to visit me here, or are you really asking me out?"

"You'd go out with me?" he said, looking genuinely surprised. "I didn't think—I mean—"

"Well, it depends on what you have in mind," she said before she could think better of it. Expecting to turn him down, she'd been caught off guard by his apparent lack of intention.

"I haven't lived out here long enough to know the cool spots."

"Is there someplace you've been wanting to see?" she said, her mouth running way ahead of her prudence and good sense.

"I drove over to Fisherman's Wharf once," he admitted, "but I was by myself and didn't want to sit alone to check out any of the restaurants." He arched his brows, daring her to be enthusiastic about such a touristy outing.

"Scoma's is my favorite," she sparred back. "You have to walk down this little alley behind some other buildings to find it."

"Since you know your way around, maybe you could point out some other things to do."

"It's the greatest city in the world," she said. "My favorite place is the Museum of Modern Art, that or the M. H. de Young. Both have fabulous collections."

"Wherever you like," he agreed. "I'm driving up to Santa Rosa to submit a résumé, but I'll be back this afternoon. Um, what time do you get off?"

"How's three o'clock? Pick me up here?"

"Right on time." He looked very pleased, nodding good-day back toward the desk where Marva pretended to glance through an art magazine. He hesitated as if resisting the impulse to touch Phrekka, then turned to leave.

"One question," she interrupted. "Did you make him face the wall?"

He paused, actually looking a bit hurt by the insinuation. Slowly, earnestly, he shook his head no, then disappeared into the sunshine, a shimmering flare of blond and gold.

"Marva," Phrekka said, still gazing into the street long after he'd gone. "I'd like to pretend I live with you so I have a place he can bring me home."

Marva smiled, flowing out to where Phrekka stood, taking her by the hands, tilting her head to study the younger woman. "Oh my, did I just hear Miss Churán agree to go out on a date?"

"I'm going to learn something from him," Phrekka admitted, surprised at herself. "I've never seen somebody so oblivious to art, yet so moved by a piece as he was by the drawing of that boy. I knew there was something about that sketch."

"I've said so myself."

Phrekka looked toward the street again, absently twirling a sun-kissed lock of hair. "He hasn't figured it out yet."

"No, not yet."

"I have a feeling he will."

"The San Francisco Museum of Modern Art," Grandmamá announced. "Would you like that?"

Young Phrekka nodded. Anywhere Grandmamá wanted to take her would be a treat. Phrekka dressed in her nicest pantsuit and adorned her long hair with pretty butterfly barrettes in preparation for her entrée to a very adult place, her comportment befitting a precocious and sophisticated child, her behavior precisely as the grown-ups would expect of her, nothing more, nothing less.

She found the excursion to be thrilling, the majestic museum imbued with a sense of the spiritual, filled everywhere with marvels in multiple dimensions, some tiny and delicate, discreet and understated, while others dared to be big and bold, loud and confident. Phrekka had never felt such sensations, such curious impressions coaxing emotions both familiar and new.

"I wonder how this would look if I were upside down," she mused absently in front of a particularly effervescent abstract.

"Then you shall be upside down," Grandmamá decided, a mischievous twinkle in her eyes. She found a curator who retrieved a velvet cushion and helped the little girl stand on her head, much to her surprise and delight.

Phrekka laughed and pronounced, "Everybody should have the chance to see it this way!"

The curator laughed, too, and promised, "We shall see if it can be arranged!"

Later, relaxing over teacakes and lemonade at a nearby café, Grandmamá asked, "Do you think you would like to discover and collect artwork someday, my sweet child?"

"I should think I would not be very good. I do not understand why or how these images affect me so."

"Ah," the elder said, "that is the secret. You see, an artist begins by creating what you see, but then she infuses it with a very special power, tapping the energy and essence of life to reach out and touch those who look upon the work."

"Then even if I am not to become a collector, I would still like to discover this energy."

"Yes, child, I understand." Grandmamá's gentle face shined as she gazed lovingly at the little girl enjoying her teacakes and lemonade. "I discover it more with every new piece."

Phrekka enjoyed her visit to Fisherman's Wharf with Geoffrey Drousseau. For an uncultured, naïve Midwestern fellow, he at least endeavored to carry himself with some degree of refinement, a mix of formality and barely concealed delight at such a picturesque setting and so many exotic flavors—chilled Dungeness crab with spiced mayonnaise his favorite. Though his fleeting hesitations belied a lack of confidence in his manners, his surreptitious glances to ascertain nuance—like which is the proper fork—made him seem more genuine, more endearing, more real. For a young man unpracticed in the minutiae of etiquette, he tried very hard to show his respect for her, thus proving that he considered her opinions about him very important.

Rather than speaking about themselves, they centered their discussion around the city, its history and diversity, reputation versus reality. It became clear that Geoffrey truly preferred not to visit the museum, nor would he be coaxed easily into viewing or commenting on any of the artistic esoterica at nearby places like Ghirardelli Square or even Pier 39. Much to Phrekka's relief, he appeared equally disinterested in the *Ripley's Believe It Or Not* museum.

They walked westward together, meandering their way around the piers and plazas, past the maritime museum, following a footpath along the rocky shoreline. The sun hung low in the swirling-misted sky, weeping brilliant hues in amber and orange, the great bridge glowing with a corona that painted its towers blood red. He seemed profoundly moved by the view, increasingly obsessed with finding the best place and the perfect angle at just the right time for optimum composition.

Finally, Geoffrey strayed from the path to climb out among the jagged rocks of a jetty, peering westward, his face the picture of wonder. He helped her climb out for a similar vantage point, holding her firmly yet tenderly. They sat among the sharp stones and watched. At that moment, the sun dipped just below the bridge's roadway and, splayed through wisps of distant clouds, fanned out into a flaming peacock's tail that filled the sky and reflected across the strait, a kaleidoscope of violets and reds and yellows all washed in a gauze of translucent, shimmering orange and gold, its radiance absorbing all trace of azure from the water as it danced forward and licked, like the lapping waves, at the rocks before them. A lone sailing yacht disappeared into the brilliance, slowly emerging scrubbed and renewed from the other side.

"If I could capture this on my computer," Geoffrey whispered, "I would remove those buildings and the people walking over there."

Phrekka took a deep breath, imagining how this might look on the wall of a photo gallery. "I would take all these ugly rocks away," she said, "so the water would come to the bottom of the photo."

"No," he disagreed. "No, you need the rocks. I might even add some."

"But they're so harsh and dirty—"

"But they make us safe. They're all that's between us and the edge of the world. You see, there's the span that crosses over, allowing scared people to pass safely; and there's the daring sailboat, chancing a cautious look, wary and careful not to go too far; and here are the rocks, piled high so the waves don't erode the shore, protecting us from the water and the water from us. But in the picture, these rocks are the barrier between us and the setting sun, its serpent's tongue reaching out to draw us in, closer and closer, until it's too late, and we can never come back . . ."

"Without the rocks," she whispered, "we might suffer the fate of Icarus." She wondered if this simple Midwestern man would understand the reference.

"Yes! Except that we'd float too close to the edge of the world, then fall into the sun, consumed and carried off by the light."

"How does an artist give his picture power, Grandmamá?" young Phrekka asked later that night, the wonders of the Museum of Modern Art still swirling her thoughts and casting them to scatter just beyond what can be seen or known.

Grandmamá put her arms around the delicate child and rocked her gently back and forth. "Ah, this then must be a secret. The artist must understand her audience, be they the whole world or one small child—or even if it is just herself for whom she creates. You see, most people are like mirrors, and in the presence of artistic power, they must reflect it away, never to see, never to know. Others are like obsidian, absorbing all color and sensation and keeping it close to their hearts, only for themselves, to share with no one. But the most interesting people, those with depth of soul and love for all essence of life, they are the artists who learn to embrace this power, then to enhance it, and to spread it anew to others. They can find beauty in the ordinary, excitement in the mundane, love where there is hate, joy to triumph over all pain."

"Wow," the small child whispered. "What are those people like, if not like mirrors or obsidian, Grandmamá?"

"Your grandpapá was one. He was my prism, capturing the powers of light and color, then sharing the splendor with those around him, showing us a new way to see each part of what is too bright for us to see all together, each new beam of light and hue imbued with a new power of its own."

The little girl felt enchanted, her eyes wide, her lips pursed. "How will I know who these people are, Grandmamá?"

The elder woman smiled, that same twinkle in her beautiful eyes; then she turned her granddaughter around and held her close, the girl's silky hair at her cheek, whispering in her ear, "Some you will know right away; others you must look very closely—but it's not with your eyes that you will see—"

"I won't see them?" she whispered back.

"Sweet Phrekka, when you discover one, you will feel him touch your very soul."

CHAPTER 4

The time had come for Phrekka to visit the boy.

Over the past week, Geoffrey Drousseau demonstrated pronounced tenacity in his attentions to the enigmatic Miss Churán, lingering with her for a time each day at the gallery, allowing her to study his varied reactions to the pieces on display, together discussing artists and artistry. He had resisted any temptation to make romantic overtures toward her, reluctant to risk her rebuff, preferring instead to nurture the slightest notion of potential, to preserve the promise of possibility.

This hesitation seemed new for Geoffrey, a young man usually prone to impatience in his pursuits of companionship. He cherished his tenuous bond with Phrekka too much to risk misguided attempts at making it more than it might become on its own. He learned this lesson during boyhood excursions to hunt quail. Too often there is only one chance, one shot, for upon revealing one's intent, objects of desire will scatter to the wind, and that briefest moment of opportunity will be transformed irrevocably into one either of consummate success or of forfeited expectation. Exploring without his gun one day, he had discovered that with patience and diligence he could slowly ease even closer, then simply watch the birds, sharing their world, and in this he achieved a sense of belonging which he came to appreciate more than any conquest. Now he valued simply spending time in the company of Phrekka too much to risk trying to make her his own.

Geoffrey and Phrekka planned to celebrate. She had located another sketch, one offered by a small gallery in the French Quarter of New Orleans, this find the result of considerable time and energy—and probably more of her patron's money than she cared to admit—scouring the catalogs and listings, posting bulletins for the galleries and auction houses, placing ads in periodicals, plus accessing numerous web and resource sites, all in search for any reference to this mysterious name, the unknown creator, a woman called Sara. Asking $400, the seller offered them an opportunity to consider a facsimile, but Phrekka suggested, and Geoffrey agreed, to make the purchase based solely on its description, to wait and view the piece in person, to savor their initial impressions unfettered, uninfluenced. The second sketch in Geoffrey's Sara collection would be the drawing of a young boy, maybe four or five years old, given the appearance of silky blond hair, lying on his rumpled bed in a deep and contented sleep, this time complete with a title, the words neatly penciled above the artist's name:

Sweet Dreams.

So to celebrate, Phrekka accepted Geoffrey's tentative invitation, agreeing to come as an afternoon guest to his apartment, to bring her suit for a leisurely swim, to relax for a time and visit the boy. He found her waiting in front of the co-op she shared with Marva, her light cotton dress flowing in hues of aquamarine and magenta, her eyes and cinnamon hair sparkling in the sunshine, an ornate satchel slung over her shoulder. Driving north toward Mill Valley, he enjoyed watching Phrekka's impromptu tour, her fascination with various points along the way—buildings and landscapes and even the people they passed—Geoffrey seeing for the first time so much of what he had never before noticed, shared observations from a new perspective.

"Very nice!" she reacted to his place, and this pleased Geoffrey very much.

He showed her his view from the balcony, surprised by how awkward he felt, admitting, "Um, the sketch—it's in my bedroom."

"I like that," she said. "Such an interesting choice. That must be where you are those times when you want to see him."

"Well, I usually don't pay it much attention, but when I'm tired and ready to read or relax, when the place is quiet . . ." He shrugged, looking at her sheepishly, reluctant to admit it, but hoping if anybody could understand, Phrekka would. "It seems like somebody else is here with me, but of course it's only him. So I wind up looking at him, and he looks at me . . ." He felt embarrassed, like maybe he shouldn't have tried to explain.

"You tell him good night, don't you?" She moved close to him.

"Yeah."

She sighed, seeming almost—relieved? "Oh good. I'm glad somebody does."

Prompted by her reaction, though still a bit self-conscious, he tried to explain how he'd come to feel about the sketch, a secret shared among trusted friends. "If I try to ignore him and just go to sleep, it seems like he's waiting for me to say it. It's like I don't want to hurt his feelings."

"Why, Geoffrey," she teased, "it's only a sketch." She reached out and gently touched his cheek. "But I like that you care."

"So do you want to see him?"

And there he stood, displayed prominently over Geoffrey's desk, the picture of contentment, this unadorned boy pausing amid his cattails, unfettered, uninfluenced.

And the boy looked back.

"It's like having a pet," Geoffrey said, smiling with self-mockery.

"More like the mirror from a fun house," she countered. "If you look closely, you can see yourself, but in that very act, you've been transformed."

"That's the risk we take," he added, more serious than he intended.

He offered her the desk chair, but she chose to sit beside him on the edge of the bed. They gazed upon the boy, his world now so familiar to Geoffrey, trees swaying in the breeze, the chirps and buzzing of the birds and the insects, the fragrance of flowers and pine pitch and rotting logs, all strokes and shades of charcoal that almost seemed, if one looked closer, to shimmer into vivid colors. More than just an indifferent boy, this cheeky lad had dared to share his special place, and Geoffrey almost believed there could be more, something else this child would offer him, to be accepted gratefully only when the time was right.

Phrekka asked him for his thoughts, and he considered trying to describe that feeling, but mere words would never suffice. She seemed to understand, saying, "You won't be able to show me the way in until you've learned how you're finding it yourself."

"How did you know I'd be so mesmerized by this sketch—or am I so interested just because you convinced me to buy it?"

"Does it matter?"

He shrugged, smiling. "Not anymore, I guess."

She matched his smile, leaning closer as if to share a secret. "I could tell right away," she admitted, now that it didn't matter. "When you came into the gallery, he stopped looking at me so he could watch you."

"Have you ever found an art piece just for yourself, one that seems to—I guess how they usually describe it is: one that speaks to you?"

She glowed with the pride of a child who's discovered there's a man behind the curtain. "He talks to you?"

"Oh no, I didn't say that. It's just—I wonder if you have your own favorite."

She closed her beautiful eyes and tilted her head closer, her hair brushing his shoulder, her breasts rising and falling with several deep breaths. "Yes, I have one, too. It's an abstract painting, a favorite of my father's."

"Is your dad a pretty good guy?" Geoffrey asked, surprised by how important this felt to him. Phrekka seemed so delicate, so sensitive, so pure and natural, in many ways like the boy in the sketch, and the word *father* to him invoked so many impressions of power and control, of disapproval and punishment. He couldn't allow himself to imagine her being mistreated. "Do you love your father?" he whispered, a question more probing than he intended.

She turned to face him, searching his eyes, tears beginning to well in her own. "Very much. Sometimes I think he's the most important person in my life."

Geoffrey felt the knot in his chest ease, but a new and unfamiliar tightness rose in his throat, and the tears in Phrekka's eyes seemed to wash over him, leaving him somehow cleansed, yet exposed and vulnerable. "Do you still see him sometimes?"

"Only when I look at his painting . . ."

"Where does he live?"

She took another deep breath, closing her eyes again, the teardrops squeezing free to linger on her cheeks, and she whispered, "My father died."

"Your father might be dead," Billy Marloney whispered to young Geoffrey, the two eleven-year-olds standing in the Calhoun living room. Mrs. Marloney lingered in the bedroom, hovering over Geoffrey's mother, comforting the distraught wife, something about a wall collapsing in the quarry out at the concrete works, at least one man killed, others hurt, still more possibly trapped, nobody knows for sure.

Your father might be dead.

Geoffrey felt confused and worried, wanting someone to reassure *him*. Suddenly the whole world might change, and though his own corner had always chafed with tension, it nevertheless wrapped him in the cloak of familiarity, the uncomfortable fit of stiff fabric worn so long as to escape notice.

Geoffrey tried to go to his mother, but she ignored him, gazing through her window at the cloud-swabbed sky, maybe searching for angels who would trumpet that all will be right, that God truly had looked after his disciple, her husband, Geoffrey's father.

"Go stay with Billy," the neighbor woman urged him, no doubt sensing his mother's distance, understanding there would be no connection. At least she'd brought her son to be the worried child's companion while everybody waited, each in his own way anticipating the fated revelation, good news or bad.

The eleven-year-olds sat awkwardly there in the living room, both avoiding each other's eyes, Geoffrey on the couch where his mother normally smoked cigarettes and drank coffee and read romance paperbacks.

"Maybe he's all right," Billy offered, but his voice echoed without conviction, no confidence that Ernest had survived his trial by stone, no hint that Billy Marloney, any more than Geoffrey Calhoun, even wanted this to be true.

Geoffrey sat stoically, nervous that so many feelings lurked just below the surface, that they might in an instant make themselves known, betraying him with proof that Ernest's son did indeed care.

Billy had tried from the very beginning to become the Calhoun boy's best friend, and Geoffrey appreciated both the intent and its result; but they had drifted apart over the past year ever since, as rambunctious ten-year-olds, they accidentally started a small fire in the Calhoun barn. They easily extinguished it, but couldn't hide the damage. Ernest came in and caught them, flaming into a rage not so easily doused. Billy Marloney stood to the side, wide-eyed and terrified, watching as the pious man grabbed Geoffrey by his shock of blond hair and hauled him upright, pawing madly at his jeans until the button tore loose, yanking them and his underpants down to his calves. The slight boy squirmed and cried as Ernest removed his belt and whipped him mercilessly, striping his bare legs and buttocks with raw, stinging welts while Billy sobbed and pleaded for him to stop. Geoffrey tried desperately to escape until, unable to control his bladder, he wet himself and collapsed, crumpling face-down in the urine-soaked dirt to writhe, squalling and gasping, until the final lashes signaled it had finally ended—for now.

Geoffrey's humiliation stemmed not just from being punished or having his nakedness exposed in front of his friend—the boys had showered together at the Marloney's many times after coming in from the fields covered with mud—but rather because Ernest had exposed his very soul, the last vestiges of his dignity taken against his will. Geoffrey felt ashamed around Billy after that, and he knew that Billy remained embarrassed by what he'd seen.

From that moment, for years to come, neither boy would risk revealing the privacy of his feelings in front of the other. They never again showered together, their innocence replaced by self-consciousness, a new sense of vulnerability. Geoffrey felt grateful to Billy for withdrawing, and this had become the new basis for their friendship, respecting the other's boundaries, offering the time and space so desperately needed to rebuild self-esteem, unfettered, unchallenged. Geoffrey had learned yet another fear, the knowledge that within any submission to scrutiny there lurks the potential for degradation, and he decided never again to allow anybody the chance to look too close.

"Your father might be dead," Billy whispered there in the living room, waiting for any word, any sign from the concrete works.

Geoffrey could tell that Billy savored the idea, a forbidden thought now more real.

"You boys okay?" Mrs. Marloney wondered, peeking in.

Their reverie interrupted, Billy jumped up and assured her, "Yeah," then proceeded to fiddle with knick-knacks on the mantelpiece.

Geoffrey slid down onto the floor, sat Indian-style, propped his chin on his fist, and stared into an uncertain future.

"There might be a funeral," Billy said without turning.

Geoffrey wrapped himself in this new reality, and he dared to enjoy the fit, wondering how he would dress for the service, who would come, how many would hug the child who had lost his father. Then he and Billy Marloney could be friends again, and Geoffrey would grow up without fear, learning new ways to invent himself. He would never again have to be Ernest's boy.

He would be Geoffrey.

Billy dropped down onto the floor beside him, rocking back and forth, not saying anything for a minute.

"Yeah," Geoffrey agreed, "there might be a funeral."

"Maybe after," Billy suggested, "you could, you know, come sleep over?"

The boy over the desk stood patiently there among his cattails, watching as Geoffrey sat quietly on the bed with Phrekka. She seemed distracted for a moment, maybe remembering her father, maybe even mourning his death.

"I'm sorry," Geoffrey said soothingly. "When did he die?"

"Six weeks after I was born," she said, much to his surprise. "I guess that's why I miss him so much: no memories to carry with me."

Geoffrey felt the slightest pang of jealousy as he considered the advantages of having a father who gives life, but who then goes away forever, blinking out of existence before the harm can even begin.

Phrekka explained, "My friend Danicia, who writes fiction, says that when I try to imagine my father, it's like the way she creates the nuances of her characters. That's how they become real to us. But then she gets frustrated because, to keep the plot moving, she has to leave out a lot of the detail."

"I'd only be interested in whatever about them matters to the story, anyway."

"Yeah, but only she knows what's important, because she knows what's going to happen and how it's going to end. If my father is a character in the story of my life, how can I know what there is about him that matters to me?"

Geoffrey offered her the hint of a wry smile. "Turn the page and find out?"

She chuckled in spite of herself, challenging, "Wouldn't you want to know more, I mean if the story were about you?"

"Geez, I already have enough trouble with my own plot." It was a joke, one that didn't reveal too much, nothing she could take from him. The truth was, nothing about his past interested him anymore. He had been firmly focused on looking ahead, growing up fast, getting out fast, having a girlfriend and then a wife, living his own life, fast.

She rolled her eyes, then looked pensive for a moment. "No matter, I guess, because what's passed is past. Grandmamá always said to keep moving forward. Figure out where you are, then head toward wherever you want to be."

"That's because we're real people, not somebody a storyteller makes up. We have to live our lives in the order it all happens. A writer can start with something interesting, then go back and forth in time, filling in the background. We take it as it comes."

"But what about my father? He was gone before I had my chance. That's why I used to insist Grandmamá tell me about him, and sometimes she would, even though it was hard for her. Sure, we have to move ahead, but living requires momentum, and sometimes you can't adjust your course until you plot it, and that means looking back to see whence you came."

"So can't you just dig into your father's background—do some investigating?"

"Oh, I already have. I pretty much know the story of his life. It's those parts of his character that never made it into the plot—into my plot—which intrigue me most."

"The parts only your grandmother could tell you," he said quietly.

"And she's passed away."

"So what do you do now?"

She glanced at the boy in the sketch, then offered Geoffrey a knowing smile. "I guess I turn the page."

"Oh Geoffrey," Mrs. Calhoun had moaned, "what will I do?"

Somebody was coming up the drive, so Mrs. Marloney and Billy rushed out to learn the news. Geoffrey had gone in to check on his mom, but she didn't want to be touched, nor could she bring herself to touch him.

"What will I do?" she repeated.

Geoffrey felt angry. This woman never thought of anyone but herself, even in this time of crisis. *You'll read romance books!* he wanted to shout. *You'll drink coffee and smoke cigarettes and read your books! That's what you'll do!* But he stood silent, feeling sorry for her. She would want him to take care of her, and he would. He would make her coffee and bring her more cigarettes and see to dinner . . . *You'll do what you always do,* he wanted to tell her. *You'll focus on yourself.*

And Geoffrey thought maybe he would try that, too. He could focus only on himself, on how his life might be. He could finally stop being afraid, and everything Ernest believed in—and even Ernest himself—could all go to hell. There, he'd thought it, and that was as good as saying so, and he felt liberated.

And sick to his stomach.

To think such horrible thoughts, to stand before God and imagine that Ernest might be dead, and to want so much for that to be true . . . It became a part of him he could never forget, one he must carefully put away, wrapped in layers of gauze, softened from the glare of scrutiny, there in its place where nobody would see, though he would always know it dwelled there.

Mrs. Marloney hurried in with the news. "He's fine! He's all right!"

Mrs. Calhoun started to cry. Mrs. Marloney cried with her. Billy just looked at Geoffrey, sympathy in his eyes, and in that glance they admitted what they'd both dared to hope.

And the gauze stripped away to leave Geoffrey standing naked before the realization that Ernest would come home again.

There would be no liberation. For Geoffrey, this meant he would return to his practiced role embodying all that is bad and wrong. He tried desperately to recapture how he'd felt when he imagined the possibility of a funeral, that he would sleep over at Billy's and start fires in the barn with impunity, but the very idea diminished to little more than a flicker, and he couldn't risk fanning it for fear it might wink out and he would lose the flame forever.

Then Geoffrey realized he didn't feel quite so afraid anymore. He had found the first suggestion of Ernest's vulnerability, discovered that the pious man could be vanquished, that maybe not even God could protect him . . .

That maybe Ernest's brand of God never existed.

At the center of the world lived a skinny eleven-year-old boy with blond hair and blue eyes named Geoffrey, small but growing bigger, weak but getting stronger, and he would remain at the center no matter what because nobody, not even Ernest, could push him off this mountain.

He could put the notion of his father's death safely aside, maybe dust it off and polish it from time to time, never again for it to feel so powerful as the strength Geoffrey would draw from hating him. He would resist this man. He would rebel against everything he stood for. He would never become what God's harsh-handed messenger wanted him to be. Ernest could live forever, and he could belittle and mistreat this vulnerable child, but he would never break him, for Geoffrey needed this force against which to push.

Geoffrey would answer to no one except himself.

You can have your God, he thought, *and I will be my own.*

Later, after the Marloneys had gone, only Geoffrey and his mother remained in the house. She made coffee, found her cigarettes, and situated herself on the couch, her book within reach. She studied her son curiously, then shook her head, saying, "I don't know what I would have done."

That's when Geoffrey finally dared to say it. Before he could stop himself, before he could think twice, the words tumbled from his mouth.

"You would think about yourself, Mother, like you always do."

Geoffrey watched Phrekka prepare to dive into the cool, clear water of the pool. She'd changed into wisps of bikini, he into his trunks, their soft towels and robes arrayed on plastic chairs off to the side. The area appeared nearly deserted, their only company an auburn-haired young girl playing in the shallow end, her sullen teenage brother propped against the balustrade, hidden behind sunglasses.

The light shimmered through Phrekka's hair, threads of spun cinnamon teased by the gentle breeze. She arced gracefully, slicing into the depths to radiate concentric ripples; then she surfaced near the girl, exhilarated and renewed, her arms lifted in a spray of vaporous angel wings, her tresses now refracting hues of cocoa and bourbon and root beer.

"You have very pretty hair," the girl said.

"And yours is quite beautiful, too," she said sweetly. She showed her how to submerge to her nose, then tilt her head back and gently spread her locks across the surface to capture the sunshine. They both started to giggle, these strangers sharing a moment of understanding; then Phrekka kissed her cheek and glided up the stairs for another dive.

Geoffrey followed next, substituting exuberance for grace, and swam to her, enveloped by the chill rush, invigorated. They relaxed for a bit, took turns diving, cannonballed together, practiced treading, and tried floating perfectly limp, immersing themselves in the moment.

After some time, Geoffrey went inside for cold drinks, returning to find the girl and her brother gone. Phrekka reclined in a chaise-longue, shiny droplets glowing on her tanned skin. She accepted the iced mango nectar with a smile, closing her eyes for a lingering sip, breathing in the ambience, her breasts rising and falling, her face toward the sun. He sat close to her, pretending to concentrate on combing his hair, enveloped by her beauty, this first occasion to witness her in pristine form, so pure, so unadorned. He vowed to remember every nuance: the downy soft wisps of light chestnut on her arms; the delicate pucker of her navel cradling a shiny droplet of water; the smooth symmetry of her sleek, streamlined calves; the rounded teardrop contours of her breasts, nipples firmed by cool water, impatient against the satin sheen of bikini top; the inviting mound of her pubis, wayward cinnamon curls peeking shyly from behind the curtain, the clinging moist cloth pulled tight into a crease at the center . . .

He grew acutely aware of his own pulse, the urgency of his heartbeat, the shallowness of his breaths, the rhythms of his body, the taut fabric of his shorts. He watched as a drop of water trickled down her thigh to join with another, then another. He noticed her suit starting to dry, but it clung damply at the center where she parted ever so slightly, a door ajar, a portal to her soul. He wanted to touch her, to practice the art of seduction and discover where she might take him.

To Geoffrey, women seemed most receptive when focused on themselves, even as his mother had found bliss in losing herself in the realms of literary romance, barely aware of her home and her family. Rarely could he hold her attention for more than a few minutes, but if he brought her more coffee and more cigarettes, then allowed her to dwell undisturbed where she found her own private source of contentment, he could sit with her for hours, even cuddle close and feel as if he shared a small but important part of her.

He discovered a similar trait in girls during middle school, something he studied in his quest to move closer to them: what they wanted was not to touch Geoffrey, but to be persuaded to allow themselves to be touched by him. He and the other boys scrutinized photos in magazines, filling their fantasies with every detail, extending their senses to imagine the warmth and the softness and the fragrance . . . but it seemed different for the girls. They would never be aroused by the image of a nude man, these young women emerging like fragile butterflies from the chrysalis of menarche. They cared too much about their own bodies, worrying over their development, focusing on their appearance, on their hair and skin and nails and their budding breasts; their pride over burgeoning pubic curls giving way to an obsession over its spread to unwanted places; their quest to master the tools of womanhood, of makeup and perfumes, of shavers and stylers, and of perfecting the techniques of conditioning and moisturizing and absorbency. The women in Geoffrey's high school and junior college proved somewhat more sophisticated and experienced, but still they tended to focus most on themselves. They responded to seduction, first to gestures like "going steady" or an invitation to the prom, then to the right touch at the right time.

Geoffrey learned well, practicing whenever he could, rehearsing in his dreams, finally believing he'd mastered the art when his girlfriend Melanie moved in, only to discover there still remained much to understand. He would do better with his next lover, demonstrating his newly honed finesse, methodically moving her toward intimacy, hovering so close that she would lose herself in the tension and kiss him first; then he would kiss her back, gently for a moment, then with escalating passion. Next he would ease his hands toward her breasts . . . but hold back, stroking around them to build anticipation and focus her expectations, for to progress too quickly would risk arming her defenses and scaring her away, making her uncomfortable with letting a man dare familiarity where she could not. When he sensed her readiness, he would touch her there; then he would move lower, and even a woman who started with lesser intent could be seduced, immersed in the heightened awareness of her own needs and desires, wanting him to join with her and dwell for a time at the center of her being.

The books called this *foreplay.* In Geoffrey's world, foreplay differed substantially for the woman and the man. For her, it meant the journey of him carrying her there, until she became ready, until there existed no place else she could be. For the man, it simply meant drinking in the scenery, savoring the ambience, making the trip last as long as possible. Geoffrey suspected that his father must not understand this, that Ernest should be better at helping Marjorie find her own place; then maybe she wouldn't spend all her time in worlds created by somebody else.

As much as Geoffrey had believed this true for all people, he suspected it would never work the same with Phrekka, the first woman in his life whose focus seemed to encompass everything. People and their creations, the elements like water and sunshine and the air we breathe, the sounds of calling birds or traffic passing, the fragrances of flowers and trees and the rushing sea, all of the flavors that are life—these created the place where Phrekka dwelled as aware of herself as all that surrounds her, no more, no less. She might allow her spirit to pass through another realm, even one found in the pages of a book, but anyone who moved close to her would then be written on the pages, to be read at her own time, on her own terms.

The droplet in her navel dried, but the supple mound remained moist.

Geoffrey lay back in the next chaise-longue, aware she had sensed his gaze, grateful she allowed it, sure she understood. He tried to be as aware of himself as of her, to listen for all sounds, to breathe in all fragrance, to taste the flavors of their shared world.

Without even touching her, he already felt closer to a woman than ever before, and the sensation consumed him.

Eventually, they went up to his apartment. She changed out of her swimsuit in the next room, the door slightly ajar. He imagined how she must look, and in that instant he lost himself in the obsession that for a moment she would be completely nude, this close to him and so stunningly beautiful. Then when she emerged suddenly, adorned in her flowing turquoise dress, she startled him, and he knew she could see it in his face, his thoughts and feelings betrayed.

Like a hunter who's spooked his bird and sees her scattering to the winds, he aimed without thinking, stepping forward, then reaching out to touch her.

She intercepted and cupped his hand, gently brushing his fingers with her lips, touching his face, lingering just for a moment, then releasing him, disappointment in her eyes.

She had said no.

And he felt naked standing before her, a lump rising in his throat, ashamed and unsure if he should pretend misunderstanding or admit his mistake and seek forgiveness.

"Your new Sara sketch will be shipped out tomorrow," she said, and he knew this was her way of reminding him what they did share, nothing more than a budding friendship, a relationship built on one common interest. He no longer desired to touch her as much as to find hope that when they concluded their business, she would at least agree to visit the boy, that she would still want to spend time with the man.

"I want to pay you," he said. She tilted her head curiously. "You can stay with the gallery, but when you have extra time you could be my employee, not only looking for more Saras, but helping me find the artist. Will you agree to that?"

She allowed the hint of a smile, clearly intrigued by his offer. He hoped she wanted to do this, but if needing the money had to be her motivation, for now that would suffice.

"Is this important to you, Geoffrey?" She wanted the truth.

And it *was* true. He had lain awake too many nights watching that innocent child cavort with his bugs and his birds there among the cattails, wondering about the mysterious artist who could capture such a moment, how much more Sara had seen, how much more she could know. "Yes," he said earnestly, his voice cracking.

She nodded, softly answering, "I would like that."

"I'm sorry," he blurted without thinking, still embarrassed for what he'd thought moments before, for what he'd tried, hoping she wouldn't ask him to explain.

She looked deep into his eyes with a profound sincerity, reaching up and brushing his cheek; then she smiled. "Learning is always to be cherished."

He never said why, and she never said what.

"Okay, then," he said. "Tomorrow I'll come to the gallery—"

His phone rang, probably about a job, maybe his friend from the graphics firm, maybe Melanie asking to come back. Frustrated at the interruption, he excused himself and answered, surprised to hear his mother's voice.

"Geoffrey," she said, "I need you to come home." She exhaled like she'd been holding her breath.

"I can't do that," he said. "I have too many—"

"I don't know what I'm going to do. There's too much—"

"Can I call you back?"

"Ernest pulled over to the side of the road," she said, her voice far away now, her attention focused on something else. He heard her taking a drag from her cigarette, and he resented the interruption.

"What do you mean he pulled over?"

"Coming back from the concrete works last night . . ." She trailed off.

"Where is he now?"

"That's where they found him this morning."

"What happened?"

"Oh, Geoffrey, I don't know what I'm going to do."

"Is Ernest all right?"

"People driving by couldn't see. They didn't know he laid down on the seat."

Another woman's voice came on the line. "Geoffrey? This is Billy's mom—Mrs. Marloney? I'm sorry, Geoffrey, but it seems your dad passed away sometime last night."

CHAPTER 5

Just a boy.

Phrekka watched from the other room as Geoffrey talked quietly on the phone. Struck by his boyishness, she noted that eager-to-please demeanor, his awkwardness and immaturity. He impressed her as one still struggling, like all boys invariably must, to wear the trappings of manhood, an uncomfortable fit for a time, a outfit invariably so large as to allow plenty of room for growth. Though his character at times rendered her at least curious, if not fascinated, his clumsy advances traced that all-too-familiar pattern, one which betrayed his carefully tailored persona, revealing that he truly had been cut from the same callow cloth as common boys. She couldn't feel angry with him—disappointed maybe, but certainly not surprised by his misstep. To his credit, he had sensed her reticence and withdrawn immediately, allowing his overtures to be construed as possibly innocent, even charming in a juvenile way, at least not yet imbued with the intent and determination that would render his affections dangerous.

She studied his physique while he conversed so earnestly, his soft voice a murmur in harmony with the *tick-tick-tick* of his clock and the urgent hum of his freezer's ice-maker. His silky hair clung damply at the top, the sides feathering outward as it dried. He'd been neglecting to shave ever since losing his job, his mustache honey-colored, an accomplishment so far insufficient to warrant public display. Highlighted by the window-gauzed sunlight, his cheeks and the underside of his chin revealed similar patchy wisps, evidence that it would likely be many years, if ever, before his wannabe beard might threaten the sovereignty of that territory between nose and lip. The t-shirt he'd pulled over his smooth, nearly hairless chest showed the faint impressions of nipples against soft cotton fabric, the only prominent features of that entire region. His swimsuit remained damp in places, clinging in a way that outlined the contours of his modestly proportioned masculinity. She caught herself wondering just how much of a pubic tuft he'd managed to cultivate through years of early-teenaged angst, imagining a precisely bordered smallish patch of soft fuzz cordoned off from the smooth skin of his lower abdomen like so many silky stalks of golden wheat grass planted in a tight little circle around the stubby tinkling-cherub fountain of a private garden.

Considering that wet spot at the front of his trunks made her smile, recalling her first impressions of school-aged boys' bodies. It occurred the summer of her twelfth birthday while visiting her friend Cerise in Santa Barbara. They swam for a time in the family's improbably situated pool, a fiberglass enclosure supported by stilts at the edge of a small valley. The girls had sunbathed for a time before retreating indoors to brush their hair in front of the bathroom mirror. Cerise's first-grader smidgen of a little brother chose that moment to relieve himself. He traipsed in unconcernedly, garbed in nothing more than his favorite cartoon t-shirt and briefs, then positioned himself in front of the toilet, dutifully lifting the seat—this gesture of consideration no doubt the result of countless hours of training and no small number of admonishments. Oblivious to the presence of the older girls, unaffected by the faintest glimmer of yet-cultivated modesty, he peeled down the front of his superhero undies to reveal a pinkish round snail shell, its occupant jutting forward as if to model its lavender beret. The boy sprayed an exuberant amber stream against the porcelain, splashing the rim and even the tile floor. This finally slowed to a dribble before, with one final exclamation to make its point, he quickly tucked away his peeper snail. The lad flushed, leaving the seat up as if training for married life, then trotted off to his diversions, indifferent to the half-dollar wet spot where pressed the snail's head.

How easy it must be for boys, Phrekka had thought, her curiosity giving way to amusement. So easy, she decided, as to discourage even the least interest in hygiene—at least not until little boys grow much older and demand more attention and greater degrees of satisfaction . . .

Which is when they become more dangerous.

Watching Geoffrey on the phone, still smiling about that wet spot, she imagined his fuzzy and water-chilled snail withdrawing, as much as it may, to the sanctuary of its wrinkled shell, and she considered the clumsiness of his attempts at intimacy, these impressions making it easier to relegate his behavior to the ranks of childish games like pretending to be a cartoon superhero, or even playing dress-up or doctor. In Phrekka's short life, there had been many boys, and it seemed no matter how old she grew, those her own age would always be just boys. Men were the kind her mother used to seek out for companionship, manly men, large and hairy and brusque and powerful, commanders of lesser men, the stars around whom their women orbited. Geoffrey seemed different from them in every way: smallish and soft-spoken, wiry and baby-chick downy, observant and deferential and polite . . .

Geoffrey hung up the phone, took a deep breath, and appeared to be lost in thought.

"Is everything okay?" she asked, flowing quietly into the room.

He shook his head once, then looked at his feet. "I have to go home for a few days," he said quietly.

Home. She understood he meant his boyhood home in Coon Rapids, Iowa—home to his parents and his bedroom with the high-school pennants and model airplane, where he would snuggle in the soft bed that concealed mattress-pressed and tattered copies of pornographic magazines. Boys might go off to school, or they might move halfway around the world, but as long as they remained boys at heart, Mom's kitchen and hearth would always be the center of home. "To Iowa?" she asked.

He nodded. "I have to help Mother. My father died last night."

The words seized Phrekka's breath, burning her chest and spreading in waves with each throbbing pulse. She felt herself falling, shivering in a rush of cold yet consumed by heat, dizzy and disoriented and nauseated. She wanted to cry, to fib and assure him she understood, to hold and comfort him in his time of profound grief—but she dared not, for this simple act of compassion would include physical intimacy, and Geoffrey was still too much a boy, his passions still dangerous. Unsure, unprepared, she stood there blinking.

He looked at her, took a deep breath, then scowled, his cherubic face marred by the sadness in his eyes . . . Or was it something else? Frustration? Anger?

"I'm sorry," she offered, but it sounded insincere, though she couldn't summon the words to express what she really wanted to say.

"Yeah, me too. I need to help Mother, uh, handle her affairs for a couple of days. I guess I'll fly out in the morning." He took a deep breath. "Maybe I should take you home now," he said apologetically, "so I can start making arrangements."

"I'm sorry," she said again.

He looked at her, and she could see that he appreciated her sympathy, this much she believed.

During the drive back to Sausalito, she found herself studying this grief-stricken boy who seemed so inexplicably unaffected by tragedy. She ventured to ask what had happened, growing all the more frustrated by his detachment as he described how Ernest had been found in his car, sprawled on the seat from an apparent heart attack, having pulled over on the way home from his job at the concrete works.

They rode in silence for a time, and she wondered if maybe he had postponed expressing any pain until he could be rid of her, if he would drive along the shoreline that separated their homes and pull over even as Ernest had done, there to suffer his own grief-attack, crying for the father he loved, mourning for the heartache and loneliness his mother surely must endure. But no, Geoffrey seemed to be marshaling very little, if any, effort to contain his emotions. She tried to reconcile how this young man could have developed and refined the talent of erecting walls around his vulnerabilities, a skill her mother's magnate men had practiced to perfection. The more she considered this disparity, the angrier she felt. Maybe he really had been a fraud, his impetuous advances calculated, and beneath his thin veneer of innocence he possessed none of those qualities she adored in the face of that child in Sara's sketch.

"If you can get a few days off work," he said, "I mean, if you want—I'll pay all the expenses—"

"I have to work," she answered softly, saving him from actually asking. For the briefest moment, she thought maybe she could put aside this mystery and steel herself to experience vicariously the ritual and ordeal of burying a father . . .

But no, she couldn't fathom Geoffrey, and she felt like she barely knew him. She would carefully limit their association to helping him pursue the sketches of Sara and, hopefully, to achieving a new level of understanding about the powers of artists and how their accomplishments affect others. While she might also learn more about this enigmatic man-boy in the process, that must not become chief among her goals in this otherwise frivolous endeavor.

"I'm so sorry," was the last thing she said, standing there in front of Marva's co-op, declining his offer to walk up with her, nevertheless secretly wanting him not to leave.

"That means a lot," he told her sadly. And he spoke the truth, this she believed.

She watched him drive away, then turned and ran upward through the winding streets until, panting from exertion, she stood before the ornate iron gate that protected her enchanted castle. She stabbed her security code into the keypad to gain entry, then hurried to the mist-shrouded refuge, easing quietly inside and creeping to her father's room.

She closed the door, then sat on the bed and stared at the floor until she could catch her breath. Finally, she looked up and into the painting over his desk, and she reached out for the man she never knew, and she waited for him to come to her.

After a few tentative moments, a familiar serenity passed around and through her.

She wondered where Ernest had gone, if now he dwelled in some unseeable and intangible realm with her own father, but she couldn't sense his presence, and she saw no sign, and she heard no answer.

She wondered how Geoffrey would fortify the now-tenuous bond with his father, if he might find some connection through a symbol or objet d'art, or maybe with an article of clothing or just through his own impressions and the fleeting images conjured from memories. She wondered if Geoffrey would reach out to his father, if there might be some glimmer of acknowledgment or form of communication, if he would even want this, if he would be willing to try.

Geoffrey remained innocent and naïve, regardless of his deceits and frauds, in spite of his façade, this much she understood. She recalled and pondered the image of him on the phone as he learned the heartbreaking news . . .

Standing there looking so vulnerable.

Just a boy.

"New Orleans, Charles," Phrekka explained. "Can you make the jet available for a few days?"

"Certainly so, Miss Churán. Do you require a car and overnight lodging?"

"Yes, someplace near the French Quarter, if I may."

"Would this trip be of a business nature?"

"Why, I guess it would. I'm to take delivery of some artwork from a gallery there, and I think I might explore and attend some exhibits, as well."

"Please allow me to arrange for an attendant to accompany you, someone discreet who will see to your personal safety."

Phrekka smiled into the phone. "Oh, Charles—I'm quite sure I will be fine, thank you, but I appreciate your kind thoughts."

"The quarterly report will be released in your absence. I understand the numbers are to be very impressive, indeed."

"Aren't they always, Charles? Our success gives credit to the substantial capabilities of your team. Watch out—if I discover a treasure trove in New Orleans, I may just squander the profits adorning our various worldwide headquarters with expensive displays of artwork."

"When you take a notion," Charles said affectionately, "we look forward to your cultural contributions. Commerce too often tends to run roughshod over aesthetics."

"One pays for the other," Phrekka countered with a mischievous chuckle.

They concluded the arrangements for her trip before disconnecting. Phrekka dawdled at the gallery desk for a few moments, watching as Marva consummated the sale of a large painting to an elderly woman who had been admiring the acrylic landscape during occasional viewings over the past several months.

"It takes me home," the woman had whispered to Phrekka during one of these recent visits.

"You have lived in a place that looks like this?"

"No," the woman answered. "I've never been to the country, nor most certainly have I ever visited a setting this beautiful." Turning to Phrekka with a twinkle in her eye, she added, "To the young, home is whence you come. By the time you're my age, home is where you want to go."

Phrekka watched as Marva promised delivery the very next day. She and the customer hugged, the ancient woman lingering for a last wistful gaze before disappearing into the long shadows of the street.

"I have arranged to pick up the Sara sketch in person," Phrekka explained to Marva, standing to leave. "I depart in the morning."

Marva sat on the corner of the desk, regarding the young woman. "I suppose that will be fun. I confess, when I heard you making travel arrangements, I rather hoped you had reconsidered and would be accompanying your Mr. Drousseau to his father's funeral in Iowa."

"No, oh no—I couldn't. In New Orleans I can scout for other Sara sketches, maybe discover people who know more about her. I should think my Mr. Drousseau—as you call him—would be quite thrilled for me to surprise him with the opportunity to meet the artist whose work so fascinates him."

"Yes, but that can wait, Miss Churán. I suspect his thoughts are occupied by more important matters at the moment."

Phrekka took a deep breath, glancing off toward her collection of treasures. "I don't know him well enough," she said quietly. "It's not like we're close friends."

"Close enough that he wanted you to accompany him."

"I don't even *want* to be his friend." She felt surprisingly exasperated, uncomfortable with the subject. She took a deep breath, looking up into Marva's face. "He's just a *boy*."

Marva cupped Phrekka's face in her hands and smiled. "And you, Phrekka Churán, are just a girl."

Gargantuan redwoods towered above the timberland thick with assorted hardwoods, soft firs, and giant ponderosa pines. A profusion of needles in shades of ochre and olive littered the ground. Pine cones lay scattered about, live grenades waiting to explode in the lightning flash of hot summer fires. Here and there showed patches strewn with the fiberglassy threads of shredded orange sequoia bark. Caravans of ants and beetles buzzed along invisible highways, pausing at the mushrooming tollbooths tended by toadstool-sheltered slugs, the forest floor a multi-hued mosaic of lichen and moss and leaves. Young Phrekka's indifference to the minutiae of this world was unusual. She ignored the carnival-barker calls of taunting birds perched in their tree-branch berths, just as she missed savoring the natural fragrances of old-growth forest swirling around and through her.

She felt too nervous.

After all, she was barely twelve, and walking the woodsy trail and holding hands with a much older boy named Kieran—one all of fourteen—a *teenager* already sporting the dark hint of downy-soft mustache across his upper lip. He had convinced her to accompany him on a pine-cone-gathering expedition, but she suspected—and secretly hoped—that he intended a brief romantic liaison. She liked this boy and enjoyed entertaining the possibility that on this special occasion she might experience her first *real* kiss as a young woman held in the arms of a young man, no pressure from friends.

Phrekka had come to Sequoia National Park as a guest of her friend Cerise—of Cerise's father, really. He brought both girls and the little brother who routinely stained his superhero undies with amber circles. They would enjoy nature for a week, an annual respite from Cerise's mother's myriad ailments and complaints, which the girls understood really served as the father's clever guise for a rendezvous with his mistress from Bakersfield. Sometimes he left for long periods during the day; evenings he encouraged the children to sleep outdoors, down along the shallow stone river near the outhouses and horse trails, while he entertained "guests" or "business associates" in the cabin. All in all, it had proven a glorious vacation, the girls communing with this mystical, magical world, their chief supervision provided by towering grandfatherly leviathans, their companions the critters who followed them here and there on their journeys. The only drawback was the constant presence of that little brother. Such a sweet boy, he never presented any real obstacles or strife, but he needed watching and had a remarkable capacity to explore and wade in and climb and touch whatever and wherever he shouldn't, all in the blink of an eye.

Phrekka had met Kieran during an afternoon trek along a well-maintained trail that boasted "a thousand giants"—a natural exhibition of the most magnificent triumphs of the forest, some having withstood fires and storms and the encroachment of man since before the time of Christ. A handsome ninth-grader from Akron, Ohio, he was vacationing here with his parents, a contentious pair who left their son mostly to his own devices so they could concentrate on bickering in exciting new vistas beyond the tire capital of the world. Kieran's family had parked their camper at a hook-up just upriver from the cabin rented by Cerise's father. Phrekka enjoyed his polite flirtations for several days, but always in the company of Cerise and the little explorer, too much shadow and scrutiny for budding romance. Kieran's parents would be moving on to Yosemite the following day, so he suggested that Phrekka steal away with him to collect pine cones, just the two of them, their first and only walk alone together through the forest. Both wore shorts and t-shirts, he carrying a pillow-case to collect their specimens, the day hot and humid but pleasantly cool under the shifting, shady canopy. They held hands, strolling quietly, called to by the warbling carnival barkers watching their progress from the trees.

Finding a small clearing, they stopped and sat together on ground cushioned with soft needles and tufts of spongy grass. Phrekka had her legs up, her chin resting on her knees, her arms encircling her calves. Kieran scooted close and put his arm around her, gently caressing. After a time, she relaxed some and allowed him to pull her closer, to cradle her against his chest. He gently turned her face up and kissed her, tentatively at first, then parting his lips ever so slightly and coaxing her to respond. It all felt very tingly, really, and quite good, this wonderful setting, a handsome boy, and such grown-up expressions of affection, intimacy shared, a first-time memory to cherish.

He eased her back so they could lie beside each other, cuddling close, watching the shifting canopy and catching sparkles of peeking sunshine on their faces. He kissed her again, his fingers stroking downward to caress her budding breasts. She carefully cupped his hand with hers, guiding his arm around her back, and she whispered, "Please, just kissing."

"We don't have to go all the way," he whispered back, and for his understanding she felt grateful, but as he held her close, his hands kept straying, casually brushing her nipples, cradling her bottom, tracing fragile lines across her abdomen to scatter fairy-dust tendrils of tickley tingles . . . but moving inexorably lower with each pass, his hands with determination and purpose of their own.

Nervous and unsure, but trusting he would honor the spirit of her request, she let him.

This was more than just kissing, but as the time passed, she felt safer, and she enjoyed the sensations, and he seemed careful not to go too far, so she relaxed her vigilance.

Then she felt something unfamiliar against her leg. She glanced down to see a stiffness pressed outward from his shorts, the fabric pulled aside just enough to reveal a tuft of ominous dark curls and a wet spot. Before she could react, he guided her hand there, and she was awestruck by its size and inflexible hardness, reminding her of the valve stem jutting from some overinflated tire, how it would bend only slightly—but not too far lest it break—and how even the slightest touch in just the right place would unleash all the power and pressure from within.

She pulled her hand away, squirming to escape, panicking now, that enlarging wet spot on his shorts scaring her with fears of pregnancy and herpes and AIDS. "Please," she whispered. "Please, I said just kissing—"

But he held her tighter, and his hands were groping her, and she started to cry.

"Come on!" he complained.

"Please," she sobbed quietly.

And he released her. He was breathing hard, his cheeks flushed, his shorts bulging and jutting out in a way irreconcilable with her vision of the cute peeper snail Kieran had surely once cradled in his underpants. She pulled her legs close, burying her face in her knees, hugging her calves, and continued to cry softly.

"I'm sorry," he pleaded. "I thought— I'm sorry. Please don't cry. It's okay."

And she did feel a bit better, for she could tell he now felt as scared as she. He sat close, but not touching her, his words soothing, reassuring. She realized she'd been trembling, and that didn't seem very grown-up, so she willed herself to calm down.

"Are you okay?" he asked.

She felt silly, embarrassed, immature. She offered a weak smile. "Yes. I'm sorry. I'm okay now."

"You're sure?"

"Yes."

"Well, I have to use the bathroom," he said. "I'll be right back." With that, he disappeared into the woods for several minutes. When he returned, the bulge in his shorts had shrunk to normal, but he seemed self-conscious about the unerasable wet spot, holding one hand in casual concealment. He helped her up, and they walked for a time, but they never gathered any pine cones, and they didn't hold hands, and they certainly never kissed again, finally parting ways as they approached the campground.

"Yes, we kissed, but that was all," Phrekka confided to Cerise later that afternoon.

"It was kind of icky." That was all she would say, ashamed that she'd allowed such an awful experience to debauch what should have been the most wonderful moment of her young life.

That night, the girls and their tag-along little explorer slept in the tent, a tiny battery-powered nightlight glowing from the upper corner. The heat and the humidity weighed heavily upon them, pressing them down onto their sleeping bags. The girls wore panties and pull-over sleep shirts, the little boy nestled between them in his underpants—Batman this time—his trademark half-dollar yellow stain scarce reassurance that months had passed since he last wet the bed. A summer storm gathered over the forest, occasional rumbles in the distance, the intermittent *pat-pat . . . pat-pat-pat* of droplets piercing the canopy to tap impatiently against the roof of their old-fashioned canvas tent.

The little boy twitched, then whispered something in his dreams, finally sighing as he drifted with each soft breath farther and farther into enchanted realms.

Phrekka closed her eyes and replayed her sojourn with Kieran, allowing herself now in the safety and sanctity of her tent to explore the emotions she'd felt during such an exciting though disenchanting experience, disappointed she had allowed herself to become scared. She wondered if there might have been some middle ground that would have satisfied both their desires without violating each other's limits, and she grew curious about what he did when he disappeared, frustrated, into the woods . . . what she might have learned had she followed him and watched.

The patter of rain grew more urgent, the humid air caressing her exposed arms and legs, her whole body rippling from the warmth.

She recalled Kieran's surprising erection, now as an afterthought seeming more impressive than alarming, the sensation of feeling it pressed against her leg, the rhythmic pulse of its urgency, the slippery secretion touching her bare skin . . . and she touched herself there in the exact same place, rubbing gently, then breathing in the fragrance from her fingers, testing for the lingering presence of Kieran's masculinity. She retraced the route his hand had followed as it explored her body, caressing her abdomen, lightly brushing her nipple. Her skin tingled, cascading waves washing over her even as the growing storm outside churned and raced among the trees, the winds tugging at a thousand giants towering above her, each massive tree yielding only slightly in its stiff defiance of nature, never so much as to break.

She fantasized about that first kiss again, the simple expression of intimacy, pretending Kieran might have been some wild forest-dwelling boy emerging tentatively from the brush to caress her, then to carry her back to his lair. She touched her lips with the back of her arm, the sensation of soft hairs reminding her of Kieran's downy mustache. She licked her lips, then her fingers, Kieran's moist tongue probing tentatively. She allowed her other hand to stray again, this time moving lower, wondering how it might have felt had she not stopped him, her fingers—his fingers—now sliding purposefully under the elastic of her panties. Kieran probed farther, and she shuddered as he touched the first silky hairs, goose bumps spreading through her body. She allowed him to move closer, stroking her soft curls . . . and she remembered how scared she had felt.

But this time she remained safe.

She paused and waited, her apprehension passing slowly until she understood it wasn't fear that had gripped her, but rather the uncertainty of expectation, the overwhelming pull of sensations new and unfamiliar, the possibility that a boy's slightest touch might expose her greatest vulnerabilities.

She retreated for a moment, pausing for several deep breaths, then moved her hand back, easing her fingers under the elastic again just as Kieran had, and it seemed more natural now, as if with time she might learn to embrace his caress, to feel secure during such intimacy, and to enjoy touching him and exploring the contours and the rhythms at the center of his being. The storm blustered outside the tent, gusts of rain showering the canvas, wind-swept evergreen needles pawing at the walls like some wild forest boy scratching to be let in.

Phrekka stroked lower, the tops of her fingers lifting the smooth fabric already mounded up by the cinnamon curls of budding womanhood. She touched the upper fold of her crease, and she felt moisture there. Thunder roared across the sky, echoing through the forest, the great trees trembling under its power. Cerise and the little Batman-boy breathed softly, each in solo rhythm, unaware, indifferent, innocent. The wind tugged urgently at the tent flap, Phrekka's protection holding fast. She spread her thighs ever so slightly, the rush of moist air tickling her. She wondered how it might have felt for the tip of Kieran's stiffened snail to touch her there, exploring even as his tongue had probed her mouth—

But the apprehension returned—

She could feel him thrusting suddenly inside of her, and he gave her no alternative, no middle ground, no escape. The wind pulled at the tent flap, stinging droplets of driving rain spraying through the narrow slit to spatter her sleeping bag. She squeezed her legs together tightly and covered herself with a protective hand, and the tent held firm while the storm thundered dangerously through the forest.

And Phrekka understood.

She understood how wonderful it could feel to immerse herself in the liquid ebb and flow of shared pleasures, but that in others' desires there lurks the potential for shame, the risk of taking chances with the wrong person, and for Phrekka to allow herself to experience true intimacy would require the confidence and reassurance found only in the deepest, most abiding love. To be swept away by passion—not resisting, but surrendering to its inexorable will—would require the trust earned by protecting her precious vulnerability, a lover who she must know in her heart would help bring her safely home.

A drop of water clung tenuously under the roof of the tent, a wet spot like the dribble from some impatient little snail. She rose to her knees, then reached up tentatively to touch it, releasing it to splatter on her face. She lay down again and watched as another droplet formed and dripped onto her abdomen, then another, now splashing lower, probing her with neither assistance nor consent. Then another . . . and another. Phrekka had been warned never to touch the canvas during a rainstorm, but there didn't see to be much harm in it. She lay very still as drop after drop soaked the front of her panties, and she felt cleansed, and safe to experience the sensuality of the water's touch even while the storm raged just outside the protective layer. A tingle spread through her body, rippling across her skin, and she felt warm, then cool, then warmer yet . . . and finally, cold and wet.

And still the droplets formed and splattered.

And she felt the chill passing around and through her, the drop in pressure lifting her, and she listened to the creaking sway of giant erect trees threatening to topple and crush her, and she felt scared again.

She scooted over, trying to escape the *drip-drip* she had unleashed but could no longer control. She gently eased the little boy closer to Cerise to make room for herself, gathering the loose end of her sleeping bag, pulling it over herself to ward off the cold and wet, to escape the determined and invasive touch, to protect herself from the splatter.

The storm sounded dangerous now.

The little boy shifted in his sleep, cuddling close to Phrekka, his warm back nestled against her.

She put her arm around him and held him tentatively, this little guy so unaffected, so indifferent to the probing eyes of big girls watching surreptitiously while he splattered the tile and stained his drawers, this child who remained, for this one special moment, the essence of pristine serenity.

She closed her eyes and listened to the dangerous storm, the *drip-drip* of bad judgment pooling on the floor behind her, and she knew she would be safe only as long as she dwelled in the sanctity of her shelter, the protective flap tied securely, trust and security and childhood and innocence cradled close to her heart.

"It's time to wake up, Miss Churán," the co-pilot said softly, nudging the luxurious recliner where Phrekka slumbered during the flight. "We'll be landing soon."

She sat up and blinked, took a deep breath, and contemplated the fleeting sensations of her bad dream, of tumbling down a slope in an avalanche of wet pine cones, buried in a narrow canyon. She looked out the window, pulled her cinnamon hair back, then fastened her seat belt, the fading dream yielding to the anticipation of yet another art-gallery exploration.

A man driving an electric cart met her on the tarmac. He retrieved her travel bag, then ferried her through several gates until they arrived at a silver Cadillac CTS-V Coupe, greeted by a handsome man dressed rather smartly, not in chauffeur's uniform, but in a tailored suit of elegant European cut.

"Miss Churán," he said with an affectionate smile.

"James! It's been so long." She embraced him briefly.

"We always enjoy when you take a notion to visit our part of the country."

James delivered Phrekka to the Sheraton, leaving the car idling while he insisted on carrying her bag. He supervised her check-in, then offered her a tiny pager, explaining, "I will be nearby, day or night. I hope you've a mind for long drives during your stay," he added with a twinkle in his eye.

She squeezed his hands, kissing him on the cheek, then let the bellman escort her to the suite.

She stood in the great window and looked toward the French Quarter, catching a glimpse of Bourbon Street, the wrought-iron trellis adorning an aged balcony, a horse-drawn carriage rounding the corner, the mist rising from newly-scrubbed streets . . . all backlit by the long rays of mid-morning sunshine filtering between buildings steeped in history, the enclave of countless, sometimes bawdy, stories. She unpacked her ward-robe, choosing a summer dress in muted earth tones, shot through with threads in fuchsia and chartreuse that curled into miniature flowers here, into dainty peacocks' tails there. She added delicate highlights to her make-up, donned some elegant ear buds with cut stones sparkling of honey and molasses, then brushed her long hair. She considered weaving some threads of colored silk into her tresses in celebration of the festive mood of the Quarter, but she decided not. She had come here on business and, even though she carefully resisted the impulse to ponder Geoffrey's circumstance, this day nevertheless remained a solemn occasion which at least deserved some measure of dignity, a modicum of decorum, the slightest gesture of respect.

She strolled along Bourbon Street for a while, the carny-barkers of various establishments bird-calling for her attentions. Each time, she would smile and chuckle, then hurry on. Finally, she turned south and walked toward the galleries, gradually sensing the presence and power and magnificence of so much creative expression all gathered in the narrow confines of these few blocks. Delaying her mission to retrieve the latest Sara sketch, she strolled into the first place she spied, a small display of etchings and acrylic paintings. She felt immediately welcomed into the fold, absorbed into a world of visions and imagination, each piece telling its own story of deception or truth. Over there, a landscape, possibly by a young woman visualizing the faded memories of home, or by an older woman longing for the serenity of vistas she hopes one day to see. Here, the scene along a seaside quay, no doubt drawn from the experiences of a young man who enjoyed the water but, unable to afford the time or expense of indulging his whims, instead reveled in the vicarious pleasure of creating this world on canvas. There, a cityscape, somewhat abstract and not very good, created by the scratched and faded shell of a man who nurses grudges against the scenery of his failures, the world that surely rejected him; instead of capturing its essence or celebrating its form, he'd chosen to depict its dark exteriors, scarred and raw, to appease his burning spite and to feed the hunger of his malice toward the world of men. Ah, here beckoned an underwater scene, a coral reef, and this lived on as a labor of love by a man who had been there, precisely to this exact coral head, and who found joy in sharing it with others. Phrekka could feel the gentle pull of the current, felt herself floating in neutral buoyancy, watched as the curious queen angels studied her, laughed when the selfish yellowtails surrounded her with hungry curiosity, then found security in the ubiquity of sergeant-majors patrolling this vibrant neighborhood.

There were no more than forty or so pieces in this display, but Phrekka spent hours there. Tourists wandered in and out, each earning a friendly *May I help you?* from an older woman, the custodian of these treasures who quietly watched Phrekka with understanding, leaving her to explore unfettered, uninfluenced.

After a time, when Phrekka had savored all this small gallery could possibly yield, she approached the woman and held her hands. "You offer a wonderful collection," she said, gazing into the radiance of the caretaker's eyes.

The woman squeezed back, misting up, a single tear gathering the will to break free. "Isn't it? I'm so glad you appreciate them. They—" She looked embarrassed, leaning closer to whisper. "They take me away from here."

Phrekka whispered back, "And today, they took me with you."

Both women laughed, then hugged each other, exchanging cards and promising they would travel together again someday, to visit images already as familiar as old friends, and to discover new visions to welcome into the fold.

Phrekka wandered the streets, finally settling in at a little cafe to enjoy some crawfish étouffée, watching the tourists stroll past, so many wrapped in banners proclaiming allegiance to theme parks and musical acts and sports franchises, one little boy's shirt extolling the prowess of Spider-Man. She inhaled the warm sunshine, the mingling aromas of horses and beer and ships churning the Mississippi Delta.

Next she explored some of the mask shops, finally discovering a decrepit-looking place with a series of rooms extending into the back, a million masks and various oddities on display, specimens stacked and racked from floor to ceiling. She found a grizzled old proprietor sporting a bounteous frazzled beard. He worked at a messy bench like some fisherman tying delicate flies, carefully doing the featherwork of an exquisite mask to capture the attentions and admirations of Mardi Gras revelers. He set down his work and beheld the young woman before him, his eyes lighting up even as he studied the contours of Phrekka's face.

"You *must* allow me to help you explore new ways to express yourself with a mask," he offered, but it sounded more like a plea, because he spoke the truth.

"Yes," she agreed, "you absolutely must."

Delighted, he pulled over a comfortable chair for her, then he studied her some more, finally setting to the task, lapsing into a trance-like state as he worked feverishly, hurrying about to gather scraps of this and sprigs of that. The masterpiece taking shape before his gnarled fingers reflected a natural theme: the soaring grace of feathers from pheasant and quail, the woody sanctuary of an evergreen spray, the crescendo of stair-step pine cone petals, the breezy flutter of a tiny silk moth, the smile of a mischievous doodlebug bright orange with her telltale spots. Two tufts rose owlishly from the corners of the eyes, extending their graceful lines to reach out toward a thousand giants towering in the sky. There, along one side, jutted two tiny cattails, a small butterfly perched at the tip of one, with tendrils of silk bouclé trailing below. He carefully fitted the mask to her face, gently weaving the bouclé into her hair until he achieved just the right effect, then he handed her a mirror, proud of his achievement.

"It's beautiful," she sighed reverently, studying her reflection. "You have seen in me what I too often forget to reveal. You have coaxed me out," she added, giggling.

He looked ecstatic, virtually dancing a little jig. "It is my gift to you," he insisted.

"Oh, but I couldn't—"

"Ah, but you must," he countered, carefully helping her remove it.

She laughed. "Yes, I must. But I would like to become one of your patrons."

He looked thoughtful for a moment. "Only after you accept my gesture of affection," he insisted.

"I accept." She smiled, clasping his hands, mischievously kissing his rough, grizzled cheek. "Now," she insisted, "I would like to purchase one-thousand dollars' worth—" She counted out hundred-dollar bills from her purse. "—Of whatever would add to your collection in a way that allows you to create more art for others."

"Such a generous patron!" he exclaimed.

"And you must accept!"

"Yes, I believe I must!"

Phrekka left carrying the treasure in a small box, this mask not for concealing, but for reflection, to highlight character, to amplify nuance, to shift perspective and add fragrance and flavor and sensation.

The time had finally come to visit the gallery, time to discover if the blond-haired subject of another Sara drawing would be the same boy who so fascinated Geoffrey. The sketch awaited her at one of the larger shops just one street over, attended by a severe-looking woman, one who chewed some sort of bubble-gum which she insisted on popping with distracting regularity. Without introducing herself, Phrekka tried first to explore the many pieces on display, but the insufferable woman insisted on following her around like a security officer preventing some juvenile shoplifter from slipping a painting under her dress and spiriting it away, rescuing it from the stifling confines of a gallery that wouldn't allow its subjects even to breathe.

"Can I help you?" she snarled.

"No," Phrekka said quietly, moving on.

"Are you just looking?" snapped the fierce protectoress, ever vigilant to deter the intrusions of tourists seeking I-heart-New-Orleans memorabilia.

Phrekka stopped and studied her, this nuisance demanding more of her attention than all the artists and their work in residence. "Right now, I am talking to you," Phrekka said quietly. "I cannot do both."

"Well, we have a time limit if you're not going to buy anything." *Pop!*

Phrekka felt profoundly sad for the pieces around her, now seeing them as so many children without friends, never allowed to come out in the sunshine and play, never embraced and loved by another soul. "Then I will take delivery of the sketch I have on reserve, and I will leave quickly before I risk discovering another I might like to purchase, thus upsetting the delicate balance of disharmony you have achieved in this collection."

"Oh! You must be that Phrekka woman. I'm sorry." Too late, Madam Gumwad had already spoiled the moment. She led her customer back to a desk where a framed piece, wrapped in brown paper, leaned forlornly against the wall. "The money arrived this morning," she said, "so here's your receipt." She set the sketch on the desk. "You wanna see it?"

"No," Phrekka said quietly. She looked around sadly, adding, "Not here." She took her sketch and her mask box and retreated into the sunlight. The Cadillac glided over to the curb, James stepping out to take the packages.

"How do you do that?" she asked playfully.

"Do what, Miss Churán? I'm sure I don't know what you mean. Would you like to go somewhere else now, or maybe visit another gallery?"

She sighed. "I was having such fun until this woman spoiled it all. I think I'll go to the hotel and rest for a while, thank you."

He drove her there, then carried the wrapped sketch up to her suite, propping it on the desk. "I'll be downstairs," he said by way of taking his leave.

"James, I should appreciate it if you would go back to that mask shop for me."

"Yes?" He obviously knew where she meant.

"Tell the man with the great beard that his newest patron would like for him to make you a mask."

James flashed a wide, handsome grin. "Why thank you, Miss Churán. I believe I shall."

She freshened up, then studied the room-service menu, and the furniture, and the carpet . . . finally walking over and gazing out across the city, the late-afternoon shadows casting a maze of contrasts along the streets and avenues. She opened the box and explored the beauty of the mask, imagining what her artist must have seen within her that inspired such wondrous creativity.

Finally, the sketch.

She sat in front of the brown paper and considered waiting until she could unwrap it in the presence of Geoffrey, a chance for them to savor the flavors of their virginal impressions simultaneously, but the siren call of the mysterious boy proved too compelling, the temptation too great. She reached out and pulled it close, then carefully unfastened the paper at the back and unwrapped the framed piece.

And there he slept.

No question remained; she looked upon the same silky-blond little boy as the other Sara sketch, maybe just a bit younger in this drawing. Phrekka first reacted with annoyance at herself for letting the woman at the gallery bother her so. Although she'd been assured there were no other Sara sketches to be found, still she had hoped that with enough exploration, and by asking the right questions, she might nevertheless glean some helpful clue that would set her on the trail of the enigmatic artist who so beautifully captured and conveyed the innocent images of this delicate child. She felt like the real little boy languished back there in the gallery, hiding between the aisles, watching nervously while Phrekka bristled at the rude woman, and that she had left him behind, his only remaining hope now to slip out on his own, unseen, into the streets, to disappear lonesome and unwanted into the madding crowd.

She studied the sketch.

The boy slept peacefully, arrayed atop his twin-sized unmade bed, adorned in outgrown brief-style underpants and a tank-top undershirt slid up to expose his belly. With his feet to the right, one leg dangled off the side, his bare foot not quite touching the floor. His head and shoulders formed a curious image, for there were three versions of his position, superimposed lightly atop one another, creating the illusion that he moved in his sleep. One showed his face tilted upward, his mouth barely open. The next showed his head turned slightly this way, his shoulders shifting downward. The last angled his serene face entirely toward the artist, his mouth closed, his button nose breathing warmth and security even as his tiny chest rose and relaxed with the rhythm of childhood at rest.

The artist had rendered this sketch, like the other, in graphite and charcoal, a match in style and technique. Phrekka admired how light wisps through the boy's hair gave it the appearance of shimmering blond silk. Faint lines and shadows in his chest suggested the contours of muscles, the tiny nipple of his right breast. She followed the lines down, found his navel amusing—an "outie," just like Geoffrey Drousseau's—like a button carefully fastened to cloak the exuberance of youth. She traced down to the mound over his pubis, the fabric pulled tight, the lines and shadows suggesting a small but determined snail crawling toward the boy's belly. A faint spot showed there on the cloth, and Phrekka had to laugh at the suggestion of a damp circle or maybe a stain. She traced farther, down his calf, to his stubby little knee with its small scrape and scab, a badge of uninhibited exploration, stung by Mercurochrome and kissed better by a mother's love; then farther down, his dirty foot and ragged toenails, a country boy.

It was a wonderful sketch. Where the other had captured the child's bliss as he romped in his natural playground, his immodest demeanor lacking any hint of self-consciousness, his fascination with the physical world and his adoration for the artist, this sketch showed him utterly at peace, drifting into a realm of dreams, not bundled protectively under the covers, but sprawled where he may, confident of the love and protection of his family, no monsters under the bed.

Accents included the faint outline of a dresser against the wall, some rumpled clothing on the floor, and the grain of slatted hardwood trailing down toward the title and Sara's name, disappearing under the edge of the slim frame matte. This annoyed Phrekka to no end. How could such an amateur cover up part of the sketch while mounting it? This piece deserved to be set off by a much wider matte, preferably layered, with at least a half-inch of space around the farthest fringes of graphite and charcoal.

She examined the back, then called for a bellman to bring the proper screwdriver that would allow her to disassemble this travesty of packaging. Tools in hand, she set about releasing the slumbering child, giving him the freedom and space he deserved, promising she would find him a more suitable home.

The offending material discarded to the side, she studied the drawing again, and there she discovered, along the very bottom edge, some writing:

First appeared a date showing this sketch to have been rendered some fifteen years before.

Then came a notation: *Geoffrey taking a nap.*

Finally, a byline, a neatly penciled signature: *By Sara Drousseau.*

Young Phrekka rose at dawn and, there in the damp tent, struggled into her jeans. She pulled on her hiking shoes and added a light jacket in deference to the cool morning air, then hurried up the banks of the stream until she came to the area where so many trailers and campers sprouted like toadstools in the moist earth.

She found Kieran and his family packing to leave.

Shyly, she approached them, surprising the fourteen-year-old, asking if they could walk, if only for a minute. His mother agreed when he promised to return soon. His father grinned licentiously.

They strolled farther upstream until she knew no one could hear.

They paused awkwardly, neither speaking for several minutes. Phrekka looked at the ground a moment longer, then raised her face to look into Kieran's. She had fresh tears in her eyes. "I wish you hadn't said we were going for pine cones," she said sadly.

Kieran wouldn't look at her, staring instead at his shoes, picking at a thread on the leg of his jeans. "Me, too," he said with the tiniest voice. "I wish I didn't, I mean—that I hadn't made up the part about pine cones."

"I had hoped we would kiss," she said, tears spilling out to dampen her cheeks.

He looked at her again, relieved maybe. "Me, too. I swear, that's all I expected. I don't know why— I mean . . ."

"It scared me, because you tricked me. I'm not angry because you got carried away, just because I thought you intended to."

"I swear—"

"I believe you now, but that was my first real kiss, and you ruined it." She looked at the ground again, and so did he, still tugging at the thread of his jeans.

"I shouldn't have tricked you," he repeated, "and I was wrong—but at least it was for a good reason."

"What was that?"

He looked at her, his own eyes now brimming with tears, and she knew he spoke the truth. "I just wanted to be closer to you, but I didn't know how."

She watched as he looked down again, still picking at that thread. She reached out and touched his fingers, gently pulling his hand into hers, now holding it affectionately.

He looked at her, then closed his eyes.

She leaned forward and kissed him gently, tentatively.

He hesitated for a moment; then, sure of her intent, he kissed her back.

They held each other for a full half-minute, both trembling, both swept away by the moment.

When she stepped back, they both smiled, and they wiped the tears of uncertainty and regret from their faces. She turned to leave, pausing next to the stream and glancing at the boy from Akron one last time. "Thank you, Kieran. That's the one I'm going to count as my first ever *real* kiss."

How could he lie to her like this?

Geoffrey Drousseau had sent her on a wild-goose chase for pine cones and Saras, tricking her into believing he'd been honest. No wonder that sketch in her gallery moved him. It showed *him* as a little boy, drawn when he was that age, by a relative of his.

He was using her.

And lying to her.

Why would he do this? Why wouldn't he admit the truth? What did he have to hide?

He gave himself away when, in his apartment, he reached out to touch her. That's what he wanted all along, a way to get on her good side, an excuse to know her better so he could seek out her vulnerabilities, a sophisticated way to plan his move, not the awkward bumblings common to shy and inexperienced teens. Geoffrey Drousseau had played her like a violin, drawing his stiff bow across the strings linked to her very soul: her love of art, her fascination with artists, her curiosity about impression and interpretation, her empathy for the man who would pause to notice the boy who looked back. He was a fraud, hiding the truth from her . . . Like she had been doing with him.

Like she had pretended to be just an employee of the gallery.

Like she had pretended a lifestyle of modest means.

Like she had pretended to be interested in Sara's work when she really wanted mostly to study Geoffrey's reactions to it.

Like she had been pretending to care about him . . .

And failing miserably when tragedy struck his family, when he wanted a friend but she couldn't pretend to care enough to overcome her own discomfort, thus to empathize with someone who had loved and lost a father.

She looked at the sketch of little Geoffrey slumbering in his undies, sprawled without a care in the world, no fraud, no deceit, all boy, what you see is all he is. When had he lost this innocence? And why did he play this game with her? She reasoned that she had conjured the false image of herself as protection from people who could never see beyond her wealth. But Geoffrey had admitted he has his own money.

No, the secret Geoffrey hid, maybe out of shame, maybe for amusement, maybe for some reason Phrekka couldn't yet fathom—the secret Geoffrey protected must be Sara.

And he'd played this game just to spend time with Phrekka Churán.

And to be close to her . . .

And that felt good, in a way, but it wouldn't be right unless she knew the truth. She would find him out, expose him to the light of day, root out his secrets and decide for herself if he deserved friendship or disdain.

She picked up the phone. "Charles? I would like to alter my itinerary. Please schedule the jet for departure early tomorrow morning. I'll need reservations at the closest hotel, and of course a car, and some help identifying the correct address."

"I see," he answered. "Has something come up?"

"Yes. It's to attend the funeral of a friend's father. I want to be in Iowa by late morning."

"Where?"

"Coon Rapids."

CHAPTER 6

It felt like backing blindly through the quagmire of his past, the twisted trail linking boy to man, a path used only once, then abandoned to sink into the kind of deepest mud that warns against any attempt to return.

Geoffrey glanced around at the other passengers, assorted travelers packed into the small twin-prop airplane, the sod-jumper leg from Kansas City to Des Moines. Discreetly, he searched for clues revealing why each person would make this trip, maybe one or two chasing the luxuries of ambition and desire, most more than likely tethered by the necessities of duty and obligation. After all, to Geoffrey places like Iowa are never where one goes, but rather what one leaves behind.

He found the young adults most intriguing, wondering if they had truly escaped the scenery of their childhoods, now returning to embrace fond memories and revisit the places and people they would always love. He tried to guess which, if any, might be pursuing new goals. Or were most retreating from failure?—returning to the security of "home" until they can muster the nerve to escape again. Geoffrey knew how to confront his own trepidation: he clung tenaciously to the conviction that very soon he *would* leave. This trip would represent only a temporary pause in his forward momentum, too brief for him to sink again into the sense of helplessness he once fled.

Ernest had died. There would be a ceremony, followed by a procession, the rites of burial. Eventually, the meticulously mounded grave site would turn to muck—

Again Geoffrey found himself distracted by an image of mud too pervasive to wash away, seized by the panic one feels upon realizing he might become hopelessly stuck. He recalled one of his earliest memories, a sequence of shifting images, the first glimmers of grown-up purpose, watching helplessly as the sincerest desire to please others failed, good intentions crushed by false assumptions. The episode occurred in the springtime, with new corn sprouting in the fields. A surprise rainstorm thundered relentlessly across the land, washing out roads and bridges, flooding fields, damaging crops, and—duly noted by the worry-prone little boy—causing concern among the nervous adults. When the rain finally subsided, the black clouds swirling into clots of gray as they danced across a peek-a-boo backdrop of cerulean sky, Ernest reported that some of the tender stalks had been lost, and that a portion of the field would need to be replanted lest a smaller yield adversely affect the family's finances. Unfortunately, he had to work double shifts at the concrete works, something about damage from the flood, an emergency at the worst possible time.

Geoffrey formulated a plan that would allow him to prove his worth and demonstrate the responsibility of a big boy, a way to help his family and win respect for himself. He stripped to his shorts to avoid muddying his pants, then stole barefoot out to the barn and filled a sack with seed kernels, dragging it toward the back lot, Johnny Cornseed on a mission to sow anew. Squishy gunk whoosh-sucked between his toes until he arrived where the drainage ditch along their property line had overflowed, its embankment washed away, a veritable pond spreading where corn should be growing. The water seemed magical to the little boy, the rippling surface reflecting images of patchwork sky spinning grape cotton candy in the swirling clouds. God surely must have sent this ephemeral playscape to the Calhoun farm just for Geoffrey, so the enthralled child decided to postpone his mission for a while and, dropping the sack of seed, waded into the shallow pool.

The result proved disappointing, certainly not as fun as he had expected. The water seized him with its coldness, turning murky wherever he stepped, like the dregs of coffee he once tasted from Mother's dirty mug after it fermented atop the counter overnight. The water deeper and muddier than it appeared, he realized he was sinking more with every movement, the darkening ripples now lapping at his shorts and soaking his bottom. He turned to retreat, hurrying frantically as he felt the panic rise, but it became increasingly difficult to pull his legs free . . .

And then he couldn't move.

He squirmed and struggled, only to find himself mired even deeper. He tried not to cry, but he grew increasingly scared and distraught, surrounded by a flood powerful enough to destroy roads and bridges.

Ernest spewed fury when he found him. "You had no permission to come out here. You will get your own self free and take responsibility for your mistakes. Never should we have accepted such a disobedient and foolish child."

Ernest turned and walked away. Geoffrey cried for help, shivering from the chill, wrenching against the mud in desperation, the icy water now above his waist. With no way to escape, and no chance of assistance, Geoffrey knew he would remain there until the big black birds came—even as they do when a dead 'coon is found in the road—to peck out the boy's eyes and pull out his guts and consume his flesh until the flies swarmed and the maggots would finish whatever remained of this disobedient and foolish child. Exhausted, Geoffrey tried to sit, but the water splashed into his face and mouth, causing him to strangle and spit between sobs, wondering why God would let him die this way, and if he would still go to heaven, having failed at saving the family crop, a bad boy after all.

He looked up to see Ernest standing there again, this time wearing hip-waders. The big man stomped out into the muck, then grabbed Geoffrey by the arm and pulled him free, depositing the now-squalling child on the high furrow along the side.

"What was you thinkin'?" he demanded.

But Geoffrey couldn't answer, couldn't speak, couldn't breathe, couldn't explain he'd wanted to surprise his father by replanting the corn, how desperately he truly wanted to be nothing more than a good boy.

"Your mother put a towel and some clothes on the back porch. You hose off and don't track no mud in," Ernest warned, leaving Geoffrey there crying and shivering.

It occurred to Geoffrey that he might run away, that he could turn the other direction and run and keep running until he found a new life and a new home and a new family to call his own, but his body obeyed Ernest, trudging dutifully toward the house, though his heart remained mired there in the muck, buried too deep to escape, waiting for a time when the mud would dry and crack, when Geoffrey could step across it and walk away for good. His childhood moved in fits and starts after that, but his determination grew indelibly until he could never again be Geoffrey without it. His ultimate destination never seemed important, his goals never clearly defined, for the indistinct fantasies he would conjure of arriving at someplace new were always overshadowed by the narcotic anticipation of finally just leaving the old one behind, of getting away from Ernest, permanently shedding the man's disappointments and disapprovals, regardless of where that may lead.

That day in the cornfield marked the last time Geoffrey tried to please his father, choosing instead through the coming years to sow and cultivate his own convictions, and to demonstrate his obstinance by rebelling and doggedly pushing away. While Ernest believed in God and church, Geoffrey blamed such relentless devotion for tarnishing the man's soul and blinding him to life in the real world. Where Ernest demanded the ritual of schoolwork, Geoffrey skirted his studies at every opportunity, his grades ultimately relegating him to probationary admission at the community college in Des Moines where he realized too late that graduation from Stanford or Cal-Berkeley would have empowered him more and conferred the greater opportunities inherent in choice. Ernest loathed reading for pleasure as an idle waste of time, so Geoffrey immersed himself in every book he could find, swimming the rivers and streams that flow though fiction, the stories of deception and truth, of people and places beyond the town and the schools and the open fields of Coon Rapids. Ernest pronounced that any artwork not for the greater glory of God must necessarily be profane, so Geoffrey parlayed his talents for graphics and design into an associate's degree and a fledgling career in advertising and naked commerce.

By returning to Coon Rapids for the funeral, Geoffrey would be doing exactly what everybody expected of him. He could have manufactured an excuse, lied his regrets—pressing matters, you understand—and asked the Marloneys to ship him the records so he could determine how best to help his mother avoid fiscal worries and legal concerns. But no, obligation in the Calhoun family had always been most about appearances, doing what is considered appropriate, not allowing people the chance to whisper disapproval for leaving his mother to fend for herself, so heartless as to abandon his only surviving relative in her time of greatest need. Ernest always worried too much what others might think; never mind what his wife or son preferred, but let the church elders offer an opinion, along with the people at the hardware and the farm supply and the concrete works. They were the ones who always mattered most.

In time, Ernest's obsession with appearances became Geoffrey's greatest weapon, the key to his escape from the choke-hold of parishionership. Long after Geoffrey had rejected the congregation's hypocrisy, their stilted and oppressive views of the world, Ernest still forced him to attend, to participate in the ridiculous rituals with people whose outward appearances hid the troubled lives they truly led. Geoffrey allowed his disdain to become increasingly obvious, the opinions he brashly expressed escalating to heresy, until Ernest finally decided he preferred for the teenager to remain at home than to continue embarrassing the family. Geoffrey won that confrontation, and several others in the coming years, but he ultimately conceded and submitted to most of the rules and requirements that mired him, preferring to choose his battles carefully, discovering on more than one occasion that victory often leaves the winner with results unanticipated and too often undesirable.

So Geoffrey flew to Des Moines and rented a car and drove to the small Iowa town of his past, there to put his mother's affairs in order and preside over the interment services of his father. He would greet visitors and accept their condolences, representing his fractured family and keeping up appearances, one more time for his indifferent mother, one last time for Ernest. Geoffrey would earn everybody's respect, and nobody would find fault in doing his duty on this solemn occasion.

It felt like backing blindly into mud, but he was determined to look steadfastly ahead, and he would escape once again before he could sink too deep.

Quiet strains of organ music welcomed Geoffrey into the funeral home. Most of the planning had already been handled by telephone, but there remained the selection of a casket and coordination with the Presbyterian church to conduct the service. Ernest had purchased burial plots some years before, two beside each other, a package deal through another of the church's deacons, assurance that certain members of the faithful flock would ultimately dwell together for all eternity, thus preventing the encroachment of those less pious.

Brother Mickey arrived as Geoffrey signed various documents guaranteeing full and timely payment for all services in regard to the deceased. Brother Mickey's approach to congregational ritual had been the only reason Geoffrey ever looked forward to attending Ernest's church. A twenty-something carpenter's apprentice who taught Sunday School and organized activities for the young teens, Mickey always strove to keep the lessons relevant and fun, and he understood how to talk-with rather than down-to his small but loyal cadre. He always imbued his sermons with hints that no trespass they might conceive could exceed what Mickey had already committed by the time he reached their age, back before he had found the Truth and the Light. Because Brother Mickey became the only devout person Geoffrey ever trusted, he looked to him as a role model, seeing in him the possibility that faith could be embraced on one's own terms without having to sacrifice autonomy and individuality to the manipulations of hypocritical proselytizers.

Geoffrey found comfort in this relationship, and relief from Ernest's constant pressure to conform, until not long after his thirteenth birthday when he started to feel increasingly uncomfortable with Brother Mickey's unflagging interest in whether or not the young teen might have developed the habit of touching himself in ways, you know, other than for proper hygiene. As Mickey warned during frequent impromptu private conversations, allowing unnatural acts like masturbation to flourish unchecked would cause spiritual debilitation, blinding the unwary to the purity of God. Geoffrey always lied and assured him that he avoided the practice, but Mickey never seemed to believe him, the young teen sometimes wondering if maybe there were some way Mickey could tell. There existed no acceptable middle ground, Mickey warned, and no absolution achievable through perceived loopholes, not even for causal touching at night, or unnecessarily prolonged washing, or in believing wrongly that some method to avoid the use of hands might not count. This nasty habit, especially in concert with impure thoughts, was so shameful and heinous that it would draw the harshest wrath from the Lord, Geoffrey's only possibility of commutation to be found through confessing the precise details of such aberrant behavior to his good friend Brother Mickey.

Geoffrey had no interest in discussing such a personal subject with him, not with anyone, not even his best friend Billy Marloney, the one who had only recently taught him about the exciting capabilities of their burgeoning masculinity. This lesson was imparted in Billy's bedroom one afternoon during the previous winter, the wrinkled pages of a magazine as visual aids to establish an atmosphere for learning and mental stimulation, with Billy matter-of-factly explaining what little he understood, proceeding to the laboratory practicum on his own while Geoffrey endeavored to catch up, neither actually watching the other, both somewhat embarrassed afterward. Geoffrey under-stood that this awkward moment of intimacy had involved more than Billy just showing off or sharing a revelation, but rather a rare opportunity to bridge the uncomfortable chasm between them, if only for one day, and for Billy to give his friend a gift that only the two of them would understand. Billy had trusted him with something personal and private, even as Geoffrey trusted Billy to keep secret how he had wet himself after Ernest exposed and beat him. This gesture gave Billy a way to prove that he regarded Geoffrey as having matured beyond that humiliation, and that he cared enough to teach him the ultimate way—at least for a twelve-year-old—to prove to himself that he had become a man, something Ernest would never see or touch, something so central to the core of Geoffrey's being that Ernest could never take it away.

Geoffrey eventually gave up trying to reconcile his perception of God with the image Mickey painted, refusing to believe the Lord and Savior would care a whole lot about such harmless pursuits. Would it be acceptable if he imagined that he loved the girl in his fantasy?—that she practiced religion, that they had been joined in holy matrimony, and that she thoroughly enjoyed having him touch her? Geoffrey even tried, because he trusted Mickey, to relinquish the noxious habit on several occasions, but his resolve always dissolved rather quickly, until ultimately he gave up, unable to understand what could possibly be accomplished by such unnecessary sacrifice. He finally decided that if Brother Mickey would spend a little more time taking care of his own private needs, then maybe he would spend less time worrying about Geoffrey's.

Apparently, several of the other boys shared similar opinions, because rumors started floating and Brother Mickey suddenly found himself relegated to passing the collection plate during adult services. Geoffrey lost his role model—just in the nick of time, he decided—for he could no longer trust *anybody's* version of how to be a better person, especially from someone who dared claim to speak for God. He would stop feeling guilty about benign diversions that simply felt good, instead seeing them as learning how to share himself someday with the woman he would love, and though his liaisons would be limited for a time to those of his own imagination, he sure looked forward to the day when all that practice would pay off.

"Geoffrey!" Brother Mickey greeted him at the funeral home, flashing his seductive smile and offering a firm handshake. "It's such a blessing that you could be here for your mom."

Geoffrey had to resist the impulse to ask, *That's quite a grip there, Mickey—you been working out?* "Have arrangements been made for someone to conduct the service?"

"Yes, Brother Walker offered to officiate—in a manner Brother Ernest would have wanted," he quickly added, a not-so-subtle hint that Geoffrey should act the part of devoted son who accepts guidance from those who shared his father's faith, not to interfere as some back-slider nursing a grudge, one who insists on unconventional practices gleaned from the pagans he'd met at college or, worse yet, the hippies and homos and God-knows-whats out there in San Francisco.

"Good," Geoffrey confirmed, nodding. He felt uneasy with the way Brother Mickey studied him, those suspicious little close-set eyes, the sheen of perspiration beading along his receding hairline. Recalling how Mickey had once asked the young teen, *Have you started, you know, to grow hair yet?*, Geoffrey had to resist the impulse to demand, *Hey Mickey, have you stopped, you know, growing hair?*

"We'll all be attending, helping to usher, whatever is needed," Mickey assured him.

"I appreciate that," he responded, much to the older man's obvious relief. "I have but one request." The air grew suddenly thick with tension, a possible threat to the propriety of Raccoon River Presbyterian, maybe the expectation of some bizarre nipple-piercing ritual followed by LSD-sniffing and, God help us, circle-jerk group masturbation. "No recruiting—and no guilt."

"I don't understand."

"A nice service where Brother Walker quotes from the Scripture, leads a few prayers, and talks about what a good man my father was will be sufficient. I don't want anybody guilt-tripped—especially my mother or me—for not attending regularly, and no trying to convince other mourners that they should join your church, or attend more often, or tithe more. This is to honor Ernest, not to provide a soap box for Brother Walker."

Geoffrey felt he owed at least that much to his mother. She had grown tired of being one of the church women, constantly held up to scrutiny, relentlessly advised on how to live and raise her child and even what to think, until she finally decided simply not to participate anymore. The tension in their home escalated to shouting matches over this, but the issue of *appearances* won out, the image and perception of indifference preferable to one of acrimony, rebellion, and spousal defiance. Her obstinance indirectly wound up mapping Geoffrey's route of escape from the church's choke-hold some years later, just as an older sibling often fights the battles that ease restrictions for younger brothers and sisters. For this, Geoffrey would always feel grateful. He would not allow these people to bully her, especially at a time when grief had rendered her so vulnerable, when focusing on her own needs must take precedence before satisfying the expectations of demagogues espousing the presumed commandments of a petulant deity they created in their own pathetic images.

Brother Mickey considered Geoffrey's request for a moment, then sighed and nodded. "I'll have a talk with him. But just between us—" Geoffrey flinched at the phrase, recalling how many awkward conversations had begun with the whisper of those words. "This *is* a sign, you know."

Geoffrey took a deep breath, frustrated, annoyed, angry. He fought the temptation to suggest where Mickey might insert his beliefs, but he prudently decided to let the man have his say for now, hopefully to get it out of his system. "A sign of what?"

"The Lord works in mysterious ways. He brought you home, brought you and your mother together again, and He's given you both another chance to accept Him into your lives."

"God planned all this?"

"It's like how He made sure I got lots of overtime these past two weeks, even though business has been slow lately. My water heater gave out, and I couldn't afford to replace it, so the extra hours—"

"God gave you *overtime*?—to pay for a water heater?"

"Well yes, but—"

"Why didn't He stop it from giving out in the first place? Then you wouldn't need the overtime, and you could spend those extra hours helping the church—"

"Well, that's not important. What matters is this chance He gave you and your mother—"

"Are you saying God *killed* Ernest, his deacon and faithful servant, so my mother and I would start going to church? He left her a widow, alone for the rest of her life. What if I start going but she doesn't? Will He kill me then?—to get to her?"

"Geoffrey, please."

He shook his head, furious with himself for letting Mickey rile him like this. He forced a calm demeanor, fixing Mickey with his eyes and evenly stating, "I will pay a generous honorarium for Walker to conduct the service, but *not* for what you just did. I'll cut him off if he does, and take over myself if I have to."

Mickey bristled at the threat, standing awkwardly for a moment, but then he smiled, donning that tailored mien of seductive charm that Geoffrey recognized with a shudder. "Whatever you wish." He nodded, shook the younger man's hand quickly, then turned and walked out.

At that moment, Geoffrey realized the irony of being the one to orchestrate Ernest's final religious service, but he found comfort in believing that his father would be eulogized the way he would have wanted, a service befitting his devotion while carefully preserving the dignity and fragile emotions of the woman he had taken for his wife. Ernest was a stubborn and determined man who had many faults, but Geoffrey, at that moment, standing there chest-deep in a sea of empty coffins, listening to the familiar-but-discomforting strains of organ music, realized something placed his father at least one notch above Brother Mickey, the beady-eyed savior who fretted so much about how often young teenage boys might be touching themselves . . .

At least Ernest had finally learned when to quit.

Geoffrey stopped at the florist's to order a casket spray.

He stopped at the cemetery to look at the burial site, a backhoe reaching toward the muddy soil, its scorpion tail poised to strike.

He stopped in front of the high school, then parked facing the road, studying the forlorn building in his mirror.

He slowed in front of the hardware, but decided not to go in. Bill Marloney would be working there with his dad—now business partners who bought out Old Man Willikers. Mr. Marloney could no longer work the farm since his accident, so he let the Hansons lease their farmland for corn-cropping, and decided hardware had been his true calling after all.

Geoffrey stopped at the clothiers and bought a conservative silk tie, grateful he'd not yet been recognized by any of the locals.

He stopped and put gas in the rental, nine dollars and change.

Then Geoffrey ran out of places to stop.

He really didn't want to see his mother yet, but couldn't figure out what to say, and felt apprehensive about how well she might be coping. He didn't feel ready yet to greet people, to keep up appearances, to parcel out solemn intonations of mutual mourning. He wished Phrekka had come, but then he wondered just what he'd been thinking when he invited her. Imagine how complicated this would all be if he had added a guest to the mix, an outsider, a stranger in a strange land, some sensual enchantress who couldn't help but soar above these Iowa townspeople, these common folks who take pride in being so grounded yet live by the dictates of ancient spiritual conjurers.

Geoffrey had returned to Coon Rapids as a man with no job, a fizzled career, no real friends, no love. Phrekka Churán was the one person he thought about night and day, but he persisted in his determination not to fall in love with her, not to risk again marring the sheen of friendship he'd so methodically polished. He found it difficult to admit such weakness, that he had wanted her to come along as a talisman from his new life, a reminder of who he had become and how much more he wanted to be, for her to be the sparkling point of tomorrow's light who keeps his sights focused ahead, a beacon to show him the way home. The fragile construct of his life still teetered unsteadily, unbalanced, unsupported; he'd been so busy running from Ernest and Coon Rapids that his goals remained murky: any graphics job in California, not necessarily fulfillment wherever it may lead; a live-in girlfriend, even if she wasn't his one true inamorata; companions to reflect the image he projected, not real friends he could trust with his vulnerabilities . . .

Unsure of how Phrekka might change his life, Geoffrey realized that in some elusive way, she already had.

Finding a dozen or so vehicles parked around the Calhoun house, he pulled in slowly, the crunch of gravel under tires announcing the return of the itinerant child. Mrs. Marloney burst out the door, hurrying to the car to greet him, tears in her eyes.

"Oh Geoffrey," she whispered in his ear, enveloping him in her arms. He noticed how much shorter she seemed, the images of his childhood colliding with the realities of this day. There had been so many Mrs. Marloney hugs through the years, so many times her blond-haired neighbor boy had secretly wished his own mother were more like her, or that Billy's mom would adopt him, and he would have a brother . . .

"I'm glad you're here," he said quietly, not wanting to let go.

Finally, she stepped back, looking up into his eyes. "You're mom's doing okay, I guess, all things considered. I don't think it's quite hit her yet. That happens you know, in stages they say. I've seen it myself, like when my daddy and Uncle Teddy was killed. It don't seem real at first, but then it does, and then it seems too real for a long time . . ." She looked off into the distance, but then seemed to snap out of her trance. "It's good you could be here. Your mom needs you—oh, and you need her, too. You need each other."

"And you," he said, and she liked that. "We both need you."

They walked toward the house, arm-in-arm. "Billy's gonna leave work early and come out to see you," she said, pleased about that, too.

"That'll be great," Geoffrey said, and he meant it, sort of. It would be awkward—neither had made the effort to keep in touch—but Bill would offer, well, some solid ground, the one person who could understand how important it was that Geoffrey not become mired in the past.

Inside the house loitered nearly a score of people, most older, all speaking in solemn whispers, plus a brigade of women working in the kitchen, plying the guests with platefuls of noodle-rice-meat-veggie casseroles, the table piled high with food, each dish labeled with little pieces of tape. The room fell quiet. "Geoffrey's home," Mrs. Marloney announced.

People gathered around, hugging, clasping hands, lots of "How you holding up?", no sign of his mother.

"He shore did love you, son."

"He was always bragging on you."

"You was the first Calhoun went to college, you know."

"And you got a big important job all the way out in California!"

"I'm Eldin—from the church. I'm a deacon, too—just like your father. He was a good man—talked about you a lot."

"If there's anything you need, son, you just let us know. I mean that now, you hear me? I mean it. Anything."

Once everybody had discharged their opening volleys in this ceremony of helpless concern, they all stepped back dutifully, shaking their heads, wiping tears from their eyes, patting him on the back, clasping his shoulder. Mrs. Marloney led the fatherless son to the master bedroom. There sat Marjorie on the bed, a hankie clutched in her hands, staring forlornly out the window at roiling gray clouds scrubbing all color from the sky. She glanced up, appeared to be confused for a second, then seemed to recognize him. "Oh Geoffrey, I don't know what I'm going to do."

He sat beside her on the bed, took a deep breath. "It'll be okay, Mother," he reassured her.

Mrs. Marloney lingered for a second, then quietly eased out, pulling the door nearly closed behind her.

They sat close, but neither offered to touch the other, the awkwardness still carving the canyon between their worlds.

"Are you back to stay?" she asked, looking at him.

He shook his head. "I can't."

"No, I suppose not." She looked out the window again. "He took care of the money, the business—everything, you know."

"I'll help you sort it out. I'm sure there's plenty in the bank. We can let out the farm—maybe to the Hansons—like the Marloneys did, and that'll bring in more than enough for you to live on—unless you'd rather move to a condo or something. I have my trust fund, too, if you need more."

"I'd rather stay here—if you'll make sure I can afford to. I don't know what I'd do without you."

He nodded. "Why did you schedule the funeral for tomorrow afternoon?"

"He didn't like 'em long and drawn out. Always said get 'em in the ground and get back to work. Don't do anybody any good standing around a funeral home all week, he always said."

He nodded again. "Visitation starts in a couple of hours. If you want, we can go in first, by ourselves."

She shook her head. "No, I'll go when there's a lot of people there. I don't like funeral homes, so I'll just do what I have to for appearances."

"That's fine then."

They were quiet for a minute or two; then she looked at him again. "He loved you, you know."

Geoffrey closed his eyes. He wanted to float away, just catch a breeze and swirl into those clouds through the window. Maybe she believed herself, but he couldn't, and he never would.

"I know it didn't seem like it sometimes," she pressed, "like when he was hard on you, but that's just how he showed it."

He took a deep breath, shook his head, and felt himself pulled back to the room, sitting there on the bed. "There are better ways."

She looked at her hands, folded the hankie, then shook it out and folded it again. "He just wanted you to grow up right."

Geoffrey didn't want to have this discussion. He had recited this stilted dialogue before, usually during desperate attempts to convince her to intercede in Ernest's outrage du jour, but now he flew on autopilot, and the words came easily, and maybe this would be the last time they had to be spoken, these thoughts expressed, these feelings scrutinized. Maybe this conversation between mother and son would be the eulogy that finally laid Ernest B. Calhoun to rest. "I was never the kind of son he wanted."

She actually chuckled at this. She'd never done that before, improvising her part like that. "Oh, Geoffrey, I don't think anybody's kids ever turn out like they expect. In spite of not takin' to the church, you still grew up to be a good man, and he knew that, and he told it to anyone who ever mentioned your name."

"But not to me."

"No," she sighed. "No, he wasn't good at that."

"It's 'cause I wasn't really his," he blurted, regretting it as soon as the words tumbled from his mouth, a new line for him, too.

"That's not so!" She looked genuinely surprised that he would believe such a terrible thing. "No, he thought you were a blessing from God. When it turned out I couldn't bear children . . ." She hesitated at the pain summoned from some dusty nook in the manse of her regrets. "His only fault was tryin' too hard with you—" Quieter, she added, "—And maybe not being so good at knowin' how."

Geoffrey considered how much better it must be to do nothing than to do something wrong for not knowing better. At least, well, he believed that to be true, but then maybe it wasn't, and then maybe nothing made sense right then. "He sure *thought* he knew what he was doing," he grumbled.

She looked at him, her features softer now, and this reminded him of those infrequent times she had hugged him, when she'd allowed those rare glimpses of her love to shine in her eyes. "By the time you got older, he wasn't so sure anymore that he'd done right."

"He gave up."

"No, Geoffrey, he realized you were turning out pretty good anyway, just your own way is all, even though it wasn't what he expected. These past few years, since you've been gone, I could tell he was sorry for being so harsh on you."

Geoffrey started picking at a string on his Dockers, his throat constricted, tears threatening to well in his eyes. He didn't want to paint a human face on Ernest, not now, not after all he'd been through with the man. He'd grown too comfortable carrying his resentment and hatred close to his heart, and there would always be room for it there, no matter how much she tried to push it aside with even the slightest suggestion that something else, something unfamiliar, something unrecognized might have dwelled there all along . . . maybe disguised, maybe misguided, but nevertheless very real. "He never did anything to make up for it," he said softly.

She reached over and lifted his face, searching his eyes, tears tracing lines down the rough contours of her cheeks. "But then he ran out of time, didn't he?"

Set and setting, backdrop and props, this was the scenery of life on the Calhoun farm. Geoffrey stood in the back doorway, then decided to take a walk, respite from so many consultants gathered in the name of Ernest, all contriving the futures of Widow Calhoun and her only child, now the man of the family.

"Might be good you move back for a while," one had whispered.

"It'd sure help your mom," the advisory council agreed.

"Good place to marry and settle down," offered the site locator.

"Lots of nice young women here," agreed the matchmaker.

"Plenty of room in this old house, plus a live-in grandma to help watch the young'ns," pronounced the specialist.

Geoffrey stepped from shadow to sunlight, and first he noticed the odor, that familiar balmy aroma of springtime rains leeching freshly turned soil; then he heard melodies, the breeze sighing through trees, shuffles of tussock-grass along the hedgerow, a plaintive personal ad from some lonesome cricket; and he imagined the flavors, freezer-cranked homemade plum ice cream, steamy Silver Queen sweet corn drenched with butter and salt; and he recalled how it felt in late summer, swaddled in a blanket of warm God's breath, swatting mosquitoes as butter dribbled down his arm to drip from his elbow, his neck and arms sore from shucking corn and stuffing so many burlap sacks. He blinked, reluctant to look, steeling himself for the retro-tug of this place where he had laughed and cried. He wanted to erect a tent around himself, a translucent cloak of invincibility with portals to look out but screens to prevent touch, protection from memories threatening to swirl around and through him. He would observe all this with the detachment of an impartial scientist.

Geoffrey smiled, thinking about Phrekka and her fascination with his reactions to artistic images, always puzzling over the power of association and interpretation. Yet here he stood, moved profoundly by this uncaptured and unremarkable scene, resisting its hold over him even as he submitted to its will. Would the director film its stark reality or paint the abstract impressions evoked by this still life, this past life? The elements arranged themselves picture-perfect, neat and organized, Ernest's defense against the cluttered worlds of cluttered minds. Mother's potted plants lined up for inspection, the Wandering Jew reaching out tentatively, testing the rumor that Ernest's shears had been stilled, this patio ceded to the citizens who dwell there. Stacked railroad ties played Lincoln Logs, bricks and patio blocks hosting a pill-bug convention, some unknown project never realized. There stood the propane-gas grill, and Geoffrey just had to stroke his fingers along the contours of the white tank he was never allowed to touch. There waited the picnic table, stained and sealed and varnished, then varnished again and again, arranged just so, but with a twig atop it, and a leaf, interlopers out of place. Geoffrey flicked them away, just for Ernest.

He walked toward the small garden over by the barn. The vegetables were flourishing, beans climbing gym-class ropes of twine, caged tomatoes reaching through prison-cell bars, squash and melon vines conducting clandestine sorties into each other's domains, zucchini taunting the cukes with *Mine is bigger than yours*, radishes and carrots playing hide-and-seek with the potatoes, cabbage and lettuce sunbathing side-by-side, onions awaiting cleaver therapy for a good cry.

He glanced up at the bracket still affixed atop the light pole, rusting some ten or twelve years now, the last sprig of failed birdhouse, like a barren tree, its leaves stripped by tornadoes of frustration and regret. The pole didn't seem so high as it once did, not very high at all. Geoffrey searched the eaves of the silo, and there he found it, a lone blue jay watching him curiously, not the same bird from his youth, but one with the same attitude, accusing Geoffrey of obligations unfulfilled.

The corn looked good, knee-high—high as your eye by the fourth of July. The stalks lined up like so many obedient school children—some taller and more robust, others slight and shy, or maybe just unsure of themselves—each as important as the other, all imbued with possibility and potential. Geoffrey liked how sometimes the smaller ones can surprise, their tufts of blond silk dancing majestically in the breeze, drinking every drop of sunshine until their tender nectar explodes with every bite, sweetest of all. Given the chance, even the smallest can grow bigger than life. *Like little boys*, Geoffrey thought.

Like me.

He found himself drawn to the back corner, that acre which tended to flood. He walked along the scrub bordering the field, rabbits scurrying this way and that. A lone pheasant ran ahead, playing *Catch me if you can*, pretending he couldn't fly, Plan B held in reserve. A bevy of quail flushed from their solemn conference, scattering to the winds, evading his shot, remembering.

The soil gave way to mud, caking Geoffrey's shoes, too messy to ford, circumnavigation not worth the bother. He turned and looked back toward the house, not so far away as he remembered it. The field was shrinking. Mrs. Marloney was shrinking. The light pole, the imposing presence of Ernest, the whole world—everything seemed smaller than it should be. He studied the mud again, so deep and ominous, turning to quicksand before his eyes, and a cold chill passed around and through him. Better to move on, to walk away.

He paused under the silver maple he and Billy used to climb. Ernest always warned them down: "Ain't nothin' to see up there, gonna get yourselves killed." Then Billy fell and broke his wrist the summer they turned fourteen. Mrs. Marloney rushed him to the clinic, Geoffrey riding along. Billy tried to be strong, determined not to cry, but when Doc Waverly set the bones, it proved too much for him to bear. Mrs. Marloney held her son tightly, and when the doc went out for supplies, she looked up to see that her son's friend was crying, too. "Well bless your heart, Geoffrey," she whispered, pulling him into a three-way embrace, which meant he was hugging Billy, too, and that was okay under the circumstances, all things considered, especially since no one else would ever know.

Geoffrey let himself into the barn, then stood there in silence, holding his breath. So many scenes had played out in this abandoned theatre, stories of adventure and conquest, mystery and suspense, comedy and tragedy, tales of deception and truth. Spotlights shined from the eaves, choreographed specks of sparkling dust dancing in and out of the golden sunlight. There stood the tractor, center stage, draped in the blue-tarpaulin curtain of intermission. Kettle drums of insecticide rested silently in the orchestra pit. Instruments of creation and repair, Ernest's tools reposed along the workbench mezzanine. Hay bales provided extra chairs, sacks of seed an audience, onions and taters watching from their private boxes. They had all laughed at Geoffrey and his friend playing, nodded approval while Ernest and the reluctant son worked, wept for the disobedient child who danced the lead in Ernest's macabre ballets of discipline and degradation.

Over in the corner he could see the scorched boards, carefully varnished, then varnished again to minimize further damage, silent testament to the sins of regretful past. There above the workbench hung the leather strap Ernest had purchased after that fire incident, wielded many times over the following four or five years. It looked smaller and not so thick now, like it had been shrinking, worn along one side, unable to heal like the welts of freshly strapped skin. He lifted it off, rubbed his hand along it, squeezed it tightly the way Ernest used to, testing its pliability. What a powerful tool this must be, making even Billy cry from just watching his friend suffer its lashes.

Geoffrey realized he was trembling. He squeezed his eyes shut, trying to fight it off, but he'd been gripped by currents pulling him inescapably into heart-pounding rapids, sinking in the riptide of panic and fear, that wrenching certainty each time it poised to strike again— He fought it off, clinging to the solace of knowing its time had passed, afraid to leap for the life-raft victory inherent in facing one's fears, proof he can emerge unscathed from the other side and float safely home, no matter how much, no matter how long, no matter what.

Even as he decided to avoid this posthumous confrontation, the choice was made for him, his heart drawn into the maelstrom, just as Ernest had never allowed him any alternative.

And he remembered.

It came vividly . . . the pain, the desperation, the humiliation, measuring endurance in micro-increments, clinging desperately to the hope that it would be over soon . . .

And then it *was* over, and he knew it would never come back, and that the only way it could ever hurt him again would be if he let it. He decided to package this anguish in a box and shove it on the back shelf in the darkest closet, there to gather dust, benign, ignored.

"Geoffrey?"

He started, snapped from his reverie, embarrassed at first, then determined not to be.

Bill Marloney stood in the doorway, watching as the blond-haired twenty-year-old clutched Ernest's tool of disapproval and reproach. They looked at each other, neither speaking for a moment, and the most profound sense of understanding passed between them. Bill wouldn't need to cry for his friend this day, for this moment would purge his soul, too.

"Good to see you, Bill," he said quietly, casually hanging the strap back in its place.

"I was gonna clean up and go to the funeral home for a while; then I can cover the store tonight and let my dad go."

"It'll be good to have you there," he said, the words inadequate to convey how much he meant it. "Your mom has been a gem."

Bill smiled at that. "Her heart's always in the right place, even when her head's not." Then, more seriously, he confided, "She says it still hasn't hit your mom yet."

"Nothing ever hits her very fast," Geoffrey sighed.

"Maybe it's best that way."

"Reality in doses small enough to swallow."

They stood there for a second, then Bill said, "You owe me a sleep-over, you know."

Geoffrey smiled at that. "Aw, come on. I stayed over lots of times after—you know."

"I mean *me* visit *you*. You're out in California now, with that fancy apartment and big job."

"I messed up and lost the job," Geoffrey said, somehow relieved by the confession. He'd come to town intending to deflect or obfuscate or outright lie about that.

Bill shrugged. "You'll get a better one."

"Yeah."

Silence.

Bill glanced toward the strap on the wall. "Is there anything I can do?"

Geoffrey took a deep breath, then had to chuckle. "What else is there?"

Bill spread his hands and allowed a smile. "I'm gonna go round up my mother—that should take a while—then get ready and see you over there." He turned to leave.

"Bill?"

He paused. "Yeah?"

"I do owe you a sleep-over."

Bill fixed him with that sneaky expression that always used to signal conspiracy, and Geoffrey knew his friend intended to collect, which they both wanted, maybe even needed.

Geoffrey stood there alone for several more minutes, looking around, trying to recapture that feeling of helpless panic . . . but it was gone. The more he tried, the farther away it seemed. He knew what it looked like, how it made him feel; but it slipped just beyond his grasp, another fading memory like the photos in a tattered album. He understood that what matters most happens after the picture is taken. So what's the next shot?

He took the strap down again, shook his head in awe of its power over the mind, so much more potent than any damage it may inflict on the flesh. Like Phrekka's paintings, more than strokes and splashes of color in acrylic or oil, what matters is how people feel when they draw near.

Geoffrey carried the strap out into the sunshine. He looked up at the blue jay, and it seemed the bird knew what had passed around and through the Calhoun farmyard this day, and that made Geoffrey laugh to himself. Phrekka must be rubbing off on him, to think such silly ideas.

He paused before the trash bin, lifted the lid, and buried the strap deep among the discarded debris of everyday unremarkable lives. He closed the lid, sealing its casket, a wordless eulogy as it passed from the physical world, never again to hurt the little boy Geoffrey would forever cradle in his heart.

Geoffrey had won after all.

Time to prepare for a funeral, he paused at the back door and wiped the mud from his shoes.

Chapter 7

Geoffrey led the pilgrimage to the funeral home, there to preside over public visitation. Mrs. Marloney stayed behind to look after his mother and serve as receptionist in charge of accepting food deliveries, answering calls, dispensing schedules and directions.

Impressed by the large crowd and heartened by their pledges of support, Geoffrey traded some of his initial cynicism for relief, confident that when the time came for him to move forward again, chasing new job opportunities up and down the west coast, his mother would continue beyond this pause between chapters, friends helping her resume turning the pages of her life. Marjorie would immerse herself again in the passion-filled worlds of Charlotte and Lance while the people of Coon Rapids hovered just a phone call away.

Ernest reposed stiffly in the open casket, dressed in one of his church suits. Geoffrey quickly surveyed the scene and, satisfied all was in order, decided to avoid approaching the flower-festooned tableau, circulating for a time and receiving visitors near the entrance to the viewing room. People filed in dutifully, pausing to introduce themselves, hugging Geoffrey, sharing anecdotes, remembering *When you was just a little thing, all blond hair and big eyes* . . . They would march slowly and solemnly down the big aisle, maintaining a respectful distance until the area cleared, most arm-in-arm, some with arms around shoulders, supporting the elderly, whispering instructions to the young; then they would approach Ernest, catching their breaths, shaking their heads, wiping their eyes, some touching the deceased man's shoulder as if to confirm this elegiac reality.

"How you holding up, Geoffrey?"

"And your mom?"

How you holding up?

More people waiting, the mourners would move aside, commenting on the flowers, checking senders' cards, nodding approval, looking around to see if their own arrangement had arrived yet.

"How you holding up, son?"

"How's your mom holdin' up?"

A delivery boy brought in more, another van pulling up in front. Organ music wafted from strategically mounted speakers. Smokers eased their way outdoors, a small group standing around to the side. The funeral director checked in discreetly, assured that everything's okay, that yes, mom's holding up okay.

"He shore was proud of you, son."

"Bragged on you all the time."

"He was a good man and a good Christian."

"Are you holdin' up all right?"

Mrs. Marloney arrived with Geoffrey's mother. People gathered in the outer foyer, hugging and consoling, offering anything, just name it, anything. Finally, they propelled the grieving widow forward into the room where stood the coffin, everybody stepping back respectfully, busying themselves with each other so as not to stare awkwardly. She held Geoffrey's arm as he walked her to the front, there to stand before the catafalque and inspect Ernest.

She gasped, stifling the sound, then let her breath out slowly, shaking her head. She touched his arm, her fingers lingering for a moment. Then she leaned in a bit, turning her head toward his face, probably comparing him to the myriad images from her life. Her hand unsteady, she straightened the knot of his tie, then aligned it carefully, arranged just so. She adjusted the handkerchief in his breast pocket, unfastened the bottom button on his vest, and made sure the points of his button-down collar lay even with each other. She took a deep breath and searched his face. She used her fingers to comb some loose strands of his silver-streaked hair, but her hand shook and Geoffrey reached over to touch it, to hold it, to pull it back gently, to keep holding on. She took another deep breath and nodded just perceptibly, then nodded again.

Goeffrey glanced at Mrs. Marloney hovering close by, permission to approach.

"They done a good job on him," his mother said quietly. "He looks good."

Mrs. Marloney stood at her other side, all three now inspecting Ernest. "They done a very good job," she agreed. "He does look good."

"He does, doesn't he?"

He looks dead.

"Looks like he's just asleep is all," Mrs. Marloney decided.

"Doesn't he though? It's 'cause they done such a good job on him."

Mrs. Marloney nodded. "He looks good."

Waiting for Geoffrey to comment, they wouldn't be satisfied until he'd agreed.

"Yes," he said, "he looks good."

Appearances mattered a lot to Ernest. He and his family must at all times project the right image to their community, especially to their church's parishioners. That his teenage son so often ignored this along with his other obligations and responsibilities frustrated him to no end.

Geoffrey Calhoun, at fifteen years old, disagreed with his father about nearly everything, obligations and responsibilities in particular. It seemed Ernest considered his own obligations to be feeding, clothing, and sheltering the boy while his responsibility lay in correcting every little thing about him. Geoffrey cared little about Ernest's obligations, maybe even taking them for granted, but he argued often and loudly that a father's responsibility should be to respect his son, to see him as a separate person who would someday have to make his own way in the world, on his own terms, for now an equal member of the family who deserved encouragement. Ernest countered often and loudly that Geoffrey's obligations were to do as he was told. As for responsibility, well, the boy simply didn't have a lick of it.

This conflict erupted yet again late one autumn evening as a storm blustered outside. The obstinate teenager had failed to take responsibility for cleaning and storing the miscellaneous farm equipment after completing his chores. Since nobody else was home, he took a break and stretched out in his bedroom to spend a little private quality time with a magazine featuring somebody named Candi or Cherri or maybe Cootchie, after which he fell asleep. Earnest returned home, found the equipment out in the rain, and burst into Geoffrey's room clutching a broken shovel handle, then flew into a rage and started swinging when he discovered exactly how the boy had squandered his time, evidence right there in plain sight, a shameless affront to the commandments of God. Geoffrey managed to dodge or deflect most of the rod's blows, but then he blurted some profanities.

On these occasions Geoffrey risked the greatest danger of being pulled across his own line, where first he would lose awareness of his surroundings, and then even of himself, like he had gone somewhere safe to wait for the onslaught to end. Upon returning, he would usually discover that Mother had intervened.

This time proved different. He scrambled back across the bed, Ernest coming at him and connecting with several bruising blows. Geoffrey fell to floor, looking up in time to see the staff raised toward the heavens. Desperate, without thinking, he clawed under the bed and found his powerful air-pellet pistol, aiming toward his berserk attacker.

Ernest froze, sputtering spittle, panting his rage—

Then he swung!

Pfoom! Geoffrey fired past him, trying to scare him off.

Ernest jumped back from the bed and stood there amazed, unbelieving, his eyes darting between the trembling teen and the lower-corner pane of French window now sporting a small hole and the spider-web of several radiating cracks.

Geoffrey stood up, lowering the pistol, but still clutching it tightly, not sure if he was safe. Terrified of what he'd done, furious at Ernest for making him lose control, profoundly ashamed for letting him . . . he dropped the weapon and stood there trembling.

"You would see me dead!" Ernest bellowed, the steam rising again.

Geoffrey closed his eyes, impotent, helpless, but then the trembling faded away, and he braced himself.

Nothing happened, then still nothing.

He opened his eyes, and there stood Ernest, tears lining his sun-flecked cheeks. He had never seen the man cry before, never realized he even could.

"I'm sorry," Geoffrey whispered, and the sound snapped Ernest back from wherever he'd gone. He stormed out of the room, slamming the door behind him.

Geoffrey kicked the pistol under his bed, then studied the cracked pane for a moment, finally moving his lamp in front so he wouldn't have to look at it. He turned off the light, then stood there in the darkness, waiting until he felt sure it was over. He felt icy cold shivers, so he peeled off his jeans and snuggled into bed, pulling the covers up tight, burying his head under the pillow, aghast at what he'd done, at what he'd become. His social-studies class had discussed how abusive behavior often becomes a repeating cycle with each new generation, but he had scoffed about this to himself, listening while the teacher prattled on about other people in other worlds. *Not me. No, not me.*

What he had just seen in himself was a piece of his father. Worse yet, Ernest had seen it, too, and Geoffrey's façade of self-righteous superiority had crumbled to dust. He never intended to shoot him, not that a piddly air-gun would do much damage, and to this conviction he clung desperately, though he never imagined he could even brandish a weapon at Ernest in the first place. He had seen how rage can cause people to lose sight of their own limits, but he never comprehended that fear might do the same—not just moving the boundaries, but removing them completely. For the first time in Geoffrey's life, he feared himself.

In that, he found a hint of empathy with Ernest, the suggestion of understanding, like maybe he could forgive him, a fleeting notion without substance, never fully grasped. Maybe he'd realized that Ernest did, at least, have limits, too, which must have been why he'd given up and left the room. His father might lose control of his rage, but Geoffrey had to admit that never, not once, had Ernest ever made him fear for his life.

But Geoffrey had made *Ernest* feel mortally afraid, and in that he committed a worse offense than his father ever dared.

Geoffrey twisted his body, gripping the covers so tightly that his hands cramped. He wretched and gagged, trying not to vomit, waves of cold tingles washing over him, wracking him with cramps and nausea.

He would never hurt Ernest because it wasn't the man he hated, but rather how he treated Geoffrey and the fact that he refused to love his son, disapproving or not. Now, with what Geoffrey had done, the secret hope he always nurtured, that glimmer of possibility he rarely dared admit even to himself, that chance of someday reconciling with Ernest . . . would forever be tainted.

Geoffrey had lost after all.

Geoffrey vowed that he would never hurt anybody for the rest of his life, no matter what. Succeeding, he would find redemption, and he would deserve the confidence that he'd become a better man than his father. He knew what it looked like from the other side of his own limits now, and though it might haunt him in his dreams, at least he would recognize it, and the next time he would know what to do, and he would be ready.

If he ever again, driven by desperation, found a weapon in his hand . . .

He would turn it on himself.

Geoffrey bid good night to the last mourners departing the Calhoun home while Mrs. Marloney and Bill busied themselves in the kitchen, sealing and refrigerating covered dishes, carrying others out to a chest freezer on the enclosed back porch, boxing the overflow to keep chilled at their house until time to set up again after the funeral the next day. There would be lots of people gathering then, and lots of food.

"We're going now," Mrs. Marloney said, her son standing there awkwardly, loaded down with boxes. "I know you're checked in at the motel, Geoffrey," she said quietly, "but it sure would be good for you to stay here with your mama tonight. You think about it. It's good to see you home again, Geoffrey—I just wish it was under better circumstances." Bill nodded agreement.

Geoffrey walked them out to the car, thanking them for their help. "I'll stay here," he assured her, though he didn't want to. It would be the right thing, though. He'd move on soon enough, back to Mill Valley and an empty, lonesome apartment. He couldn't leave his mother alone tonight. Not tonight.

They sat in the living room for a few minutes, she in her customary place on the couch, he in a chair. Ernest could be at the concrete works . . . He offered to make coffee, but she shook her head.

"I've been drinking coffee all day." Apparently reminded of the other half of that endless cycle, she disappeared into the bathroom for several minutes, then returned and lit a cigarette. They sat in silence for a while, Geoffrey trying to figure out what to say. "Mrs. Marloney sure has been great," he offered.

She nodded and lit another cigarette off the last one, glancing at him occasionally. Finally she asked, "Will you stay long enough to go through the records, to see what needs to be done?"

He felt relieved. She'd confirmed again that she understood he would leave soon. "Of course. I'll make sure everything's set up so all you have to do is balance your checkbook and stop at the bank whenever you need money." He wanted to say that she needs to learn how to handle everything herself, that he'd help her for now, but what if something ever happened to him . . . But no, she'd been dependent all her life, and she had too many other painful adjustments to make now without adding that kind of stress to her concerns, and he felt protective of her, knowing how intimidating money and mortgages and lease arrangements can be, and how scared she would be of messing up. He would do this for her, for the rest of her life if needed, because then she would never have to worry, and he wouldn't worry about her.

He watched her smoking the cigarette, wondering at how she would cope. Her whole world would change now. The star at the center of her orbit had flamed out, leaving a dark void threatening either to suck her in or repel her to float listlessly beyond the outer reaches. He expected she would try to maintain her momentum, to revolve as if nothing had happened, like maybe Ernest had simply taken a nap, everything okay, nothing to fear.

She stubbed out the cigarette, then stood and flicked ashes from her solemn dress, crossing to kiss him atop his head. "Good night, Geoffrey." She used to do that sometimes, kissing him on the head like that.

Good night, Geoffrey.

He crept up to his room.

Nothing had changed. Somebody put fresh sheets on the bed, and had made an effort to dust in anticipation of his stay.

He felt tired, but wide awake—numb, sort of. Maybe he felt uncertainty, or maybe a sureness too real, like getting an ugly tattoo and knowing it will be there always, or suffering a disfiguring amputation. It felt like that instant of dropping a priceless heirloom, grabbing desperately, losing control, watching helplessly as it shatters on the floor, too late.

Geoffrey sat on the bed and looked around. Despite his determination, he felt the pull taking him back to the years he'd slept there. He didn't mind it, but rather found it kind of amusing in a way, like visiting a museum or watching a film, peeking at something for a while before moving on. He got up and walked around, pausing at the dresser, looking in the drawers, now storage for spare blankets and linen. Underneath, he could feel the slot where he used to hide magazines, smiling at how lurid he'd once considered them. There stood his desk, sandwiched between chest and wardrobe, smaller even than he remembered it, his own private place where he studied and did homework and read stories of conquest and adventure. He colored at that desk in third grade, learned algebra in junior high, word-processed reports and created graphic layouts in high school, and as the years went by and the seasons came and went, he would sometimes pause and look out, watching through the window, noticing how the world constantly changes.

He turned off the light, then sat in darkness at the desk and gazed out. Leaves were budding on the silver maple he and Bill used to climb. An owl perched on the eaves of the barn, his head swiveling this way and that. The corn looked like the tines of giant combs lined up in even rows. Stars twinkled in the sky, freckles surrounding the lopsided smile of meniscoid moon. Peace blanketed the farm, and quiet. Calm.

This was Ernest's world, and it suddenly struck Geoffrey that Ernest would never walk here again. He had never made it home from work the other night, carried off to the hospital, the funeral home, soon to the cemetery. It seemed unjust, cruel, vindictive. He resented the corn and the barn and even that owl for acting so casual about what had happened, so uncaring, not even noticing the passing of the man who dwelled here for so long.

Geoffrey pushed the lamp aside, dreading what he expected to find: a tiny hole in the lower left pane of the French window, the radiating spider-web cracks of Geoffrey's brief bout with desperation, his flirtation with insanity. Why had Ernest never replaced that pane? To remind Geoffrey of his sin?—or maybe his own stubborn refusal to acknowledge what had passed between them that fateful night?

Geoffrey knew why he'd never replaced it himself: it wasn't his fault that it happened, and he wouldn't take responsibility for it.

He pulled out the drawer and could see, cast in moonlight shadows from the window, that it still held his pencils and pens and paper clips and glue. He found the stain from his sudden nosebleed, the holes where he'd repeatedly jabbed his stylus, the mascot icon of his high-school team ballpoint-tattooed into the wood.

He closed his eyes and lay his head down, feeling that nauseating wave of reality washing over him again, the stark realization of what had happened, why he was drawn here to the scenery of his past. He wanted to do something about it, to solve the problem, make it go away, and save his mother . . .

And save Ernest.

His throat hurt, and his nose started running. Not now. No, not now . . .

He got up suddenly, renewed with purpose, then pocketed his keys and gently slid open the side window. He stepped out onto the fire escape, sneaking out even as he had so many times in his childhood. He started the engine of his rental, hoping the noise wouldn't betray him, then pulled out slowly and drove down the road. As he approached the Marloney place, he turned off the headlights, eventually pulling over where tall cattails lined a roadside ditch. Leaving the engine running, he slipped out and skulked up through the Marloney yard, around the back, to the shed under Bill's window. He climbed up on top, even as he had so many times before, and tapped their code ever so quietly on the glass.

The curtain rustled, and Bill's face appeared, bigger than life. He looked at Geoffrey with a sly expression, then smiled. He quietly lifted the pane and whispered, "I wondered if you'd show up."

"I need to go into town. You game?"

"Let me get my pants on."

"Make sure you bring your store keys."

They sneaked away, retracing Geoffrey's route, for the first time in their lives not scared about getting caught.

An awkward silence hung between them as they drove toward town, so many things to say, no starting point. They missed the ebb and flow of conversation that used to swirl around and between them, the way they finished each other's thoughts, both thinking the same identical idea next. Arriving at the store, Geoffrey parked around the back. Bill let them in, asking why Geoffrey wanted to come there, of all places. Embarrassed for a moment, he blurted it out, then tried to explain it, then tried to explain his explanation. Bill helped him with the words until, by the time they set to their task, the conversation returned, as strong and clear and as real as it had ever been. When they finished the job, they pulled chairs together and fired questions at each other. Geoffrey admitted he'd blown his employment for being stubborn and obstinate, for insisting the designs should be done his way—the better way—rather than what clients wanted, and how his boss had pulled rank on him and that infuriated Geoffrey and he had offered unsolicited opinions best kept to oneself. Bill talked about wanting to come out west after Geoffrey settled in, maybe to go to school if he could afford it, or to find a job if not, but his family had become dependent on him after his father's accident. He despised farming corn, and there wasn't enough money to be made from their small spread for him ever to afford his own house and support a wife and family, so his dad had suggested letting the Hansons farm it so together they could take over the hardware, and it seemed like a great idea at the time, and still did, except that Bill was trapped in Coon Rapids now, visits to be his only hope for getting out to California.

"Or to open the west-coast branch of your hardware chain," Geoffrey joshed, more serious than not.

"How are the women out there?" Bill asked.

Geoffrey told him about Melanie, about how he'd lost her, how he'd never truly felt close to her in the first place. Then he told him about Phrekka. "She's the most beautiful, most exquisite jewel you could ever imagine. She's not into anything romantic—which I sort of had to learn the hard way, almost blowing it—but I think she's turning into a good friend. At least I hope so."

"You got any other new friends?"

Geoffrey shook his head. "The few I knew at college all drifted away; they were never really friends. Not like—you know."

"I work all the time now, but at least I get to meet people who come into the store. That's how I found Monica Ridley. She lives in Council Bluffs, but comes out here to visit her aunt." He grinned. "I drive out to Council Bluffs most Sunday afternoons and stay 'til she leaves for work Monday."

They talked some more about Monica and Phrekka, eventually acting like two old men who've exhausted the present and now have to dip into the past, taking turns regaling each other with exploits from their school years—the happy times, anyway.

Geoffrey hadn't realized there were so many, and in talking through the wee hours, they barely scratched the surface.

"I need to get back, try to get some rest," Geoffrey sighed. It felt like warm fog spreading around and through them, the palpable solemnity of returning to the harsh present. They both stared at the floor for a moment, neither speaking, nothing more to say.

They drove back to the Marloney's, Geoffrey parking down the road again as if getting caught even mattered. There they sat, like neither wanted this to end.

"God, Billy, I've screwed up so much." He rubbed his eyes with his palm, then sighed and shook his head.

"Like what?" Bill asked, genuinely puzzled.

"I needed to get away from here."

"And you did."

"But I left *everything* behind." Then, in a tiny little voice from far away, he added, "And every*one*."

Bill shrugged and looked uncomfortable for a moment, hurt feelings betrayed in his face. "I figured you'd done better, getting out in the world." Bill seemed embarrassed to admit that, and Geoffrey wondered if he feared saying the wrong thing would ruin what they'd found again this very night.

"How could I possibly do better?" Geoffrey said quietly, not looking at him, but watching out the corner of his eye.

Bill looked relieved, satisfied . . . then he snorted and pronounced, "That's what I decided."

They both chuckled, then sighed at the same time.

Bill said, "Um, you know, that's . . . It goes both ways."

"Cripe, took you long enough to say it—leaving me hanging like that."

"Okay, so I won't anymore," Bill sniffed with a hint of smile.

"Actually," Geoffrey said tentatively, "it was a good time for me to hear it."

They looked at each other, and they reached a very important agreement without saying a word. Bill shook his hand, then stepped out and closed the door.

Geoffrey rolled down his window, quietly asking, "Are you gonna be there tomorrow?"

"Yeah, we're closing the store."

"You don't have to do that."

"Dad wants to go, and I have to."

"No you don't . . ." Geoffrey trailed off, both young men looking at each other. "I guess you do."

"Don't forget, Geoffrey Whatever-your-name-is, I'm the one who's been there all along."

The lopsided smile of crescent moon hung low in the sky. A solemn barn owl watched as the blond-haired interloper sneaked around the picnic table and past the propane grill there behind the Calhoun house. Geoffrey glanced up toward his second-floor childhood bedroom, the glowing tic-tac-toe albedo of its nine-paned French window a satiny sheen betraying its injury in splintered refractions. The imperfect lower-corner square whispered down to him, its grievance the shame of disrepair.

Clutching his Marloney & Son Hardware sack, Geoffrey climbed the fire escape and eased quietly indoors, gently closing the window, now insulated from the outside world's winds of shifting expectation. He sat at his boyhood desk and reached for the light, then decided to linger for a while longer in the darkness, pushing the lamp aside to study the cracked pane. Five years that window had remained thus, to Ernest a symbol of rebellion and defiance unleashed, to Geoffrey a horrible mistake he'd tried very hard to forget. Determined now to ignore history, he regarded it as nothing more than a damaged sheet of glass, some object of intended home repair, a five-minute job, ten at the most.

He carefully unwrapped the custom-cut replacement pane, then unpacked the tube of caulk and a small putty knife. Though intending to proceed immediately, the better to be done quickly with this long-overdue task, he paused to catch his breath, feeling dizzy, distracted by fleeting visions of disparate intent lurking in the tenebrous shadows, some reminiscent of security and hope, most remindful of desperation and fear. He felt warm, feverish, a dull pain at the base of his skull, and he swallowed hard several times, willing his stomach to settle, his breathing to calm.

The shadows swirled around and through him, bringing with them images from just after his eleventh birthday, of the illness he had suffered the night he learned Ernest had emerged unscathed from the quarry where a wall collapsed. Doc Waverly pronounced the boy physically fit, whispering to his mother something about stress, the trauma of worrying about his father, that he would be fine with time and healthy doses of love and reassurance. Eavesdropping through the door, Geoffrey found in this diagnosis the smallest measure of assuagement for his guilt, albeit intangible and indistinct. Later that night, snuggled under his duvet, he dared to replay his fantasy that Ernest had indeed perished, and to savor the euphoria in imagining himself as the unfortunate child eligible for sympathy and love and support, but the waves of nausea returned, and he felt shame for harboring such malice toward another, resigned in his heart that forever he would be cursed as the demon seed undeserving of God's love, no better than his father. Without warning, he vomited on himself, spattering his bed, then wretched repeatedly until his mother hurried to her weeping child. He feared he might be punished for the mess, but Ernest just stood awkwardly in the doorway, confusion and concern twitching in the rough-hewn features of his face.

Mother gave Geoffrey several sips of ginger ale, then led him to the bathroom and opened the tap to fill the tub with steamy, soapy water. She started undressing him, mortifying him at first—eleven being much too old for such a breach of his modesty—but he nevertheless submitted, finding comfort in the warm suds while she gently cleansed from him the dregs of his shameful thoughts, and he secretly wished this moment, this feeling, would last forever. After a time, she helped him from the tub and dried him with a great fuzzy towel, dressed him in fresh flannel pajamas, then held him with unaccustomed tenderness and walked him back to his room. Ernest had stripped the soiled linen and cleaned the spill from the floor, remaking the bed with fresh sheets and blanket, a plastic bucket at the side in case of future accidents. Mother fussed over him, tucking him in tightly, Ernest watching from the side. Finally, they left him there in the darkness, and he felt much better, lying awake for some time to recall and savor the warm embrace of sudsy water and the gentle touch of his mother, his father distressed but supportive . . . from a safe distance.

Geoffrey picked up the putty knife and considered how to proceed, trying to divert his attention from the rising nausea. He would find relief in repairing that which he had inadvertently wrought, and thus take responsibility for his actions, but with that determination came a palpable sadness that Ernest would never see this handiwork, would never know, could never approve. Ernest had waited five years for him to achieve this level of maturity, probably willing to purchase the materials at even the slightest hint that Geoffrey had decided to make amends, expecting to linger discreetly elsewhere while his son made right what had for so long remained wrong.

Geoffrey shifted uncomfortably, his hands and arms variegated by the glass-splintered refractions of taunting moonlight. He swallowed hard, reminding himself that completing this minor task would bring redemption for the sins of his past, but this led to surprisingly profound apprehension, a sense of hurtling toward disaster, a runaway toboggan careering toward trees, a tipped canoe swept into the rapids . . . because he knew the anticipated result would prove too elusive, that there would be no coasting safely home, and no relief, for what mattered most about this broken window was that it didn't matter anymore. Ernest was gone.

All that remained after repairing the glass would be to clean out his father's clothing and personal effects, then to listen and watch while others spoke the solemn words and sealed the varnished coffin. The man who had spent his last moments of life faithfully driving toward the safety of home would, instead, lead a procession of mourners to a muddy rectangle in the fertile Iowa soil. Paid strangers would cover his father, then scatter seed to the ground and set the marker, Ernest's monument, tangible granite-and-bronze proof that a man had ever lived. The strangers would return to water and mow—mowing as each year yields to the next, as the seasons come and go—until the burial ritual would be repeated and Ernest's wife would join her husband. Geoffrey would dutifully attend his mother's interment, then clean out the house and list it for sale, the story of a repaired bedroom window left unspoken. He would visit the graveyard, offering tribute with a spray of durable silk or plastic flowers, wiping dust from the markers, then standing by helplessly while the grass grows and memories of lost parents shimmer into the ever-elusive fleeting images of life, each dancing away, one by one, on the winds of denied expectation, never to return.

Then, someday, one of those trips would be Geoffrey's last . . .

The window whispered to him, and it spoke of mortality and squandered grace. Geoffrey searched the shadows for meaning, sitting there at the desk where he'd grown from boy to man, and the waves of vertigo washed over him, leaving him balanced on a tightrope, poised between youth and old age, between birth and death. He had always hurried, accelerating over the pits and crevices of growing up, faster and faster to pass each successive milestone, but now he hurtled with too much momentum, steering blindly in the absence of clear direction, and he missed too many opportunities to chart his course because he'd foolishly ignored the blur of important signs as they zoomed by. Now he wanted to slow down, to remain forever young, to soar with his dreams and ambitions with the confidence that he would always manage somehow to arrive safely home. He wanted to measure every increment of his life against infinity, but realizing the inevitability that one moment would finally be his last left him shaken, covetous of precious time, daunted of spirit, fearful of exploration and uncertainty . . .

And afraid of death.

His social-studies teacher had warned about the risk-taking tendencies of youth, teenage indifference to mortality, the mindset of behaving like lifetimes are boundless and only old people ever die. Geoffrey finally started to perceive himself as having a beginning and end, the early years lost in a haze of indistinction, the balance an immeasurable, unpredictable interval rushing him headlong toward his own demise. He had listened to the siren call of religious faith, those carefully crafted tenets designed by mortals to deny the finality of death, the oft-preached promise that enchanted realms await only the pious, but try as he might, he could never hope so desperately as to believe, not even in his bleakest moments, for Geoffrey understood that his mind and body are one, and that when he returned to the dust his spirit simply would be no more. Instead of reaching disconsolately for some implausible reward, he would focus his attentions and aspirations only on what he could see from this side of his mortality, and he would rejoice in the achievement of a long and full life, blessed with time enough for understanding, time enough for love.

He thought of Melanie, how she might have contributed, the glorious conquest of convincing her to cohabit, his ignominious defeat when she fled his nest . . . Melanie never fit into Geoffrey's world, which now seemed quite small and very precious, and the valuable time he spent trying to love her had been wasted unless, at least, therefrom he learned how and why never to replicate that mistake. Geoffrey hoped he would someday share his life with another, but with this new vow to live for every moment, he knew he would rather be alone than settle for less than the deepest, most abiding love, the one woman with whom he could share everything, cherishing her as they grow old together, even until the day one is buried beside the other.

He considered the importance of friendship, and the rediscovery of his own with Bill Marloney, the one who had "been there all along." Bill had seen Geoffrey at his best, stood beside him for the worst, and had never offered anything less than acceptance and friendship, no matter what. There was no remorse with Bill, and no shame, and no apologies. How many friends had Geoffrey found in his first twenty years?—and how many had he kept . . . One so far, and with Phrekka Churán, hopefully two.

The window whispered of memories, the shadows a montage of episodes, of comedies and dramas, the calm between crises, a scattering of tacit approvals, moments of awkward affection. The images rushed at Geoffrey, playing faster and faster until only one remained, a scene demanding unwavering attention: the last occasion he saw his father alive. Three months before, Geoffrey had marched in his graduation procession, berobed in pomp and circumstance, his parents four rows up in the bleachers watching the first in their family ever to earn a college degree. When he heard his name called, he stepped up onto the dais and accepted his diploma, then glanced out toward the audience . . . and saw Ernest. His father stood up, the only person to rise, his head held high, clutching his hat to his breast, radiating unparalleled pride for his son's accomplishment. Puzzled, surprised, pleased, Geoffrey looked to his father, and Ernest nodded approval.

At least you lived to see it.

Geoffrey wanted Ernest to live long enough to be proud of him again, for him to know his grandchildren and watch them grow and attend their graduations, maybe even to stand there beside him, together, proudly. For the first time, he suffered pangs of regret for changing his name from Calhoun back to Drousseau, knowing how much it had hurt his father, ashamed that wanting to hurt Ernest had formed the basis of his intent. Now there would be no more chances for Geoffrey to prove that labels and names never matter as much as deeds, and that he still had every intention of growing into the kind of man who would make any father proud. He pondered how many times and how many ways Ernest had given up in their battles of will, and for the first time he considered that maybe his father had not retreated, but rather capitulated, that he had begun to learn how to accept his son just as he was, not compared to how he wanted him to be. Geoffrey wondered, had Ernest not died so prematurely, how much more they would have learned together, and how much approbation between father and son they might have achieved.

Geoffrey had tried to despise him for the punishments, assuming malice fueled their intent, but in retrospect, though he would always consider them inappropriate and harmful, he knew his father simply didn't know any other way, and that this humble man honestly believed it to be an effective method of guidance for children. Now, try as he might, with all threats long since removed, Geoffrey could no longer hate Ernest for his ignorance, and he wondered if it might be possible ever to forgive him, but even for that, the time and opportunity had passed.

Ernest was gone forever, consigned to memory, his image fading in people's minds even as the echoes of his footsteps fade from the landscape of his world.

The sense of loss overwhelmed him.

As Geoffrey's eyes brimmed with tears, what he saw there in the shadows was no tenebrio, but rather Ernest, a frangible but principled and determined man, his hat held at his breast, standing proud to watch his only son accomplish what the father could never achieve. Geoffrey tried to reconcile that image with all that remained of the man in the coffin, but that could never be, for one held promise and hope, the other mortal defeat. He rested his face in his hands and wept, the grief washing over him in waves, the whispers from the window relentlessly reminding him of what he could only begin to understand, what he tried very hard not to believe, the palpable sense of despair pulling him further and further until he allowed himself to cross over the line, and nothing else mattered. Nothing anybody had ever inflicted on Geoffrey, no punishments, no humiliations—not even the excruciating rend of indifference—nothing had ever hurt him like this, nor left him feeling more helpless and afraid, the promise of better days floating beyond his grasp.

In that moment, angry with himself for never realizing this, or maybe just for failing to admit it even to himself, he reached out in desperation, but all he could find, all he could touch, was the regret of a son who had discovered too late how much his father meant to him.

Geoffrey tried not to spatter his desktop as he cried, but he could find no solace, no meaning, and no sympathy, so he allowed himself to weep, hoping enough tears might cleanse from him the dregs of his anguished remorse. In this release he found the suggestion of acceptance for all that must come to pass, and with that dawned the first hint of relief, for he could finally admit that he loved the man, that he always had, and that he always knew that his father loved him.

After a time, he willed himself back from the brink of despondency, but an important part of him had been left behind, the loss of his father opening a wound that would never heal, marking him with a scar that would never fade. He wiped his face, then stared at the broken window, shattered even as the shards of his life, but still stubbornly resolute, holding together as one, fortification against the winds of expectation and the rains of squandered opportunity.

Geoffrey wondered how long he would live, and how many more regrets he would collect, and which of those might someday allow him the chance to make amends.

The window whispered again, and this time he heard the voice of his father:

Move on, Son . . . What's done is done.

Geoffrey opened the desk drawer and carefully stored the caulk and putty knife and new pane of glass, maybe for another time, maybe never.

He wiped his eyes, resigned to the inexorable wellspring of his grief, and he gazed out the cracked window as he had so many times in his short life, watching each year yield to the next, while the seasons come and go.

CHAPTER 8

Asia, Europe, Australia, Africa . . . Phrekka Churán had been around, and she always proved adept at adapting to any culture, her savoir-vivre and plucky intrepidity honed during Grandmamá's many far-reaching excursions. But how does one comport herself in Coon Rapids, Iowa?—especially during the funeral of a man she never met, his son an acquaintance she no longer trusts.

A twinkling light signaled permission to move around the cabin, so she unbuckled and explored the luggage bins there in her private jet's lounge, setting the wrapped Sara sketch aside to remove several clothing boxes brought in from Los Angeles earlier that morning. These outfits, one of her favorite designers had assured her, would be appropriate for conservative, Midwest religious services. She found tailored dresses in muted hues, matching accessories, and modest accoutrements—everything needed to effect several ensembles. It surprised her to discover a petite cross on a gold chain, a religious icon she would eschew displaying because she considered this symbolic pledge of false allegiance to be excessive, not necessary simply to show respect for the customs and conventions of people whose hospitality she would accept. Otherwise, she liked the selection, especially how the complement reflected glimmers of her personal style—all in an Iowa sort of way.

Several resonating marimba tones announced an incoming telephone call. "Hello, Miss Churán," greeted the familiar voice.

"Why hello, Charles. Have we been successful?"

"The information is being transmitted as we speak."

Phrekka glanced toward a page emerging from the shipboard printer.

"The delay," Charles explained, "was caused by a *nom non sequitur*. The decedent is Calhoun, not Drousseau as we surmised—Ernest B. Calhoun, survived by his wife and son, the latter named Geoffrey Drousseau. The services are scheduled for one-thirty this afternoon."

"Will there be visitation?"

"Until noon, then the viewing parlor will reopen at one for seating. The map I included directs you to a motel at Guthrie Center, Iowa, plus the funeral home and cemetery in Coon Rapids. As you requested, a rather unostentatious vehicle will be provided for you in Des Moines. I wish you would reconsider and accept a driver—"

"No, I'm sort of under cover. The last thing I want is to arouse curiosity."

"I could arrange a discreet escort—"

"Oh Charles, it's just Coon Rapids," she teased. "I'll be fine."

"You know your welfare is always in my thoughts."

"You mean you always worry about me. I do appreciate your concern. My father couldn't have had a better friend."

"Nor he a better daughter." He sighed, a sound grown familiar through the years. "If you think of other ways I may assist, you have only to call. Regardless, I hope you find that which you seek."

"Thank you, Charles. It's no wonder I've always adored you."

"Something I count on."

After disconnecting, Phrekka took the faxed material to her seat and studied it, trying to envision the environs of Coon Rapids. Her gaze drifted out the window to the patchwork quilt of farmland passing below, fluffed pillow-clouds shadow-casting across an enormous duvet blanketing the Missouri countryside. A small pond amid the sheeted fields, the enuretic accident of a giant youngster, coaxed from her an amused smile; but then the image of an oversized little boy reminded her of Geoffrey, the man who presented himself as unaffected and innocent, in reality a shrewd manipulator who sensed her vulnerabilities and schemed to exploit them.

Geoffrey had intentionally feigned ignorance about Sara, trading on Phrekka's curiosity about his fascination with the first sketch, a blatant ploy to win her attentions. Then he raised the stakes when she demurred after his first pseudo-clumsy pass, brazenly offering her employment in order to claim the prize of her companionship. It wasn't pine cones Geoffrey Drousseau wanted to collect.

On this journey she would call his bluff. She would seize whatever opportunity presented itself, just like she had once prevailed by exposing Daryl, the boy with whom she had won seven minutes in the kissing closet during one of Cerise's parties back when they were thirteen years old. Daryl proved himself an affectionate though clumsy kisser, but he persisted in groping her no matter how much she protested. Finally, exasperated, she pretended to relent, fumbling with the buttons on his jeans and suggesting he remove his scratchy sweater. Just as he tangled with it over his head, she quickly yanked down his pants and undies, then turned on the light, opened the door wide for all to see, and walked out. It was a fine prank, she had thought, and well deserved, but even though the initial laughter subsided fairly quickly, the teasing and taunting Daryl suffered persisted for months, and she ultimately regretted having inflicted a punishment far more egregious than intended.

A small patch of business district passed below the jet, reminding her of how Cerise's little brother used to create Matchbox Cars cities on his patchwork-quilted bed, there to spend the day *vroom-vrooming* about his miniature world as its invisible citizens lived their busy invisible lives. She wondered if Daryl lived down there somewhere, and if he was happy now, and if he had ever forgiven her . . .

Phrekka tried to savor the anticipation of besting Geoffrey at his own game, but the image of Daryl's blushing face intruded too vividly, the eighth-grader not angry as she had expected, but embarrassed nearly to tears, hurt that she would do this to him. She didn't want to injure Geoffrey, but rather to prove she had uncovered his deception and thus teach him the forfeit earned through dishonesty. After all, she deserved the same respect she had afforded him.

Deception, dishonesty, disrespect—the more she hurled these weighty appellations at her kaleidoscopic image of Geoffrey, the more they succumbed to the gravity of Phrekka's own hypocrisy. Like bright light suddenly illuminating the shadows of a kissing closet, she remembered again that she had been as guilty as Geoffrey, pretending to be somebody she was not, feigning affection for him while her curiosity about the powers of a Sara sketch had outweighed her interest in developing a new friendship. Having huffed and puffed her ballooning outrage, she suddenly deflated, all air of righteousness leaked from her enmity.

She gazed down at the squiggle of Missouri River passing in and out of her view, an enormous barge moving goods upriver, or maybe downriver, pushed by a tug imbued with its own direction and purpose, navigating the twists and turns and obstacles of a natural course, going with the flow. How easy it must be, she thought, to know one's purpose, and to know the way.

To justify her deception, Phrekka had to remind herself how the costume she had so carefully woven to wear in proximity of potential suitors served as a garment of security, insulation against others' greed and their desire for influence and power, armor against those maneuvering to gain control of her purse. She considered these ends to be justifiable as long as the means were born not in malice, nor of intent to inflict harm. The prank she had played on Daryl failed these criteria, yet Geoffrey's deceptions appeared to meet them. Admittedly, the ultimate motive for his guile seemed to be simply to spend time with her; his request for help in locating sketches had been couched by his offer to remunerate her efforts; he had consummated two purchases so far without bargaining for discount or suggesting they be obtained through subterfuge or fraud. No harm, no foul—and Phrekka was forced to concede she had remained as uninjured by Geoffrey's assertions as he had by suffering hers . . . so far.

Amid this balance lay her failure to consider one other possibility: maybe Geoffrey had his own very legitimate reasons for disingenuity. After all, he had admitted, without flaunting it, to having amassed some modicum of financial means, and he freely confessed being dumped by his girlfriend and failing at his job, so maybe to reveal the secret of Sara would engender some measure of risk either to the artist or to himself, thus forcing him, even in the blossom of new friendship, to stem his trust and forthrightness, at least for now.

Both were bluffing with secrets, but Geoffrey must have expected to reveal his if she accepted the invitation to visit his hometown, there to witness his grief, to meet his family and, at least incidentally, finally to learn the identity of Sara and the story of her sketches. Maybe Geoffrey simply didn't want to play the game anymore, the stakes having grown too high to gamble, and he'd taken a genuine chance, the risk of hoping that in revealing himself she would like what she saw. Maybe inviting her to Iowa had been a test.

Therein lay the chance for Phrekka to practice the charity Cerise had so often warned she possessed too little capacity for extending to others; she would allow Geoffrey the benefit of the doubt. How dare she exploit the occasion of a funeral to expose him pants-down in the closet of his vulnerabilities, such disrespect undeserved by a trusting victim who truly had respected her limits, the gentle soul who asked for nothing more than her company during a very personal and painful ordeal. She resolved to focus only on her original goals, to satisfy her curiosity about Sara, to learn whence springs the power imbued in her art. She would do this as a forthright acquaintance, without deceit or fraud, truly sympathetic in this time of grief, neither suggesting nor implying further obligation or commitment. Thereafter, the arc of this friendship would pass.

The plane began its final descent toward the small airport at Des Moines. She stowed the outfits and accoutrements, then carefully replaced the wrapped sketch of a dreaming little boy known only as *Geoffrey*. She buckled in and gazed out the window, watching as the quilt of Iowa countryside yielded to a Monopoly board of railroads and houses and hotels.

Asia, Europe, Australia, Africa . . . The time had come for Phrekka Churán to visit Coon Rapids.

Poised on the threshold, Phrekka gazed out through the open doorway, studying Iowa's heartland. At the asphalt lot's entranceway flashed a sign alerting travelers to its coffee house's pancake/egg special. Beyond that, across the two-lane road, stretched an impressive expanse of cornfields, miles of symmetrically rowed stalks standing like troops awaiting inspection, the platoon's outer flanks fading to infinity in the distance, the entire tableau back-lit by midmorning sunshine and shimmering in the still, humid air. She had come to this region expecting quaint antebellum towns, but wound up disappointed by cookie-cutter intersections encrusted with national-chain outlets for fast food and gasoline, geometric constructs growing like the sea-salt crystals that appear on sun-baked jetties during low tide. Where she hoped to discover picket-fenced farms with their pastures demarcated by blushing Mail Pouch Tobacco barns, she had found instead chain-link or electrified wire and pole barns of gray and gleaming aluminum—all very functional, plain and repetitious.

She longed to return to the majesty of coastal California, to stand atop the cliffs south of Big Sur; or to watch the sun set behind the Golden Gate; to sample Dungeness crabmeat from paper cups while strolling Fisherman's Wharf; to nibble chocolates across from Ghirardelli Square; to meander through museums and galleries, Chinatown and Haight-Ashbury; then to ride the last cable-car run of the night and pause at the turnaround while the blind saxophone player breathed new life into plaintive strains of "I Left My Heart In San Francisco" . . . but she had come to Iowa, and now she stood poised to explore Geoffrey's world, a simple place awash in the universal values of all mankind, where the greatest events are birth and baptism, varsity football and graduation, marriage and children, retirement and death. Spread before her lay a sturdy tapestry woven of wheat stalks and corn-silk, its story painted with sweat and blood, the scenery plain, a subject all too familiar, but frightening nevertheless.

She dreaded attending Ernest's funeral. She had read about Anglocentric-traditional death rites, even heard friends describe them from experience, but Phrekka had never participated in any. Her experience with Grandmamá's passing had followed tenets of Buddhism, the elder Churán embracing many of the beliefs inculcated during her own childhood in Korea. Grandmamá had used her prolonged illness to practice bodhiccita, experiencing her pain as a path to enlightenment for all sentients, accepting the sufferings of mankind in order to give happiness to the world. They spent their last moments together with Phrekka reciting elegant poetry, the sickbed surrounded by paintings they both loved, so Grandmamá would die in a virtuous state and her conscious principle, expected to linger in the body for three days, would achieve the extreme void of pure, colorless light.

A public memorial drew crowds, a tribute in conjunction with Grandmamá's bequest to the art museum, but the private service was limited to a select few: Charles, who had been Grandpapá's and later Father's partner; Marva, manager of their art empire; Miss Cilla, the Churáns' Korean housekeep-supervisor and friend for more than forty years; Doctor Laventer, Grandmamá's personal physician; and Phrekka, the granddaughter who loved her more than anybody in the world. Grandmamá had asked that her ashes be scattered to the waters near Sausalito so her remains might complete this cycle of incarnation, flowing with the currents of earth and sea, buffeted by the forces of the moon and the stars, carried by the tides and the winds and the rains, hopefully someday for a small part of her to touch again the shores of her native Korea. They gathered on Charles's yacht at sunset to honor her wishes, sailing under the great bridge toward open sea, sprinkling the glorious Pacific with rose petals and gardenia, then scattering Grandmamá to the splendor of the natural world she savored during every minute of her life, no longer the visitor ephemeral, now one with the scenery, eternal. Phrekka never considered herself Buddhist, but she found solace in hoping that eight Bodhisattvas did, indeed, come to lead her grandmother to a new life in another form, and that their souls would always be somehow linked as they traveled through life, beyond death, toward rebirth and spiritual purity.

Now she stood on the motel-room threshold and wondered how it must feel to say good-bye to one's father, his body committed to the soil, the mourning child inheriting his place in the world, a legacy of fading memories. She feared that standing near Geoffrey, sharing his grief, would engulf her in the loss of her own father, the soul she could touch only when seeking meaning from the abstract dabs and strokes of color found in the painting over his boyhood desk. Anticipating this funereal trepidation, she had tried to prepare herself, determined to maintain her composure, to prevent being overwhelmed by circumstance beyond choice or control. She took a deep breath, anaesthetized by the distance inherent in never having known Ernest, and she crossed the threshold into the blinding glare of Iowa sunshine.

She drove northward, past Springbrook State Park, then west toward Coon Rapids until she found the turn-off and located the cemetery. She had decided to familiarize herself with the burial site in advance, a course of systematic desensitization, imagining what to expect as she gradually tested the floodtide of rising anxiety, there to locate the stepping stones that would allow her sure and swift egress. The grounds appeared quite beautiful, surrounded by brick wall and wrought-iron gates, shaded by maples and crab-apples, dressed with concrete benches, statues, several mausoleums, and a small chapel. She drove through very slowly, circling toward the back where she found a lovely oblong pond fed by a small stream, dozens of colorful ducks and a quartet of regal swans gliding its surface, turtles clustered on a small island at the center, all supervised by majestic cattails lording over tussocks of tall grass along the shallow end. Every spark of life sharing this parcel of tranquility seemed somehow respectful, accepting of their roles reminding mourners to discover beauty in the world, and to remember that people, too, must always move on. Phrekka had never embraced any particular religion, but she hoped somehow a part of her father still dwelled somewhere in the world, maybe in a setting as serene and beautiful as this, gracing the reflective, glassy waters of a peaceful, idyllic pond.

She turned into one of the winding roadways, passing close to where a large green canopy cast shadows on a solemn man setting up folding chairs, a pattern no doubt practiced and familiar and functional. The gaping rectangle of open grave scarred the earth, chert-colored soil piled to the side. Some kind of tractor, a backhoe maybe, lowered a vault, spider-webbed in chains. She watched as the concrete tomb disappeared into the hole, there to await the remains of Geoffrey's father . . . the final resting place.

Phrekka's father never had the chance to be cremated or buried, lost instead at sea when one of his company's small freighters sank in a violent storm. Rescuers saved several people and recovered some of the bodies, but they never found Mr.

Churán. Grandmamá had once tearfully confessed she feared her son spent his last moments scared, that negative thoughts might have prevented him from achieving the next level, but she found solace in Phrekka's conviction that surely he must have been remembering the joy of holding his baby girl, his own tiny spark of purity and light, the child who would always carry his love in the warmth of her heart. The ache from lingering unanswered questions abated somewhat over the years, but it wasn't until after her grandmother's death that Phrekka discovered the sense of renewal achieved in fulfilling her final wishes. Though today's ceremony for Ernest would be very different, probably involving Christian recitations and tossing clumps of soil onto the casket, she hoped Geoffrey would find similar comfort in presiding over Ernest's memorial service.

Realizing she'd squandered her extra time, Phrekka hurried toward the funeral home, sighting it a scant ten minutes before the close of visitation. Her heart started palpitating, her breathing growing rapid, and she had to will herself to calm. There would be no time to wait, to steel her courage, to imagine and mentally rehearse her dignified entrance or Geoffrey's gratified surprise at her arrival, the explanations and commiseration, a dead father waiting for her to pay respects. Only a dozen or so cars were parked near the front, but she pulled around the side to avoid notice and, before apprehension could overshadow resolve, she stepped into the bright sunlight and walked purposefully to the entrance.

Several people milled about inside the foyer, all pausing from their conversations to nod acknowledgment to the obviously foreign stranger. Her fears of committing a sartorial faux pas were allayed by confirmation that she had, indeed, dressed appropriately, and this reminded her how often the proper costume is more effective even than an invitation for gaining entry to exclusive, private affairs. She moved quickly to the viewing room, hoping to find Geoffrey there and thus avoid self-introductions and awkward conversation. The myriad flower arrangements overwhelmed the room, the resplendent splashes of vivid color enveloping her, and she stood there transfixed for a moment, wrapped in the expressions of mourning, transported by fragrances redolent of wildflowered meadows in the springtime.

There stood the open casket, a man lying peacefully within. Phrekka noticed his suit: conservative, vested, with gaudy cuff-links and polyester tie. She looked around, but seeing no sign of Geoffrey, she felt her anxiety escalating to near panic. She swallowed hard, frustrated over arriving too late to meet him in advance of the service. Nobody seemed to be paying her much attention, so she used this momentary semi-privacy to approach the catafalque. She started trembling, but the open box whispered to her, assuring her safety to pause and observe. She resisted for a moment, then finally yielded and found herself standing before the late Ernest B. Calhoun. He did not appear, as she had feared, to be an older, lifeless replica of Geoffrey. She considered the lifetime just concluded, envisioning him as a gentle man, cradling his baby son in his arms, later wiping the boy's nose and drying his tears, teaching him to ride a bicycle, helping him tie his tie for the junior-high prom . . .

Her eyes filled with tears, and she surprised herself by feeling so . . . *jealous?* A new emotion for her, it felt very different than simple curiosity about Geoffrey and his story. She pondered this and finally decided it must be empathy, a sincere desire to reach out and comfort somebody who had suffered the kind of loss few, like she, could understand. Geoffrey would never see his father again, and though he was lucky for the years they had shared, now he must move on, sustained by gingerly nurturing the memories in his heart.

Ernest looked nothing like the photos of Mr. Churán, but somehow in her mind the faces melded, and she could imagine her own father there in the casket. As she searched this vision, it faded into brush strokes in browns and grays reflecting off the surface of a golden sea, the image framed by condolence flowers whose blossoms opened delicately to drop petals on the shimmering, sun-flecked waters. In this vicarious farewell, at this very moment, Phrekka felt closer to her father than ever before, and she experienced his loss more profoundly than she ever thought possible. Tears streaked her cheeks, and with trembling hands she reached out and touched Ernest's fingers. They felt cold, and stiff, and lifeless . . . and dead. She realized she'd begun to cry, and all the fathers in the world were dying before her eyes. She felt herself washed into a sea of helplessness, desperately clinging to her surroundings, fighting her way back, this time reaching out for the consolation of strangers here in this world where she never belonged.

She sensed a woman standing beside her now. Phrekka felt self-conscious, embarrassed by her own discomposure, uncomfortable with the sudden scrutiny. The woman put an arm around her, held her close, whispering quietly. The stranger offered her name, but Phrekka couldn't hear clearly, though she did find reassurance in the woman's gentle, understanding voice.

"I'm sorry," she whispered back. "I didn't hear—"

"I'm Opaline, dear child—friend and neighbor of the Calhouns. Opaline Marloney."

Phrekka avoided offering her own Calhoun affiliation, too ashamed of her behavior. It had been a mistake to come here; she knew this now, and she wanted very much to leave before Geoffrey ever learned she had tried.

"Are you a friend of Geoffrey's?" the woman asked.

Phrekka felt like an outsider despite her gray wool skirt-suit with proper accessories, betrayed by her own frangibility. She knew her escape must come now or never. "I'm sorry," she whispered, wiping her face with a lace handkerchief. She squeezed the woman's hands, thanking her for the comforting words, then quickly turned and walked out with all the dignity she could muster.

She hurried around the corner, fumbled so awkwardly with her keys that she dropped them twice, then managed to crawl inside her car. Nobody had followed her, so she sat for a moment and willed herself to calm somewhat before starting the engine and driving casually from the lot. Her hands still shook, her eyes blurry with tears. She stopped across the street, parking at the side of a new strip mall, then turned off the engine so as not to attract attention. Her anxiety slowly yielded to anger at herself as she watched the comforting woman come out and drive away in a dilapidated station wagon. Several others departed . . . then Geoffrey came out!—walking with an older woman, probably his mother. He looked handsome in his dark suit, his blond hair shimmering in the noontime sunshine. Phrekka's heart started beating rapidly again, her palms damp where she gripped the steering wheel. Geoffrey looked so sad, so solemn, standing there talking with several people, oblivious to the woman who had traveled so far to be here, she who feared her own feelings too much to let her presence be known.

Geoffrey looked her way.

She scrunched down behind the steering wheel, peering over the dash. He kept glancing toward her, never exactly registering recognition, but appearing distracted, maybe peripherally aware of her. He held the car door for his mother while she stepped in; then he walked around to the driver's side of the big, dark sedan, opened the door, and paused. He looked her way again, but then peered around as if searching for the source of unseen whispers beckoning for his attention. He sat on the car seat, shook his head, and finally closed the door and started the engine.

Phrekka held her breath as his car slowly pulled out, and she feared Geoffrey would drive across and into the lot, then pull beside her to confirm it was she who had intruded . . . but he turned and drove away, Sara's subject receding in the distance, enveloped by midday sunshine.

Phrekka finally accepted that she could never endure the funeral ceremony, and she felt a profound sense of dislocation, of not belonging, of having no right to be there. Her appearance would alter the natural course of events unfolding in this small Midwestern town. Her motives now seemed selfish, the mystery no longer important, Geoffrey's world mutually exclusive of her own.

She started the engine again, then drove slowly into the downtown area of Coon Rapids, a foreigner in a foreign land surrounded by foreign people all busily living their busy lives. She stopped at an old-fashioned diner and sat in a faded booth, its duct-taped cushions whispering stories of squirming children dripping mustard and ketchup, sweethearts holding hands after a school dance, farmers forecasting weather and crop yields, retirees scrimping their dollars for an occasional meal out. She ordered a soft drink and the fruit-salad platter with a world-renowned sticky bun, and she sat for a long time watching people come and go, returning nods and smiles, a friendly and relaxed demeanor greater camouflage than rude indifference.

She watched the old rotary clock by the cash register, but time passed too slowly, and though she wanted to linger until after the service had begun—until after the procession and burial, even until the town of Coon Rapids had returned to the simple grace of everyday life—she knew she could not. Paying the check and leaving a generous gratuity, she stepped into her unassuming rental car and left Coon Rapids forever.

She would compose herself as she drove straight to her motel at Guthrie Center, then call Charles to see if the jet could be made available sooner than planned, to save herself from Iowa, to go home, but the route took her past the cemetery, and she thought again about her own father. She wondered if a part of him really still existed somewhere in the world, if he had been reincarnated even as Grandmamá believed, or if he now dwelled in some sort of heaven. Maybe his spirit soared free to mingle with the winds and the rains and the sunshine; or maybe, like the regal swans, he really did grace the glassy surface of some idyllic pond; or maybe she had been drawn to this place because, after all this time, she would find her father . . . here.

She turned into the cemetery, slowly driving past the waiting gravesite of Ernest B. Calhoun. She parked, then walked to some nearby markers, pretending to visit a lost loved one, drinking in every detail of the scenery where Geoffrey would stage the final act of laying his own father to rest.

Silence settled around her . . . no sound of birds, no rustling of trees, no gurgling of water over stones, no cry from the ducks or swans, no Bodhisattvas waiting patiently to lead the dead man to a void of purity.

The man with the folding chairs returned, and Phrekka felt self-conscious, still out of place. She strolled as casually as she could to her car and drove around to the other side of the cemetery, then parked again. She wandered to a lovely bench beside a great grandfatherly copse of regal shrubbery that dripped gobs of lilac buds and dusted the air with twinkling bursts of springtime forsythia. She sat in the shade and watched, drinking in the surroundings, and she began to notice more life here among the dead, robins and sparrows gadding about, a lone hawk circling overhead, an iridescent beetle trundling along the ground, a ladybug landing nearby to reflect for a moment before flying away, an inchworm measuring the side of the bench.

She reached out for her father again, and though she couldn't touch him, she recalled the life she had found in his painting. She imagined the pooch waiting for attention, so she lifted him to her lap and cradled him. She scratched his ears and rubbed his belly and nearly giggled at herself, amused at how much she loved this little guy, for her dad had given her this gift. The puppy paused his gyrations, fixing her with his innocent little face. He looked into her eyes and whispered that the time had come . . .

The procession suddenly appeared from the roadway and eased through the wrought-iron gate, somber cars adorned with tiny flags humming their funeral dirge as they led each other toward the gaping grave. Her pulse throbbed as she watched the shimmering image of Geoffrey in the distance. He led the grieving widow to their front-row seats while scores of cars parked the length of the road. Mourners drew forward, some holding hands, arms around others, small groups joining to form larger ones, the condensation of grief trickling down the cold windows of mortality. Once everybody had settled into place, six sturdy men lifted the casket from the hearse and carried it to a rack that straddled the green-blanketed hole. She couldn't hear the words, but she felt the gravity and emotion of their ceremony as it passed around and through her, and she wept. She cried for Geoffrey, sitting there by herself among the lilacs and forsythia. She watched until the beetle trundled off to new horizons, and the inchworm finished his work for the day, and the lone hawk made one last dive before disappearing from the sky, until the last straggling cars of the departing procession wended their way out through the wrought-iron gate and faded into the sunbathed countryside. Several workmen moved in, the chairs folded, the canopy collapsed, the casket lowered into the ground as the backhoe rumbled its way down the road and scooped the great pile of chert-colored soil into the hole. Shovels finished the job, then wire-racked flowers sprouted around the mound, and the workers disappeared, leaving Phrekka alone, her tear-streaked cheeks glistening, a young woman cradling an imaginary puppy in her lap.

She gave the puppy another hug, then released him to run free as she paused to bid farewell to the turtles and ducks and swans. She hadn't found her father, nor could she tell him good-bye, so she left the cemetery without looking back and drove to the motel where she called Charles on the room phone.

"I am sorry, Miss Churán, but the jet is almost to Tampa by now, and our captain will have exceeded his allowable flight hours for the day. I will find another pilot, though, and try to have the jet there by morning."

"I'll stay by the airport and wait for your call. I'm sorry—"

"Please, do not feel bad. I understand, and I will do the best I may. Is there anything else I can do?"

"I could never hope for a more wonderful friend, Charles. You do indulge me so."

"I am just glad you let me."

As soon as she hung up, the room phone rang, probably Charles with some new information, but when she answered nobody spoke, apparently a wrong number. That made her feel very alone, the realization that only Charles knew her whereabouts, and that nobody would be calling to cheer her up.

She sat there for a few minutes, wondering how she might pass the time, but her thoughts kept returning to her failure. She had come to solve a mystery, then fled at the first possibility of confrontation. She had resolved to offer Geoffrey a gesture of support, only to leave him to fend for himself. She had looked forward to showing him the new Sara sketch, but now she planned to retreat on the wings of regret and disappear into the twilight of Iowa sky without him ever knowing she had come.

Reframed and rewrapped in brown paper by Phrekka's small-gallery friend in the French Quarter, the dream sketch leaned against the motel room's wall, quietly whispering for attention. Phrekka longed to gaze again upon the childhood image of Geoffrey's innocence, the sleeping little boy sans care or concern, safe and content, at home, where he knew love. She carefully unfastened the covering and lifted it away . . .

The child slumbered so peacefully, unaware she watched him across time and from another world. This young boy asked nothing of her while the grown boy who just attended his father's funeral offered to share a personal part of himself during his time of profound vulnerability, without terms or conditions. She had let him down, but at least she could find solace in having honored him as best she could by watching from afar, even as she would have been willing to tuck in the sleeping child, careful not to wake him . . . But still, she could have done more, and in that she realized that the need to confront Geoffrey's lies had been her own self-deluding excuse. Back when her initial anger abated and her focus shifted to the mystery of Sara, the pretense of traveling to Iowa to learn about the enigmatic artist had also been nothing more than an excuse. She didn't come for Ernest or Sara or even to sample the grief of others and search for her father . . .

She came for Geoffrey.

And tears spilled from her eyes again, but the opportunity had passed.

She opened the door and looked across the shimmering Iowa cornfields, and the whole world mocked her selfishness. The asphalt baked in the scorn of revelation, the sign flashing its utter disbelief, the fast food restaurant denying nourishment to her charity-starved soul, every corn stalk awaiting the at-ease order for her to make amends, and there at the door appeared a young man with dark-brown hair, and he looked very nervous as he asked if it really was her, and she couldn't hear him for a second, but she told him yes, it was she, and he introduced himself.

"I *knew* it was you. I'm Geoffrey's friend—Bill."

CHAPTER 9

Geoffrey circulated through a small after-funeral assemblage gathered at the Calhoun house. He noted that everybody's initial responses to the tragedy finally started to wane, the phase of bringing food and ordering flowers and the stunned *What can I do?* offers of assistance slowly giving way to well-intended platitudes. Soon, as the community adjusted itself to the loss of Deacon Calhoun, the final phase would unfold: reference avoidance—pointedly not mentioning him in the presence of his family, misguided attempts to avoid prolonging their grief, inadvertent but tacit implication that Ernest never existed, never mattered. For now, Geoffrey and his mother would suffer people's hypothetical scenarios constructed upon layers of "at least" phraseology, homilies intoned with the gravity of prophecy, comparisons with layers of metaphor, and finally the assignments of new roles for the bereaved.

"*At least* he didn't suffer none," Mrs. Beasley allowed, "—like Edna's brother who died of the cancer."

"*At least* he managed to pull off to the side of the road before causing a crash that mighta hurt someone else."

"*At least* your mama won't get put out of her home thanks to that insurance policy I sold him."

These attempts to establish a new base-line for evaluating tragedy, thus to diminish the gravity of real events, impressed Geoffrey as, at best, pathetic. The man had died, and the true base-line should have been a long and full life, another day in the sun, arriving home safely every night. Religion works the same way, he thought, conjuring fantastic reassurances to blunt the harsh certitude of mortality in an indifferent world.

"Life must go on," the waspy Widow Warner buzzed.

"Life is for the living."

"Time heals all wounds."

He wondered if anybody would go home and embroider these sage words on a sampler for his wall. A live bird in the hand is worth two dead ones in the bush. A life saved is a life earned. You can't teach a dead dog new tricks. Life's a bitch, and then you die.

"I went through the same thing," Brother Johnson empathized. "My first cousin had two heart attacks before he got the bypass."

"I know how you feel, Geoffrey. My brother-in-law died in a hunting accident."

"When the mighty oak falls, the tiny sapling has room to grow—"

"It's like the Scriptures say—"

Nobody experiences grief the same, Geoffrey understood, and nobody can truly claim to have walked the same path in another's shoes. If a metaphor could be found for Geoffrey, it would not be about trees, nor would it be found in the Scriptures.

"Your mama's gonna have to make certain adjustments," the fat bakery woman advised, "—bein' a widow and all."

"—To get out more, maybe volunteer at the church or—"

"I guess you'll be movin' back home now, and takin' over the farm . . ."

Geoffrey handled these remarks politely, nodding with gravity, shaking hands or hugging, agreeing or evading, always feigning gratitude for the generous support of whichever abstract splashes of dark-hued grief passed before him. He noticed that once the mourners had dispensed their advice, they always moved on, setting about the arduous task of enjoying themselves, visiting with each other, greeting sporadic acquaintances, forecasting weather, telling stories, planning their own futures, renewing their humble appreciation for life. For a wake, this gathering grew uncomfortably festive, more like a party, and this surprised Geoffrey, then annoyed him, then angered him. These people were supposed to be here to honor Ernest, yet everybody acted like he had already been packed away, relegating him to one of the neatly stacked boxes of dusty mementos and fading memories in the cobwebby attics of all that's passed. His mother appeared inappropriately chipper, too, emerging from her chrysalis to revel in the attention, a social butterfly flitting from bloom to budding-friendship bloom, sampling the nectar of outpouring support, spreading her widowy wings and testing the winds of anticipation.

Where were Geoffrey's friends? Left behind, that's where, one by one, un-nurtured bonds neglected to wither in his mad rush to flee the scenery of his traumas, to explore alternative paths through uncharted life, traveling light, with minimum baggage, and no porters. He had called a few friends after learning of Ernest's death, chums from his community-college years in Des Moines, and he'd been pleased to find their names on the sterile mass-market condolence cards of Florist Raybud's $15.95 bereavement arrangement (basket or vase—your choice), but none had shown up for the funeral, or come to the house, or mentioned getting together again anytime in the near future. None had offered Geoffrey an entrée back into their lives, not even a platitude or homily or metaphor . . . A simple "at least" would have meant a lot.

He wanted to steal away with Bill Marloney right then, if only for a few minutes, to elude the scattershot bursts of impromptu laughter that mocked Ernest's passing, but his friend had disappeared right after the cemetery service. Some hardware obligation had probably distracted the younger Marloney partner, maybe receiving a stock delivery, or an emergency order, so he felt confident his friend would arrive eventually, if not soon.

Geoffrey sighed. Unwilling to shrug off his yoke of social duties, he circulated again to endure more volleys of sympathy, all the while imagining himself rushing to Sausalito to find Phrekka, admitting to her how he really felt about this trip and these people, confident she would understand, but that would have to wait, at least for another day. He caught himself glancing out front with nervous frequency, watching for Bill, yearning for his assistance to make this frenzy of obligation and proper appearances less cumbersome, a burden easier carried when shared with a friend. He felt selfish for wanting Bill's attention now during a crisis, especially after ignoring him so much over the past few years, but maybe that's what friendship was all about: mutual selfishness, forged in circumstance, tested by adversity, and finally—rarely, luckily—elevated to affinity.

The opportunity finally presented itself for Geoffrey to slip upstairs and linger in his bedroom. He closed the door, then sat at his desk and stared out the damaged nine-paned window, watching the seasons and the years, and he pondered the irony of feeling like the one person who seemed most to mourn Ernest's passing. He misted up, unsure why, burying his face in his hands and trying to maintain his composure. Lonesomeness gathered around him, watching his inability to find solace in solitude. There would be no comfort in family communion; his normally indifferent mother was having too much fun enjoying her moment in the spotlight, the hapless victim deserving of love and sympathy and support. Geoffrey no longer belonged in Iowa, but nothing awaited him at home except a stack of want ads and a beautiful young woman he'd distanced with a clumsy pass, a fascinating and tolerant soul he couldn't quite fathom . . .

And the sketch of a boy standing innocently amid cattails in an idyllic pond.

Determined from the onset not to become mired by the events in Iowa, he had paused here too long, and he felt overwhelmed. Tears spilled inexplicably down his cheeks—

The stairs creaked.

"Geoffrey?" he heard Mrs. Marloney whisper. He didn't want her to catch him crying, but before he could answer, she slipped inside and closed the door.

He couldn't believe she walked right in, but then he smiled in spite of himself, recalling the summer he and Billy turned eight. They were in Billy's bedroom, changing into swimsuits for an afternoon playing with the garden hose. Mrs. Marloney burst unexpectedly through the door with fresh towels just as they stood there buck naked. Billy never flinched, but Geoffrey freaked and tripped over himself trying to grab his clothes and cover up. Mrs. Marloney just laughed and tousled his hair, reminding him, "Oh Geoffrey, I've seen your little bum-bum more times than I can count. It wasn't too long ago we couldn't get you to keep your clothes *on*; every time we'd look up you'd be running off somewhere nekkid as a jaybird!" No form of chagrin ever survived Mrs. Marloney's disarming affections, always replaced by feelings of comfort, security, love.

"Geoffrey?" she whispered. "Are you okay?"

He stood awkwardly, wiping his face, his cheeks flushed, glancing at his shoes, trying to avoid letting her see. He couldn't believe he'd actually sort of started crying yet again, more often these past two days than the last however many years combined, and he couldn't even understand what had triggered this awkward outburst.

She sat on the bed, patting beside her, an unspoken summons. He joined her there, still looking away, and the sense of security bolstered him.

"Don't ever be ashamed to let your feelings show, hon," she admonished him. "Remember in seventh grade when you scraped all the skin off your finger playin' on that ol' tractor? You wanted me to fix it up, but you were embarrassed about cryin'. I told you that's okay 'cause big boys *do* cry and all it would do is make you feel better."

Geoffrey had been punished by Ernest many times for crying. *I'll give you something to cry about.* Tears were acceptable only during whippings because they proved Ernest had gotten through, that his electric lashes had completed a circuit that triggered the floodgates and sounded the wailing alarm. Geoffrey learned that holding back only prolonged those ordeals, but all other times required rigid self-control, a skill never quite mastered, most attempts miserable failures.

"I never loved you more," she continued, "than the time Billy broke his arm. I was tryin' to look strong so he wouldn't get scared, but you was hurtin' as much as he was and—bless your heart—you didn't care what anybody thought about you cryin' right then."

He looked at his lap, but noticed her studying the side of his tear-streaked face.

She leaned down to gaze up into his eyes. "You ain't turned into somebody else now, have you?"

He smiled even as another tear trickled down to linger on his chin. This strange mix of emotions couldn't be for Ernest, nor did it seem like feeling sorry for himself. He wasn't *that* hurt or angry about the escalating party going on downstairs.

She pulled him close to her, cradled his head at her bosom, and stroked his hair like she had so many times when he was a boy. The momentary release left him feeling better, increasingly buoyant as the suffocating pressure bled away.

After a few minutes, he sheepishly lifted his head. She produced a hankie from somewhere and wiped his face, insisting, like she had a million times before . . . that he blow his nose.

"It was a lovely service," she whispered.

He grimaced, nodding agreement. "They seem to be having an awful lot of fun down there, though," he complained.

"It's no disrespect, hon. You know how they say funerals is for the living. People can only let themselves feel bad for so long, then they have to move on—or at least pretend to. Remember, this is also a reunion, a chance to see people some ain't seen in a long time."

"I appreciate how much you're looking out for my mom."

"Well, I'm her friend. That's why I've been steering clear this afternoon."

He had noticed that and wondered why. He looked at her, puzzled.

She explained, "Your mama needs to get out more and get on with her life, and yes she needs more friends." She glanced away, continuing, "I don't need to get in the way just to prove I was there all along. She knows that." She looked at him again. "Sometimes friends need to be there for you, and sometimes they need to be somewhere else for your own good."

Geoffrey understood, and he smiled. "Oh yeah? Is that why Bill ran off after the funeral?"

She returned his smile, fixing him with a mischievous twinkle in her eyes, squeezing his hands with hers. "Yes."

The hallway resounded with the *swish-thump swish-thump* of Mr. Marloney using his cane to struggle up the stairs. "Are you in there?"

Geoffrey hurried to open the door.

"Billy's back."

Mrs. Marloney stood behind Geoffrey now, holding him by the shoulders, propelling him forward, guiding him around her husband and down the stairs.

The living room fell quiet, everybody pausing to watch. A path opened before him, revealing two figures standing in the doorway. Bill Marloney displayed a goofy grin of self-congratulation. Beside him, looking just a bit nervous, but radiant and beautiful, stood a vision with long cinnamon hair and sparkling eyes.

"Geoffrey," the Widow Calhoun whispered. "Who is this?"

Geoffrey smiled, and his heart started pounding, his palms suddenly very sweaty, and his voice squeaked like it did that summer before junior high.

"Don't you recognize Bill?—that's Billy Marloney."

Several people chuckled.

"No, silly—*the girl*."

"Oh, she's my friend from California."

Their eyes locked from across the room, and he felt exhilarated like never before, and he didn't care if anybody saw how he felt right then.

"Hello, Geoffrey's friend," his mother offered, her son standing there stunned.

"Please, call me Phrekka."

Word spread fast; they said her name was Belinda Mayroth, and they called her a stone fox. She had just moved to the Coon Rapids area less than a month before the high school's junior prom, just days after eleventh-graders Geoffrey Calhoun and Tracey Collins had "broken up," an unfortunate and somewhat acrimonious end to their relationship.

Geoffrey and Tracey went steady through most of eleventh grade. He had been straightforward and honest with her from the very beginning, describing his interest in graphic arts, his aspirations to earn a college degree and eventually leave Iowa, his belief in the need for couples to support each other's goals equitably, his disdain for violence and rigid social norms and organized religion. She assured him she shared his feelings and beliefs, but her actions often contradicted her words, and it became increasingly clear she had launched a campaign to reform him, her methods subtle at first, eventually escalating to cajoling and pouting and withholding access to the normally free territory of her breasts. Geoffrey would be free to pursue any career he chose, but only after he worked for her father's butcher shop and saved enough money to support her while he pursued his fanciful whims—and then only briefly, just long enough to get them out of his system. He could even choose to remain a heathen if that suited him, but the children would be raised strictly as God-fearing Methodists.

Geoffrey realized the improbability of this relationship enduring, but he decided to wait until after the junior prom before exploring others. This plan changed abruptly when he took Tracey home after school one day and found her fifth-grader brother snooping in her room. She went berserk, grabbing the boy by his hair and shaking him violently, even slapping the squalling youngster viciously across the mouth. Geoffrey grabbed her wrist and rather indelicately forced her to release him. She whirled, spewing venom, and slapped Geoffrey. Geoffrey called her behavior inappropriate and cruel; Tracey assigned blame to the little brat and her permissive parents and even Geoffrey for interfering in matters not of his concern. The outburst escalated to slamming various objects, an eruption of remorseful tears, the reiterated recitation of others' culpability, and just before Geoffrey walked away for good, the severing of all obligations and expectations.

Belinda appeared at school the next day, a vibrant face among the stagnant throng, a stone fox. Mysterious and aloof, pouty lips and round emerald eyes, delicate features lightly brushed by wayward strands of long peroxide-blond tresses . . . He noticed how her petite body moved with feline grace, the way her breasts threatened to spill from her V-necked knit pullover, that her threadbare stone-washed jeans pulled into a slight crease in the middle that appeared, from behind, to delineate her buttocks like tandem teardrops.

Catching her attention earned admirers the wizened expression and mischievous smile of a girl who had been around and knew all the routes. Several boys immediately vied for her attentions, but she responded most to Geoffrey's earnest charm and sincerity. Moved by how she stirred something deep inside him, he quickly discovered how easily she could be focused at her own center, and he anticipated how passionately she would eventually be seduced. After several days of blissful communion, he invited her to accompany him to the prom, and she accepted.

In the coming weeks, he told her much about himself, and she always approved, offering that mysterious smile of hers, voicing similar convictions and even loftier dreams. She described a handsome sum of savings earmarked for after graduation when she intended to strike out from Iowa and start a new life in some exotic location. Although she resided in the affluent area southeast of town, she steadfastly discouraged him from visiting her home, refusing even to rendezvous there on the occasional evenings Ernest allowed him to use the pickup. Describing her mother as rather stressed out and paranoid, adjusting to new medication, Belinda thought it best to let some time pass before testing the often-turbulent waters of her family with the introduction of a new fish.

Three days before the prom, she suggested they explore a very personal way to demonstrate their love and cement their bond. A friend had lent her the keys to a trailer concealed behind an abandoned barn, its owners moved away. Their love nest turned out to be tiny and dilapidated, dirty and decrepit, and it stank of soiled linen and spilled vodka, but it offered them complete privacy. She insisted they practice dancing for the prom, and they did, without benefit of music, finding their own synchronous rhythm, melting into each other, commingling with tingling sensuality.

They danced their way to the mattress, stretching out and lying very close together. She guided his hand under her blouse, then unfastened her jeans and moved his other hand there. She opened his trousers next, then slipped her fingers into his underpants with a series of gentle strokes that made him throb and stretch the fabric. He flushed warm, and waves rippled across his abdomen wherever brushed her wrist or sleeve. She eased his hand lower, spreading her legs to accept his advances. He explored her with his fingertips, and he found soft curls, a gentle crease, and moisture . . . and she shuddered, easing his hand back out, maybe too much, too fast.

With a mischievous giggle, she playfully undressed him, singing a little song and making a game of it. Then she stood up and, pretending to be a club stripper, undulated to silent music and undressed herself one garment at a time. He palmed a condom from his wallet and watched, his interest and approval painfully evident, his desires pulsating with the rhythm of her movements. He reveled in the sensation of complete nudity with a woman, his short résumé of limited encounters always having involved the awkward tug and pull of restrictive clothing. He tore open the packet and started to roll the condom onto himself, but she only laughed and pulled it off with a snap, insisting she used the pill and, besides, she didn't have any diseases. What did he think, that she was dirty or something?

Geoffrey let her draw him in, and for once the woman set the pace and called the plays, but he felt uneasy at first, unsure how to proceed without reliance on his own seductions, for she required no focus on herself, eagerly accepting his explorations with profound approval while *she* focused at *his* center. Whenever he tried to kiss her, she would withdraw, guiding his mouth instead to her neck, her breasts, or even lower. He tried again, but she moved to his chest, licking his nipples, then traced a glistening trail of saliva down his abdomen—

This felt too fast, for he missed the intimacy of moving there together, and he wanted to express his affection, to show her that he loved her in every way. Growing frustrated, he finally resisted, slowing her down, holding her tenderly, telegraphing clearly that to kiss her was all he desired at this moment, for now. She started trembling, and her eyes welled with tears.

He panicked, afraid he'd acted wrongly, that he might be hurting her despite his best intentions, but she never moved to escape, submitting to him, trusting him. And he kissed her, awkwardly, quickly, a brief experiment before retreating to neutral corners. Then he kissed her again, and this time she responded tentatively, still trembling. Then she kissed him back, holding him tightly.

He stopped thinking about what he was doing, though he would remember every intense detail later. They moved together until exhausted, cradled beside each other, and she suddenly wondered about the time. Realizing he had barely thirty minutes to return home with the pickup, he scrabbled up and hastily pulled on his clothing. She insisted she had hours, that she would straighten up their mess and call a girlfriend for a ride. She walked him out to the pickup and kissed him good-bye with more passion than he ever imagined possible.

The next day at school she acted very cool toward him, even avoiding him. Later, he spotted her openly flirting with one of the more affluent students, a varsity football player from her own neighborhood; then he saw her leave with him in his new Chevy after school.

The following day, the eve of the prom, she didn't show up at all until after classes when she appeared in the parking lot, apparently waiting for the end of football practice. Geoffrey confronted her, trying to understand this befuddling transformation. She evaded his questions, asserting that he shouldn't blame himself, but rather her. He promised they could work it out—whatever it might be—hopefully *soon* so as not to mar the romantic reverie of attending their first prom.

Her face softened, and she searched his eyes, then she summoned a scowl of indifference and announced her intentions: "I don't *do* proms."

She left with the football player, and never looked back.

Geoffrey stood there and watched her go, and it hurt him more than he could ever imagine to know she had lied to him, had deceived him, had used him . . .

But still, he loved her anyway.

He went home and sat at his desk and looked out the window and watched the culmination of his junior year, a series of disparate and disconsolate images all passing before his very eyes. Another big event, another opportunity, another fond memory . . . all lost.

Lonesomeness gathered around him, collecting on the investment of his heart, his proceeds the worth-denying rend of indifference.

The deposit on his tuxedo was non-refundable.

Geoffrey quickly excused himself so he could slip out back with Phrekka and Bill before the inevitable onslaught of interrogations. Several smokers lingered in the patio area, enveloped in hazy gray clouds that looked like shrouded hats undulating in the still, humid air. The trio walked toward the barn, pausing beside the garden.

"You came," Geoffrey breathed, his exhalation the purge of a pressure valve.

"Your friend tracked me down."

Bill interjected, "Mom said a beautiful young woman stopped by the funeral home just before noon and, well, I just knew it had to be her, after you described her and all—I mean, who else could be so . . ."

"I'm sorry I didn't notice you there," Geoffrey apologized.

"I didn't attend the service," she admitted, glancing toward the garden, maybe embarrassed.

"I called every hotel and motel within a hundred miles," Bill explained. "They wouldn't tell me if she was registered, so I just kept asking them to ring her room until the one in Guthrie Center finally did. Then I drove out there to make sure it was her."

"I was leaving to go back home," she confessed, still staring at the vined and twined vegetables simmering under the broiler of late-afternoon sunshine.

"I'll leave you two to talk," Bill said, calling over his shoulder, "Don't be long or the crowd will come looking for you."

"If you want to go—" Geoffrey offered her.

She shook her head no, her eyes downcast now. "If you want me to stay—"

"Of course, but why, how—?" he stammered, too many questions occurring to him all at once. "How did you manage to get here?—a last-minute flight must have cost thousands, and I never even told you where—"

She looked up at him, and her eyes glistened. She looked so sad that he wanted to reach out for her, to hold her, to cradle her in his arms, to cherish her . . . but he dared not, terrified of another misstep, unsure, confused.

She whispered, "I was dishonest with you."

He felt his heart palpitating, the weight of impending disconsolation settling over him. He swallowed hard, and his voice cracked as he rasped, "How?"

She took a deep breath. "I pretended to work at the gallery, when really I own it—that and a lot more. For me to arrange to come here required no more than a phone call."

Realizing he'd held his breath, he released it all at once. He couldn't regard this revelation as particularly bad news, nor did her deception reveal malign intent. Still, he felt uneasy that she had mistrusted him so much, and that he had become so infatuated with a persona, a façade, a character luring him into the unwitting role of lead man in some staged comedy—for her amusement, at his expense. He whispered, "You're rich?"

She squirmed and shrugged.

"Like—a *millionaire?*"

She grimaced at the word, then nodded forlornly. "At least several-hundred times over."

Geoffrey reeled at the figure, suddenly feeling embarrassed for having tried to be friends with somebody so far out of his league, but that made him angry, exasperated that she had planned to toy with him until she grew bored and moved on to other diversions. When comes the Belinda-style pronouncement?—the *I don't do plebes*. "No wonder you wanted nothing to do with me—"

"Geoffrey! That's not fair. These past weeks I've planned my whole life around being available to meet you at the gallery, looking forward to seeing you more and more each time, coming out to your apartment even though I felt scared and nervous about it."

"You're *scared* of me?" He grew angrier, trying to keep his voice calm.

Her eyes definitely started welling with tears now. She scrunched her mouth into a distraught pout, shaking her head. "Scared of myself."

"I don't understand."

"Geoffrey, I *have* to pretend I'm somebody else around young men. Admit it—you're already seeing me differently now that I've revealed I have money—"

"Now that you've admitted you were playing games with me," he corrected. "What do you mean afraid of yourself?"

"I thought this friendship would fade after we found out about Sara, but then I didn't want it to, except I needed to keep pretending, and I was slipping, and I knew I'd eventually give myself away, say the wrong thing, drop the wrong hint, and I'd ruin everything because then you'd want to go after my wealth . . . or you'd be angry with me for my dishonesty."

"I *am* angry," he said.

She nodded her head.

"Hurt, I guess."

Eyes cast down, nodding.

"Scared."

She looked up at him, surprised. "You, too?—of what?"

His turn to lower his eyes, he admitted, "That I would mess up." His voice broke, but he took a breath and tried to explain his jumbled feelings. "I'm not good at making friends, especially with women." He shook his head. "I have only one friend—Bill—"

"He's great."

Geoffrey smiled, glancing up. "Yeah, he is."

The sun highlighted her hair from behind, a glowing halo shimmering of coffee and honey and chocolate . . . Her eyes still brimmed with unspilled tears, each shining with a golden sparkle. He felt as if he could see into her soul, and he wouldn't look away, couldn't look away.

He blurted it all out at once: "Billy—Bill's been my friend forever, but he deserves all the credit for that because he's the one who made it work, even when I forgot—and I forgot a lot—because he always remembered, for both of us. With you, I was trying so hard—*too* hard—and I didn't know how, and I sensed that maybe I diminished myself in your eyes by admitting I lost my girlfriend—my own stupid fault—and my job—" He shook his head again. "I was showing up at the gallery every day to pester you, even though I had no job and you must have thought I was such a loser."

"You're not a loser."

"I wanted you to know I have money so you wouldn't think I was a complete deadbeat. Then I went too far at my apartment, and I tried to treat you like you were my date, and you called me on it, and I was so desperate I tried to use my money to hire you just so I'd have another excuse to keep pestering you." His voice quavered, so he tried to break the spell by closing his eyes, but he could still envision her standing there before him, searching him for answers.

"Most young men," she offered softly, "don't know how to be friends with a young woman. They try too hard to make it into something else."

"I won't," he vowed like a schoolboy repenting and promising never again.

"But you already did," she challenged, hinting at a smile.

"And you deceived me," he countered.

"Touché" she said, bowing gracefully.

They both hesitated. A monarch butterfly fluttered by, enthralling Phrekka as it landed on a squash blossom to sip nectar or maybe just to show off its regal brilliance.

"Why did you come?" he asked quietly.

She cast her eyes down again, her demeanor suggesting chagrin. "*I* was angry with *you*."

"Huh?"

"I wanted to find out about Sara, to find out the truth and prove I knew you were playing games with me. But then I didn't care about that anymore," she added quickly, "and I just wanted to come. I even made it as far as the funeral home, but that was harder on me than I expected, and I felt really out of place, so I watched the service from across the cemetery, and I planned to sneak back home without ever admitting I'd come."

"Because of your father?" he whispered.

She searched his eyes, and this time a single tear spilled and trickled down her cheek, threatening to drown his heart. She nodded, then quickly wiped away this revelation of her tender fragility.

"Maybe I could have helped," he whispered.

Emotion appeared to ripple over her, and he knew she liked hearing that. She covered her mouth with her hand, then whispered through her fingers, "But this is about *your* father."

"It's about friends coming together to show—you know." She liked that very much, this he knew, her features softening, her eyes sparkling. "Friends who know how it feels to lose a father."

She nodded, her tender feelings exposed, her face radiant, renewed. "I would like very much to stay and spend some time with you."

"I sure hope so," he confirmed, relieved.

"Honest from now on."

"Completely, no matter what," he agreed.

She smiled mischievously, searching his face. "Then when do I get to meet Sara?"

"Who?"

"Sara—the one who drew the sketches."

"Did you find her?" he asked, hopeful.

"No, silly, I assumed I would meet her here."

He was puzzled again. "I told you I've never known any Saras."

A small crowd spilled out from the house, curiosity about Geoffrey's friend overriding decorum, Bill looking sheepish in his failure to stem the tide.

"You really have no idea who Sara is?"

"Geoffrey?" his mother said. "Do we get to talk to your friend?"

"Really?"

"Honest."

Sixteen years old, only one junior prom in a lifetime, and Geoffrey would have to miss his. He could go alone, or he could accept Bill Marloney's offer to tag along with him and Mary Watson, which he found tempting at first—but no. Too angry to enjoy himself, he chose instead to drive aimlessly around Coon Rapids and hate everything about the town.

The pickup truck streaked down gravel ribbons cutting swaths between hog farms and fields of soybean and corn, a wake of low-hanging dust stirring whorls and eddys of frustration. The yellow-hot disk of setting sun baked the lemony sheet cakes of purple-frosted clouds beckoning from the horizon. Without realizing which routes he'd chosen, Geoffrey found himself pulling into the rutted dirt-tract access circling behind the old barn. There stood the trailer where Belinda Mayroth had accepted his body and soul, never for a moment hinting her intent to devour his masculinity and discard the remnants of his heart like so many scraps of gristle and bone.

Geoffrey stepped out and stood there. He and the trailer studied each other, both battered and worn, used and abandoned. A blue jay circled twice, then perched in the eaves of the barn and watched him mockingly, patiently, waiting to steal the last sprigs of his dignity.

A claptrap Oldsmobile rumbled down the road, pulling into the turnoff. Geoffrey quickly climbed into the pickup, but the car stopped behind him, blocking him in. A labor-worn woman with mousy blond hair tumbled out, kicking the four-ton car door closed and nearly losing her balance. She fished a cigarette out of her purse and lit it, all the while studying the pickup.

Geoffrey stepped out.

"Who are you?" she demanded.

"Geoffrey. Geoffrey Calhoun."

"Yeah, well, I'm Lucille Mayroth. You lookin' for Belinda?" She looked barely thirty, caked with too much make-up, bony hips, no bra, licking her lips a lot and puffing the cigarette like a dying man gulps oxygen.

He hesitated, then asked, "Are you her sister?"

She managed to laugh and scowl at the same time. "I'm her *mother.* She *said* you was a charmer. So what d'you want, Geoffrey Calhoun?" She stared directly at the front of his jeans, which suddenly felt too tight.

"Can you tell me where she lives?"

She moved closer to him, caressing the cigarette with painted lips. "Just moved back to her sister's in Mason City last night. I told her this trailer wasn't room for both of us, that I can't afford no more groceries and she never shoulda come here." She stood right in front of him now, studying him from head to toe. "She was right, you *are* a pretty one."

"I should go."

She paused and stubbed out the cigarette. "I couldn't get her in at work, not unless she quit school."

"Education is—"

"I couldn't give her no money, neither."

He nodded, opened the door, and stepped into the truck without taking his eyes off her.

She stood with her face in the window. "You shouldn't have done that to her," she accused.

He could probably fit around the trailer without getting mired in those ruts, then get out of there fast. He wouldn't take the blame for what happened. Belinda seduced *him*, and nobody got hurt—until *he* did when he found out she had been playing games with him.

"You just *had* to get her hopes up, didn't you?" she demanded. "That's all she talked about these last two weeks. We went round and round until I had to tell her get the fuck out, just go on back to Mason City."

"*Me* get her hopes up! She's the one—"

"I mean, where am I gonna get the money to buy her a goddamn *prom* dress?"

Chapter 10

Phrekka found herself at the center of attention, immersed in reminiscences of people from Geoffrey's past, and she succeeded in impressing them all. Everybody accepted her warmly, and in their unabashed efforts to learn more about her while offering unblushing portraits of themselves, she discovered a degree of singular unaffectedness charming though unfamiliar. To frank inquiries regarding her circumstances, she confided having achieved some measure of financial independence, a vague assessment not so specific as to sound immodest. To mollify those more inclined to pry, she learned that casually mentioning only one of the more familiar business trademarks under the umbrella of her holdings sufficed, for this information would be disseminated immediately through a network of cloistered whispers, encouraging approval by these curious strangers.

Geoffrey spent most of his time with her, but his obligations as the grieving son often required him to welcome arriving guests or to linger with those departing. Phrekka thought hovering at his side during these personal moments inappropriately portrayed her role as one of hostess, so she enlisted Bill Marloney to act as her escort in the interim. She liked this arrangement because she understood the importance of appearances to Geoffrey's role on this solemn occasion, and she wanted to offer her support, not to interfere. This was an important day for Geoffrey, and though certain latitude would be allowed due to the overshadowing tinge of tragedy, he would always be judged for how he conducted himself.

"Geoffrey was such a sweet little boy," oodles of old women kept telling her.

"Spent two days down at our place helping clean out the cellar after that big flood in—when was that flood, Howard?"

"I think it was—no wait, it was the year before—"

"No, you're thinkin' of—"

"He drew me a pitcher of my barn for my birthday," said another older woman, "and always used to write me little thank-you notes when him and Billy'd ride their bikes down on hot summer afternoons for some cold lemonade."

"Used to scare my little Sally with them garter snakes he'd catch. She'd throw a hissy-fit, but if he didn't come 'round for a couple days, she'd start whinin', *Where's Geoffrey?*"

Geoffrey always smiled and told Phrekka something nice about these people, after which would ensue a round of hugs and the pronouncement that he had grown up to be the fine young man they always knew he would.

Phrekka grew increasingly delighted by their concerted effort to introduce her to Geoffrey's boyhood, his pedigree from this good town of good folks. As the anecdotes multiplied, no topic seemed off limits, no information too personal, and she found amusement in the expectation that somebody, eventually, would produce a photo album to embarrass him with smiling-hiney shots of Baby Geoffrey sprawled au naturel on a bear-skin rug.

"He'd make a fine husband," sly Mrs. Patramus mused, nudging Phrekka with a wink and a nod. "The kind of good man a proper young woman such as yourself could settle down with."

Phrekka absorbed these comments with a smile rather than dismiss such speculation out-of-hand, thus allowing certain unstated assumptions to flourish; after all, that she had traveled all this way for Geoffrey in his time of need indicated no small measure of noteworthy commitment both personal and public.

"Ernest was a fine man," one fellow intoned, "a pillar of the community, a real asset to the church."

"Always doin' God's work," the man's wife agreed. Then to Phrekka, she wondered, "Are you Presbyterian, too, hon?"

"My spirituality is very important to me," Phrekka deflected.

"Out where we live," Geoffrey interjected good-naturedly, "they don't call everything by the same names."

That proved sufficient to pass another litmus test, and her approval rating continued to climb.

"Doin' God's work," Phrekka overheard the same woman telling another, "—that's what matters, not what name you put on it."

Geoffrey smiled and whispered to Phrekka, "—Unless you accuse her of being a Catholic—then watch names matter a whole lot."

"Carried me all the way to Des Moines when my sister was laid up," recounted the old woman with Coke-bottle glasses, searching Phrekka's face for recognition of her grief.

"Ernest led the building-fund drive, then pitched in and helped put up the walls," Brother Walker told her.

"Raised that boy up right, just like he was his own," Brother Mickey gushed, more evidence to support Phrekka's hypothesis that Ernest had been Geoffrey's stepfather, thus explaining the mismatch of their last names.

Ernest must have been a wonderful man, Phrekka decided after listening to so much praise, so many tales of his charity and humanity, and she felt somehow incomplete, an outsider, and sad for never having known him. She could see Ernest's qualities in Geoffrey—indeed, she found his sincere and unaffected attentions attractive and likable—and now she could understand how his unremarkable-but-loving childhood had shaped him. Though she felt happy for Geoffrey, she envied him for having had the opportunity to emulate such an extraordinary man.

Conversely, Marjorie Calhoun impressed her as rather cold and indifferent, an unfriendly woman who, though polite to Phrekka, could muster no genuine enthusiasm for the intrusions of this interloper. She considered several hypotheses for this: disapproval for Phrekka's obfuscations on the subjects of religion and money; resentment toward an outsider drawing so much undeserved attention from the grief-stricken widow; rejection of Phrekka's part-Asian heritage, these ethnic and cultural variances falling outside a mother's preconceived boundaries for her son's presumed potential mate; or maybe the threat of another woman stealing Geoffrey's affections. Phrekka kept allowing these ruminations to exacerbate her own discomfort, but seeing how much Geoffrey relied on her support encouraged her to persist, bolstering her confidence, proving her selfish journey had accomplished something positive after all.

Mr. Hanson introduced himself, a giant of a man, gentle and polite. "Geoffrey, you know I got more sons than I can keep count of, none of 'em with a lick of smarts, but all strapping boys who work hard. If your mama wants, we's ready to do the same deal we got with Marloneys and the Widders Higgins and Donohue. We'll take a small share for harvestin' this year's crop, then next year we'll provide the supplies and take care of everything, then give your mama a third for using her land."

Geoffrey smiled and shook his hand. "That'd be just fine," he said with a hint of Midwest-speak, sealing their deal.

After he'd wandered off, Phrekka offered, "Charles could provide an agri-business specialist to evaluate the suitability of his offer, plus an attorney to draw up an agreement that covers all contingencies."

"No thanks," Geoffrey whispered back. "Mr. Hanson couldn't cheat somebody to save his life. If any problems arise, he'll figure out the fair way to account for them. If I insisted on anything more than a handshake, he'd think I didn't trust him, that maybe this arrangement wasn't such a good idea."

"I'm sorry—"

"Oh, please don't be, Phrekka. You're just used to the ways of the corporate world. What Mr. Hanson offered wasn't a business deal, but a social obligation—to look out for my mother while giving his sons the benefit of working a farm they couldn't afford to buy on their own. I'll bet they're saving every penny hoping someday to buy out these farms whenever they go on the market, homesteads to earn an honest living and raise their own families."

The crowd had thinned down to a handful by late evening when Mrs. Marloney gathered several of the women to organize and clean up after the ersatz smörgåsbord of covered dishes. Having taxed the limitations of his bad leg, Mr. Marloney appeared to be suffering quite a bit of pain, so Bill left to take him home just as his mother shooed out the last of the helpful women. Mrs. Calhoun lit a cigarette and seated herself on the living-room couch, then proceeded to critique everything about the service and most of the people who attended.

"At least Walker didn't use it as a chance to make me feel guilty for not going to church," she mused. "I was afraid I'd have to tell him off in front of everybody." Geoffrey seemed pleased by this observation, though Phrekka couldn't conceive of anybody delivering a eulogy laden with implications and accusations toward the survivors.

Mrs. Marloney motioned for Phrekka to join her in the kitchen. "Listen, child," she whispered, "I can see you've got a good heart, and Lord knows Geoffrey does, too, and I'm not one of them gossipy busybodies assuming what ain't my business or tellin' others how to live their lives—" She took a deep breath, searching Phrekka's eyes. "I just want to thank you for bein' here; I can see how much it's meant to him."

Phrekka nodded, unsure what to say. "Well, I'm—"

Mrs. Marloney put a finger to Phrekka's lips and smiled. "I know I'm overstepping my bounds here, but I wanna make sure you understand something about him. That boy's so full of love that anything hurtin' somebody else hurts him just as much—if not more. I first noticed this when him and Billy was real little. Billy broke my good platter climbin' on the counter when I told him not to. After his daddy walloped him a good smack on the butt, Geoffrey tuned up and cried just as much as Billy, and it's been that way ever since." She lowered her voice even more, glancing toward the living room. "Geoffrey's had the worst of it growin' up, but he's always tried to keep his own hurt to hisself. Look at today; he's worryin' so much over his mama and everybody else that he ain't—well, you know. I don't want you to think he ain't hurtin', too, just 'cause he keeps his inside." Her gaze never wavered, and she watched Phrekka very carefully, gauging her words precisely, her eyes glistening now. "I just hope someday he feels safe enough with someone . . ."

The phone rang, and Geoffrey came into the kitchen to answer it, Mrs. Marloney's thought left unfinished. He listened for a moment, then disconnected and explained, "Bill said he had to run to the hardware for somebody whose water heater quit and needs some emergency parts. He'll be back in a half hour to pick you up. I can take you sooner," he offered, "but I hope you'll stay. You've been so helpful all day, I'd like to see you actually sit for a while, just us four."

"I *would* like a chance to get to know your new friend," she agreed, winking mischievously at Phrekka, the interloper who had already decided she liked this woman—a lot.

The newcomer wound up doing most of the talking, gently prodded along by

Mrs. Marloney—who had a remarkable knack for approving of everything said—but Phrekka didn't mind, surprised at herself for liking the attention so much. Geoffrey hung on her every word, and though he'd already heard about her years in Malibu, her mother's succession of husbands, and how she'd moved to Sausalito to care for Grandmamá, he appeared to be enthralled like there could be no more-interesting story in all the world.

"So Sausalito's the other side of the Golden Gate Bridge from San Francisco!" Mrs. Marloney clarified, obviously delighted to imagine such exotic places so far removed from Iowa and the scenery of her life.

"I can see the city and Alcatraz Island from my house. On those rare clear days, I can even see a small part of the famous bridge."

"How long did it take to fly all the way out here?" Mrs. Calhoun wondered, clearly impressed by her son's friend.

"Actually, I came up from New Orleans where I took delivery of some artwork that had interested Geoffrey."

"You have it?!" he demanded, clearly excited. He quickly explained how they had first met when she sold him the sketch of a young boy standing in a pond, and how he'd wanted to find more work by the same artist, another sketch having been located in Louisiana.

"It's out in the car."

"Is it—I mean, is he the same boy?"

She nodded.

"Well, can we see it?" Mrs. Marloney prodded.

Geoffrey walked out with her, using the chance to ask, "When is your flight back?"

Trying not to look embarrassed about it, she had to admit, "I have a plane on the way to Des Moines right now."

"You chartered a whole plane?"

She shook her head. "I have my own—a company jet."

He shook his head, remarking good-naturedly, "It must've been nice growing up with so much wealth. I'll bet you even had a famous designer custom make your prom dress."

She didn't answer, instead nodding hello to Bill Marloney, who had just parked and walked up. She pointed to the artboard covered in brown paper. Geoffrey lifted it out gingerly, then led them inside. Everybody gathered around while he carefully unwrapped it.

And there lay the gentle boy, slumbering in the sanctity of his bedroom without a care in the world.

Geoffrey's eyes softened and seemed to glow.

Mrs. Marloney did a double take.

So did Geoffrey's mother.

"Geoffrey!" Mrs. Marloney practically shouted. "It's *you!*"

His mother nodded wordlessly, stunned.

"It is," Bill breathed.

"No," Geoffrey corrected. "It's just—"

His eyes dropped to the notations at the bottom. The color drained from his face. He opened his mouth, then closed it and swallowed hard.

Phrekka suddenly felt an overwhelming sense of intrusion, of not belonging, of having sneaked uninvited into the private bedroom of this trusting little boy to watch him sleep.

"It *is* you, Geoffrey," Mrs. Marloney pronounced.

And Phrekka believed what the gentle and earnest young man beside her had been saying all along, that he had no idea the boy in the sketches was really him.

Geoffrey turned to his mother, visibly shaken, breathing hard, and he could barely choke out his words in a hoarse whisper . . .

"Who's Sara?"

Geoffrey waited for his mother to answer, every muscle tensed, his breathing labored, his attention fixed . . . but she looked away, her eyes searching for some intangible in the distance, just as she had so often during his brief lifetime. He recognized this expression as her need to escape, her refusal to confront the distraction of realities thrust before her, a longing to exist in another place or to live the life of another soul, any alternative to the heartache of dwelling forever on the periphery, consigned to turn pages for those whose lucky fates allowed them to abide in the storybook realms of fantasy and dreams. Not today, not this time, because Geoffrey would play the central character in this scene and he had demanded that his story be told.

He propped the sketch in front of the television; then he claimed the seat across from his mother and looked to each of the others, his eyes inviting them to sit, to linger as long as necessary, to listen. Mrs. Marloney hesitated, then glanced toward the door and opened her mouth to speak, but Geoffrey quieted her with a firm expression that would brook no argument, denying permission to withdraw, allowing no escape from the truth. She nodded understanding and, exchanging wordless glances with the newcomer, invited Phrekka to join her on the divan while Bill positioned himself on the floor to study the sketch. An uneasy tension settled over the room.

"Mother?" Geoffrey prodded gently. She cast her eyes down, avoiding the scrutiny of his gaze. "Mom, who's Sara?"

She shook her head. "I don't know, Geoffrey," she said without looking up, her words broken by a voice reluctant to speak. "I've never heard that name before."

"My birth-mother's name was Rachel Drousseau, right?—and my dad's was Alain?"

"That's what I saw on the original birth certificate. Rachel E—something—Elaine, I think."

Geoffrey looked to Mrs. Marloney. She nodded confirmation, encouraging him to continue, her eyes glistening with the acceptance of a moment she had to know would come, yielding to the inevitability of all moments that must come to pass. Bill shrugged slightly, tacit confession of ignorance about the details of a story he'd never heard, the reminder of friendship that never conceals. Geoffrey looked to Phrekka, searching her eyes for indulgence, and he felt safe exploring such personal mysteries in the presence of this newcomer to his life, heartened that she, too, wanted to understand, that she never feared truth, whatever that might be. Suddenly, his throat hurt too much to say the words, but he found in her a calming serenity. He steeled his resolution, determined to peer into his own past without allowing its murky images to touch him in ways he'd always feared but never understood.

Bill whispered, "It couldn't be drawn from a picture, because it shows you moving."

He nodded, grateful for any sound to shatter the palpable silence. Indicating the sketch, he said, "But I don't know that place." He quieted his voice as if to avoid disturbing the slumbering child. "—Or who could've drawn it. I've lived here since right after I was born."

Bill sat up straight, his brow wrinkled in confusion, and he exchanged looks with his mother. Geoffrey directed an unspoken question to this friend who had never offered anything less than honesty, no matter what, no matter why.

"You didn't come here 'til the summer we turned six," Bill explained, puzzled. "Don't you remember?"

No, he thought, that simply could not be, for he had never existed anywhere else.

"Just weeks before your birthday," Mrs. Marloney confirmed.

Geoffrey felt like his very identity had been nothing more than a wind-blown fantasy sand-castle, an abstract sculpture now cracking under the harsh glare of scrutiny, each facet of his self-perception crumbling, his very existence scrubbed away by the purifying tides of realization. He wanted to dig in and resist the relentless waves of revelation, afraid they would leave nothing more than a featureless expanse of immaculate beach, with no memories scratched into the surface, no footprints to prove he had ever passed . . . and he clung to what he knew to be real, the mother who raised him, the friend who embodied acceptance and loyalty, the neighbor woman who always reminded him he deserved to be loved, the new friend who believed in the treasure buried beneath his flaking veneer of fool's gold. He tried to remember, and he did recall his sixth birthday and the candle-crowned cake and the T-ball set he got from Billy and the story books from Sally who squealed at garter snakes but gave

Geoffrey a kiss on the cheek . . .

Yet nothing existed before that.

First grade, yes—but kindergarten? Had there ever been a kindergarten?—and why had he never thought about it before?

He shook his head slowly, and the insubstantial memories, if they ever existed, floated beyond his grasp.

Mrs. Marloney watched Marjorie Calhoun.

Geoffrey's mother glanced back at her, nodding just perceptibly before fixing her gaze on the sketch; then her eyes softened, and Geoffrey knew she remembered something that he could not.

"Your mama and daddy was killed, Geoffrey," Mrs. Marloney said softly. "That's why you come here to live—"

"They died *before* I was adopted? I thought— Ernest said they couldn't handle having a kid." His eyes started burning, and his chest and throat hurt, but he swallowed the waves of nausea flowing from his belly, determined to rise above emotion to consider this testimony with scientific detachment. "He said I inherited my trust fund after they died, but he acted like he didn't know when." He studied the sketch again, wondering how that unfamiliar boy could be him, and he felt weary, longing to drift into sleep and feel safe, yearning to find the serenity that innocent child took for granted—

"Geoffrey?" Mrs. Marloney called for his attention, but still he felt lost. "Geoffrey?" He looked at her, uncomprehending at first, but then he recognized the face, the woman who used to assure him all would be okay, Billy's mom who poured soothing peroxide on his scraped knees and doctored and bandaged the squalling child until she called to him and got his attention and assured him he could come back from that terrible place because the hurt would go away now and this hug would prove she spoke truth. "Geoffrey hon, Rachel Drousseau was Ernest's *sister*, his only living blood relative. He used to forbid people to speak of her because she ran off and married a Frenchman, then she renounced the church."

Ernest and Marjorie Calhoun used to be his aunt and uncle? What happened to his recollection of those early years when he called himself Drousseau?—when the only name he knew was the one he would reclaim at eighteen after discovering it on his trust fund, exercising his legal prerogative to hurt Ernest by rejecting his neo-heritage as an adoptive Calhoun.

Wordlessly, his mother got up and disappeared into the master bedroom. The sounds of drawers opening and closing filled the silence while all eyes studied the sketch. Geoffrey wondered if that really could be him, not just another boy with the same name, or maybe a fiction conjured from the imagination of some unseen artist. She returned with a time-worn envelope marked *School Pictures*, her hands shaking as she pulled out a small stack of photos, and there showed the proud smile of a blond-haired tassel-capped high-school grad, and there he posed a year younger, then a sophomore . . . The junior-high years showed a skinny, slight boy, his hair shorter, his face a mask for unspoken ideas and grand aspirations and private fantasies. Fifth grade, fourth, third . . . and Geoffrey's heart started pounding, for these images depicted more than just another time or place; they symbolized what he felt, what he remembered, and what he had forgotten.

Second grade, and Geoffrey swallowed hard, desperately trying to calm his stomach.

First grade . . .

Phrekka gasped, half out of her chair to see more clearly.

Bill nodded.

Marjorie's eyes drifted to Sara's sketch.

Mrs. Marloney watched Geoffrey.

And there could be no doubt, for there in the 8X10 full-color economy-package bonus shot posed a solemn little boy wearing a starched shirt and oversized clip-on polyester tie, with silky blond hair, and big sad eyes . . .

The boy in Sara's sketches.

Geoffrey gulped for air, tasted cotton, felt dizzy, and tried very hard to will this feeling to another place, another time, but his world melted and squished between his fingers, eluding his grasp.

Phrekka and Mrs. Marloney both appeared to be in danger of rushing to comfort him, but he glanced warning to leave him be, and they both seemed to understand. Not now, not right now, for here sat a man cradling an unmolded mixture of wet sand and modeling clay, poised to recast himself.

He studied the boy in the photo, and though it seemed like this child must necessarily be somebody else, Geoffrey needed to find some way to accept, to comprehend, that he was him. He looked back and forth between the photograph and the sketch, and the possibility of any chance of mistake slowly faded until Geoffrey began to see himself, and he could feel the uncertainty once again of being six years old with a vulnerable heart, in an unfamiliar place, with unfamiliar people . . .

Confused and afraid.

And he blushed, suddenly embarrassed, caught betrayed by his own feelings in a roomful of people. Then he actually found some amusement in the image Sara had drawn, realizing for the first time that it was he who lay there adorned in nothing more than some rather tight-fitting, anatomically revealing undies—and right in front of Phrekka, too!

"It was a chemical spill from a train wreck," his mother said, shattering his reverie. "Your father—Ernest—never would talk about it, and I didn't pay much attention; I was lost for a time because it happened right after . . ." She cast her eyes down again, then reached with unsteady hands for her cigarettes, pausing to light one and slowly inhale the smoke.

"It was a hard time," Mrs. Marloney supplied softly.

"I'd just had a stillbirth after two miscarriages," Marjorie continued, her eyes averted. "I had to have surgery, and they said I could never get pregnant again. I was laid up in bed when the call came." She stopped to smoke some more. "Ernest left and drove to Mississippi—"

"I moved in for two weeks to help look after her," Bill's mom explained.

"—Something about next of kin having to decide about removing life support and making burial arrangements. Two weeks later he came back, only he wasn't alone."

Mrs. Marloney smiled tenderly, remembering.

His mother puffed voraciously on the cigarette, then lit another from the smoldering butt and sat back, apparently finished with her story.

"Brought back an adorable little boy," Mrs. Marloney whispered as if sharing a secret.

"I wish I had it to do over again," Marjorie mused, looking off into the distance.

Distressed, Mrs. Marloney assured her, "You'd been through a lot, hon. What matters is how it turned out."

"Had what to do over, Mom?" Geoffrey asked, maybe hurt somewhat by the comment, at least unsure how to feel.

"You have to understand, I'd just lost my baby, and what he brought me was somebody else's."

"That's all in the past now," Mrs. Marloney shushed her, crossing to sit beside her and pat her hand.

"I didn't want somebody else's child," she persisted, still searching the distance, discerning the past.

"But once you started feeling better—"

"Ernest told me Geoffrey was our responsibility, that it was the Christian thing to do, but whatever the church thought I should be feeling was the last thing I wanted to hear—"

"Marjorie Calhoun, you grew to love that boy—we all did." Mrs. Marloney's voice quavered, the peacemaker trying desperately to wrestle the lid back onto an open can of worms.

"I kept trying not to love you, Geoffrey," she admitted, crying now. "I did love you—I mean, you were such a sweet little thing, and so scared most of the time—but I couldn't stand how Ernest treated you, and every time he hollered at you, and every time he whipped you, it just broke my heart and I'd have to remember you weren't really mine."

Phrekka held her hands to her mouth, her eyes welling with tears. Bill buried his face in his hands. Mrs. Marloney hugged Marjorie, whispering soothing words to her.

"You used to follow me around," she continued, "and try so hard—try so hard—"

"Hush now," Mrs. Marloney urged her. "It's all right, hon. Shhh . . . Shhh . . ."

And Geoffrey never loved his mother more than he did at that moment.

"I know you didn't understand," she sniffled.

He crossed to the couch, Mrs. Marloney moving back to make room for him, and he took his mother in his arms and whispered, "I did understand, Mom. I did."

"Oh, Geoffrey . . ."

"I did," he lied, for he hadn't understood, no matter how hard he tried, until that moment so long ago when he finally decided to give up and try, instead, to stop caring. Now he finally did understand, and he still had time, and this would be the chance he never had. "I knew you loved me," he whispered.

"Did you, Son?"

"I knew, Mom. And you've always known how much I love you, no matter what kind of crazy nonsense was getting in the way. You knew it, too."

She hugged him back, and her voice broke, but then she actually chuckled, and so did he, and Phrekka smiled through her tears, and the Marloneys smiled, too.

"Oh, Geoffrey, what am I going to do with you?" She started playing with his hair, straightening it, wiping her own eyes, reaching out to squeeze Mrs. Marloney's hand.

The last wisps of tension evaporated, and stories about Geoffrey's and young Billy's mischievous years flowed as much to entertain Phrekka as to remind everybody there had been many happy times. They passed around more photos, images capturing milestones along with the everyday events of everyday lives. Both Geoffrey and Billy found themselves blushing furiously at Phrekka's delight over a shot of them their first summer as friends, posing in the yard, arms around each other's shoulders, both wearing nothing more than clinging water-soaked underpants rendered virtually transparent by an afternoon of exuberant hose-play. She whispered to Geoffrey, teasing that she would like to have it blown up to life-size for display in her gallery. He quickly buried the print in the pile already viewed, his cheeks still burning—but not so embarrassed anymore, not around Phrekka.

The stories eventually segued into reminiscences about Ernest, and several early photos brought tears to Marjorie Calhoun's eyes. Despite the melancholy inherent in pondering a lifetime after someone's death, everybody urged her to relate the tales behind each shot, to recall how the young couple had met and courted and married. As is the custom in making trips down memory lane, they detoured the faded tenements of indifference, the blight of good intentions gone awry, and the burned-out hulks of rending regret, focusing instead on gardens blooming with promise and potential, skyscrapers towering with the pride of accomplishment, the cattail-punctuated glassy ponds reflecting moments of calm serenity.

As the hour grew late, everybody started tuckering out. The Marloneys made overtures to leave several times. Phrekka admitted she had released her pilot with an earlier phone call, confirming a suite in Des Moines for the night. Because the jet would be used for business the next day, she would have to leave before dawn or risk being stranded until later the following evening.

That's when Geoffrey uttered the words he never thought he would speak. "Another day in Iowa wouldn't be so bad, would it?"

Phrekka allowed the hint of smile, so Geoffrey affected his very best mien of boyish charm until she relented.

"Except for the sad occasion prompting my visit," she said softly, "I believe Iowa is a very delightful place, indeed." With a slight bow, she agreed to remain another day.

"Then Mother and I insist you stay here tonight." Before she could answer, he hastily added, "The guest bedroom is no suite, but I'll try to squeeze into my scout uniform and get a rickety cart to provide room service."

Bill cut in, "I didn't know you were a Girl Scout—" That earned him a playful smack upside the head, lucky that Geoffrey's sense of propriety and decorum prevented him from acting on his initial temptation to deliver that age-old traditional retaliation known hereabouts as a "wedgie."

"I will gratefully accept your kind offer," Phrekka allowed, her eyes sparkling, "if you promise no uniforms and no extra fuss."

Bill and Geoffrey scampered out to retrieve her bags, returning to find the women trading embraces. Bill weaseled his way into a Phrekka hug, no less the self-effacing charmer than his friend. Geoffrey felt the slightest pang of jealousy—while Mrs. Marloney tried to squeeze all the air out of his lungs—that Bill had just brazenly touched Phrekka more than his own apprehensions had allowed him to try.

"Bless you, child," Mrs. Marloney whispered to Phrekka, and Geoffrey could see in both faces that something special had passed between them. Mrs. Marloney hugged Geoffrey one last time, whispering, "You know we love you," and he did know it. Then the Marloneys disappeared into the night.

Mother Calhoun showed Phrekka to the guest bedroom upstairs, opposite Geoffrey's room, and set out enough spare blankets and miscellany to ensure adequate protection from arctic winter, nuclear fall-out, or worse.

"Should we get the box out now, Geoffrey?" his mother asked, "—in case you get up before me and want to look through the records?" She led him to a large carton in the top of a closet, which Geoffrey wrestled down and carried up to his bedroom. She also gave him some recent financial and farm-business records from a drawer in her room, then squeezed Phrekka's hands and thanked her for coming, bidding them both good night.

Phrekka disappeared into the upstairs bathroom to do whatever it is women do before bedtime. Geoffrey unpacked some of the bundles of records and envelopes of files and spread them around on his desk and dresser. He doffed his shoes, then carefully hung his suit, donning a pair of shorts and tank-top, and started sorting.

He found the oversized envelope marked *Geoffrey's Trust Fund* just as Phrekka emerged from the bathroom. He spread the paperwork out on his bed, plucking a yellowed newspaper clipping from the pile as he walked to the door to wish her good night. Her flowing, sheer gown, the color of shimmery buttermilk, reflected the incandescent refractions of her cinnamon hair. She looked as exotic as she did beautiful. They stood there awkwardly for a moment.

"I can't say enough—" he started.

"And neither can I," she interrupted, putting a finger to his lips, "so we won't."

Geoffrey grinned, and she smiled back at him.

"I would like a good-night hug," she offered softly.

Though brief, the hug charged him with electricity, and Geoffrey hoped she didn't notice that his heart pounded thunderously.

"What did you find?" she asked, breaking the spell, gesturing toward the faded clipping.

They examined it together, a story from a paper called the *Laurel Leader-Call*:

TRUST FUND SET FOR TRAIN SURVIVOR

Laurel—A trust fund has been established at Laurel Central Bank & Savings for Geoffrey Drousseau, 5, the "Miracle Boy" who survived last week's chemical spill when two tanker cars derailed behind his family's home at 2795 Bruce Trail north of Hwy 11 in Laurel.

The fund was established by the boy's uncle, Ernest Calhoun of Coon Rapids, Iowa, in response to an outpouring of donations from across the state. Calhoun says Geoffrey, staying at the home of Purvis and Mabel Greenstone since the accident, will return with him to Iowa. The child has been called "Miracle Boy" because he was playing nearby in the woods when the accident occurred, upwind from the cloud of ammonium trinoxinate that engulfed his family's home.

Killed in the accident was the boy's father, Alain Drousseau, 41, an oil-rig technician employed by StarrChem Industries of Gulfport. Mr. Calhoun has authorized that life-support be removed later today on the other victims, the boy's mother, Rachel Drousseau, 36, and sister, Sara Drousseau, 18.

Donations should be sent to . . .

The crescent moon offered its lopsided smile through Geoffrey's partially opened bedroom window while a warm springtime breeze strummed melancholy chords across the transom. Geoffrey pulled his door open a few inches so the air could circulate through the house, thus to waft away the odors of death's casseroles. He felt exhausted, but the answers to questions he'd never asked might be lurking in this box, and there would be no rest until every last one had been captured, examined, and tagged.

He tried to resist the onrushing waves of trepidation, the awkward hesitance between intent and actually touching Ernest's things, his legs burning with the memories of breaking his father's tools or sneaking pens from the man's roll-top desk or hauling a sack of corn seed out to a muddy field without permission. He willed away this irrational apprehension, but that meant replacing it with the still-too-vivid concept of Ernest's death and the sense of finality that weighed so heavily.

He gazed out the window for several minutes, pondering the question of why Ernest had hidden the truth. It appeared at first blush to be purely selfish: a fear of competing with a family of ghosts, the malicious and vengeful refusal to acknowledge his own sibling who strayed from God, the tyranny of controlling a fragile child by denying the support of family and friends who loved him . . . but then Geoffrey recalled Mother Calhoun's reluctance to accept somebody else's orphan as her own son, and it suddenly occurred to him that Ernest's staunch refusal to preserve any memory of Geoffrey's family might simply have been his way of trying to protect his own wife. Little Geoffrey had come to Iowa after what must have been a horribly traumatic ordeal, and he needed to forge new bonds, to welcome and encourage his new mother's halting progress toward embracing her new role. Ernest had set about diligently trying to punish all semblance of the boy's former self away, infusing him with the self-perception of a "bad boy" in need of correction, all the while prodding the desperate child to accept Marjorie Calhoun, which he did, dutifully following her around and bringing her cigarettes and coffee and sitting close to her until, sometimes, in those rare moments like when he vomited on his bed and she bathed him tenderly, he felt her love and drank from it to sustain him through the all-too-frequent periods of indifference and confusion.

And Geoffrey did forget his former self.

He forgot the faces of his mother, his father, the very existence of his sister, his home in Laurel and his friends and his bedroom and his toys and that pond with the cattails . . . and he forgot the thunderous squeal of derailing train tankers echoing through the woods where he played, the odor of deadly gas, the people who found him and took him away and never again let him go home, the wrinkled brow of a stranger who put him in a car and drove him so fast and so far that his very identity couldn't keep up, the very essence of his selfhood left in the purgatory of a world he no longer inhabits . . . waiting . . .

Waiting for him to return?

He shook his head and rubbed his eyes, frustrated with himself. Too tired for existential forays into self-identity, he had a job to do. It was time to sort through the papers, to determine the Calhoun financial status, to look out for the mother who had learned to love him after all.

The envelope of trust-fund documents whispered for his attention. Inside he found a longish *Declaration Of Trust* filled with pages of legalese, established with Ernest as trustee, the Laurel bank as custodian, and itemization:

$ 3,210	Donations
$ 87,265	Asset Liquidation
$ 180,000	Child Care (12 yrs @ $15,000)
$ TBD	Annuity
$ TBD	Interest Income

The trust specified that a child-care allowance would be paid annually to Ernest until the beneficiary attained the age of eighteen, at which time all accrued interest from that account would go to Geoffrey. The balance of financial deposits, including all interest income, also would be paid to him at eighteen. The terms of the annuity were to be specified separately. Because Geoffrey had received a lump sum of nearly $400,000 on his birthday, apparently the bulk of that money must have come from the annuity, presumably the proceeds from life-insurance policies.

He looked for anything marked *Annuity*, but found instead a packet labeled *Lawsuit*. It described a wrongful-death action, complete with a judge's signed settlement order. The plaintiffs were listed as the estate of Alain Drousseau, Geoffrey Calhoun (Drousseau) as sole minor survivor, and Ernest B. & Marjorie Calhoun as "next friends." The defendants were a well-known chemical-manufacturing company and its equally famous insurance carrier represented by a law firm out of Jackson with a long, complicated name. Geoffrey's header simply listed a lawyer's name, Peter

Gomill, address in Laurel. He read the text of the order, which consisted mostly of complicated clauses specifying non-admissions of liability and culpability, non-disclosure agreement, settlement-of-all-claims rigmarole . . . and the money: an annuity, purchased by the insurance company, which would pay Geoffrey $300,000 at eighteen . . . *another half-million at twenty-one . . . and another half-mill at twenty-five!*

Geoffrey's heart pounded. He never expected two more payments. If he didn't mismanage the resources too badly, he would become a *millionaire.* He wondered if Phrekka would assess his friendship differently now, but he decided she would never be that kind of person; then he hovered between chagrin and self-reproach for momentarily ascribing such petty values to her. He regarded her as a sensitive soul, and he remembered *her* fear that others would judge her materially.

Once the high of new-found wealth abated, he hurried through Ernest's financial and business records, quickly discovering the man had maintained his affairs meticulously, eschewing loans where payment could be made, retiring obligations ahead of schedule, amassing an impressive portfolio of conservative investments. The simple Iowa farmer apparently didn't really need to work at the concrete works after all. The widow would live quite comfortably, owning her home and property free and clear, even without the seasonal benefit derived from the Hanson boys' corn-cropping.

Geoffrey's CDs, the envelope said. Inside he found twelve certificates of deposit, purchased one per year over a period of twelve years, the principle of each at $15,000, the beneficiaries listed as Ernest and Geoffrey, jointly or severally. Ernest had never spent a dime of the money he received for raising an orphaned nephew, saving it instead for the boy to use after he'd reached adulthood. This saddened Geoffrey. He wondered why a man would drive off to the concrete works every night, ignoring his adoptive son rather than accepting the very payments designed to help him afford to spend time with the growing child. Maybe Ernest's pride won out, his determination to fulfill the responsibility he had assumed, to support his new son without assistance. Maybe guilt interfered, his refusal to profit in death from the sister he'd abandoned in life. Maybe it signified making amends, Ernest returning to Geoffrey all that remained of a world irretrievably stolen from the boy. Maybe Ernest kept the job because he hated the punishments and belittlements as much as Geoffrey, but knowing no other way, he chose instead to stay away as much as he could—distance to dampen the kindling wherein too often sparked rage, the resulting conflagrations burning dan-ger-ously out of control and, in different ways, consuming them both. As much as Geoffrey had found some measure of relief every time he watched Ernest drive off to his job, sitting here now in the bedroom of his youth, he didn't want this money.

He wanted Ernest back.

Why? Rational explanation eluded him. Maybe to say, "Take the money, Dad. Don't work yourself into a heart attack. Use it to take Mom on a romantic trip to someplace found in one of her books, or quit your job and use that time to show me what I did wrong with my birdhouse. I think I understand you better now, and if you'll let me learn more, I'll try my very best not to make you angry with me . . ."

His throat hurt and his eyes blurred a little, but he decided not to succumb to maudlin feelings, so he pressed on . . . and he found the *Last Will and Testament.* It specified that everything Ernest owned or was owed would go to *my wife, Marjorie Calhoun.* In the event his wife did not survive him, the entire estate would go to *my son, Geoffrey Calhoun.* The last name had been lined out and changed to *Drousseau*, initialed and witnessed in the margin, the notation dated some twelve years after the original filing during the summer of the boy's sixth birthday.

Suddenly overwhelmed, he lost himself for a moment in his grief, in his guilt, in his regret, but he looked at the cracked pane of French window and it whispered to him again in Ernest's voice, reminding him:

Move on, Son. What's done is done.

Geoffrey had returned to Iowa determined not to become mired in his past, his final tribute for Ernest B. Calhoun one last homage to keeping up "appearances," playing the proscribed role, acting as expected of him, no shame, no dishonor . . . yet now he realized the irony that doing what Ernest would have wanted turned out to be what the adopted son had truly wanted to do. In the process, he had waded into the quagmire with both feet, but he no longer felt afraid, for he knew the way out, and he could count on friends like Bill to push him and Phrekka to pull him. No matter how much he once tried to deny it, he now realized that a part of him would always dwell here, and he could accept this, if not embrace it.

The last envelope was marked *Cemeteries.* It held the deeds to Ernest and Marjorie's plots, plus a packet from a funeral home in Laurel, Mississippi with receipts acknowledging payment for three full interment packages, a single family headstone, and the deeds to three grave sites at a private cemetery along Horse Creek. The deeds listed three Drousseaus: Alain, Rachel, Sara.

For the first time, these people started to seem real. More than abstract concepts or the subjects of some folklore fiction, Geoffrey's birth family had once gone about living their everyday lives, but then they had died, and now he knew where they were buried. As much as that hurt, he yielded to the sensation of floating recklessly through other people's pasts, and in that he found acceptance, he found connection, and he found the glimmer of possibility that he might come to know them after all.

He eased into the hallway, crept down the stairs, carefully avoiding the floor creaks whose locations he'd learned through years of trial and error, and he slipped into the living room. He studied the sketch propped in front of the television, then lifted it carefully and carried it back up to his room. He left the door open just enough to allow the warm springtime breeze to dance mischievously through the house; then he propped the sketch on his desk chair right beside the bed. He turned off the overhead light, leaving the nightstand lamp to bathe the slumbering line-and-shadow boy in its soft glow, and he stretched out on the bed to study his long-lost sister's rendering of her sleeping little brother.

He yawned wearily and tried to remember. He tried desperately to find Sara's face, but no image would come. He longed to hear her voice, but the breeze offered only brief crescendo gusts of minor chords to mock him. He closed his eyes and tried to conjure her fragrance, the sensation of her hand holding his as they walked to the pond and listened to the birds and felt the warm sunshine on their faces . . .

But Sara was lost to him.

He studied the sketch, and he tried to imagine Sara there in the room with him, watching him and waiting for him to sleep before she would leave. Then, without effort or intent, the strokes of graphite and charcoal seemed inexplicably to come alive, and little Geoffrey breathed gently, his chest rising and falling with the rhythm of life.

He reached out for Sara's touch, the young woman he would never again see, and he felt overwhelmed by the power of circumstance beyond choice or control, and he knew Sara would never have left him, but that she had been taken from him. In this literal rendering, there existed the suggestion of hope that someday he would remember. This moment, this connection, this would be his opportunity to believe, and to love her back, no matter how far away she had gone.

And he could almost feel her gentle arms around him, holding him tenderly, then slipping away into the night, lingering for a moment to capture the image in her mind, and he wondered what she must have thought, and how she must have felt.

As he drifted into a dreamworld of wonder and bliss, he glanced one more time at the sketch beside his bed and whispered, "Sara, what else did you see?"

Phrekka nestled under a light bedsheet, the lingering aroma of reheated casseroles mingling with the farmland fragrances of corn and soybean, faint hints of sheep and cattle and hogs all swirling around and through her as she drifted in and out of slumber. Each time she floated across the escarpment between waking and sleep, gliding into the vale of dreams, she would find herself back at the edge again, peering over the precipice into the real world, watching the light glowing from under her door, listening to Geoffrey rustling papers across the hallway, imagining what he must be thinking, how he must feel.

Phrekka had thoroughly investigated the life of her own father by the time she was thirteen or fourteen, poring over papers, studying photos, talking to people who knew him, hiring an investigator to compile the official records. The journey toward knowing him had frustrated her every step of the way, for with each new revelation she moved forward a few steps, only to watch the indistinct object of realization fade farther into the distance. This culminated the summer before ninth grade when she had exhausted every scrap of information she could uncover, and she found herself alone in her room, nestled under a sheet, holding a photo album of blurring snapshots, tearfully reaching out to bridge that chasm between life and death, between curiosity and understanding . . . finally realizing that no amount of facts or data could bring him back to her, for any connection between Phrekka and her father must necessarily live on in her heart. He'd touched her that day she discovered his room and looked upon his painting, when she'd dwelled for a time in the scenery of his world, and nothing since had helped her feel any closer, so she would accept that a touch must suffice, and she vowed to nurture and cherish this tenuous bond to sustain her always.

She knew this would be true for Geoffrey, too. Maybe sooner, maybe later, maybe at this very moment, eventually he would reach out for the family he'd forgotten, for Sara, the sister who loved him so much that she captured his very essence in images that even now span time and cross the threshold between life and death, she whose sublime touch had been there from the beginning, even before he knew, before he understood. Geoffrey would go to Mississippi, and though Sara had been dead for many years, there he would search for her, and there he would seek to rediscover his lost identity.

Phrekka hoped he wouldn't ask her to accompany him because that would entail too personal an exploration, be too much to share with him, and it might resurrect too many memories of her own search. She could try rationalizing such a trip as the ideal opportunity to seek more sketches, to learn more about Sara-the-artist, to study the effect of her work on posterior audiences, but the more Phrekka pondered this, the more she admitted she could never succeed, for to participate in this foray with Geoffrey would inextricably link her purpose with his, and there could be no delineation between her artistic temperament and the emotional trauma of having spent so much of her life yearning to love the father she never knew.

And she feared Geoffrey would be unable to keep separate his search for lost family from his feelings for Phrekka.

She considered the first sketch, the impact of which had formed the basis for this unique friendship, the boy standing naked and unashamed, absorbed by the idyllic scenery of his childhood, and it made her sad to know Geoffrey had outgrown that innocence, that he'd become a dangerous young man, buffeted by his physical urges, his interest in Phrekka clouded by the hormonal surges that drive all men. Once a young man has reached this state, he must see his female friends differently, and he can never return them to their former grace. He will want nothing more than to possess one of them or, worse yet, believe he already does, forcing her to hurt him in a way that hurts herself, to push back in self-protection even like Phrekka had in the kissing closet when she humiliated an affectionate boy whose only crimes were desperation to become a man and his desire for Phrekka Churán.

Geoffrey had acted the perfect gentleman ever since his first stumble, and she liked to think that he would forever remain thus, but to continue to delve with him into such personal explorations as a shared trip to Mississippi would surely present . . . The big-eyed little boy standing in his pond had looked so sweet and innocent, and if Geoffrey would only stay that way, then she might learn to trust him completely, and then she could hold him tenderly, and they would cuddle together in a tent of safety while the storms of passions-run-amok raged through the forest, leaving them untouched, unharmed.

Geoffrey had crept downstairs during these ruminations, returning after a few minutes. The rustling of papers stopped, the light under Phrekka's door dimming to a soft glow, and the house fell quiet except for the hum of breeze strumming curious chords across the transom.

She eased from under her sheet, slipped quietly into the hallway, and stood poised before Geoffrey's slightly ajar door. He appeared to be asleep. She whispered his name, then pushed the door farther open. His breathing sounded deep and measured, emanating from a dreamworld of wonder and bliss, and he lay sprawled on the bunk in tight shorts and white tank top, one leg over the side, his foot on the floor. Beside him, propped in the incandescent radiance from his night-table lamp, slumbered the little Geoffrey of Sara's sketch, in the same position, the boy from the past in contrast with this man in the child's future. More than ever, she could see the connection, and Geoffrey did seem to have grown beyond some callow boy struggling his way toward manhood, but he no longer appeared to her as someone who had crossed a distinct line between innocence and danger, and she realized that maybe Geoffrey would be different, that he simply existed as a point moving along a continuum, that he might learn to add new dimensions without sacrificing the grace from which he emerged. In that, she found hope that Geoffrey might still encompass all the qualities he once embodied as a boy rather than trading them wholesale for the dangers of a man.

She moved closer to the bed and studied the contours of his body in contrast to the sketch, his slightly broader shoulders, the ripples of his chest, his genitalic outline now grown way beyond the innocent peeper snail of a little boy, the sleek and muscled leg now reaching the floor rather than dangling, the smooth once-scabbed skin of his knee proving that all wounds heal with time and gentle care. She liked to think that all children are born with an unlimited capacity to love, but that circumstances beyond choice or control cause too many to lose various amounts of this blessing, and she wondered how true this would be for Geoffrey. Could she believe, could she trust his demonstrated loyalty to his family and the earnest respect he had shown her? Had Geoffrey retained his capacity to care?—and would it prove strong enough to override his other desires so he could remain Phrekka's friend on mutually ascribed terms? Did she care enough for him to take that risk?

She reached out tentatively, and she touched his silky hair, and she stroked along some feathered strands ever so gingerly.

She closed her eyes and imagined holding the child from the sketch in her arms, and then she imagined holding the man . . . but then she felt scared.

She opened her eyes again, and she studied Geoffrey, and she experienced something new and unfamiliar deep inside herself, and she knew the answer to the only question that mattered . . .

Geoffrey would be worth taking the chance.

"I'll go with you, Geoffrey Drousseau," she whispered. "If that's what you want, we'll go to Mississippi together."

CHAPTER 11

Geoffrey felt like a comet blazing across the sky, the itinerant wanderer intersecting the orbits of many worlds, envious of those tranquil moons who routinely trace their own familiar orbits.

He prepared to leave Iowa again, on different terms this time, imbued with equal parts of relief, ambivalence, and apprehension. He'd fled this area once, trading the scenery of trauma for one of both personal and professional failure, but then he'd returned to bury the past, inadvertently resurrecting evidence of a previous life he had lived and forgotten, people he had loved and lost, their fleeting images flickering beyond substance or realization even as mysterious fireflies twinkle in velvet twilight fields of wonder. Now another sphere loomed before him, Phrekka's world, affluence and luxury, leisure and unimagined choice. He had invited her into the expectations of his, only to find himself drawn into the potential of hers.

Geoffrey wanted to be more than a mere curiosity, a puzzle to be deciphered, but what could he offer her that she couldn't easily acquire for herself? What manner of birdhouse would attract a free spirit who already owns the sky? She had accepted his invitation to visit Mississippi and honor the graves of his birth-family, to help him find his original home and the couple who kept him those first weeks after the tragedy, to seek more sketches by Sara while he sought snatches of distant memories about his sister, but rather than traveling with him on *his* journey, circumstance had dictated that it was he who would accompany her, on her jet, in the manner to which she had become accustomed.

A uniformed fellow waited beside an older woman in a golf cart outside the airport, no red carpet, no phalanx of hand-servants, no trumpeting heralds to embarrass the kept man who passed—suspiciously, to all outward appearances—around and through the domain of this rich and beautiful young heiress. He wondered how many other suitors had passed this way, what price her protectors customarily offered to send them away.

"Good evening, Miss Churán, Mister Drousseau," the woman greeted them.

"Mrs. Jamasol! It's been so long!" Phrekka clasped hands with her, standing beside the rental car, both smiling like old friends reunited.

"I couldn't pass up a chance to see you off this afternoon," gushed the woman.

"Geoffrey, this is Linda Jamasol, an associate and good friend."

"Mrs. Jamasol—" he started to greet, accepting her hand.

"Please, call me Linda."

Phrekka interjected, "First names for us, too, Linda—you know that."

Linda held their hands, grinning mischievously in her perfectly tailored business suit, a buxom heavyset woman with a swoosh of platinum blond hair and brightly painted lips. "I know, hon," she admitted, looking Geoffrey over from head to toe. "I just wanted to use up my daily quota of formality in front of your handsome friend."

The man loaded their bags onto the cart; then with a nod from Linda, he stepped into the rental car and drove away.

"And how is *Mister* Jamasol?" Phrekka asked as Linda ushered them into their seats.

"Still fat and lazy, fat and lazy," she snorted, adding a cackle of laughter for effect, "and I still keep him nearly as happy as he keeps me." She climbed behind the wheel, turning to warn Geoffrey, "Hang on tight, hon, I'm a wild woman." And off they zoomed. Still blatantly eyeing Geoffrey while somehow managing to navigate her way around the terminal without mishap, she teased, "The rumors of you being a looker don't do you justice. I hear you're quite the charmer, too."

Geoffrey felt his cheeks flush.

"Linda!" Phrekka protested, also blushing.

"Let an old woman have her fun, hon."

They zipped toward a gleaming Gulfstream poised alongside the tarmac, its stairs lowered in anticipation. Linda zoomed them up next to the modern version of a gangplank; then she reached into a satchel and handed Phrekka a packet. "You wouldn't let Charles arrange an escort, so here's your get-around kit. A sedan, but no driver, is waiting at the Laurel Municipal Airport, and two suites are reserved downtown at the Sawmill Ramada. Frankie said tell you the area's quiet and laid back, the kind of place where fun is watching 'em pump gas down at the fillin' station on a Friday night."

Somebody from the jet gestured toward the bags, so Phrekka turned to answer his questions. Geoffrey wanted to blurt out that he could afford his own plane ticket, that he would insist on paying for their hotel suites, that it was he who had invited Phrekka, expecting nothing more than a friend to stand beside him while he confronted something undiscovered about himself, a shared view from his own past.

Linda used the opportunity to sweep Geoffrey into a breast-crushing hug, whispering, "You know, Geoffrey Drousseau, you're taking our little girl someplace she's never been."

He thought at first that she meant Laurel, Mississippi, but then he understood, and he whispered, "It's okay," and in that moment something passed between them, and Geoffrey knew that each had made a promise as indistinct and undefined as it was important.

Phrekka turned back too late to hear them. "Thanks so much, Linda, and tell your husband I said hi."

"I will, hon," she said, deep affection in her eyes. Then she hugged the younger woman, whispering something Geoffrey couldn't hear. It made Phrekka blush again, and for some reason, Geoffrey liked that. "Go on now; get out of here." With a wave, then a sly wink for Geoffrey, she jumped into the cart and sped off.

"Miss Churán, Mr. Drousseau—if you're ready—" the man in uniform offered, gesturing.

They boarded the plane, and Geoffrey nearly gasped aloud when he saw the cabin. Expecting mundane rows of seats, instead he discovered what looked like a luxurious lounge with plush recliners facing each other across low tables, a compact work area, entertainment and business electronics. He found it rather impressive.

Phrekka let him select a seat, then settled into one opposite him, both strapping in. The Gulfstream pressurized and taxied, then lifted off immediately. They both watched the sun-drenched quilt of Iowa countryside until the jet banked and headed southward, leaving them blinded by late-afternoon laser-orange glare from across the horizon. Geoffrey's return to the Midwest had been fraught with trepidation, but now he found himself feeling a sense of loss, of leaving something behind, of losing home. This seemed different than when he'd first escaped to California, the ink still wet on his new diploma. This time he'd finally confronted the beast who lurks in the shadows, and though he held no desire ever to live in Iowa again, he'd proven he could visit without being eaten alive, and that by daring to peer into the dark crevices illuminated by Phrekka's confidence and support, he'd found a certain simple beauty in the scenery of his childhood.

He chased away those thoughts and studied the cabin, still awestruck by the trappings of wealth, feeling an odd mix of awkwardness and delight over having been treated with the same deference as Phrekka, everybody knowing his name and even calling him "Mister Drousseau," Linda seizing the chance to draw Geoffrey into her intimate circle, Phrekka's endorsement the only requisite for acceptance. Nevertheless, like a country bumpkin who wins the first-prize weekend-in-the-big-city vacation, his first excursion into Phrekka's true lifestyle left him admitting that more light-years separated their worlds than he'd realized, and he considered how much more at ease he'd felt, how less intimidated, when he perceived her as a gallery employee needing to sell sketches to pay rent, an intoxicating young woman fascinated by the young man who could afford to buy them. He felt sheepish, remembering how he'd accused her of financial motivation underlying her sales pitch, this chagrin yielding to outright embarrassment as he remembered all the subsequent hints he'd dropped about his own modest wealth. He really had played the rube, the show-off with a pocketful of change trying to charm a match girl secretly clutching her own purse full of gold.

Flying above the clouds, they chatted about their day in Coon Rapids; their luncheon excursion with Geoffrey's mother and Mrs. Marloney; visiting the hardware store so Bill could play the proud tour guide; and one last trip to the cemetery where they had hugged briefly, unexpectedly, without expectation or intent.

Suddenly, Geoffrey blurted, "That's not where you live, is it?"

She confessed the co-op belonged to Marva, that she really owned the gabled mansion atop the hill. "It's lonesome sometimes, so I spend a lot of time down at the gallery. My friend Cerise is in Malibu, but she's busy with school and a new boyfriend."

"I'm sorry I teased you about your designer prom dress," he offered, "but I'll bet you *were* the most beautiful girl there."

She looked at him affectionately, but then she glanced away, a far-off look in her eyes, and she appeared wistful. "I never attended my prom," she sighed. "I did have a stunning dress, but . . ." She studied him, searching his face.

Sensing she'd recalled a painful memory, he tried his best to project assurance, understanding.

She hesitated, then continued, "He told me he rented a hotel suite—you know, for afterward." She looked away again. "He told me this two days before, at his house with nobody home, and he said we should *practice* so it would be perfect after the prom. You believe that? *Practice!* Then he started pawing me, and he wouldn't stop. He even tore my—" She caught her breath. "I left, but not before he called me a bitch and said he'd find somebody else for the prom."

Geoffrey clenched his fists, fighting the urge to demand the man's name, but he forced himself to calm. In that moment, their orbits passed very close to each other, and their worlds seemed not so very apart at all. As much as shame and embarrassment would prevent him from ever revealing some parts of his own childhood, he wanted to know every moment of hers, the good times and bad, and to show her he would've helped, if only he'd known, however he could. Every time he saw something new in Phrekka, it mattered very much, and he wanted to see more.

"I don't know how I misjudged him so," she admitted. She shrugged, shaking off the feeling; then she unbuckled and went to a storage locker, carefully removing a small box. He followed, sitting beside her at the table. She opened it to reveal an exquisite Mardi Gras mask.

Geoffrey instantly recognized the pheasant and quail feathers; then he noticed the miniature cattails and tiny butterfly, and those reminded him of the Sara sketch. "Wow," he said.

She gazed at it as if searching for something. "My prom date masked his true intentions," she said quietly, lifting out the feathered masterpiece and setting it in front of Geoffrey.

"Wearing masks can be dishonest," he said, examining it, noting the doodlebug, the moth.

"But sometimes you have to," she countered.

He looked at her, puzzled.

"You might have to appear happy for a friend," she explained, "even if you believe she's made a bad choice. Disappointed teachers need to encourage effort, even in the face of mistakes, so their students will persist and improve, especially when all they need is confidence. Sometimes, parents have to look stern to make a point, like to show disapproval for foolish risks, even though secretly they're relieved the child wasn't injured."

He looked at the mask again, then back at her. "Then you shouldn't wear masks to *conceal*."

"Aren't those examples of concealing?"

He shook his head. "No, they're showing something deeper, loyalty to a friend, faith in a student's desire to learn, unconditional love for a child . . ." He swallowed hard, and somehow this felt very important to him. "Any little boy or girl who knows how much you love him won't forget it when you need to put on your stern mask, and he'll understand."

She considered this for a moment, then tilted her head and nodded slowly. "I've never dressed up in a costume mask before, always thought it rather silly, but I like this one, and now I think I know why. It doesn't—like you said—*conceal*, but rather it helps express who I am."

Geoffrey had never experimented with unfettered self-expression; the oppression of a seen-but-not-heard childhood still weighed heavily upon him. The very idea of revealing himself had always felt too risky, like a loss of control, the betraying of one's weaknesses. Wondering exactly when unmasking his most private feelings had come to feel this way, he considered the full spectrum of his experiences, and he realized that by looking to his past he could also find scattered exceptions when personal revelations *had* left him unscathed, and that he owed those to the confidence that he could trust the witness, his friend, Bill Marloney. Billy was the one person who had earned that trust, the only one who had proved he would always accept Geoffrey and remain loyal, whatever he'd seen, whatever he'd heard, whatever he knew, no matter what. He wondered when he and Billy had crossed that line; if it was shedding unabashed tears over a broken wrist; or blushingly exploring wondrous new sensations evoked by the wrinkled images from a magazine; or worrying together that Ernest might be dead, both knowing the other secretly found relief in imagining it might be true.

Suddenly, memories of the worst moments of his life washed over him, and he could see his young friend watching from the side, crying pitiably, and he vividly recalled the defeat of being exposed against his will—not just his body, his pain, his anguish . . . but his greatest vulnerability, the admission that he was powerless to protect even the last vestige of his dignity, his autonomy, his very self. He tried to chase these morbid ruminations away, embarrassed to recall such awful secrets in the presence of Phrekka, frustrated that reassuring visions like any remembrance of Sara's face still proved too elusive to grasp, and he wondered how much more he had lost, how many fleeting impressions of another lifetime even now were being eclipsed by the controlling grip of Ernest's pious and punitive ministrations. Still, he couldn't shake the image of Billy's tears, and he remembered how his friend had always steadfastly refused to flee, and though Geoffrey would have been hard pressed at such a tender age to explain Billy's obstinance, deep inside he had understood, and he had counted on that simple guiding truth of their friendship:

They were in this together.

That's how Geoffrey had learned to find reassurance, not shame, in Billy's presence. Billy had never abandoned him, but rather loved Geoffrey enough to take some of the agony upon himself, helping his friend survive by being there to guide him back to safety once the danger had passed. Now, after all this time, Geoffrey's gratitude for that powerful expression of true affection overwhelmed him, and he recognized the glimmer of his greatest victories rising from the depths of his bitterest defeats, the possibility of loving others and being loved unconditionally, friendships built upon the immodest foundations of naked trust.

He glanced at the mask, then he found himself gazing into Phrekka's patient eyes.

He swallowed again, and his throat hurt. "I used to pretend to be who Ernest wanted so he would stop hurting me—but it never worked, so when I got older, I started pretending instead to be whatever made him angry, just out of spite. Now I'm tired of pretending."

"Me, too," she said. "I've been hurt so many times by the naked avarice of potential friends that I can't help but be secretive, if not ashamed of all this." She gestured awkwardly around the cabin.

"I *would* feel better paying my own way," he said, regretting the words even as they tumbled out.

"And I'd feel better giving your mom a million dollars to enjoy life, then donating her corn crops to a homeless shelter, but I respect your world too much to interfere, and now I'm trusting you with mine. I can't help what I have, or how that affects the way I live, and though I could send the jet home and book commercial fares with you, that would worry the people who look out for me, and I doubt it would make you feel better."

The words gave Geoffrey pause, and he knew she spoke truth, but he kept his eyes on the mask, and the feathers reminded him of a beautiful bird, and he recalled building the birdhouse, offering sanctuary so something exquisite would come and want to remain a part of his world; and in that moment he finally understood Phrekka's alternative, that she embodied a free spirit who had invited him selflessly to soar with her, if only for a time, to see the world from her vantage-point. "I feel like such a fraud," he admitted, shaking his head.

"Maybe you've pretended too long that your life in Mississippi never mattered," she whispered. "But everything in life matters."

He rubbed his eyes and shrugged, sheepishly admitting, "I'm kind of afraid, really—I mean, I don't know . . ." His heart palpitated, and it seemed suddenly warmer there in the cabin. "Part of me doesn't want to go back."

"But you have to."

"Why?"

"Sara deserves that much."

His eyes dropped; then he closed them, and he looked again for Sara's face, but the image always eluded him.

Softly, Phrekka said, "The boy in the pond looked right at you that day you stomped around my gallery wearing your don't-need-anybody mask," she whispered. "He knew that was a lie and, once he called you out, so did you."

Waves of insecurity and apprehension washed over him, and he felt swallowed by something too big to conquer, a black hole too powerful to resist.

And he knew in his heart that he didn't *want* to resist . . .

But Phrekka's world hovered so vulnerably close, and he feared she would be drawn in with him, and he would be the one who hurt her the most.

"You can trust me," he promised in his tiniest voice, his profound sincerity the briefest flash of meteoric hope streaking the endless skies of infinite promise.

"I do," she admitted, her eyes glistening.

And for that moment, he knew his mask had dissolved, that she had seen the truth, that this risk would be worth taking, even if their worlds eventually drifted apart, even if he would lose her. "If I get down there and start freaking out, you don't have to stay. You can leave if you want."

"You're afraid I won't like what I see in you."

"What if you don't?"

"Geoffrey, I've seen who you really are. I've seen it from the very beginning."

He looked up, searching her face. "But how?"

Phrekka smiled the radiance of a rising sun, her eyes the sparkle of majestic stars. "Sara showed me."

"Where's Geoffrey?" she squealed. "Where's my big guy goin' on his first trick-or-treat?"

"Raowww!" the costumed little boy growled, running menacingly into the room. "Raowww!"

"Oh no! It's a monster! What happened to Geoffrey?! Did you eat Geoffrey?"

"Raowww!"

"Geoffrey done been eat up by the monster!"

Little Geoffrey giggled, lifting his mask. "Here I am!" Crawling into her lap, he wondered, "You wasn't scared, was you?"

"No, sweetheart, I knew it was you."

At dusk the spiral began.

Geoffrey felt himself descending into the mysterious depths of memory's long-sealed catacombs, a series of wondrous chambers where linger glittering sparks of insubstantial associations, those tauntingly vague impressions always swirling just beyond reach, fleeting images stubbornly unformed, unexplained, uncaught.

He settled into his Gulfstream recliner, buckled and cinched his seatbelt, and watched below as the flickering lights of Laurel, Mississippi coalesced into the first tangible depiction of scenery from his lost childhood. He held his breath, the expansion popping his ears against the change in cabin pressure, and he gripped the armrests for one last rollercoaster upsurge and plummet, sighing with relief when the jet touched down.

Phrekka offered a reassuring smile while they taxied to a tranquil, apparently deserted service building. The pilot unsealed the hatch and activated the stairs as a golf cart threaded its way from the small terminal. Geoffrey moved to retrieve their bags, but Phrekka gently reminded him that somebody had been assigned that task, a subtle hint about the etiquette of allowing others the honor of fulfilling their responsibilities.

As they stepped down to the tarmac, Geoffrey felt a blast of hot, humid air, the warm breath of Mississippi countryside settling over him with a heavy security blanket that evoked cozy sensations of recognition and belonging, touching him with practiced familiarity, caressing, soothing, welcoming. The fragrances of Laurel probed him tentatively: the pungent rain-washed potpourri of lush forest, the nose-wrinkling odor of livestock pastures, the bouquet of wildflower blossoms fringing the cool waters of swift creeks and placid ponds, the swamp-gas skulking malevolently on unwary wisps of restless breeze, the stench of industry and autos and trash bins . . . all demanded acknowledgment and competed for dominance in the sweltry air. His heart palpitated, his breaths quickened, and he tried to calm himself. He looked around, but the scenery paused with deceptive stillness, the trees little more than depthless dark brush strokes painted on backdrops haphazardly bordering nature's stage, order imposed by the beckoning rows of rising runway lights, a tableau trimmed by burnt-orange muddy ruts along the pavement's edge and decorated by hundreds of pinpoint yellow lights flashing intermittent reminders through a gauze of rising mist.

Phrekka introduced the man in the cart as Frankie, and Geoffrey was pleased to meet him—in a polite but somewhat distracted way. She indicated a preference for walking, assuring Frankie she and her guest would be fine while he took their luggage to the car, promising to meet him there shortly. Geoffrey sensed Phrekka's awareness, her understanding that he had been overwhelmed for a moment, and it made him feel self-conscious, sheepish, awkward.

The bag-laden cart disappeared into the gloom. The pilot nodded recognition and retreated to the maintenance building.

Phrekka and Geoffrey were alone.

"Wow," she whispered, following his gaze.

The purple bruise of evening sky descended across the horizon, dissolving the ephemeral hues of iridescent cobalt that haloed the tree-line, and the field came alive with the fairy-village display of thousands of flickering lights.

"Fireflies?" she asked, barely audible, reluctant to disturb the delicate wonder of such a transcendent scene.

Geoffrey nodded, then closed his eyes to capture and preserve those first impressions lest they slip beyond his grasp. He breathed deeply, and this time he tasted the flavors of pecan ice cream and fresh-sliced watermelon; and he felt the sensations of soft cloth gently brushing his face and of warm sand squishing between his toes; and he could hear the melodies of songbirds rising in syncopation with percussing crickets and cicadas, counterpoint to the basso of bullfrogs and the cymbal-brush of snakes in the tall grass . . . but a numbing sense of panic suddenly spread over him, and he swayed on his feet, refusing to open his eyes, desperately trying to find something lost deep inside himself, resisting all distractions from the real world, poised between the intangible apparitions of before and the palpable touch of all that is now. He felt himself spiraling again, descending deeper into the mysterious depths of memory's long-sealed catacombs, and in that series of wondrous caverns where linger the glittering sparks of insubstantial associations, something familiar swirled just beyond realization. He reached toward it, desperately hoping to touch whatever had eluded him, to make it more real, but instead his hand found Phrekka, and she put her arm around his waist, offering support, assurance. His eyes still closed tight, he watched as the pinpoints of light swirled faster and faster until they formed a nimbus through which peered the briefest glimpse of a gentle face with love in her eyes, but that dissolved just as quickly, and it left him reeling. He opened his own eyes to find himself and Phrekka enveloped in a glittering sea of myriad fireflies all bobbing on the currents of expectation.

He took another breath and, buoyed by Phrekka's willingness to risk this moment of intimacy, he dared to put his arm around her shoulders. He felt a moment's hesitation from her, but then she accepted his gesture, and for this instant in time that would be enough.

"They're beautiful," she whispered, the shimmering glow of dancing life reflecting deep in the glistening hazel depths of her eyes.

He nodded, floating, pulled toward the lights but holding tightly to Phrekka, anchored to priority, connected to life, linked, tethered.

"I've never seen them in real life," she breathed.

Geoffrey could hear her speaking, but he also listened to another voice, a song whispered among the trees, a lullaby with no words echoing through the stirring, agitated air.

"What?" he asked the sky.

"I said I've never seen them before," Phrekka answered.

Phrekka Churán . . .

He listened to the crickets and the frogs and his own heartbeat, then felt the rhythmic pulse of Phrekka's life-blood.

"They're a kind of beetle," he said.

The voice whispered again, rising and falling in familiar melody, and Geoffrey waited for it to come closer and embrace him, but the indistinguishable strains faded, quieter, softer, farther away, maybe calling for him to follow, maybe saying good-bye, until he could hear the voice no more, and all that remained was Phrekka by his side and the sparkles of a trillion fireflies watching over Mississippi's lost son and his new friend, winking, waiting, sad somehow, forlorn, expectant, resigned.

"Do you want to see one up close?" he asked.

She shook her head and sighed. "They're prettier this way."

"What are they?" the wide-eyed little boy asked.

"Lightning bugs!"

The sparkling lights twinkled reflections in the glassy surface of the pond.

"Bugs?"

"Beetles. You wanna catch one?"

She led him to the closest one, a blur hovering tentatively in the air, a shadow intermittently illuminated by its own yellow beacon. Afraid of it, he shied away.

She laughed, assuring that he would be okay. "Watch me," she said, reaching out and cupping the firefly in her fist. She formed a peep hole with her thumb so little Geoffrey could look.

He approached gingerly, but not too close, and he saw the briefest flash of radiant wonder before the beetle escaped and flew away.

"Catch one, Geoffrey."

He reached out, but then he pulled his hand back, unsure.

"It's okay," she whispered, and she put her arm around his waist for reassurance.

He reached again, hesitated, then dared to cup the intriguing little fellow, feeling it crawling in his hand. That startled him for a moment, but he remained stalwartly brave because he trusted her with all his heart and he knew she would never let him risk danger, would never let him be hurt, would always protect him and love him, no matter what. He kept his fist closed so it couldn't crawl out, gazing across the pond at the mirrored fantasy of a million pinpoint lights reflecting in the glassy surface. "They're just bugs," he said, maybe somewhat disappointed to understand the truth behind the magic, maybe proud to unravel another mystery of the grown-up world.

"But they're still pretty, aren't they?"

He nodded, glancing this way and that, the entire clearing coming alive and shimmering with the loving glow of more and more lightning bugs all watching over the little boy. "Oooo," he whispered.

She giggled. "You still like 'em, don't you, Geoffrey?"

"If you do."

"Look closer," she urged.

He formed a peep hole and peered into his fist, delighted to see it illuminated by the comforting night light that chases phantasms from the shadows of his room while he sleeps.

The skinny, orange-headed beetle crawled out onto his thumb, mesmerizing the captivated child, then it spread its wings and lifted into the air, a bright yellow flash signaling departure.

And it whispered a silent good-bye to its very own enchanted little boy.

Geoffrey reached for it, but it disappeared among the mysterious firefly twinkles in the velvet twilight clearing of wonder. "Aw, he's gone."

"That's okay, sweetheart, there will always be more."

CHAPTER 12

"We need to talk about your new stepfather," Charles said quietly.

Arriving at Cerise's house full of ideas about her own upcoming sixteenth-birthday celebration, young Phrekka was surprised to be greeted by the CEO of her company, the gentleman who had been her father's business partner and lifelong friend. Behind him stood an unfamiliar fellow in a very expensive suit, Cerise and her father off to the side. "Why hello, Charles. Why did you come *here*?"

"To keep this meeting secret from your family," Charles explained. Then he introduced the stranger. "Miss Churán, this is Aaron LeBraugh, your attorney. Your grandmother exercised her prerogative as the close relative of a minor and hired him on your behalf."

She greeted LeBraugh politely, asking Charles, "Why do I need an attorney?"

Charles hesitated, clearing his throat. "It might not be appropriate for me to participate in this discussion, or even to remain here—"

Mr. LeBraugh interjected, "You're attending at my request, to facilitate, and if my client wants you to be present . . ."

"I do," Phrekka asserted.

Cerise's father showed them to the living room, offering drinks before disappearing into the kitchen, urging his daughter to follow. Phrekka's friend ignored him, taking a seat next to her on the couch.

"It's about your new stepfather," LeBraugh began. "I'm afraid he's taken some legal action."

Charles looked very upset, and Phrekka felt a rising sense of panic. For Grandmamá to hire an attorney, this must be very serious, but for Charles to appear so flustered and to act like he shouldn't even *try* to help her . . . Charles understood everything and could accomplish anything, and he had always been available to support Phrekka, her bedrock of stability beneath the shifting sands of an unstable home life, of an endless succession of indifferent or interfering stepfathers, of Mother's pathetic attempts to mold her into a materialistic social butterfly, of a lifetime longing for the father she would never remember, of too many painful lessons proving she could never trust the motives of boys and men . . .

And now Charles looked very worried . . .

And that made Phrekka suddenly feel very scared.

"I'm afraid you and I both will be hurt considerably by this," she heard Charles say, and she felt tears in her eyes, afraid to hear the rest. Quickly, Charles knelt before her, offering his handkerchief, assuring her. LeBraugh shifted uncomfortably, glancing around the room. Cerise put an arm around her, and Phrekka felt embarrassed, frustrated that she had acted like a child during an important meeting. Then she found solace in reminding herself that here among friends she would be safe to reveal her vulnerabilities. Charles had dried her tears many times in the past, no matter their cause, and she always loved him for that. He had also taught her to stand up for herself, and now came her chance to prove she learned well. She would draw a line in the sand, and she would meet whatever challenge lay before her. She would succeed because she could count on herself, on her determination and diligence, and because she could count on Charles and Grandmamá, their loyalty and support, no matter what. Besides, she had her own attorney now, a notion that finally coaxed a hint of smile from her because anyone Grandmamá would hire, someone Charles would endorse, must be the best, and he would be fiercely loyal, unwavering, a brick amid the shifting sands.

"What kind of legal action?" she asked.

LeBraugh answered, "He's filed two petitions with the court. The first is for approval to legally adopt you."

Phrekka reeled at the notion of becoming Larry's daughter. She found the very idea repugnant. How dare Larry attempt to usurp a role he never earned and could never deserve. "Why would he even *want* to adopt me?"

Charles returned to his seat, answering, "We think it's a ploy to bolster his other claim. He's also trying to assume conservatorship of your trust."

Phrekka held her breath, and she could see the sand-castles of her charmed and enchanted life crumbling to dust. The accomplishments of two generations of Churáns were being rendered as frangible as footprints crossing the beachhead that separates stilled pools of remembrance from the tides of oblivion, Phrekka's tangible proof that her father and, before that, Grandpapá had once passed this way now about to be obliterated by the corporate tsunami of a man referred to in newspapers as "Liquid Larry."

"But he can't do that," she breathed.

LeBraugh disagreed. "If he can become your guardian, with his business track record, he might very well succeed in wresting control of your trust from Charles."

"But what would he gain? It's not like he can take my shares and keep them for himself."

"It's not your shares he wants," Charles said, "but the right to vote them. The very control of our company is at stake."

"But my trust holds only forty percent," she said, "and even though you vote it by proxy, you don't really need to. With the forty percent your family owns, Grandmamá's twenty percent gives you the majority because she always goes along with your recommendations."

Charles smiled, reminding her, "Your grandmother did disagree with me that one time over an environmental issue—and she persuaded me to vote your shares against myself. She's a very determined woman."

"One who trusts you and won't let an outsider convince her to support anything that hurts the company or diminishes my trust."

"Actually, her votes might not be enough. Remember, my cousins own half of my family's shares, and even though I currently hold their proxies, too, I now have reason to believe they're allied with your stepfather. If they transfer their proxy to him after he assumes control of your trust . . ."

Phrekka was crestfallen.

"Can you guess what he's likely to do then?"

"Yes," she replied sadly, "he's called Liquid Larry because floundering companies bring him in to slash costs and increase profits—or to divest them, breaking up and selling off their holdings so the shareholders can cash out."

Charles looked proud of her. Always encouraging Phrekka's interest in business, he eventually grew so impressed by her savvy that he started treating her like his protégé, providing her information, seeking her input whenever possible, honoring her wishes. "I believe our company is his next target."

"If he succeeds, he can tear down everything our families worked together to build." She rubbed her eyes, flabbergasted, flustered, flummoxed.

"And as long as my cousins are satisfied with their windfall profits, he can write himself a contract to collect tens of millions of dollars for the privilege of dismantling your inheritance."

"But Grandpapá set things up to prevent this from ever happening. That's why despite letting Father run the company at nineteen, he put those shares in trust for him until age twenty-five."

"Do you know why he raised the age so high?"

"Because Father got engaged to Mother when he was only twenty, and Grandpapá didn't trust her, even had her investigated and found out she was still having an affair with her high-school boyfriend. I know she cheated on him, Charles, even after they were married, and I know that wanting to share my father's future stake in the company is the reason she married him."

Phrekka had understood this for years. Her mother used to vent anger about the trust arrangement on a regular basis, especially when she'd had too much to drink, spitting venom about how the Churán family had screwed her out of her dead husband's fortune. Her father had died at twenty-two, which meant he never actually got to own those shares, and that her mother couldn't inherit them. Since he did leave his family substantially well off with other assets and life-insurance policies, Phrekka decided long ago that her mother never deserved the company, even before the young teen understood concepts like fidelity and naked avarice.

Charles hesitated, then said, "I have information suggesting Liquid Larry targeted our company even before he met your mother. Frankly, I think that's why he courted and married her."

Phrekka looked him right in the eye and said, "She's wanted to gain control of my inheritance all my life, and Larry presented the best opportunity to accomplish just that. I think that's why *she* married *him*."

LeBraugh interjected at this point, stroking his neatly trimmed beard, musing out loud, "Unfortunately, ulterior motives, especially without evidence, might not be relevant. If I am to look out for your best interests, who's to say Liquid Larry—as you call him—might not serve *your* ends better with his plan?"

"Charles," she asked, "if he did a fast, basic liquidation, how much cash do you think he could get for me out of my shares?"

Charles shrugged, thinking for a moment. "I don't know—at least three-hundred million, maybe three-fifty."

Crash!

Everybody jumped, startled by the shattering sound from the kitchen, a "Sorry!" from Cerise's father suggesting he'd been listening and found the figure rather impressive.

"Mr. LeBraugh," Phrekka announced, "I intend to take over the company someday—whenever Charles grows tired of it. I consider that my birthright, and that to me is worth infinitely more than any amount of cash Larry could obtain from it for me."

"Good for you," Charles practically cheered.

"And if he tried to pay himself a fee out of my proceeds, I could fight that, couldn't I?"

"Why yes," LeBraugh agreed. "It would open channels for me to charge conflict of interest—"

"And Charles and Grandmamá, as shareholders, would be entitled, in advance, to copies of any contracts written in that regard, true?"

"Well, yes."

"Then we could charge conflict and seek an injunction *before* he could damage the company."

Charles considered this, then pointed out, "It would still be worth his while if my cousins were willing to pay his fee out of their portion."

They sat in silence for a moment, and Phrekka looked to Charles, noticed him gazing at her with pride and determination. She felt for the briefest moment like she might be losing her footing, but something old and familiar passed between them, something only they could ever understand, and she knew she would stand firm against any attempts by Liquid Larry to erode the substance of her dreams.

"We can beat this," she said quietly.

"I think we can, too," LeBraugh agreed, "but you might have to pay a steep personal price."

"How?"

"Well, for starters, your home life may deteriorate. Plus, your mother has the right to prevent you from having any contact with Charles—"

"No!"

"Yes, and she can enforce it with legal action. The same is true with your grandmother. In California, grandparents have no right to visitation."

"I won't abide by it."

"Acts of incorrigibility diminish your position in the adoption petition, plus Charles and your grandmother would be liable to criminal sanctions if they're caught violating a court order."

"What if I move out, get my own place?"

"If you were seventeen, you could probably get away with that, but at not-quite-sixteen, no. That would make you a runaway."

Phrekka thought of her home life, of her indifferent mother, the woman's interests focused on constantly berating her daughter and bemoaning her lack of social aspirations. She thought of living with Larry, and of the cheap gifts he showered upon her in what now seemed an obvious attempt to bolster an image of selfless generosity. Her heart started pounding as she grew increasingly furious with the man who too often grabbed her in awkward, uncomfortable hugs, holding her too close, his hands straying too far and lingering too long. She felt those hands touching her now, probing for loose change in her pockets, reaching for her purse, pushing away the only people who truly loved her and looked out for her. Rage washed over her in waves, not only because this man would take advantage of her family in order to seize a piece of the Churán fortune, not even because her mother's duplicity would abet this end, but that Charles and Grandmamá would be hurt in the process and the dying wishes of Grandpapá would be thwarted. Grandpapá had lost his only child to an early, tragic death, his son's greatest gift a baby girl named Phrekka Churán, and he wanted his empire to pass into the hands of this granddaughter he would never live to see grow into womanhood. She had inherited a sacred trust, and nobody would take that from her, especially not Liquid Larry.

She thought for a moment, then decided to risk asking the next question, embarrassed about the subject, but summoning her courage. "What if I testified that I'm uncomfortable with how he touches me?"

Charles leapt to his feet, his face crimson, his fists clenched. LeBraugh shifted forward, eyes wide. "What's he done to you?" Charles demanded. Then, just as quickly, a tenderness spread over his features, and his eyes softened. "Wait, not now. We'll go talk to—"

"I'm okay, Charles. He's probably not done anything illegal—that I know of." She rubbed her eyes and hesitated, feeling embarrassed but determined to go on. "It's just that he's always pushing too far, and I woke up once and found him sitting on my bed. He scares me sometimes, but I've never said anything, not wanting to interfere with Mother's marriage."

"I'll pound him into a bloody pulp," Charles growled.

Phrekka shook her head no; then she looked up at him, and she loved him more in that moment than she ever had before, understanding that he had always loved her as if she were his own. "No, Charles. I'll stand up to him now, and if that damages or destroys their marriage, well, business is business, and their partnership will just have to be nothing more than a deal gone bad. I would never lie, or even exaggerate accusations, but now I'm angry enough to make it very clear that his adoption scheme might force me to raise questions about his character, questions that would hurt more than this—this . . . this *business deal*," she spit out, "that forms the basis of his becoming a part of my family."

LeBraugh had his hand on Charles's arm, urging him to sit, to calm himself, to listen.

"You can't appear to be involved in that personal part of my life, Charles," she said quietly. "Your motives would be questioned, anything you tried to do cast under suspicion of self-interest. I'll take care of myself at home," she vowed, "and you help Mr. LeBraugh win the legal battles."

Charles looked at her, his fists clenching repeatedly, his breaths coming too quickly, until finally he settled down some. Then he sighed and nodded. They gazed into each other's eyes, lost in unspoken assurances. LeBraugh stood to leave, passing a business card to Phrekka, urging her to call him any time, day or night, and let him know of any developments she might even remotely consider relevant. The attorney shook everybody's hands before he left. Cerise disappeared down the hallway so Phrekka and Charles could be alone.

Charles stood there awkwardly. Phrekka moved closer, and they tentatively embraced, then held each other with conviction. She felt safe, protected, and in that instant, it seemed like she had become closer to her own father than she ever thought possible. Charles was his best friend; they had grown up in tandem, the scions of industrial giants, their families traveling together, moving in the same worlds. The young men had loved each other, this she knew in her heart, had heard it in Charles's voice all her life, had seen it in his eyes, even feeling it with his tears the only time she'd ever exhorted him to speak of the accidental death, the investigation, the aftermath. Her father had been lucky to have Charles as his friend. Now Phrekka was the lucky one.

She told him this as he prepared to leave, and she knew it meant a lot to him. "No matter how this turns out," she whispered, "he can't come between us and what matters most."

The girls decided to have a sleep-over, just the two of them, so later that night, bathed in the warm lamp-glow of Cerise's bedroom, they dared to review the day's developments.

"You can't ever get married," Cerise said, "not unless he's also super-mega-rich."

Phrekka shrugged, agreeing, sort of. "Charles is the only man in the world I can truly trust. The rest all seem to want something from me."

"So stay single and take something from them. Have your pick of buff young lovers every night and live the good life."

Phrekka shook her head, but didn't say anything.

"You should just say that bastard tried to fondle you," Cerise urged her.

"Cerise?" came a voice outside the bedroom, her ten-year-old brother, the handsome little guy who still wore superhero undies—not that he would ever admit it.

"What, brat?"

He pushed his way in. "You got the cable guide?"

She tossed it to him, and he started to retreat, but Phrekka called him over, reaching for his hand. "You're gonna marry me someday when we get older, aren't you?" she teased him.

"Oh, sure, what the heck—if you got a good game system to play." She leaned over and surprised him with a fast kiss on the cheek, but he wrinkled his nose and pulled away, declaring, "Ick! Not if you're going to act like that!" He rubbed the cooties from his face and disappeared out the door.

Phrekka laughed.

Cerise snorted. "He'll change his tune in a few years."

"They all do," both teenage girls agreed simultaneously.

"You're right, though," Phrekka said, pulling the duvet up over herself, settling into the soft comfort of the twin bed. "I can't ever get married. Marriage is supposed to be an act of love, but the way it works legally, it's a business deal. Pre-nuptial agreements ruin the romance, and they never hold up in court; then you eventually wind up hating each other." She shook her head and closed her eyes, trying to imagine the scenario Cerise had suggested, a series of lovers . . .

But that could never be.

"You need to quit being so weird about sex," Cerise urged her. "Find somebody cute, make him jump through a bunch of hoops to prove himself, then go for it."

"Like you have a lot of experience—once going almost all the way with James."

"Hey, I let him play with me sometimes—if he does what I want. He'll do anything for a chance to finger me."

"Sex is supposed to be an expression of love," Phrekka whispered.

"It doesn't have to be," Cerise's voice murmured from far away.

"It should."

"Guys don't know the difference. They fall in love with whatever makes them get hard."

"I don't want that to be why . . ."

"Come on, Phrekka, you can't stay a virgin forever."

Phrekka kept her eyes closed, and she drifted through time, seeking the sensuality of her body, finding only the danger of men's and boys' impulsive lust. She touched her breasts, lightly brushing her nipples; then she traced a line down through her navel, slipping her fingers under the waistband of her panties, and she felt the dancing whorls of passion stirring in the sere dust scattered haphazardly by her apprehensions. She tried to imagine herself on a tropical beach, approached by one of those buff young lovers, but the sands beneath her shifted and crawled with invisible denizens, feely-bugs touching and probing her body, and no matter which way she squirmed, she could find no escape. Waves of panic washed over her, threatening to pull her into the deepest abyss of degradation, and she could feel the terrifying threats of Kieran's arousal pressed damply against her leg; of Daryl's hands groping her undeterred in the closet; of Timothy tugging at her jeans in the back of James's car, the clumsy teen growing angry when she resisted, then scared of her when she cried; and she could hear her stepfather calling her "little girl" and feel him holding her too close, laughing at her discomfiture when she pulled away, refusing to treat her apprehension seriously.

Phrekka crossed her arms over her heart, turning her head so Cerise wouldn't see her tears glistening in the warm lamp-glow of vulnerabilities revealed.

And the dust settled upon her gentle soul, insulation against the fears of a young woman in a dangerous world bereft of sympathy and understanding.

Amused by Geoffrey's infatuation with the majestic pair of wall-mounted sailfishes framing the couches in her hotel suite, Phrekka agreed that, yes, the gulf tide would have to rise quite high indeed for them to escape and swim free. When he turned his attention to her king-size canopy bed, she admitted sleeping in one as a child, her magical haven trimmed in frilly princess-pink. She liked his idea of finding a carnival so he could win her a menagerie of stuffed animals to prop among the pillows, and she was in the process of negotiating to secure this promise in writing when a uniformed fellow arrived with a food-service cart and started setting a table for them on the private balcony.

"I got the information for the cemetery," Geoffrey finally said, "and I found a P. Greenstone in the phone book." Using his best hillbilly twang for the names, he added, "I wasn't sure if that meant *Purvis* and *Mabel* Greenstone or not, so I tried calling, but it was disconnected. At least I have the address."

"Shall we visit both places tomorrow?"

"Yeah, if that's okay—maybe even drive down Bruce Trail to find the house, too. I'd like to get this over with. Did you find anything interesting in your get-around kit?"

"Oh, lots, including the Lauren Rogers Museum of Art; plus there's a private gallery just blocks from here."

"In *Laurel?*"

"Art is a universal language, Geoffrey, which touches everybody in different ways, and has ever since people learned to decorate crude pottery and draw on the walls of caves, aesthetic expression you'll find in one form or another anywhere and everywhere you go." She could say so much more about art and about how it affects people, but Phrekka understood that other matters preoccupied Geoffrey.

"How about if we just play it by ear?—maybe take a break in between and visit the museum or something, see how everything goes."

He looked so earnest, so determined to defer to her wishes, so gentlemanly . . .

The waiter bowed, indicating their meal awaited, so they moved to the balcony and took their seats overlooking the glowing kidney-shaped pool. The dinner-theatre crickets struck up an overture from the courtyard orchestra pit while the murmur from other balconies signaled fully seated loges, but the stage remained draped by the star-sequined velvet curtain of twilight night sky. Phrekka breathed deeply, the aromas of their entrées and the warm Mississippi air swirling around and through her with an ambience both familiar and new. A sense of déjà vu came over her, not of having visited Laurel, but of eating the same meal on the same balcony overlooking the same pool many times during her childhood travels with Grandmamá, except on this occasion one important difference reigned, sitting across from her discreetly crossing out her room number and writing in his own before signing the room-service check.

Geoffrey lifted his glass in toast and gazed at Phrekka in a way that somehow touched her, his expressive eyes elevating her. "I don't know how to do this," he said quietly, "being a farm-boy and all, but a moment like this is so perfect, sitting with somebody as extraordinary as you, that it seems like I should say something profound to christen our impending adventure."

"How about, *To the boy in the pond,*" she suggested, clinking his glass. Ha!—extraordinary, indeed.

He smiled. "And to the girl who returned with him many years later." He clinked hers, and they drank, amused by their own cleverness.

As they ate, Phrekka noticed that Geoffrey still seemed self-conscious about his lack of savoir-faire in proper dining etiquette, the result a mostly concealed but clumsy awkwardness. He dallied with each course, observing and mimicking her, buttering his bread the same way, positioning his wine glass just so, holding his salad fork precisely—all with the unintentional effect of making her self-conscious, too. She wanted to urge him to relax, to assure him that such nuances of grace and decorum are unimportant and often go unobserved during intimate occasions among friends, but she feared that acknowledging his discomfort would only exacerbate it.

"I'm sorry, Geoffrey," she admitted as part of her plan to put them both more at ease. "I've been so overtrained to comport for mother's snooties that sometimes I forget to relax and enjoy." She reached across to steal a shrimp from his plate, licking her fingers. "May we dispose of all these extra dishes and flatware—and will you promise to call me out if you catch me slipping into snobbish formal behavior?" She offered him her best smile, and it worked, his relief washing over him with an audible sigh.

"We didn't even have forks in Iowa," he joshed. "We'd just wipe the tractor grease off our hands and sharpen up a big ol' stick."

"Well," she parried, "*we* always used the *pre*-sharpened sticks."

After dessert, Geoffrey suggested they stroll toward Mayhaw Place and locate the gallery they hoped to visit during viewing hours. They enjoyed the quiet as they walked, admiring Laurel's serene sense of dignity, a traditional southern town beautifully styled with antebellum architecture and lush landscapes, much of its charm now displayed in full springtime bloom. Phrekka found Geoffrey's exuberance for discovery to be endearing, the way he pointed out curious minutiae for her benefit. She thoroughly enjoyed his narrative, laughing at his jokes, sharing his appreciation for the artistic balances struck between the influences of nature and man.

When they found the gallery, Geoffrey peered through the window for several minutes, but Phrekka decided to wait for the opportunity to enter unencumbered and savor the proprietor's presentation as intended. Geoffrey finally looked away, disappointment clouding his features, and she understood that he had searched for more sketches by Sara but failed to find any new images echoing from his past, any tangible proof that a sister he couldn't remember had ever passed this way.

They sat for a time on a bench, watching occasional traffic pass them unconcernedly. Still melancholy, he sighed and admitted, "It seems like I keep forgetting why I'm here."

She wondered what clouded his purpose as he gazed across the horizon and studied the sky, lost in his own thoughts. Phrekka had come to Mississippi sure in her own mind of what Geoffrey should accomplish, but sitting here now, so close to the links between his memories and his mysteries, she succumbed to a moment's hesitation, a lack of clarity, their plans suddenly unfocused. She vacillated between wanting to avoid involvement and a reluctant willingness to fulfill the obligations of a tour guide who had navigated similar waters many times before.

"It's like," Geoffrey struggled to explain, "—like I don't even *want* to think about why I'm here."

You came because I pushed you, she wanted to confess. *Because I know you can't see through the looking glass until you first study your reflected image.* "You came to seek," she said quietly, "but you're afraid of what you might find."

"I want to know if the life I left behind was better than the one I got," he decided. He looked at her this time, and his eyes betrayed intense gravity, considerations deeper than detached curiosity. "My family deserves for me to find out who they were. I mean, I try to put myself in Sara's place, and suddenly some horrible tragedy happens, and my little brother is playing in the woods—" His voice broke, so he closed his eyes and took a deep breath, then continued quieter, "It's like, I realize I'm dying, and there's nothing I can do, and I'm desperately hoping my little brother is okay, but I don't know for sure. Maybe I'm dead, and maybe I'll never find out . . . or maybe I can float free and watch him be spirited to safety, a new life somewhere else, but then I realize he doesn't even remember me. It's as though I never lived."

But you would remember, she thought as he glanced her way, the twin irises of street-lamp reflections glowing transcendently in his glistening eyes. She knew he had touched something in himself, unrecognizable refractions splayed from the prism of hazy memory, the obverse of pure, colorless light. Geoffrey had awakened the Bodhisattvas by drinking from Sara's mortality, and with that he embraced his own essence of life, seeking enlightenment as a virtuous being.

She whispered, "You would want your little brother to come back to that place, if only for the briefest time, no matter how many years had passed."

He touched his temples and breathed deeply of the warm Mississippi air, breezes redolent of the mingling fragrances of then and now. "They deserve that," he said quietly. "Sara deserves for me to make as much effort to find her sketches as she put into drawing them."

"I like to believe she drew some of them for you," Phrekka said, almost regretting the words when she saw how they moved him.

Geoffrey covered his face with his hands. "She did," he whispered, and with this, she could see he spoke the truth. "That must be another reason I'm here."

"Sara will always exist, and part of her was meant to be within you, except she's been lost, so you've come to find her."

He nodded wordlessly, slowly moving his hands from his face, the curtain lifted, a whorl of determined moths flailing themselves against the street lamp reflected in his eyes. "It's loyalty. Families deserve loyalty, even when they don't earn it."

"You've had *two* good families."

He shook his head, admitting, "I don't know if Sara drew fantasies or the truth about the world I lost, but the family I found wasn't very good at all."

"Geoffrey, how can you say that?"

He took a deep breath, glancing away, maybe uncomfortable facing her. "You don't understand. What little you saw during and after Ernest's funeral—he and my mother spent all their time ignoring each other, and he never approved of her because he loved his religion and the people at church more than his own family. I spent all my time either begging for my mother's attention or trying to avoid Ernest's, but I succeeded at neither."

"Why would you avoid your father?"

Finally, he looked right at her, searching for something, perhaps practicing his response and imagining her reaction. He started to speak, then thought for a moment, eventually looking toward the light as he answered. "Because he only paid attention to me for two reasons: to find things wrong with me, or to punish me for who I am." He breathed hard now, cold steel forged in his glowing eyes, his lips clenched defiantly.

Her breath caught, unformed images flashing through her mind. Afraid of the answer, she nevertheless wanted to know. "You mean that Marjorie didn't exaggerate, that you really were *hit*?"

He snorted derisively. "Hit? More like severely *beaten*—whipped, strapped, switched, punched, kicked . . ." The grievous list of iniquities flowed like venom, then just as quickly subsided under the weight of helplessness such recollections must engender. "—Dragged around by the hair, tied with nylon cord, locked in a dark closet . . ." He lowered his head and closed his eyes. "—And . . . And more."

She tried to imagine these things, suddenly seized by a flood of terrifying visions, her desperate desire to protect Geoffrey colliding with the harsh reality of somebody hurting him. She started trembling, sinking under waves of revulsion, watching from somewhere in the distance as he raised his head again and looked across the horizon, his eyes a glaze of self-preservation. He had plunged to the depths of defeat before her very eyes, but then he quickly fought his way back to the surface, held his head above water, breathed deeply of the sustaining Mississippi air, and swirled in a nimbus of buoyant determination. She wondered how much effort must have gone into learning to escape those feelings, how many times in his life he had been pulled under while clinging doggedly to the saving conviction that he would eventually float free.

"I'm sorry," he whispered, his words echoing regret for what he'd said, what he'd done. He reached out tentatively, gently using the backs of his fingers to wipe a tear from her cheek.

She couldn't articulate how she felt, so she nodded assurance, and she touched his fingers, but they electrified her and she started, letting them slip away, afraid to be so close, fearful of being hurt. "You're a good soul, Geoffrey."

He tilted his head and studied her, then wryly noted, "Not by Ernest's standards."

"Then by mine," she breathed, not intending to say it, not sure whence it came, though it felt right, and she meant it.

He smiled, then nodded wistfully, gazing across the horizon of her eyes. "I would love my wife, not ignore her; and I would love my child, no matter how he or she came to me. I would take care of my family and protect my children and play with them and teach them, and I'd let them teach me what I've forgotten . . ." He sighed and shook his head, maybe overwhelmed by the possibilities, maybe embracing them, maybe floating beyond them.

Geoffrey had never appeared more vulnerable, nor had he ever shown such inner strength. Something about him, some quality, maybe his empathy and determination—something she had just seen made him more of a man than any of the giants who had passed through Mother's life, and this reminded her of Charles.

"So how was it, growing up mega-rich?" he asked, suddenly turning the subject to her childhood, most likely for relief from the intensity of his own flashback, possibly out of sincere desire to learn more about her.

"It brings more obligations than freedoms," she said, dabbing her eyes with a tissue.

"Are you in control of your fortune—I mean, is it all tied up, or can you spend, like, *any* amount you want, on *anything*?"

These kinds of questions always made her uncomfortable. She tried to convince herself of the innocence in Geoffrey's curiosity, but he sounded too alarmingly like that insufferable succession of suitors she'd reluctantly allowed to pass through her life, shallow men professing their love before ever plumbing the depths of her soul, opportunists as blinded by the glitter of her gold as were the aroused boys who groped for treasure beneath her dress. Now she wished she'd never revealed her circumstances and thus rendered Geoffrey so ineligible for her affections.

"I don't pay much attention to that," she lied, all at once ashamed for treating him so disrespectfully after he had honestly shared a past she could hardly imagine, let alone fathom revealing. She held desperately to the conviction that her deceptions continued as much for his sake as her own, shading the truth to save him from the distraction caused by shiny baubles of opportunity.

"Who's the Charles you always call to make arrangements?" he wondered. "Is he like your secretary or personal assistant or something?"

She chuckled at the characterization. "Charles is the CEO of a multi-national conglomerate which owns the companies in my family and his."

"A *CEO* books your reservations and handles your details?"

"No," she said defensively. "No, he has people do that. I just call him to set it into motion. Oh, you don't understand." She resented him reminding her of those times she felt like a nuisance to Charles. "He was my father's friend and business partner—" she blustered.

"Then he must be *your* friend," he interrupted quickly.

"Well . . . yes—"

"It sounds like he's probably very fond of you and *wants* you to call, even if he has somebody else do the actual work. That's how he stays in touch and looks out for you, making sure you're okay."

Suddenly, the vague sense of being a pest, which she'd always tried to push aside, yielded to the affectionate compliment of knowing Charles loved her as if she were his own daughter. Still, she vowed that her next call would be simply to let him know how much she appreciated him.

"Thank you, Geoffrey," she said, relieved that he understood, buoyed by his reminder of a truth she'd foolishly hedged.

They strolled back to the hotel, lingering in the hallway for a moment to say good night. She sensed how much he wanted to touch her, to hold her and maybe to kiss her, but he seemed to understand how uncomfortable it would make her. She felt grateful for this, confident he wouldn't try to breach their unspoken boundaries so soon, the value ascribed to their friendship too high for him to risk misguided attempts at remaking it into something it could never be.

He brushed her cheek with his finger, just as he had dried her tear earlier, and he whispered, "Good night, Phrekka. Sleep tight, pretty princess-in-pink." Then he scurried down to his doorway, waiting to be sure she found her way safely inside.

A princess, indeed.

She closed the door behind her, then stood with her back to it and touched her own cheek, replaying the moment, the whole evening, admitting she liked how it made her feel. She gathered her hem and danced a simple pirouette, then bowed gracefully and flowed out onto the balcony to pause and listen to the crickets' song, their lifeblood rhythms swirling around and through her. She gazed into the rippling depths of the kidney-shaped pool and recalled her afternoon swimming with Geoffrey at his apartment, the awkward moments, his invitation to see Coon Rapids, the trust inherent in daring to let her glimpse a world stained by the bruise of violence and degradation.

She wondered how such a gentle young man could have learned to cope with so much. Watching him earlier this evening, after his past pulled him under for the briefest of moments, she drank from the profound gratitude in his face when he gasped for air and discovered her waiting to breathe sustenance into his soul. Phrekka had spent so much of her life afraid somebody would hurt her, yet she just passed an evening being charmed by a man who *had* been hurt, countless times, in ways that made her own soul cry out and weep not for what he had lost, but for what might have been.

And Geoffrey, through it all, had sought to make *her* feel good about herself.

Extraordinary, indeed.

Again she stroked her cheek with the backs of her fingers and recalled how she felt when he dried her tear, recapturing and savoring the sensation. Like no other time in her life, this simple gesture, bereft of threat or omen, had cleansed her, and she realized she had desired his touch as much as she feared it. He had sensed this and understood, respecting her boundaries enough to avert his gaze from his own expectations in order to embrace the delicate and wondrous sparkles refracting from a single chance droplet of her vernal faith.

She took another turn around her suite, and she noticed the ubiquitous sense of déjà vu had been washed from her thoughts. This place she just discovered existed in a realm she had never before explored. It took her breath away, and it proved the time had come for what she had always known she must eventually do. To preserve and cherish what she achieved this very night would mean strengthening her resolve to prevent its otherwise inevitable debauchment. Geoffrey would never be satisfied with a friendship forever channeled by her limitations, and the deeper she allowed his passions to pool, the more they would both be hurt when those boundaries eventually crumbled under the eroding impatience of his tenuous self-control. She would fulfill her commitment to visit the cemetery with him, to meet the Greenstones and search out his childhood home; then she would say good-bye to him forever, for Geoffrey Drousseau had proven more dangerous than any man she'd ever known.

In a way she never imagined possible, she had actually started to trust him, and in that incalculably risky gamble, she discovered she could no longer trust herself.

She dialed the lights low and flowed forlornly into her magnificent canopy bed. She breathed deeply of the warm Mississippi air wafting from her balcony, one last hearty draught of the intoxicating elixir for this young woman who knew her own limits.

And still the majestic pair of wall-mounted sailfishes waited patiently for freedom in tides that would never rise.

CHAPTER 13

Geoffrey Drousseau had entered the maze.

Studying himself in the vanity mirror of his hotel suite, he considered his next move. He noticed his hair didn't lie quite right, so he wet his comb and adjusted it, a lifelong ritual of futility. Feeling the kind of nervous anticipation that precedes a junior-high dance, he looked closer, wondering how he might appear more attractive for Phrekka. He touched his face where he'd shaved, stroked his soft mustache, and gazed deeply into his own sapphire eyes where reflected a lifetime's worth of vulnerability cradled protectively to the bosom of steeled new-found determination. He wondered what Phrekka might see in him, if she sensed the honest sincerity inherent in his clumsy devotion, and he worried that revealing his traumatic past had portrayed him as flawed and therefore less desirable, but he decided to trust her understanding and willingness to accept him as he is, holding fast to his faith that she would embrace the very same conviction he'd honed during a lifetime suffering Ernest's humiliations, for on those too-frequent occasions when he found himself nearly convinced of the futility in aspiring to become the boy good enough to deserve love, he would rediscover his oft-tapped secret reservoir of sustaining reassurance and believe in his heart that he already deserved more than his family could give.

As is the custom with most adolescent boys, Geoffrey had become infatuated, obsessed even, with the very concept of moving toward intimacy with a succession of young women, never truly knowing or understanding them, but nevertheless wanting very much to attract one he might claim for his very own. He would endeavor to look nice and to appear charmingly masculine, first to entice, then to captivate, drawing them into the labyrinth of his dreams and desires so they might come to know him, encouraging them at every turn with the rewards of attention and affection.

But Phrekka Churán proved very different from anybody Geoffrey had ever known, a free spirit who moved where she may, on her own terms, immune to the lure of tangible rewards. Her every move so far had come of her own volition, and she had demonstrated a preference for pausing after each and allowing him, in measured steps, to move that much closer to her. That ill-fated day in his apartment when he had reached out impulsively, desiring to hold and caress her, to probe her deeply and intimately . . . that had been cheating, crossing a line, moving too fast, his rampant imagination craving overmuch. Not until he had come here to Laurel with greater purpose and no amorous expectations did he discover that simply brushing her cheek with his fingers would cause static ripples to flow over his body in a way he had never conceived possible. Geoffrey understood that for Phrekka to navigate the maze to his heart would be simple, the route a short, straight line. Everything he could offer, all that he would give, hovered within her reach, and all that remained for her to claim his prize would be to touch him and hold him, even when he electrified her, never to let him slip away.

He wondered how much further and by which route he must travel to earn full admittance to her heart. She offered a challenging complexity never before encountered, enticing layers of mysterious and convoluted passageways in multiple dimensions, the promise of a journey through exquisitely enchanted realms. He vowed to take every precaution for avoiding any possibility of misstep, never to cross lines, no wrong turns, no mistakes requiring him to track back. He wished he could predict how fast she would allow him to move.

He sighed and decided to give up on his hair, wondering if she would like it better cut and styled differently, smiling at the notion of just how far he might be willing to go to please her. He might wind up looking very strange, indeed.

And she would be worth it.

He opened the door and glanced toward her suite, hoping she would hurry over. Leaving the door ajar, he moved to the table and spread out the Jones County map, a maze of lines weaving through colored boxes and numbered landmarks. A few simple turns just beyond the southwest border of town would lead them to the cemetery, only minutes from the address for P. Greenstone. Bruce Trail didn't appear on the map, but the concierge had helped him locate it, drawing in the approximate site of a cul-de-sac just beyond the northeast fringe of city limits, alongside the fateful railroad tracks. The gravity of this impending tour suddenly weighed heavily on him, distracting him from the giddy anticipation of learning new ways to approach Phrekka.

He heard her door open and close, so he rushed to meet her in the hallway. "Good morning!"

"Hi," she said, and she glanced around awkwardly.

He instantly sensed a palpable distance, invisible barriers surrounding her, new lines added to the maze. "Did you want to have breakfast here?—or we could go could for a walk, stop at one of those places we saw last night."

"That would be fine," she committed non-committally. "We have a lot to do today," she added by way of suggesting they proceed with diligence, dawdles and distractions notwithstanding.

As they walked along the street in early-morning sunshine, the fiery highlights smoldering in her long, cinnamon hair enthralled him, but he could tell she found his scrutiny discomforting. He tried pointing out minutiae along the way, the kind of impromptu tour of the inconsequential she had enjoyed so much the night before, but now she could muster only polite indifference, nodding occasionally, once or twice offering a murmured "That's nice" without enthusiasm.

They navigated the maze of downtown streets until aromas wafting from a quaint storefront diner drew them inside with the promise of flavorful delights. Geoffrey tried to sustain some conversation while they ate breakfast in lime-green vinyl booths, but the more he tried, the more frustrated he felt, eventually falling to silence and wondering how he had alienated her, regretting mistakes he could neither list nor describe.

As they walked back to the hotel to retrieve their car, he realized the lamentable truth, the fatal error he could never undo: though Phrekka had learned to enjoy spending time with him, he had foolishly blurted out his humiliating secrets, the result of which had been to make her cry. She would always view him in a different light after that, an image he could never reclaim or replace. Whereas Billy Marloney had actually witnessed those horrific events, the young friends had ultimately used their conjoint adversity as a springboard for achieving new levels of shared understanding, non-judgmental acceptance and a more intimate and enduring friendship; but Phrekka demonstrated unwillingness, if not incapacity, to undertake such a profound leap. Now at twenty, not the least bit stereotypically macho but still wanting very much for Phrekka to see him as a man with integrity, Geoffrey had inadvertently painted for her the portrait of himself as a defeated child.

"I let Charles know we'll probably be ready to fly out in the morning," she finally said, breaking the tension-rife silence as they drove to the first destination in a maze that promised passage into the kaleidoscope of Geoffrey's past.

Anxious to leave, he thought sadly.

His last day with Phrekka would offer no chance to paint fun new scenes together, for him to replace the dark hues of traumatic stain with the bright colors of mutual attraction and the enjoyment of amusing activities shared, their brief remaining time on this trip squandered instead by his foolhardy insistence on wallowing in the childhood he now regretted ever letting her glimpse.

"If you don't want to do this—" he tried to offer.

"We've come this far," she countered, the slightest hint of exasperation swirling around her words, unspoken implications in the tautness of her shoulders, her hands nervously clasped, her body stiff as if to avoid breaching the invisible shield.

The cemetery proved easy to find, a contradiction of tragedy and grief splayed across an otherwise idyllic wildflower-bloomed meadow fringed by an irregular line of trees, the meandering orange-banked and sand barred creek forming an ornate, jeweled border. The maze of plots existed in planes above and below the ground, a mix of mausoleums, graves, flat markers and stand-up headstones. A certain effort at groundskeeping could be seen, but the lawn lacked the meticulous care of the memorial gardens where Ernest Calhoun had been laid to rest. A small cinder-block *Office* appeared locked and deserted, so Geoffrey and Phrekka drove through the winding, circular drive, silently reading markers from the car, unable to identify their target. Finally, they parked and stepped out to continue their search on foot.

The blazing disk of rising sun crested the treetops, casting long shadows among stones and crypts, dark and forbidding lines drawn across scattered passageways through this maze of single and family parcels. Choruses of birds foraged for insects and grubs in the spongy damp grass. The faceless stories of lost loved ones whispered to Geoffrey: the clip-art tale from a tiny marker depicting a little boy knelt in prayer, Jesus' lamb called to heaven at the tender age of four; an old man, veteran of the Korean War, reserving space for his devoted wife below their double stone, the date announcing their reunion left blank until someday etched by the sand-blasting winds of time and destiny; a teenage girl recently mourned with delicate silk flowers and a school photo taped to her bronze vase, a corner peeled away in the damp, humid air; elaborate engravatures of verse framed in marble; the plainest of simple stones encrusted with lichens and mosses.

Geoffrey paused and closed his eyes, resisting the pull, refusing to sample any more of the macabre offerings laid out in this smörgåsbord of mortality and grief. He opened his eyes again, and he could barely discern Phrekka looking at him, not ten feet away, yet somehow from far in the distance. She tilted her head to draw his attention to something, but he kept looking at her, making her flinch uncomfortably, penetrating her barriers just for an instant. She tilted her head again, and his eyes drifted in the direction she'd urged. There, for all the world to see, patiently waited the name he had come to find:

Drousseau

The polished granite headstone reflected the horizon in shades of gray, presiding eternally over a domain of three graves demarcated by small gray cornerstones. Under the name, listed left to right to identify where reposed each person's remains:

Alain ` Rachel ` Sara
Husband *Wife* *Daughter*

He tried to conjure even the slightest glimmers of memory to recall the images of his family, but nothing would come. Instead, he kept seeing the flower-framed depiction of Ernest lying in his coffin, and he wondered how Sara and his original parents had appeared, if they'd been laid out for viewing, if people had come to mourn, or if they were simply boxed without ceremony and lowered into the ground to be covered over by indifferent workers laboring with shovels under the hot sun, seeded and occasionally mowed as the years pass by and the seasons come and go.

Did you look good, Sara? Did they 'done a good job' on you, make you appear to be sleeping, resting in peace?

His eyes stung, the sun too bright now, the birds alternately mocking him and warning him away, no time among the living to suffer further intrusions from the dead.

A name was missing:

Geoffrey
Son

He wanted to lie in the grass beside Sara, to see how it would feel to assume his rightful place, to let her know he'd come home, the boy who never should have survived all these extra years.

Geoffrey felt himself spinning, rotating faster and faster as the world revolved around him in contrary and contradictory motion, and he clung tightly to his purpose the better to prevent being flung into the meaningless expanses of space.

What if he dared to let go?

He could see Phrekka.

"Why am I obsessed with Sara—and not the others?" he asked, his voice echoing like a pinball ricocheting from one stone or crypt to the next.

"She talked to you through the sketches," Phrekka answered, but she sounded too far away for her words to compel.

"She talked to me only when she was alive," he argued, injecting his customary scintilla of substance into the surreal. He took a deep breath, looking again at the name on the marker. "She's dead now," he pronounced, revelation for those not paying attention, those too stubborn to accept the truth.

"Grandmamá believed they could still speak to us. If Sara died worrying about your safety, then she suffered an impure and unhappy death, so maybe she's not ready to move on to the next plane."

"And she's calling for me?" The echo grew eerily: "—for me? —for me? —for me?"

"Waiting to see you again, maybe right here, right now, to be assured you emerged from the disaster safely, that you're okay."

"But I'm not," he said. "But I'm not okay."

Phrekka hesitated out there in the distance, wherever she hid. Then her voice came again. "But you are."

"*You* don't know *what* I am," he accused, angry now, the world spinning too fast to see anything clearly. "My sister's not floating around Mississippi any more than your father's living in that abstract painting you inherited! If Sara wants something from me, why doesn't she come tell me?! Why doesn't your father come to the world outside that painting and show you what he knows?!" His voice broke, but he wouldn't let grief find him, touch him, watch him. He reached out for Phrekka in defiance of the spinning world, but he grasped insubstantial air, the fleeting wisps of concepts less real than the phantasms of his unrealized attempts at recollection.

Geoffrey turned around and gazed at the shimmering brush strokes splayed across the backdrops of this scene, turning faster and faster, spinning his body now, dizzy, floating, then suddenly falling to his knees before the *Drousseau* headstone, touching Sara's name, he and his dead sister spun into their own secret cocoon of invincibility.

The outside world didn't exist, so nothing in it could matter, and nothing else could ever hurt the indomitable man come full circle to the scenery of his introductions to life-affirming love and heart-rending loss.

Phrekka had disappeared, consigned to dwell among the long-lost fleeting associations of his past, or maybe still awaiting the full realization of her preordained role in his future.

Sara couldn't be here in this cemetery. She had never come here, had never waited here for him, had never wanted him to come.

He'd found the center of the maze, a place he never wanted to be.

Alone, he could find no way out.

"Geoffrey! How come you to keep spinning around like that? All you do is get dizzy and fall down."

"'Cause it's like goin' someplace fun."

"Oh, Geoffrey, what am I gonna do with you?"

The disk of blazing mid-morning sun rose high above the tree-line, affording itself a better view. Like so many granite sponges, the precision-plotted imbroglio of monuments and crypts and statues slowly absorbed their myriad shadows, opening newly lit pathways for Geoffrey and Phrekka, alternate routes leading away from the scenery of former lives, from these clustered parcels of death memorialized.

Geoffrey stopped turning, then stood very still, but the world kept spinning, his fleeting glimpses of Phrekka remindful of a friend watching from the midway while unwary riders tumble head-over-heels in the Rock-0-Flip, cotton-candy and caramel-apple nausea rising, loose change and a pocket comb jangling in the cage. He extended his arm, stretched his fingers away from the sun, and focused his eyes on this static point in time and space. He cupped his hand and turned it toward the sky, then concentrated his will and forced the axis of gyration away from his reeling inner ear, down along his arm and into his palm where he held it gingerly, feeling the heat of its friction, gazing raptly at the concentration of energy and light, transformation and momentum. He turned his head to see Phrekka more clearly from this new vantage point, and he noticed that she appeared uneasy, maybe even frightened, like she felt trapped too close to the vortex of his swirling domain, confused by this simple gesture with his hand.

"There is nothing of Sara here," he told her.

She nodded wordlessly, her mien of apprehension replaced by a mix of relief and patient anticipation.

"Thank you for coming," he added, sincere gratitude clear in his words.

"I wanted to," she said very quietly. A chipmunk scurried close and studied her, his head tilting curiously before he scampered off to continue his explorations.

"It turned out to be more taxing than you expected," he said, the sound of his voice resonating like the tender strokes of a bow across the taut viola vines of fringing trees. "More than *we* expected."

Agreement in her eyes, she lightly touched her cheeks as if to remind herself that she really existed in this place, one of a pair of opposing static points anchored just this side of her own unexplored limbo, all while Geoffrey's world continued its oscillation around the palm of his outstretched hand.

"I'm sorry," she said, glancing toward the Drousseau monument.

Geoffrey curled his fingers tighter, a firmer grip on the nexus between this moment and all others. He had succeeded in removing himself from the maelstrom by holding it apart, but Phrekka still appeared to be wary of the whirling morass, probably because she could never understand it. Drawn unprepared into the pathetic game that had become his life, so overwhelmed that she needed to deploy layered barriers of defense, she had opted to remain as close to the sidelines as possible, determined not to be swept into his unpredictable plays. He could reach out with his other hand, or with his words, or with his mind, but he would always fail to connect as long as this threat spun so close. The penalty for failure too great, he knew he must guide her away from this dangerous place where he dwells, seeking permission instead to enter and discover the serenity of hers.

"The gallery at Mayhaw Place," he said. "Let's go there next."

Her eyes lit up for an instant, then she looked away. "We don't have to, not for me."

"But I want to."

"You've never before shown interest in attending an exhibit."

"That's because I don't know how," he admitted, his eyes downcast, embarrassed at his own ignorance, yet relieved somehow by the revelation. "I don't know the proper way to visit a gallery, how to act, what to say."

"Everybody's approach is different, but if you want, I'll teach you mine," she said, her face full of hope.

He glanced up, expectant, pleased.

Her eyes darted toward his outstretched hand.

He looked, too, watching for a moment. Then he brought it close to his chest, cradled it like a shivering kitten, and carefully put the spinning world in his pocket. He could see all around him again, the brush-stroked backdrop of trees, the molasses twist of creek now alive with dancing iridescent damselflies, the patchwork graves assaulted by birds flying brunch-time sorties, another chipmunk waiting patiently to search for their scraps, the headstone marked *Drousseau.* He mouthed a silent good-bye to his parents, Alain and Rachel of Laurel, Mississippi, and he wondered if he would ever find Sara, but he knew that incessantly reaching for somebody long lost to the receding shadows of past would only distract him from seeking new ways to touch somebody who might now be waiting patiently, lost in the uncertainty of his future.

He moved beside Phrekka and offered her his arm.

She hesitated.

"How do they decide which way to arrange the artwork?" he asked.

"Ah, that is the secret they strive to reveal," she said.

He watched her eyes, noting how she glanced away just for a moment before finally looking back. The distance still seemed there, might always be there, but she had just taken a chance, a small step, and she accepted his arm.

Alain and Rachel whispered good-bye, and they bid him the very best of a good life while the mute disk of blazing late-morning sun watched from high in the sky, birds heralding the interlopers' departure.

Geoffrey paused for the last time and listened for Sara, but he heard only echoes of silence amid the buzzing din of indifferent life.

Stepping gingerly through tall grass while heat waves shimmered above monuments to loved ones lost, patting the pocket that protected a boy's spinning collection of all things past, Geoffrey led Phrekka out of his world and back toward her own.

"Can I watch?" the little boy asked.

"Sure."

"That's me, isn't it?" he asked, climbing onto the porch swing to watch her shading a sketch.

"Of course it's you, silly."

"Why do you want a pitcher of me?"

"It's not for me; it's for you."

"What for?"

"'Cause you'll be big someday, and this'll remind you how much I loved you when you was little."

He wormed his way under her arm and snuggled close, resting his head at her breast so he could watch her work. "You gonna 'member how much I love you, too?"

"Uh-huh. That's what I think about when I draw."

He considered this a moment, finally pronouncing, "And that's what I think about when I watch."

Geoffrey had read about performance anxiety in newspaper advice columns, a vague concept he understood to mean fear of failure, or dread of the consequences therefrom, a nervousness that inevitably brings deleterious results. Examples commonly cited include stammering while giving a speech, off-key music recitals, forgetting learned material during final exams, pressure-induced sexual impotence . . . but he never worried about these, for the stakes never seemed so high nor his confidence so low that he would balk at chasing his desires or fulfilling his responsibilities.

Then Phrekka raised the stakes.

Just when he started to count on the tentative bond he'd worked so hard to forge between them, she had pulled away, signaled disinterest, erected barriers, and left him teetering over the abyss of outright rejection. Desperately hoping they might regroup on her turf, he had suggested they visit the gallery together, only to realize too late that the very idea made him inexplicably nervous. More than just fear of behaving inappropriately, of embarrassing himself, of embarrassing Phrekka, it worried him that this would be his first—and probably his last—real audition to prove himself capable of understanding her great passions, to demonstrate his eligibility for moving within her social circles. He'd already revealed himself as an uncultured lout who stomped around her gallery oblivious to the artistic harmony she created for visitors to sample and savor; then he'd drawn her recklessly into his own personal world like a chimp escorting the princess to baboon day at the zoo, thus exacerbating his bumpkin image.

No wonder this exquisitely cultured jewel of a young woman seemed loath to let him even touch her.

Only one gambit to his ill-conceived strategy remained, the riskiest play of all, and he had already set it into motion: honestly confessing his ignorance and asking for her help.

"The intent of each artist," she explained carefully during their drive back into town, "—the reaction he or she wanted to evoke—that's what most curators consider first. Then they arrange and display the entire collection to achieve an overall effect, whether that be to communicate a message or theme, or to strike aesthetic balance, or to lead the audience sequentially from one state of mind to the next, or maybe even to inject a sense of conflict or ambivalence. Those approaches have never worked for me, but I'm not sure why."

He considered this, keeping his eyes on the road, responding, "Maybe because you realize you can never know all the people who'll visit. All any curator can do is guess how people will react, or rely on feedback from a few."

"We're all limited to working with what we know."

"So what's *your* approach?"

"I arrange my collection in a way that groups various moods and styles. That way I can see where the patrons are drawn and watch their reactions. Ultimately, I strive to keep narrowing until I can match each person with the one piece that moves him most."

"Like trying to promote sales?—displaying the higher-priced pieces most prominently, or to appeal to certain kinds of customers you want to attract?"

"No, I don't care about sales. I turned down a lot more money for the Sara sketch than you paid because the woman who wanted it didn't truly appreciate it. You did, and I saw that. I would've *given* it to you, if that's what it took."

"Wow, did I ever misread you that day."

"What *you're* talking about is commerce, not art."

"Isn't it? They both use images to evoke reactions. If it's for sales, the results are measurable. If it's for aesthetics, you have to *guess* what others will like. In the absence of knowing for sure, all you can do is try to please yourself. It seems to me like that's all any curator can do."

She gazed out the window, watching cranes and herons in the passing wetlands, and she seemed to be weighing his words. "Pleasing oneself first," she pronounced.

"The only thing we can be sure of."

"*If* you're honest with yourself," she qualified.

"It's risky to trust others with judging your personal expressions, so you have to believe in yourself." Quieter, he added, "That's how I lost my job doing ad layouts. I kept getting conflicting instructions and unrealistic demands, so I started just doing them in a way that pleased me. Usually, the clients were impressed, but a few weren't. One went ballistic and I told him that, as a customer, I wouldn't even want to patronize his stores after seeing the confusing, negative ad he'd brought me."

She smiled slightly at that, and he did, too. "You considered anything except *your* way to be inferior. That sounds rather self-centered," she teased.

"Such is art."

She sighed, glancing away again. "At first I was frustrated with you, the way you stomped around that day in my gallery refusing to notice anything about the display into which I'd put so much thought."

"But I didn't go there to see what *you'd* done. I went there for me, and I still wound up probably being your greatest success."

She looked at him, surprise in her face, a challenge in her features. "*How* did I succeed?"

"I was mad at the world, trying not to think about what was going on back at my apartment, frustrated over my lost job. All those silly landscapes and still-lifes didn't appeal to me; they annoyed me, and they propelled me on until I did what you wanted: I discovered the one image that affected me like no other." He remembered, seeing it again in his mind, trying to keep his eyes on the road.

"The one that had already moved *me* so much," she agreed.

"The piece that brought us together." Slowing to turn toward downtown, he could see she'd become entranced by his words, considering them very carefully.

"But that sketch made you even angrier, *more* frustrated."

"Yeah, so pissed off that I had to stop pacing and calm down long enough to figure out why."

"Like you said before," she admitted, now approving of his assertions, "a personal and selfish experience."

"Just like Sara's reasons for drawing sketches of me must have been personal, too. I don't think she cared if some yahoo gallery patron would look at her drawings fifteen years later and find harmony in the balance of her half-tones, or if some critic would draw distinctions between her literal rendering of a boy and the abstract symbolic elements of the background, nor do I think she cared about the opinions of either nude-sunbathing enthusiasts or pious anti-porn crusaders when she drew reeds in front of my naked hoo-hoo, and I doubt she was making statements about neo-existential pre-apocalyptic semi-transcendental anti-Freudian non-union data-driven UFO-conspiracy mind control by the New World Order—" His voice broke in his frenzy to describe the antithesis of his sister's work. He swallowed hard, and in a very small voice, he said, "I think she drew it to show how much she loved me."

"And fifteen years later," Phrekka added, enthralled now, "that's what you saw."

He nodded, not trusting his voice, its betrayal of his loyalist sensitivities too apparent.

He turned into Mayhaw Place, then drove across the nearly vacant lot and parked close to the gallery. They sat there awkwardly for a moment.

"Phrekka," he said finally, "whoever arranged this exhibit doesn't know me and can't predict how I'll react. They had to rely on whatever *they* liked, so I don't want to go in with the weight of anybody's expectations on me." Keeping his eyes focused ahead, but watching her at the periphery, he could tell she liked that and might even be stifling a smile.

"I don't think you need any help from me, after all. You know exactly how Geoffrey Drousseau should view an exhibit."

He believed her, relieved more than he dared express, and his confidence soared for a moment, but then he lost the momentum and felt himself spiraling downward again, an uncomfortable prickling sensation where the world spun in his pocket. This would still be his audition, no matter what they decided.

Watching his face, she added, "If you felt pressure, that was my fault. Don't worry what I think."

He shook his head. "But I *do* worry. I can't pretend I don't care about losing our friendship. After feeling like we got really close last night, now you want to ditch me as soon as this trip is over—and it can't be over fast enough for you."

Her breath caught, and she looked away, her pause just long enough to lend substance to the truth of his words. She started to say something, but hesitated, and finally fell quiet.

"Wow," he said rubbing his eyes. "It's come to this again."

"To what?" She kept her gaze averted.

"I'm about to go into a gallery and stomp around, frustrated with the world because someone I really . . . because someone who . . ." He clenched his mouth, vexed about nearly saying what he'd tried not to admit even to himself, unwilling to compromise his self-respect by whining about all the rejection in his life. Phrekka owed him nothing. She had already done more for him than anybody could expect, and she had asked for nothing in return. He decided that if this were the last day she would ever let him spend with her, then he must make the most of it. "No," he pronounced. "No, I won't stomp around angry. I've been looking forward to this chance to learn about art from you, something I'd like to understand more, an opportunity with the person I'd most like to have teach me. I *am* nervous," he admitted sheepishly, "that I'll look like a fool in there, but I'm trying to convince myself it doesn't matter."

She turned toward him again, her eyes glistening. "You'll never look like a fool to me, Geoffrey."

But I'm still not good enough for you . . . "Then I won't put on an act because *I'm* entitled to my opinions as much as anybody else who walks in there. *Nobody* can leave *all* his personal baggage at home."

"Then I'm still learning from you," she said, bolder now, with nary a hint of condescension. She believed this, he knew.

"So we'll look together, and I'll tell you what I think, and you'll tell me what you think."

"No matter what," she agreed, a lilting chorus of enthusiasm added to the song.

They stepped out, melting together in the buttery saturation of mid-day sunlight. Phrekka's cinnamon hair lit up, ablaze with the fires of anticipation. Geoffrey couldn't help but wonder if any vision would *ever* move him more.

"So we judge the artwork, but not each other," she said, proposing her terms.

He shook his head, disagreeing. "There's something very important I don't understand about you, and this looks like my last chance to figure it out. Don't deny me the opportunity to try."

She looked taken aback for the briefest moment; then she studied his face and bit her lower lip, thinking . . . "Fair enough, but now *I'm* nervous. I've never before felt so self-conscious about entering a gallery."

"Maybe that's a good thing."

"But I feel like *I'm* on display."

"We're always on display."

"I'm used to viewing art as a very personal experience, something where one's awareness bridges between the self and the artist's power and the exhibitor's interpretation."

"So try making this a *shared* experience for a change. You, the art people, and the blond-haired guy who's going to steal every chance to glimpse your soul while your guard is down."

She smiled through her anxiety, admitting, "Like I was doing to you the first time we met."

"When I took a chance, and let you."

She sighed. "I've never done anything like this before."

"Neither have I."

"What if we like different pieces?" she asked, almost teasing now, maybe joking away the tension.

"I figure we will. I just hope you won't think less of me for admiring the velvet Elvis."

She smiled, her face glowing. "I've always been fond of dogs playing poker."

"I like the one of dogs playing pool."

He offered her his arm, and without hesitation, she accepted, allowing him to lead her inside where they met an older woman with dark hair wearing a beautiful, flowing print dress, adorned in native-styled turquoise and jade jewelry.

She greeted them warmly with trademark southern charm, aglow with an aura of sophistication and genteel grace. "I'll let you two explore," she offered, "and be right here if you want to talk about anything you see."

Geoffrey felt the power surrounding him, pieces whispering heartfelt stories, all calling for his attention, some rendered as messages spoken to an audience, others simply personal glimpses into the minds of artists who cared about neither display nor sale. The latter drew his attention most.

He and Phrekka moved around together, sometimes standing close to each other, sometimes drifting with their own interests. Occasionally, they pointed out pieces and described their impressions, other times studying in silent, personal contemplation. A small measure of the aloofness he had been sensing in her melted away, but he could tell her resolve to scale back their friendship had not abated. Still, he felt closer to her as a result of this experience, liberated from the pressure to impress her, free of performance anxiety. For the first time, he felt fairly comfortable moving through her world, sensing that this pleased her, that she had relaxed her defenses enough to savor the experience on her own terms.

Without trying, he had passed the test she probably never intended to give.

Not that it even mattered anymore . . .

Together they rounded a small display in the back to see the last pieces arranged on a free-standing flat—

He gasped, stumbling like his knees had buckled.

No pocket could contain his world at that moment, for there in front of him beckoned the sketch of a very familiar blond-haired little boy, his face lit by the glow of a lightning bug that had crawled out upon his cupped hand. Cheek to cheek, another face in the sketch admired the little critter with him, the soft features of a teenage girl with long tresses, both subjects' eyes sparkling the same exuberance for life.

Geoffrey felt dizzy, images of memories swirling by too fast to comprehend, the only static point in time and space now this simple sketch in graphite and charcoal. He reached out as if to touch it, his fingers spanning fifteen years, his eyes blurring even as his hand trembled.

Phrekka gasped, whispering, "Is it?"

Geoffrey nodded confirmation, and then he heard the voice, a whisper at first, then more clearly, a melodic child's song, an anthem to pristine love.

He listened, and he remembered.

The little boy inside him wept for the sister who'd faded beyond his grasp. The grown-up man standing before her finally understood that she'd been with him all along, but that he'd tucked her away and protected her so earnestly that he could never afford to think of her for fear somebody would steal even that much from him.

Never again would he let anybody deny him Sara, the wellspring of his oft-tapped secret reservoir of sustaining reassurance that helped him believe in his heart that he'd always deserved to be loved.

He closed his eyes and let Sara's song cleanse him of all the fears he'd accumulated in the years since.

"She called them *scatches*," he whispered.

"Scatches?"

He knew the voice in the melody, the one gentle soul who woke him with a song every morning and offered him lullabies every night, stroking his hair as he drifted into a dreamworld of wonder and bliss. "It's not for me; it's for you," Sara sang. "Someday you'll be big, and this'll remind you . . ."

He felt Phrekka holding his arm. "Are you okay, Geoffrey?"

He looked at her and smiled. "Yes . . . I'm big now."

CHAPTER 14

With the discovery of this new sketch, Phrekka watched Geoffrey open another door to his own past, a critical juncture buried in the dusty corridors blueprinted by his sister's indelible legacy of graphite-and-charcoal impressions, now unlocked by the key of Sara's face revealed.

Geoffrey hovered protectively near the gallery's hostess as she carefully wrapped the purchase for presentation to its rightful beneficiary. "I'll find a special way to honor it," he promised her, planning its future even as it must have pulled him back.

Phrekka imagined how Geoffrey must have felt moments before when he first looked upon the drawing, and she pondered what he might do next, what lay ahead for this young man whose steadfast determination to move forward had finally allowed him to step back far enough to hear again the lilting strains of Sara's song. Phrekka had spent countless hours gazing at her father's abstract painting, also searching for a key to unlock mysteries indistinct and undefined, and now she wondered if she'd looked the wrong direction, if what her father wanted for her really lay ahead, if the answers she sought could be found along one of the myriad paths connecting circumstance and choice, all challenging her to make the next move.

Geoffrey had confronted her in the cemetery, daring through his frustration and anger to ask why she still longed for connection with a man who could never speak to her, never share the secrets she desperately hoped he might still offer, the father who had already given her all he ever may. Maybe the time had come to accept that she would never learn what her father had seen in the montage of brush strokes in burnt-orange and yellow and blue and gray, could never hear the same truths it whispered to him as a child, that the man she longed to know had never existed in that painting after all. She had devoted so much of her life to puzzling over the power imbued in images of creative expression, yet now for the first time she found herself wondering if the true source stemmed less from what the artist offered than from what the audience simply chose to take. The cherished little girl in Phrekka's heart might still find her place in this world, not by listening for her father's voice to penetrate the void of loss and grief, but by raising her own and shouting into the blinding light, then following the echoes to navigate her way without him.

Phrekka clasped hands with the woman and complimented her on a wonderful collection. Geoffrey offered his own approval as they departed the gallery, also reminding the buoyed merchant of his interest in any Sara sketches that might yet be discovered. They stepped into brightness and warmth, a world waiting with open arms, the soft kiss of humid Mississippi breath on their cheeks.

"I'm this close," Geoffrey told Phrekka awkwardly as he loaded the framed sketch into the car, "and I want to see if there's anything else I can learn while I'm here, while the memories are fresh—" He took a deep breath, searching her face, the Medusa wisps of his sun-fired hair undulating in the late-afternoon breeze. "I'd like to stay another day, maybe two, but I sense you'd rather leave as soon as possible . . ." He hesitated, his hands thrust into the pockets of his sweats while the heart on his sleeve tentatively held the door to offer her escape, this reluctant invitation a sincere act of chivalrous honor no doubt contrary to his every instinct and desire.

Tempted to seize the chance, Phrekka considered exiting gracefully before this unexpected window of opportunity closed, but she knew that abandoning Geoffrey now would hurt him immeasurably, inflicting undeserved rejection upon the very gentleman who'd strived so diligently to respect her in every way, even to the point now of letting her go if she truly preferred. She wanted to stay, to learn more about Sara and the Drousseau family even as she might learn more about herself, to support her friend as much as she counted on him to support her, but she feared her continued presence would only further mislead him, misrepresenting her intent. Keeping one foot in the doorway to Geoffrey's world had already proven risky, his intuitiveness for her feelings surprising. He had sensed her carefully concealed, newly resolved reticence almost immediately, yet despite the overwhelming onslaught of impressions immersing him in the mysteries of his past, he had proven so unselfishly regardful as to set those aside long enough to consider her needs foremost . . .

And for that reason, if no other, Geoffrey deserved honesty.

"Would this be easier for you without my distraction—would you prefer to be left alone?" she asked, knowing the answer before she spoke.

He shook his head without hesitation.

"I want to stay," she admitted, "and it means a lot, more than I've been able to show, that you want to share this with me, but I'm worried you may expect our friendship to progress beyond that which I find comfortable, and that by misleading you now I may unwittingly hurt you in some way later." She heard surprising conceit in her words, a tendency toward assumption probably overblown, if not entirely inappropriate, but he responded before she could back-peddle.

"Are you afraid of me?" he asked in a very small voice, the firm set of his features withering like a golden-crowned amaryllis buttercup melting under the hot sun.

"No, Geoffrey," she asserted, quietly adding, "No, not of you."

He waited for her to explain, but she shook her head, mistrusting her capacity to describe clearly how she felt even as the walls started closing in around her.

"You can't tell me?"

She shook her head again, crowded into a corner, this journey toward a greater understanding of *him* suddenly way too much about *her*.

"Have I done something wrong?"

Self-conscious, she felt her heart pounding now, the heat of scrutiny washing over her in waves, the windows of evasion closing and robbing her of air. "It's not you," she attested, her voice cracking under the strain of closeted fears threatening to reveal her most private thoughts.

He moved closer to her, careful to avoid dangerous encroachment, striking balance between non-threatening distance and reassuring proximity. "Sometimes I feel scared," he confided, "and I don't always understand why."

A car pulled into the open spot beside them. A dowdy woman attired in fluorescent polyester stretched beyond the laws of physics unwedged herself from the seat, slamming the door as she reeled from the onslaught of swirling humid air, then waddled unceremoniously toward one of the boutiques, a vividly colored swatch of indifferent everyday life.

Phrekka seized the moment of distraction to consider her options. Very much the stranger in a strange land, she felt tremendous temptation to plunge through this temporary opening and retreat to her own world, but the young man who stood before her hoping she would make the right choice had turned out to be the only person besides Charles whom she ever believed might truly respect and protect her. She had already revealed more of her most personal, private feelings to Geoffrey than to any other man, but as much as she reveled in these new-found sensations of intimacy, she faced the conundrum that each step closer would render him that much more vulnerable, bringing with every stride an increasing obligation that she proceed carefully so as never to injure him even as she had feared he would aggrieve her.

"There are things that scare me, too," she admitted, "and how I might wound you in the process of protecting myself worries me most."

"Whatever happens, as long as you're not *trying* to hurt me, you can't—at least not so much that I won't heal. That's why I'm offering to let you go for now, if that'll help protect you, because I don't know what I've been doing wrong, but I do know I'll never knowingly hurt you if I can help it . . . but I can't help what I don't understand."

"But you *have* done everything right. That's what's caught me off guard, made me act so foolish."

"It's not foolish if that's how you really feel. Besides, who knows?—maybe foolish can be fun," he added, his eyes sparkling, "*if* we choose to have fun with it. It might even be good for us." Then more seriously, he vowed, "But if you think it's not, I'll try my best to accept whatever you believe is right for you."

She found profound relief in his heartfelt promise, believing he had just sworn to respect her needs, even if that meant helping her preserve the barrier behind which she so tenaciously hid, a door that could be closed when necessary, yet opened a little further whenever possible, a gateway hung solidly on the hinges of Geoffrey's promise.

He offered her a reassuring smile, his gentle face urging her to give him a chance.

"I want to stay," she said, and the unexpected hint of smile she returned cleansed her with its intoxicating liberation.

"Then help me," he implored earnestly.

The door cracked open, but its chain held firm and safe, so what harm might come from a quick peek? "I've never known anybody like you," she said, poised on the threshold.

He moved closer and regarded her affectionately, then opened and held the car door for her, handing her in like a princess. He walked around to the other side, opened his own door and peeked back.

He winked, responding, "That's because I'm the only one."

Phrekka followed Geoffrey's suggestion to dress casual for their next excursion, a visit to the address of P. Greenstone followed by a trip down Bruce Trail to look for his childhood home, possibly to scout nearby woods for the pond immortalized in Sara's sketch. She wiggled into a new pair of designer jeans and decided she liked how they fit, adding a light pullover in summer-yellow linen adorned with flowers and butterflies, then completing the ensemble with footies and deck shoes. She opened her door to find Geoffrey leaning against the hotel-hallway wall and grinning admiringly, a swatch of all-gray from head to toe in t-shirt, sweat pants, running shoes, and a blond-fringed baseball cap boasting the University of Southern Mississippi, Hattiesburg.

"Hotel gift shop," he explained, cocking his cap rakishly and striking an exaggerated model pose.

She blushed, wondering if he sensed how handsome she thought he looked at this very moment—and self-conscious about how in-tune he'd proven himself with her private feelings.

He held the car door for her, looking quite eager and upbeat about exploring the mysteries of Laurel. During the drive, she marveled at how he could act so nonchalant about all that had happened, all that was still happening, all that yet may. He seemed like a once-lost man with new-found direction.

As if reading her mind, he remarked, "You know, I'm getting these snatches of memories constantly flying at me, mostly of the times I spent with Sara, places we went together, things she taught me, and it's *all* good, but none of it feels like I'm discovering anything new." He glanced over to see her reaction.

"Maybe that's because, without realizing it, you've carried those memories all along," she supplied.

"Exactly! It's as if I just forgot where I'd put them, though it seems like a small but very important part of me has never stopped thinking about them—I don't know, maybe like when I'm asleep or daydreaming or something. It's like all those school pictures my mom brought out; you don't need to put them on display all the time to keep them safe. As long as I know where they are, I have the rest of my life to look at them."

"What about looking for more of Sara's sketches?"

"I still want to find as many as I can, but mostly so I can know where they are and maybe show them to others." Quieter, he added, "I especially want to share them with you."

They slowed to study the numbers on mailboxes arrayed sporadically along the rural road, guideposts to old farmhouses and newer clusters of rusting trailers tethered like boxfish to electric-company trotlines strung from one crooked pole to the next. They finally arrived at a vacant fire-ravaged hulk of antebellum homestead, three mailboxes on a post sharing the same number, two with other names, the bottom one designating: *Greenstone.* Behind the abandoned building stood three very run-down mobile homes, all linked by cables to a steel box mounted beside the house's cellar door.

Phrekka had visited several third-world countries with Grandmamá, but something too real about poverty right here in the United States made her feel especially uncomfortable. She and Geoffrey exchanged glances as he drove in, pulling slowly around to where several battered cars rested, one up on blocks without wheels.

Suddenly, a small boy of five or six appeared at the driver's window, a chestnut-haired moppet wearing nothing more than cartoon underpants and a threadbare cap to match Geoffrey's. "What do *you* want?" the boy drawled, his emerald eyes sparkling with curiosity and challenge.

"Is this where Purvis Greenstone lives?" Geoffrey asked, powering his window the rest of the way down.

"That's my grand-daddy," he pronounced. "He lives in Florida with Grammaw."

What a delightfully cute child, Phrekka thought, marveling at how foreign he sounded pronouncing each twanging word so deliberately.

Geoffrey turned to Phrekka for a second, his mouth open with astonishment. Back to the boy, he asked, "Is your mother named Pammy—Pamela?"

"Yessir. You want me to go get her?"

Just then, the door of the nearest trailer opened and a woman stepped into the glare of late-afternoon sunlight, squinting to see who had pulled up. She appeared to be about thirty, with hair matching the boy's, shoulder-length in the back and feathered in waves over her ears, probably home-styled but clean and uniquely beautiful in how it captured highlights from the sky. She wore faded jeans and a man's shirt, the tails tied at her belly, mended in several places but freshly laundered.

Geoffrey stepped out, his eyes wide, so Phrekka slid across the seat and joined him just as the woman approached and started to ask in a very southern drawl, "Can I help—?" She stopped a few yards short, her mouth open to mirror Geoffrey's amazement.

"Pammy?" he said, sounding very much like a little boy at that moment.

"Oh my Gawd—Geoffrey?!"

He nodded vigorously, looking very much like he teetered on the verge of bursting.

"Just *look* at you! You're *all* growed up! Well come here and let me hug your neck!" she squealed, grabbing him, then dancing back and forth with him wrapped in her arms, threatening to squeeze out all his air.

"Mawma, who's this?" the little boy demanded.

Pamela broke the choke hold long enough to announce, "This here's Sara's little brother, the boy in the pitcher you was named after!"

Geoffrey knelt before the child, his face all wonder and delight. "I'm Geoffrey Drousseau," he said, offering his hand for a shake.

Proudly, the little boy announced, "I got a Geoffrey in my name, too—Andrew Geoffrey Lanier—but they all calls me Andy-Geoff. Is you really Sara's little brother?"

"Yep! Are you really named after me?"

"Uh-huh. Mawma said you'd come t'see us someday. Where you been?"

"I've been living far away. This is my friend Phrekka," he told them both, and before Phrekka could react, she found herself uncustomarily wrapped in one of those bear hugs.

"Well ain't *you* the lucky one!" Pamela pronounced to the younger woman.

Andy-Geoff tugged at Geoffrey's shirt. "You wanna see my bike?" He grabbed his hand and pulled him over beside the trailer to inspect a rattle-trap bicycle.

"Geoffrey was the sweetest little boy you ever saw," Pamela told her. "I sure do love him bunches."

"So you knew his family?"

"Sara and I was best friends." She put her hands to her mouth, her face suddenly flush with the rekindling of long-smoldering grief. "It was terrible what happened. I was afraid I'd never see Geoffrey again, but I always hoped in my heart he'd come back someday." She glanced away for a second, then shook it off and looked expectantly toward Phrekka, taking her hands and declaring, "Y'all are gonna have to come in for a while. After fifteen years, they better nobody be in any hurry to leave right away."

Andy-Geoff rode several circles around his namesake, his new grown-up friend obviously enjoying the little exhibition. Then everybody swarmed indoors where all the fixtures appeared to be falling apart, the furniture third-hand at best, yet with everything immaculately clean, evidence of personal pride. Geoffrey set his cap on the table and sat with Phrekka on a duct-taped couch while Pamela pulled a chair close. The little one bounced around, too excited to sit. The issue of iced tea was not whether or not everybody wanted some, but how much sugar and lemon to add.

"Geoffrey," Pamela started, "you can't get away 'til you tell me where you been and what-all you been up to."

"If you'll go first, Pammy, and let me catch my breath."

"Fair enough."

As she told her story, the little boy kept studying Geoffrey curiously, sometimes coming close, sometimes retreating to his mother's side, occasionally disappearing down the hallway to return with some toy or knick-knack to show off.

"I thought that so-and-so Todd Tessin got me pregnant, so we run off to Denver where his cousin Cindy lived, planning to get a place and then get married. That was about a month before . . . you know—before *it* happened." She looked profoundly sad every time the tragedy encroached on her thoughts. She glanced away, then regained her composure and continued, "Me and Sara started writing letters back and forth—and you always drew me a picture on the bottom—then before me and Todd got around to making it legal, he got a year in the county jail for stealing car radios. It turned out I wasn't pregnant, but my parents wouldn't let me come back home, so your dad said I could stay with them. Sara was gonna send me the bus fare, but then her letters stopped coming and I didn't know why until Mama sent me the newspaper article." She paused, wringing her hands as her eyes welled with tears. She sent Andy-Geoff for some tissues. "I called Mama and said I wanted to come help take care of you, but she said you'd just left that very morning to go with your uncle and be adopted in a good home. I never even got to tell you bye," she added quietly.

Phrekka noticed Geoffrey's hands clenching. Feeling his tension, she wanted to reach out and touch him, but that seemed like it would be too much. Unable to think of a way to offer unintrusive solace, she sat very still.

"So I wound up living around the Denver area for the next ten years, working every kinda job you can imagine, some I'm not proud of. I got engaged twice but never married, had two miscarriages . . ." She shook her head, then fixed Geoffrey with her eyes, a profound tenderness from her soul. "Sometimes life ain't fair, Geoffrey. It didn't seem like things would ever be right after what happened to your family."

Geoffrey swallowed hard and rubbed his eyes, maybe unable to speak.

"Then I found one of the good guys," she pronounced, her face brighter now. "Andrew Lanier, Andy-Geoff's daddy. We got engaged—but of course I got pregnant first—" She rolled her eyes for emphasis. "This one was born real healthy," she said, gazing lovingly at the little tyke. "Sometimes *too* healthy for his own good," she snorted, reaching out to snatch him into a hug and a smooch, her cooties quickly wiped away.

"My daddy's dead," Andy-Geoff supplied solemnly.

Pamela regarded her son wistfully, and Phrekka wondered at what a challenging life Pamela must have led, so much of it on her own, all too often with no resources save her own wits, now with responsibility for a child.

"He died the same night . . . just hours after Andy-Geoff was born," Pamela said quietly. "He was riding his motorcycle home from the hospital and a drunk hit him, threw him more than fifty feet." She covered her face with her hands, breathing hard for a moment, her son standing protectively beside her, the little soldier who probably worried about her as much as she did over him.

Phrekka had to fight back tears, remembering how her own father had only known his baby girl for a few weeks, now trying to imagine a man who lived just long enough to hold his young son only once . . .

"The birth wasn't easy," Pamela finally continued, "so I couldn't work for a while, but I had Andy-Geoff to take care of. I used what little money me and Andy had saved up and come back to Laurel figuring Mama wouldn't let Daddy kick me out, not once she got to hold that little baby. Turns out they'd already bought a condo in Florida and moved away. They did send me some money; then some of the people I knew here helped me until I could work again, so me and Andy-Geoff has been here ever since. Gawd," she exclaimed, rolling her eyes and shaking her head, "I actually got out of Laurel and didn't have sense enough to stay out. Ain't nothing but old people around here because the young'ns grow up and leave and never come back—the smart ones that is."

"Do you plan to stay here?" Geoffrey asked.

She shrugged. "I got a good situation now doing bookkeeping for a couple businesses, which means I can work at home and look out for my boy, plus I'm almost through a computer accounting class I signed up for when he started kindergarten last fall. I've been saving for a better place, and was all set to rent the cottage next to your old house from Widow Lewis—she's the one used to work for that lawyer in town; she bought the property right after . . ." She trailed off, distracted for a moment. "Anyway, then she got paralyzed and moved to the nursing home. She died last month, and now her nephew's got the place up for sale, but he won't consider selling or renting me just the cottage."

Phrekka tried not to be obvious about studying the room around her, the minimal standards of basic living, a home carved out of shambles and scrap. She'd never felt particularly impressed by the power of money, but now seeing first-hand the challenges impoverishment presents to those desperately striving to improve their lot left her reeling, shaming her with the realization that a million dollars meant less to her than a hundred would to somebody like Pamela.

"Who's the nephew?"

"Gumper Lewis—"

"Gumper? The goofy paperboy with a short leg?"

Pamela laughed. "He still walks funny, too, but I guess he doesn't let it slow him down. Mama said Widow Lewis cleaned out a lot of your family's belongings and held a yard sale. She sold more than a hundred of Sara's drawings for five dollars apiece, some for less." She shook her head and looked wistful, whispering, "I wished I'd been here."

Phrekka saw Geoffrey's eyes go wide, his cheeks flush. *More than a hundred!*

Pamela noticed his reaction, too. "She once told me there's still some in the attic along with more boxes of your family's stuff. She was gonna let me clean it out and have what I wanted, but then she had that stroke."

Andy-Geoff relentlessly climbed around on the couch, testing Geoffrey's responses, seeking attention while trying not to be too much of a nuisance, so fascinated by his namesake's blond hair that he just had to feel it. Though most of Geoffrey's attention focused on the conversation, he kept an eye on the boy, reaching out to tweak him a few times, earning giggles and counter-tweaks for his effort. Geoffrey asked if a real-estate company listed the house, if he might be able to arrange a tour.

"There's a sign with the woman's phone number out front," she confirmed.

Andy-Geoff finally started to settle down, resting on his knees right beside Geoffrey, studying him very earnestly. Phrekka watched in fascination as man and child eyed each other, now face to face, then something profound and very personal seemed to pass between them. Geoffrey reached out and put his arm around Andy-Geoff's back, the child relaxing visibly under the added support as he placed his hand on the blond-haired stranger's shoulder. Wordlessly, like both understood what must happen next, Geoffrey gathered him like a delicate toy and held him in his lap, the little one settling in and closing his eyes, his cheek against his protector's heart, looks of contented bliss on both faces.

Phrekka felt wonderstruck by this vision, the fragile spark of life cradled in Geoffrey's arms, his fluttering long-lashed eyelids, his button nose and rosy cheeks and pursed magenta lips, the tiny rib cage of his nude torso swelling and shrinking with every sweet breath, the little peeper snail pressed against his underpants even as Sara had once drawn little Geoffrey's, the soft down of his lower arms and his doll-like hands with dirty fingernails, the faint outlines of muscle rippling down his sleek legs, ten little toes no-doubt loath to be suffocated by little socks and little shoes. Geoffrey must have been about the same age as this boy when he lost his family and the only world he had ever known, and Phrekka suspected he had thought of this, had seen something about himself in this frangible embodiment of love and trust, and for the second time she discovered in him a tender strength like she'd seen in no other, and she knew she'd found the paragon of what a man should be, bigger than any captain of industry, stronger than any professional athlete, more nurturing than any swaggering partner, a gentle soul with a capacity for the deepest and most abiding love.

Pamela watched, too, mesmerized, her face serene, probably recognizing the spark of Geoffrey as a child now burning brightly in the man he'd become. "It's really you," she whispered, the two of them glancing at each other, a lifetime of understanding passing between them.

"You're rich," he whispered back, holding the most valuable thing in the world.

She nodded, her face alive with wonder and joy. "Have you had a good life, Geoffrey?"

"Not as good as the one I lost, but I'm starting to realize it was better than I used to think."

She looked sad, still whispering as the little boy seemed to drift into his own dreamworld of wonder and bliss. "Did you think of Sara often?"

"No . . . I forgot about her," he admitted, the sadness in his eyes now matching hers, "or I put her someplace safe, I guess, then forgot to remember. I spent years after that trying to win attention from my new mother, and hiding from the disapprovals and harsh treatment of my father."

"Did he beat on you?" she asked, obviously afraid of the answer, but wanting to know.

Geoffrey nodded wordlessly, and he appeared to be ashamed of the admission. Phrekka wondered at how difficult it must have been the night before when he first confessed this to her, how much he'd worried that it upset her, his own feelings aside.

Pamela teetered on the verge of tears now, but she pressed on. "Sara wouldn't never let nobody lay a hand on you. There was a time me and her was hanging laundry and you slipped away from us; you climbed up on the tractor and started the motor. Your daddy lit out after you with his belt, but Sara stopped him. We took you upstairs and she talked at you 'til you cried and cried, telling you that you knowed better than to do something that dangerous, that she couldn't look out for you every minute and you had to learn to look out for yourself. She said it wasn't fair for you to make her have to worry about losing you."

Geoffrey's eyes welled with tears, but he remained stoic, holding the boy close, nodding his head. "Now I remember so much of Sara, and of us three together, but not much about my parents."

Pamela sighed, glancing away for a second. "Your daddy was gone most of the time working two-week shifts on oil rigs in the gulf. Your mama stayed in her room strung out on tranquilizers all the time. She'd had some kind of breakdown when y'all lived in Gulfport, which is why they moved up here for a quiet place in a small town just before Sara was to start school in the eighth grade. You was just a baby then, so Sara took over and practically raised you herself. When me and her become friends, we took you just about everywhere we went."

She got up, holding up a finger to signal she'd be right back, then disappeared word-lessly into another room. Geoffrey stroked the boy's hair, looking toward Phrekka with a gleam in his eye, telegraphing his gratitude, she thought, for her patience and indulgence. After a moment, Pamela returned with a framed sketch, propping it against the coffee table for her visitors to view.

Geoffrey stifled a gasp, then held his breath as he allowed himself to be drawn into the image of two teenage girls who looked like Sara and Pamela holding a blond-haired toddler between them, all three grinning at a wad of cotton candy, their mouths webbed with gobs of the sugary confection, carnival rides and fireworks in the background.

"Why did she call 'em *scatches*?" he whispered.

Pamela smiled, her eyes gleaming now, too. "She sure did like to draw, made pictures of every kid in town and most of the grown-ups, too, but no matter how old they was, she always drew what she thought they looked like when they was little, when they was what-she-called *innocent*. She said she wanted to *catch* 'em when they was still good, and if she sketched it on paper, then that was *scatching* 'em. Sometimes she'd tell 'em, 'I *scaught* you, I did.' Everybody loved her and them *scatches*."

Disappearing again, she could be heard moving things around, opening drawers, and rummaging through a closet while Geoffrey lost himself in the carnival sketch. She finally returned with several unframed drawings, explaining, "I lost most of mine when I got kicked out of my place in Denver, but Mama still had these." She moved the drinks and spread the sketches across the coffee table; one of a little girl who must have been Pamela, dressed in frills and ruffles, clutching a doll adorned in a matching outfit; the back view of a young boy and girl sitting with their legs dangling over the side of a pier, holding hands and gazing into each other's eyes, the setting sun framing them in its translucent glow—"My mama and daddy," she explained—and one of two baby girls sitting in the mud while an older Geoffrey stood over them rolling his eyes, arms akimbo.

Geoffrey looked closer, registering surprise. "That's you and Sara looking younger than me," he pronounced, glancing at Andy-Geoff to be sure his exuberance hadn't disturbed the blissful child. "Pammy, I've been trying to remember—is there a pond by the house?"

"Oh yes. Every time you'd disappear, that's where you was. Sara would dress you up and off you'd go; then we'd find you back there nekkid as jay-bird, your clothes wherever you'd left 'em, your little hiney covered with dirt from sitting on the bank with your feet in the water. That little monster you're holdin' now is the same way." Indescribable affection sparkled in her eyes as she watched her son snuggling close to Geoffrey's heart. Phrekka felt like a witness to something she could never imagine, and while the power of sketches fueled much of what passed around and through her, what people in the present did with that power, at this very moment, seemed surely to matter most.

Geoffrey told Pamela about the sketch that had first attracted his attention, encouraging Phrekka to join in the conversation and describe her gallery, then to recount how she'd tracked down the *Sweet Dreams* drawing in New Orleans.

"I remember both of those," Pamela said. "The one of you sleeping showed how you always started to twitch and rock side-to-side for a minute or two. Sara said that was how you turned on your dream machine." Pamela looked off into the distant past, wistful again, explaining quieter, "She called the other one your doodlebug phase. You'd get interested in something for a while and wouldn't leave it alone until something else got your attention. You had your lightning-bug phase, your frog phase, butterflies, snakes, flowers, minnows, you name it. The doodlebug was the last *scatch* I saw her do before I moved away."

An awkward silence coated the walls with reflection, the furniture with memories.

Geoffrey said, "Now I understand why Sara stands out so much more in my mind than my parents do. Surely, she didn't take me *everywhere*; I'll bet her boyfriends didn't want her bringing me along."

Pamela hesitated, pursed her lips, studied him for a moment, then said, "She didn't date, Geoffrey. Only once did she have a boyfriend for a few weeks in tenth grade, but he got pushy trying to mess around with her, and that *really* upset her . . ."

Phrekka felt her heart palpitating, but tried not to betray the surge of adrenaline she felt, knowing her cheeks had flushed.

Pamela continued, "She decided she'd wait until you was older, said she'd only have a few precious years to teach you how to grow up to be a good man, you with your heart of gold." She regarded him as he cradled her son, and she wiped her eyes, pronouncing, "I can see you did. She'd have been so proud of you."

Geoffrey's eyes misted up, but holding the child must have seemed more important than wiping away his feelings. Phrekka felt a lump rising in her throat.

Eyes still closed, the little boy asked, "Is you really Geoffrey?"

"I am," he answered, smiling serenely now, "but what makes you so sure you've got a Geoffrey in the middle?"

The boy sat up, jutting out his lower lip, and pronounced, "I *do* got a Geoffrey. Tell him Mawma."

"Sometimes I'm not sure *who* you is," she answered, also smiling now.

"I'm Andrew Geoffrey Lanier!" he asserted, grabbing his namesake around the neck and wrestling him, giggling with exuberance while the two of them pretended their hugs were contests of strength and prowess.

Pamela gathered up the sketches lest they be caught in the crossfire, then announced, "Well, we're gonna drive out and see the house, ain't we—before it gets dark?"

"Only if we can treat you to dinner first," Geoffrey insisted, no arm twisting required. Pamela tried to get the little one dressed, but he wouldn't cooperate until Geoffrey interceded with the promise he could choose where they ate.

They wound up at Mr. Doopey's Play Corral, eating Doopey-Burgers and Doopey-Fries, swapping stories about Laurel and Denver and Coon Rapids and Malibu and Sausalito. The adults lingered for a time and nibbled away the awkwardness of sharing intimate moments with people separated by circumstance and time, with Andy-Geoff all the while devoting his energy to winning Geoffrey's attention, recognition, approval, and touch. Phrekka quickly grew to like Pamela and her little bundle of constant motion.

They used the expressway to cross town, then exited and headed north until the two-lane blacktop merged to run alongside a railroad track. Geoffrey's hands tensed on the wheel, everybody remaining quiet, even the little one sensing the gravity of what lay ahead. Pamela directed him to turn onto a signless gravel road. They passed a wooded area, then an overgrown open field, finally slowing in front of an old two-story brick home, porticoed and gabled, with a smaller matching cottage over to the side and a barn-styled faded red shed set farther back from the road. The tracks ran maybe thirty or forty yards behind it all, a tableau cut right into the forest stretching around and beyond. The sign of a local realty company announced the availability of an important part of Geoffrey's past, for sale for the right price, memories not included.

Geoffrey stopped the car in front, shut off the engine, and sat wordlessly, holding his breath.

"I been here before!" Andy-Geoff announced, breaking the tension.

The blazing disk of setting sun peeked over the treetops, casting long shadows across Geoffrey's childhood playground. The house loomed before them, waiting patiently for their return, back-lit with an early-evening corona.

As soon as they stepped from the car, Andy-Geoff scampered off toward the cottage. Pamela studied Geoffrey, glanced at the house, then nodded with understanding before chasing after the little boy, a heartfelt gesture allowing them a few minutes alone.

Geoffrey urged Phrekka to walk with him, leading her toward the wide front porch where they stood looking up at the lifeless eyes of vacant windows. He hesitated, then took several deep breaths and appeared nervous about approaching, maybe not yet quite ready to look in, maybe remembering all those rainy days he sat inside gazing out. Instead, they wandered around the side and paused by the back porch where two weather-beaten wooden patio chairs sat forlornly. He glanced at the house for a moment, then back at her, searching her eyes, and a profound instant of understanding passed between them.

"I'd like to wait here," she whispered.

He swallowed, adjusted his ball cap, then retrieved a cloth from the porch rail and dusted the seat for her while two tiny iridescent-blue lizards scurried under the porch. "I won't be long," he promised.

"These moments belong to you, Geoffrey. Let them last as long as they may."

He nodded gratefully, allowing the hint of a smile, then turned and walked with new-found determination, disappearing around the side.

Phrekka studied the tableau around her; the old barn-style shed; a dilapidated tractor, probably where Geoffrey's play had earned him a stern lecture from Sara; overgrown shrubs with blossoms of forsythia, clusters of budding lilac and snowball; several wire-bound bales of hay, faded and frayed, rain-soaked and sun-toasted; a lone swallow-tail butterfly flitting with noble purpose from here to there. She closed her eyes and listened to the laughter of self-amused birds, the bickering of contentious cicadas, the syncopating yelps of one-upping hound dogs in the distance. She felt the warm caress of fading sunlight on her cheeks, wisps of breeze stirring her hair, the rough-hewn peeling-paint armrest pressing paisley patterns into her palms; and she breathed the pungent, earthy aroma of woods and fields and roily streams and cool, still ponds. She marveled at the twists of fate that had brought her to this place, the contradictions in pursuing greater understanding while fleeing the mysteries of what that might bring, in supporting a friend she cherished but whom she feared to keep. She wondered if this trip to Sara's home would help Geoffrey feel closer to his sister even as Phrekka had savored her father's touch whenever she sat in his childhood bedroom, that disconcerting mix of bittersweet discovery and loss, of feeling the breath of a loved one's presence just before it yields to the airless void of absence, daring to listen for a brief moment of affirming melody reverberating across time before it fades to eerie silence. Phrekka had moved forward after all, for the circumstances of her quest to reach back toward her father had conspired to bring her to this secluded homestead in rural Mississippi, to seek her answers in the world beyond her lonesome hilltop mansion in Sausalito.

There is nothing of Sara here, Geoffrey had whispered in the cemetery. What did he mean?—that no monument to Sara's death could ever capture the essence of her life? Phrekka recalled accompanying her mother to dedicate a memorial with a marble-mounted bronze plaque bearing her father's name, but the precocious little girl understood even then that her father could never exist in that unfamiliar place.

She listened for Sara's song, but the melody eluded her, never meant for her ears, an aria solely for Geoffrey.

She peeked into the real world again, glimpsed the tractor, closed her eyes just as quickly, then imagined Sara lecturing the remorseful little boy, a lesson in obligation, reminding him to care about himself as do those who love him. Phrekka owed as much to her own father, for surely all he wanted for his little girl was that she be happy, that she find her own place in the world, that she share it with people she loved, even if he couldn't be there to see her, especially if he couldn't be there to help.

She caught herself searching back through the years again, but this time it seemed like the right thing to do, that somehow she was finally ready. From Geoffrey she had learned to balance retrospection with extrapolation, realizing that both in equal measure can unlock the doorway to all that exists within, from one moment to the next, now.

Father never saw a puppy in that painting; Phrekka had, those simple brush strokes in gray transformed into the symbol of something precious she longed to love and hold . . .

Geoffrey's challenge echoed across the fields: *Why doesn't your father come to the world outside that painting and show you what he knows?*

Because her father never existed in that painting . . . All that remained of him, she carried in her heart.

She opened her eyes and the whole world belonged to her, and the painting came to life. The patches of brown and green and yellow transformed into shrubbery and trees partially obscuring a burnt-orange barn-style shed at the center; the squares of faint yellow now wire-bound bales of hay; the odd circles and shapes in faded blue coalescing into the image of a dilapidated and rusting tractor . . .

Please, Daddy, what else did you see?

And she felt his loving touch, heard his song, and finally understood that what he'd seen the last time he ever looked upon that painting, standing there holding his baby girl and rocking her to sleep, was his own beloved Phrekka grown to a beautiful young woman, stepping into the light as she found happiness and made the world her own.

She stood and closed her eyes, reaching out with her hands, the soft kiss of tears tracing lines in the warm glow on her cheeks.

Sweet Phrekka, he sang, *what else do you see?*

She opened her eyes and looked again, and there against this living background stood a young man dressed from ball cap to shoes entirely in brush strokes of gray, a soul of gentle strength poised between the traumas of his own past and the unlimited promise of an enchanted future. He came toward her, reaching out as if he somehow sensed what she needed most, and she saw in his face that he cared for her above all others.

She closed her eyes and allowed the tears to cleanse from her the stain of loss, if only for a moment, and she felt Geoffrey putting his strong arms around her, holding her tenderly as the songs of Sara and her father mingled to serenade this young man and woman swirling together into the very same dreamworld of wonder and bliss their loved ones had so long ago wished for two innocent little children.

And this, for Phrekka Churán, no matter how much it scared her, would be Geoffrey Drousseau's gift.

CHAPTER 15

A boundless bundle of chestnut-mopped energy, the little boy whose name had a Geoffrey in the middle buzzed from around the corner and interrupted the young couple's impromptu hug.

"I thought you was comin' to see the house!" he announced, demanding explanation for all this icky behavior.

"What house?" Geoffrey sparred, amused by the little one's candor. "I don't see a house."

Andy-Geoff screwed his features into a scowl, arms akimbo, fully prepared to debate the obvious differences between Phrekka and a building, but then Pamela suddenly appeared, lugging a blanket along with several towels, an ancient flashlight, and mosquito coils.

"I know where Gumper hides the extra cottage key," she explained. "If we're gonna see the pond, I thought you might like to sit awhile before it gets dark—and trying to keep this one out of the water's like asking a fish to stay dry."

Andy-Geoff's face lit up. He liberated the flashlight from his mother and rallied the troops, the guerrilla point-man locked and loaded for this mission to capture the enemy's strategic reservoir.

Not that Geoffrey needed to be led; he knew this path very well.

Several-hundred yards into the woods, they entered a small, sandy clearing, its centerpiece an acre-sized glassy pool reflecting the mirror image of back-lit haloed trees, leviathans standing sentry over flurries of iridescent damselflies dancing on the breeze. Geoffrey paused where a disgruntled fat toad hopped into a small patch of bright yellow wildflowers, tiny blossoms imbued with a purpose he recognized but failed to comprehend. His eyes drawn back to the water, he stood transfixed, vaguely aware of Phrekka and Pamela watching him as much as admiring the scene. He felt warm ripples spreading over his body, the gentle caress of fleeting impressions giving way to concrete memories, past and present paving the way toward an uncertain future.

Andy-Geoff dropped the flashlight and proceeded to strip off his shoes and socks, then his jeans—

"It's okay to get your drawers wet," Pamela interrupted him, no doubt a gesture of proprietary deference for Phrekka.

The little one shrugged, finished peeling off his t-shirt, and waded in up to his cartoon underpants, then disappeared under the surface. Phrekka started, but Pamela touched her arm reassuringly. They watched as his rippling form ghosted toward a patch of cattails in the shallows. He broke the surface silently, appearing as a phantom, now frozen, watching for unseen denizens among the reeds. The *plop-plop* of frogs leaping into the pool echoed around them, but the intrepid adventurer remained perfectly still, a wisp against the breeze, stalking his prey.

Phrekka helped Pamela spread the blanket on the sand and light mosquito coils while Geoffrey gazed around, rapt, drawn in. Teetering on the fulcrum, he felt like he might tip either direction, toward what he'd been, toward what he might become, and he chose for now to see-saw, precariously balanced between the two. He closed his eyes and remembered, a small-but-cherished part of him feeling again like the little boy who had frolicked for so many hours in this enchanted playground, who had lost his innocence here the instant a sudden storm of changing fates thundered across his world, the reverberation of twisting metal and hissing gasses exploding through the idyllic woods. He felt his heart pounding, but he pushed that impression aside and gazed again across the pond, little Andy-Geoff an apparition now shimmering at the periphery. He remembered this place, every little nuance, and though it looked smaller now, it cast him again under a familiar yet bewitching spell, and he knew this magician's-hat clearing had waited patiently all this time for the itinerant rabbit to return . . .

Pleased to see how the little blond-haired boy had grown to a man.

Andy-Geoff stood in the reeds, his delicate face a mask of gentle serenity and bliss, and he looked right at Geoffrey, curiosity and affection sparkling in his eyes. Geoffrey watched in awe as Sara's sketch came to life, real enough to touch, and in that instant he savored the first glimmers of how she must have felt watching her beloved little brother explore all this splendor right there among the cattails. The pond hadn't been calling for the young boy from so long ago, but rather for a new generation to embody the innocence of childhood, the essence of trust, the liberation of security, the reassurance of knowing one's place in the world, one's very special place in another's heart.

The bruise of encroaching dusk stained the backdrop, a reminder of the ephemeral nature of all moments . . .

And the night's first firefly twinkled amid the reeds.

Geoffrey joined the others on the blanket just as little Andy-Geoff paused in his mission, also struck by the vision. Everybody watched, transfixed, delighted as another pinpoint yellow light, then another, then hundreds of subjects in this realm of the lightning-bug god winked majestically in the twilight velvet air.

"Sara called them her dancing fairies, lighting up the water," Pamela whispered. "She loved this place so much . . . used to say all the magic in the world can be found right here." She sighed and wiped her eyes. "I wish she could see this again, could know that Geoffrey finally came home, could meet little Andy-Geoff. She'd understand how much I love him, and she'd see the magic he brings here, too."

They sat in silent veneration while some invisible sorcerer conjured a scene glittered by thousands of sparkles, and they listened for the forest's orchestra, the rhythm of their soft breaths flowing long and deep, the chorus of cicadas rising in syncopation to accompany the ballet of twinkling pixies.

"I want to see the log," Geoffrey said quietly, "before it gets too dark." He stood, offering Pamela his hand.

She glanced toward where her son stalked the lightning-bug alien spaceships levitating amid the reeds, cupping them in his hands for a peek, then releasing them with a flourish as if to scatter stardust across the skies.

"I'll watch him," Phrekka promised, waving off Geoffrey's hand. Pamela smiled and nodded, trusting the most cherished sparkle in all the clearings of the world to her newest friend.

Geoffrey guided Pamela around the low end of the pond, tracing a path through the woods to avoid the muddy shallows. He handed her up onto a huge, weather-burnished hollow log jutting over the far shore so they could sit, legs dangling, and study the scene. He could faintly hear Andy-Geoff's voice as the little hunter stalked through the reeds, B'wana Lanier explaining to Phrekka how best to catch a frog, a toad, a lizard, a snake. With a boisterous splash, the boy took one last dive below the surface, then emerged scrubbed and renewed.

Phrekka giggled, pointing at all the sand on his feet, then led him back to the edge of the water to swish them clean. She lifted him gently and carried him to the blanket where, without hesitation, he stripped off his wet briefs and wrung them out over the sand, folding himself into the towel she held for him. After drying him from head to toe, she helped him wiggle into his jeans and shirt, then hung the undies on a branch to drip dry. She fished in her small handbag and found a comb, inviting him to settle into her lap while she styled his hair.

"Bless their hearts," Pamela said quietly, her voice blending with the rising cicada cacophony. She glanced at Geoffrey with a knowing smile that hinted she'd found some way to eavesdrop on his private thoughts. Enthralled, he felt himself drawn in as he watched Phrekka nurture this small child, a side of her he'd not yet seen, something about her he liked very much. "Are you two, you know, together?"

Geoffrey shook his head sadly. "I don't know why, but she keeps pushing me away."

Pamela nodded, thinking it over. "Yet she stays with you."

"And I've given her chances to get away gracefully. It's like she's afraid of me sometimes, but determined not to give up."

"She knows you'll be worth it."

He smiled at that, recalling the Pammy who always had something nice to say about him. "I'm not sure how to make it better," he admitted, slipping into the practiced confidence that he could talk about anything with her, the concepts now more grown-up, the long-dormant flow of tender feelings still running so very deep.

"God knows I'm no expert, unless it's to say *don't* get her pregnant 'til you're both ready." Then, more seriously, she added, "Just stay as close as you can, Geoffrey, however close she'll let you be. Eventually, the time will come for her to accept you, and you'll be right there, ready."

He liked that very much: simple advice from the heart, insight that made more sense the more he thought about it.

She leaned in conspiratorially, shrugging. "Try that awhile; then give up and find somebody else if it don't work."

"No," he protested. "No, nobody else."

She smiled like an unmasked, taunting conspirator. "No, I thought not." Then she hugged him and kissed him on the cheek. "I used to imagine what you'd be like all grown into a big man—just like I try to picture how little Andy-Geoff'll be someday." She sighed. "You turned out just like I expected. I'm glad to see I was right, Geoffrey."

"Why, if something good came of me, I'm sure you deserve a lot of the credit, Pammy," he teased.

They gazed across the water at the little one now being cradled in Phrekka's lap, then finally decided to climb off the log and head back.

"My Andy-Geoff's gonna wind up raising a little hell before he settles down," she pronounced, "but he'll grow up to be a good man, too."

"He has the best mama." He knew she liked hearing that, too. Very much.

They joined the others on the blanket, one each side of Phrekka. Andy-Geoff put his feet across Geoffrey's legs, unwilling to relinquish his spot in Phrekka's lap. Geoffrey put his arm around her and embraced her briefly, saddened to feel her stiffen just perceptibly. He brought his arm back and played with the little boy's toes, earning a giggle or two, but he stayed very close to Phrekka, patient, ready.

A million fireflies swirled as the backdrop purpled to velvet and sparkles of distant stars sequined the sky. Geoffrey listened for Sara's song among the trees, her voice rising from the cool, glassy water, a lullaby dancing in the warm air, and he saw the world through her eyes.

"It don't hardly seem like she's gone," Pamela whispered.

Geoffrey listened as Sara sang a melody to welcome him home.

Then he whispered back, "Just listen . . . she's not gone."

Heat lightning flashed in the distance, warm moist air encroaching on the domain of cool spring breeze in that age-old dance of the elements, nature's forces seeking equation, immeasurable power released as two masses collide in their insatiable drive to reconcile their differences and merge as one.

Geoffrey met the waiter at the door, signed the check, than carried the room-service tray out to join Phrekka on her hotel-suite balcony, pausing for a moment to admire the distant lightning. He set the tray on a low table, then dragged a segment of the sectional couch out to the rail and invited her to sit with him, offering her first choice from the selection of dainty finger-pastry puffs, smiling when she tried to conceal a very lady-like yawn.

"It's been a long day," he summed up.

"A long week so far," she countered.

He liked the *so far*, a subtle change from this morning's distance, a promise of possibility to sustain him through what surely would be the most frustrating night of his life. "I heard there might be another Sara sketch buried in a mountaintop cave somewhere in the Himalayas—are you game?"

"0oo, can we parachute in?" she asked, rolling her eyes.

"Well, maybe we should just stick with Mississippi for now."

"I *am* starting to learn the language here," she teased. "It's similar, in some ways, to English."

"Now don't you, like, be dishing no grodiness on my homeys just because you're a gnarly Malibu chickie."

She smiled at that, shaking her head. "Valley-speak Iowa-style . . . sheesh! I do like little Andy-Geoff's southern drawl. He's so cute when he gets excited and talks a hundred miles an hour, especially the way he always demands explanations for everything." She had a far-off look in her eyes.

"I watched you helping him dry off and get dressed," he admitted, wanting to tell her he'd never beheld a more beautiful, more natural vision, but he stumbled, unsure how or if he should articulate those feelings.

She gazed off into the night sky, her face serene, probably remembering that feeling and savoring it. "Pamela is so lucky," she said, breathing a hearty draught of the torrid storm-infused air.

"Except for losing the boy's father," he said quietly.

She shook her head sadly, casting her eyes down. "Even together they would have had a challenging life, but for her to have all that responsibility alone, with no help, living in virtual poverty . . ." She sighed, lost for a moment.

"I'd like to give her some money—after all, *she* lost somebody important to that train wreck, too—but I know she wouldn't take it."

Phrekka seemed surprised by this. "You think not?"

"Oh, I'm sure of it. You heard how her voice caught when she admitted needing help after Andy-Geoff was born. She takes pride in supporting herself now, of working toward a better future. I'd have to find a way to help that isn't outright charity."

"My first thought is always to throw money at problems, or to hire people who'll solve them for me."

"Pammy's circumstances certainly give her one advantage . . ." He let the words hang until she looked up, curious. "It's easier for her to trust people's motives." He watched carefully for her reaction. "I don't think she's ever had to worry some guy was after her for the money."

Phrekka paused for a moment, then smiled demurely and pointed out, "What she has to offer is worth more than money."

"She does have a wonderful capacity to love, and she *is* pretty gosh-durn good looking," he added, suppressing what the boys in Iowa would call a shit-eatin' grin, "—and apparently generous to a fault, so if you're tabulating charm and beauty, she's loaded, but I've only met one woman in my life who was truly wealthy in that regard."

Phrekka blushed, and for a brief instant Geoffrey wondered if he'd said too much. She hesitated, her eyes averted, then asked mysteriously, "Geoffrey, are you interested in my money?"

"Well, you're on to me; I was hoping for maybe a ten-spot, you know, until Friday."

She looked at him sadly, her question more serious than he'd realized, and he tried to think of some anatomically feasible way he could kick himself in the butt.

"I feel dumb for asking, but—"

"Phrekka," he said quietly, earnest, concerned, "have I done anything that would make you suspect that?"

She shook her head, then admitted, "Still, I've known people who make a big show of not wanting small favors, thinking they're collecting the currency of obligation so they can ask for a big favor later and their motives won't seem so suspect."

"Back in Iowa, I promised I would be honest with you. I've never broken that, and I've not tried to hide what I truly want from you. If there's any subterfuge, it's because maybe I'm trying too hard, and moving too carefully so I don't scare you off—um, I mean . . ." That didn't come out right. He swallowed hard.

"Please try to understand what circumstances and resources like mine can do to a person's ability to trust."

He nodded, chuckling briefly. "After I got my annuity, several students I used to hang around with suddenly got more interested in dating me, so I got to where I worried about people being after *my* pathetic little sack of shiny baubles—and I even thought maybe that's what *you* wanted—"

"I'm *not* interested," she interrupted, suddenly flustered. "I'm sorry, that's not what I meant—"

A distant clap of thunder reverberated across the sky, a *whoosh* of damp breeze rushing into the courtyard and stirring little whorls of dust. The *splat-splat* of portending droplets spattered on the balcony. Phrekka yawned as they carried the tray and furniture back inside. Geoffrey felt his frustration rising, the time of departure imminent, knowing he should leave gracefully, against every instinct, every desire, the deepest determination.

"You're tired," he said.

She shrugged and nodded just perceptibly, then stood there in the middle of the room.

"I was gonna suggest we sit in front of the screen and watch the storm, but it *is* late . . ."

She looked nervous, yet she didn't discourage him from continuing.

"I mean, I'd like to stay, but . . ."

She bit her lower lip; her shoulders tensed, and she closed her eyes.

He knew this would be a big mistake, pressuring her to give him this chance. He knew this with every fiber of his being, but he couldn't go now, couldn't just walk out that door and leave her again, couldn't fail if this was to be her way of testing his commitment and resolve . . . but he feared discovering their hug behind the house meant less than he believed, that she'd only toyed with him before casting him aside, and he clung precariously to the conviction that she *did* want to be closer to him, that if she couldn't let him stay tonight, then it would not be him she had rejected, but something within herself. Sara had proven he could be loved unconditionally, that sometimes circumstances will fall beyond his control, that he would never be diminished because someone, for whatever reason, simply chose to seek happiness with another. After growing up believing his first family abandoned him, he'd finally learned to hold himself blameless, now understanding how they had been victimized by the harsh hand of fate. He'd never deserved the endless vitriol of Ernest's disapproval, the vented anger of a bitter man who could never accept that Rachel strayed from the fold. Mother Calhoun had struggled against loving him, not over some perceived defect, but because his very presence reminded her of her own inability to bear children. His prom date had been too ashamed to admit her poverty, his graphic-arts clients simply making business decisions without regard to the man who'd done their layouts. His girlfriend Melanie wanted nothing more than a means to escape her father, a place to live until a better option came along . . .

The birds never rejected Geoffrey, but rather the house he'd built.

Phrekka wanted to be near him, this he believed with all his heart, and if something stood in her way, then he would devote himself to understanding the invisible demon and helping her vanquish it, to remaining as close as possible throughout.

"We can sit for a little while, I guess," she finally agreed, just in time to prevent him from exploding under the pressure of ambivalence.

"We could try to get away with ordering wine," he offered good-naturedly, like the underage criminal he'd become.

She shook her head. "No, that would put me to sleep. But if *you* want . . ."

"No, no. I'll just slide the couch over here—" He started moving furniture.

"I'll freshen up," she said, stealing into the bathroom with her bag.

He arranged the sofa to face the balcony where intermittent showers sprayed indifferently. He dialed the lights down to a muted glow, tuned the radio to a soft-rock station and left it playing quietly in the background, then suddenly found himself feeling like a stereotypical wolf prepping his lair to snare a hapless victim, but before he could undo all his mood-setting efforts, she emerged dressed in a flowing gown, her hair tied back with a ribbon, radiant, beautiful, pure . . .

And very nervous.

He stepped toward her, but she shied away.

"I'm sorry," he blurted, moving off to the side. "You're afraid I'll touch you, but I promise I won't."

"I'm not scared of that," she defended without conviction.

He looked into her eyes, pleading for the truth. "But you are, Phrekka—"

"We've held hands; we've hugged—"

"But only in safe situations. Alone together, no. Holding you behind the house, other people were nearby, and you wanted to right then because your feelings had overwhelmed you. Give me a chance to prove you're safe with me alone, even when my feelings are overwhelming me."

They looked at each other, their taut reverie broken by a louder clap of thunder, a gust from the balcony, the *drip-drip* of rain forming a dangerous puddle on the balcony's threshold between safety and storm. Geoffrey moved over and closed the glass door most of the way, a crack left for screened breeze; then he stood by the sofa, the gentleman waiting for Phrekka to choose her seat.

She sighed, biting her lip again, glancing back and forth between him and the couch. Finally, she moved over and sat stiffly, her back straight, wringing her hands. "This is stupid," she said.

He moved closer, then knelt before her. "No, breaking my word would be stupid," he said.

"I mean me," she said in a tiny voice.

"You're taking a chance for me," he whispered. "Please don't call that stupid."

He looked up at her face, her delicate features radiant, her eyes shining with unrealized tears. She eased back into the cushions, then breathed deeply and closed her eyes. He wanted to hold her, to reassure her, but more than any other time in his life he understood the power of promise, of commitment, of caring so much as to resist every instinct, of putting the needs of another first.

"You don't deserve this," she whispered, looking into his eyes.

"Give me a chance, and I will."

"That's not what I—"

"I know," he soothed, offering her an innocent smile. He stretched, trying not to look like a sneaky schoolboy making his move, then casually eased in beside her. Lightning flashed the instant their legs touched, and she flinched noticeably, but didn't retreat. "I can't believe I'm in Mississippi," he said, watching the sky, drawing her attention away from the terrors of proximity, the threat of implied expectation.

"You couldn't possibly have imagined all this would happen to you."

"To us," he added. "We've been in this together, and that's part of what makes it all seem so fantastic."

Gnarled electric fingers groped great roiling clouds, the crescendo of thunder building to a final single clap of applause to punctuate the celestial performance. An exuberant spray of raindrops splattered the glass door, an impressionistic rendering that obscured their view, nature's artistic symbol for the lack of clarity inherent in examining too closely the mysteries of life. Droplets traced vertical lines in a mad race to the bottom, some choosing to journey solo, others pausing to seek assistance and tap the added momentum of joined purpose.

"There's so much for you to think about," she said, her voice drifting with the gusts of wind.

"None of it as important as what comes next," he whispered back.

They listened to the rain, nature's impatient agitation.

"You have so many choices to make," she said, succumbing to a yawn.

"Only one choice," he whispered with finality, "and it's made."

He settled lower in the cushion, resting his head back, watching the firecracker flashes of light strobing in the distance.

Phrekka closed her eyes, but her fingers fidgeted nervously, pausing, then fidgeting again.

"Are you afraid right now?" he asked as soothingly as he could muster.

She bit her lip, nodding just perceptibly.

"Of me?"

She hesitated, then whispered, "It's not you."

"I would protect you," he vowed.

She held her breath, then exhaled quickly.

"I'm right here," he reminded her, recalling the promise he'd made to himself, to remain as close as possible, to prove nothing would deter him, that he would respect her needs foremost.

The lightning and thunder subsided, the sky now unpainted black velvet, the swimming-pool lights refracting through streaking glass to paint fluid scenes across the ceiling. The pair of mounted sailfishes patiently anticipated the rising tide, the waters of potential that may never come, but maybe for them even the possibility made it all worthwhile, waiting for an uncertain future to unfold, joined in purpose, together.

Hearing Phrekka's ragged breaths, he wondered if she might be crying softly. He felt a knot in his stomach, his throat constricting as he fought back his own confusion and frustration, this close yet unable to confront denizens he could never see. Afraid to touch her, fearful his simple gestures of affection and reassurance would only make it worse, he closed his eyes and reached out with his mind to hold her tenderly, to remind her of his promise.

"I'm right here," he whispered.

The soft patter of spring rains tapped impatiently at the glass, a wake-up call for the sailfishes, the cool breeze of changing times washing through the room, searching, wondering. He listened as Phrekka's breathing softened, slower now, calmer . . . and he felt himself fading.

I built it for me, he'd protested to Mother Calhoun so long ago. He still didn't know the smartest way to build a birdhouse, but for Phrekka he would put forth his very best effort, and he would never stop trying, offering all that he could, resisting every impulse to let frustration lash out and smash even the faintest glimmers of hope, no matter how much she might inadvertently hurt him. He would build this one for her.

And within, Phrekka would always be safe.

She shifted in her sleep, her head now resting on his shoulder, supported by Geoffrey's determination.

He was this close, and he would be ready, no matter how long it might take.

I'm right here . . .

CHAPTER 16

The odor of gin wafted into the room, a shadow looming in the doorway, the shuffling sounds of stumbling, a muffled curse . . .

Phrekka awoke, focused her attention, trying to discern—

She felt something on the bed, the odor overpowering. He grunted, fumbled with her lamp, turned it on, squinting from the cone of brilliance. She'd have to get past him to reach the phone—

She froze, confused, scared. "Mother!" she called out.

He snorted. "Worthless bitch is drunk again, out cold."

"What are you doing in here?" she demanded.

"Jus' wanna talk is all," he slurred. "Patch things up, call a truce, no hard feelings."

"Get out of my room."

He snorted again. "Come on, don't be like that. You won. It's over."

She tried to scoot out the other side of the bed, but he pawed at her arm, then grabbed tightly, glaring at her.

"I *said* I wanna talk is all."

"Let go of me, Larry," she ground out.

"Long as you don't try to get away. I'm gonna say—" He belched. "—Say my piece."

Letting him speak might be smarter than forcing a confrontation, something physical, no telling what he might do. "What do you want?"

"You know all that legal stuff was because—it was because I was just trying to protect you. You know that, don't you?"

She waited.

"Answer me," he growled.

"Say what you have to say, then leave." She started trembling, her outrage crumbling to distress as she struggled against outright panic, trying to be tough, trying not to cry, not to show fear . . . and not doing a very good job of it.

"Oh, don't be afraid of me. What're you afraid of? Not of me. I was the only one—the *only* one you could really trust. Rest of your life, everybody's gonna act like they wanna be your friend, but all they want's a piece of what you got—all that money. I'm your *father*, for crissake."

You're not my father. "It's over, Larry."

"I know, I know." He put his hands up in conciliation. "Your fancy-ass lawyers won. You're free to piss it away, let yourself get ripped off, whatever . . ."

"Go now, Larry." *Please.*

"I jus' wanna—jus' wanna—" He swayed, rocking back and forth. "You still love me, don'tcha?"

"Nothing's changed, Larry. Go to bed. Good night."

Suddenly, he yanked the covers down. She started, then tried to move away, but he grabbed her arm. "Let's let bygones be bygones—you know, kiss and make up." He leaned closer, reeking from the stench of spilled gin.

"Let go! Mother! *Mother!*"

"All that money ain't the only thing people's gonna be after, you know."

She clawed with her free hand, trying to pull him loose, but he grabbed her other wrist and held tightly.

"That sweet little snatch of yours, too—that's what they'll be after. Come on, give us a kiss." He leaned closer.

She cried out, twisting and struggling, then managed to get one hand free and scratched at his face, drawing blood from his forehead before he wrestled her down and held her in place.

"Bitch! You cut me! All I'm tryin' to do—tryin' to—is be nice—"

"Mother!" she screamed. "Help!"

He slapped her across the mouth, splitting her lip. She tasted bitter blood, unable to twist free before he grabbed her wrist again.

He pinned her tightly, rocking up on top of her. She could feel his stiffness pressed against her leg, hot gin breath in her face.

Eyes afire, spittle drooling from his mouth, he growled, "You think you can stop me?"

She felt herself plummeting into a pit of despair, buffeted by the winds of terror, helpless to see through tears of anguish, unable to fight the suffocating weight. She reached out with her mind, desperately trying to find the innocent little girl she cradled in her heart, but she found only the stench of gin-putrefied air, a suffocating shadow threatening to drag her past the point of no return. "Please—don't," she wept.

"Ain't nothin' you can do now, is it?"

"Please—"

"How's it feel, you little slanty-eyed bitch?"

Still pressed against her leg— "Oh God, no—"

"I oughta fuck you right now, show you I can *take* what *I* want."

She gasped for breath, weeping for all she'd lost, all she would never find. If she could only go away, find someplace to hide, wait until it's over, then try desperately to come back and search for the remnants of herself, hoping that something of Phrekka would be left to find . . .

He pushed her away, then stood up, swaying like he might topple. "Bitch."

She cried inconsolably, begging him to leave, to leave her alone.

"You say anything about this, it'll—it'll humiliate your mother. You wanna do that to her? Huh?! Answer me! You wanna destroy your mother?"

"Get out!"

"Better keep your mouth shut, bitch, or I'll burn her. I'll burn her bad."

"Get out!"

He turned and staggered toward the door. "You passed up a good thing," he said without looking back.

"Don't ever touch me again," she sobbed, the last words she ever spoke to Liquid Larry.

The next day she moved out, dropped out of Pepperdine University, and headed north to help care for ailing Grandmamá. The danger had passed, but in Phrekka's nightmares, Larry always stopped in the doorway, then turned and came back to finish taking what he wanted, and when he was done . . .

Phrekka had nothing left to give.

"Phrekka! Phrekka, wake up!" he pleaded.

A pair of sailfishes on the wall, the sound of rain, Mississippi . . .

Geoffrey.

She cried out, twisting in her gown, trying to protect herself. She turned and saw Geoffrey very close. He wrung his hands helplessly as if afraid to touch her, his eyes wide like a scared little boy, confused and unsure.

"Phrekka," he whispered. "You're having a bad dream."

"Yes," she said. "Yes." She wiped her face, embarrassed. She felt nauseated, groping for a hand-hold against the stiff winds of helplessness.

"Am I too close?" he asked in the tiniest voice, still looking very anxious.

"No, this is good." She closed her eyes, then focused on an image of serenity in the distance, and she found a gentle soul with blond hair, his hand extended.

"I'm here," he whispered.

She opened her eyes and saw the droplets joining each other to race down the glass, Geoffrey's open hand beside her, the implication of a heartfelt offer, a gesture respectful of her apprehensions.

He reached for tissues with his other hand, offered her some, and used one to dab his own eyes. He blushed, maybe a little embarrassed by their unabashed display, but then she looked into his eyes and saw something more. There would be no embarrassment between them, not tonight, maybe never . . .

"Sorry," she said.

He shook his head firmly, clearly frustrated by this. "Sorry I'm still here?"

"No—"

"Then please don't say that. *I'm* not sorry."

Realizing she'd been trembling, she willed herself to calm. "Then you're welcome," she blurted from somewhere deep inside.

He looked surprised, and they both stopped breathing for a second . . . then he chuckled, and she laughed with him, smiling at each other through eyes still blurry from raw emotion.

They both sighed at once, the tension of their bodies bleeding away.

They watched as more droplets teased each other and danced a reel down the pane.

"Thank you, Geoffrey," she countered, almost too quiet to hear.

"You're welcome," he said, and they both smiled at that. "Does that mean I can get that ten-spot 'til Friday?"

"You'd wait 'til I got my wallet out, then ask for twenty."

"Or for something worth more than all the money in the world."

She sighed, surprised that his little double entendre didn't make her nervous at all, grateful he'd simply helped her emerge from that awful place without demanding she explain where she'd gone.

They settled back into the cushions, his hand still open, both lying there for a while as the patter of rain teased the mounted sailfishes, the cool breeze of receding past swirling through the room. As she drifted on the winds of potential quietude, she caught a fleeting image of the drunken Liquid Larry, and she started to push it aside, as always, but this time it felt somehow different. She paused, instead, and looked closer, realizing something very important . . .

Larry couldn't hurt her anymore.

She would never have to run from him again, not from all the Larrys in the world. She could take care of herself. And besides, as long as Geoffrey stayed this close . . .

He wouldn't let them.

And he wouldn't let *her* keep hurting herself.

A lone droplet crawled cautiously down the glass, seeking out a companion to finish the journey as one, the sound of Geoffrey's voice whispering reassurance in the darkness . . .

"Just remember who's here."

Phrekka must have drifted into sleep. She felt something move, then panicked for a second before realizing it must be Geoffrey. Aware of her surroundings again, she opened her eyes and noticed the rain had subsided, the sailfishes resting for the night. Geoffrey still lay in the same position, his open hand extended, waiting for her to feel safe enough to touch him.

He twitched again, rocking just perceptibly from side to side before exhaling a long breath.

He'd fallen asleep.

She studied his slumbering form, so innocent and child-like, yet strong and determined, tender, solid, a contradictory equation in precise and balanced measures.

She thought about their odyssey together, of what they'd discovered here in Mississippi, of Pamela and little Andy-Geoff carving out a life imbued with love to fortify them against the challenges, of Geoffrey's quest to find his sister's sketches and share them with others, to share what they mean with Phrekka. It seemed incomprehensible that she'd feared the glitter of her wealth might blind him, that she could ever believe his physical desires might override the patience of his affection, his respect, his honor, his promise to protect her, no matter what.

In that instant, she discovered a new feeling, something indistinct: maybe confidence, maybe trust, maybe the very essence of faith. She could count on his promise, and she knew nothing would deter him, that he would wait this close as long as she needed. She loved him for this above all else, just as she loved the innocent and injured little boy he cradled in his heart, the one he'd found the faith to let her see, and she loved him for the indomitable man he'd become, the one he strived very hard to prove deserved her.

She vowed to give something back to Geoffrey, to use her virtually limitless resources selflessly for the benefit of another, for a friend. Her mission suddenly dawned clear, and she knew what she must do first thing in the morning, something he would never ask of her.

Get some rest, Phrekka, tomorrow will be a busy day.

She'd never been so close to a man before, nor ever felt more safe.

She touched his hand, then gently placed hers inside it and felt his fingers curl protectively around her. Still sleeping, he had no way to realize she'd taken that first tentative step, a big one for her, the right one.

"I'm right here, too," she whispered.

She liked to think some part of him heard her, and she believed in her heart that wherever Geoffrey floated in his dreamworld of wonder and bliss . . .

He knew.

CHAPTER 17

A bright slash of sunlight cut across the room, kissing Geoffrey with its warm caress. He opened his eyes and looked out to see the shimmering mist of evaporating rains, a cadre of petite, colorful birds searching the courtyard for snacks, aerial marauders squabbling over matters too complex for mere humans to fathom.

Phrekka was gone.

He hauled himself to his feet, swallowed, and rubbed his eyes. He proceeded to scratch his privates, so of course the door flew open at that precise moment to reveal Phrekka.

"You gonna stand there rubbing that thing all morning or take a shower before breakfast arrives?"

"Why didn't you wake me up?"

"You looked way too adorable lying there with drool on your chin."

He absently wiped his mouth. "Where you been?"

"I rented another suite, then had a fully equipped office set up."

As she crossed to her luggage valet, he noticed her precisely tailored business outfit, an intimidating power suit. She appeared quite exquisite—and never more feminine. Thoughts of a merger crossed his mind. "An office?"

She found some papers, then stood before him, inspecting him and wrinkling her nose. "We had a deal," she said mischievously.

"Huh?"

"An employment contract. You hired me back in Mill Valley, specifically granting me full discretion in how I achieve your goals. Your statements last night implied permission to expand my responsibilities."

"Huh?"

"Since I am a contractual employee under unspecified terms, expenses are my responsibility, and the amount for which I invoice you remains still to be determined."

"What are you up to?" he asked, rubbing his hands through his hair, resisting the temptation to scratch himself again.

She exaggerated her nose-wrinkling gesture. "I'll be two doors down when you're ready." With that, she squeezed his arm and tousled his hair, then turned on her heel and marched from the room with renewed purpose.

How could he wash that arm now? It positively tingled.

Never before had he raced through his morning routine with such gusto, pointedly skipping the extensive hair-combing ritual of the day before. He dressed in a nice-but-casual outfit, slacks and sport shirt, then headed down the hallway, intercepting the room-service captain and commandeering his cart.

He caught Phrekka talking into the air. "Geoffrey just arrived, Charles."

"Good morning, Mister Drousseau," a charismatic, gentle-but-authoritarian voice greeted him.

"Um, hello, Mister—"

"Charles, please. I'm sure by now Miss Churán has forgotten my full name."

She interjected, "Just like Charles always forgets *my* name is Phrekka." Then to the air, "So did you have any trouble?"

"Simple as always. You almost never present me with any real challenges. I look forward to the day you insist on buying, say, the South China Sea—by five o'clock."

"Thank you, Charles," she said, signing off.

"You're welcome, Miss Churán."

Phrekka bowed gracefully to Geoffrey, scanning him approvingly and gesturing for him to help her set several snack trays and a bin of iced juices over on a side table, explaining without elaboration, "People will be stopping by. Care to join me for breakfast?" As they savored miniature waffles topped with gooey compote, she mentioned, "I hope you don't mind; I sneaked into your bag to retrieve the clipping about your trust fund."

"No, um, I don't—"

"Good. I couldn't remember the name of the bank."

"So what are you up to?"

"It won't be as much fun if I *tell* you."

Fair enough. As they continued eating, he could no longer resist revealing his thoughts. "You look beautiful this morning."

She paused, her face radiant, a sparkle in her eyes. "Why thank you. You're quite handsome yourself, though I'll always cherish the image of you standing there in a daze scratching your peeper."

He felt his cheeks burning, but a knock interrupted them, the arrival of Attorney Somebody-or-other, a tall black man with broad shoulders and a manicured goatee, along with four assorted crisply dressed assistants, one booting up a laptop, the rest clutching portfolios with legal pads. Geoffrey recalled the documentary-film image of schooling sharks and decided he wouldn't want to be sued by these man-eaters. Introductions and snack distribution complete, Phrekka took charge of the meeting.

"We have to be a legal entity to open bank accounts, but I need the accounts before I can consummate a deal that provides an address for incorporation."

Mr. Somebody suggested, "We'll register with the county using my office address this morning, then file a corporation later."

"By the end of the day," she specified.

He smiled. "That means two o'clock to have it in Jackson before closing."

"Good! Pick up the mission statement and rough draft of our articles and by-laws from my notes there." She gestured to some papers on the desk.

The man-eaters swarmed on the documents, feverishly scribbling on their pads and rattling the computer. Within minutes, they put several forms in front of Geoffrey for signature. Phrekka gestured her approval, so he complied without question, no point in slowing the momentum now. One of the aides snatched them up and literally trotted from the room.

Mr. Somebody spent the next twenty minutes asking Phrekka esoteric business questions, interrupted at one point by another Charles speaker-phone call informing her that he had completed preparations for the bank, whatever that meant, and that a publicist would arrive in Laurel by lunchtime. The aide returned, confirming that "the same bank" held some lien, then giving a packet of information to Geoffrey.

Before he could open it, Phrekka ushered him out so they could drive to Laurel Central Bank & Savings a dozen blocks away. They blew inside like flies finding the hole in a screen, then suddenly found themselves surrounded by very helpful employees who escorted them to meet President So-and-so, an overweight white man with tufts of gray hair fringing his balding pate. A frumpy older woman dangling '50s-styled rhine-stone-encrusted eyeglasses from a chain around her neck stood beside him.

Phrekka took charge again, a side of her that Geoffrey liked very much. He wanted to announce proudly, "I'm with *her*," but she insisted on presenting herself as "representing Mr. Drousseau."

"We've decided," she continued, "to see if yours can satisfy our requirements before we consider other banks for two reasons: you hold a mortgage we might want to retire quickly, and you handled the annuity and trust established for Mr. Drousseau some fifteen years ago."

Both bankers' faces lit up. "Geoffrey?" the woman asked, not waiting for an answer. "I just *knew* it was you." To the man, "I told you it was him." To Geoffrey, "I knew your family, hon. Such an awful thing it was what happened. My haven't you grown into a handsome young man."

Phrekka let everybody gush for a minute before returning to business. "Mr. Drousseau would like to register a master business account, including unlimited sub-accounts and checking, for a charitable foundation to be established here in Laurel." She gestured for him to surrender his packet of papers. "If that is something you can accomplish in the next thirty minutes, establish it under this legal authority." She let them tear through those papers for a few minutes before sliding another across from her satchel. "We have no authority in this separate matter, but Mr. Drousseau requests the courtesy that you assume, confidentially, that this mortgage will be paid off this afternoon, that you prepare all the necessary calculations and documentation for expedience."

"We can do that," he agreed. "What shall we use for funds to open these accounts? The minimum requirement is—"

A buzz interrupted him, a voice telling him something relevant to his meeting just arrived. A young fellow rushed in with more papers. The bankers took one look, then reeled. Geoffrey jumped to catch the woman in case she fainted outright.

"That must be from Charles," Phrekka said. "I think our first corporate patron has made a donation. Will that be sufficient?"

"Sufficient?" he declared, nearly gasping for air. "*Two-million dollars?*"

Phrekka looked surprised by this, but then she smiled, rolling her eyes. "That Charles—I only asked for *one*—"

"And here's another," the banker said, reading off the name of a different company. "Two-hundred thousand!"

Phrekka seemed very surprised, but enjoying herself immensely.

"And another here for three-fifty—"

Phrekka laughed. "He promised he'd shake the tree down at the club, but I didn't expect first thing this morning."

Mr. So-and-so appeared to be resisting every urge to crawl across the table and kiss his new clients. "Thirty minutes," he declared, "and *anything* else you need—"

"Please send it all to Mr. Drousseau's office at the Sawmill Ramada. We really must go; we're late for another meeting. Will you be available for some verbal approvals over the phone?" He bobbed his head. "—And have a courier on standby to run a draft down the street in the next little while?"

"Bring it myself, if need be."

After a round of handshakes followed by a brisk walk, Geoffrey found himself three doors down sitting in a real-estate office, fawned over by a skinny middle-aged woman with big hair and a cackling laugh. She held his hands, her eyes glistening with the possibility of outright tears, declaring, "Bless your heart, child. Sara babysat my Darlene a couple times, drew lots of pitchers of her, most I still got put away somewhere."

One of the legal aides arrived to join their meeting. Back to business, Phrekka inquired about the properties in question.

"You know we hold the one listing," the agent answered. "The other's owned by the bank, but I have authority to negotiate it, subject to approval." She mentioned the name of their new banker friend down the street, and Geoffrey strongly suspected that whatever Phrekka planned would proceed with much facility.

"We have another site already selected, but the purchase agreement specified closing by end-of-day today, and now they're causing delays. If we can do this—" She gestured toward the papers the woman held. "—*Faster*, then the sale is yours."

She nearly gasped, bobbing her head, then seemed to think of something. "Oh, I'm not sure."

"I can get all this drawn up in time," the aide offered, "but a title search and inspections could take longer."

"Mr. Drousseau will waive both," Phrekka said.

"No title insurance?" the agent gasped.

Phrekka asked the aide, "You found no other registered liens, correct?"

"Yes—"

"Mr. Lewis is an honest man, is he not?"

"I'll vouch for him," the woman said.

"Good. Mr. Drousseau can afford to devote his life to ruining Mr. Lewis's if any illegal misrepresentations are made." Everybody smiled. "That settled, let's agree on price." She looked at the paper, shook her head, then said, "We could get him on the phone, spend the next half-hour negotiating, then settle for ten-percent lower, but Mr. Drousseau will agree to these figures if you'll provide the courtesy of having the utilities activated today. In particular, we need a phone number confirmed for our paperwork by this afternoon, one that can be expanded to multiple lines, plus a separate private number in the cottage. Mr. Drousseau will authorize the bank to provide whatever funds are needed for this."

It wouldn't take a clairvoyant to read the agent's thoughts.

The attorney told her, "I'll start on the sale agreement, deed, and tax filings while you contact the utilities."

"Yes. Yes! I'll call Gumper and get him down here from Tupelo for the closing." Then she realized something. "Oh my, there's a mortgage involved, too."

"The bank is already preparing for that," Phrekka said, surprising her. Then to the aide, "Now you have the address to list on the corporate filing."

He nodded and smiled, obviously enjoying the efficient pace of Phrekka's calculated and deceptively casual style.

The meeting broke, the aide off to his various tasks, Geoffrey finding himself in the car as Phrekka drove toward Pamela's trailer. She gave him another paper, explaining, "We need to convince her, and she knows and trusts you more, so I think you should be the one who makes the offer. Feel free to change anything there you want."

He grinned at that, her letting him have some fun, barely giving him time to study the information before they arrived.

Andy-Geoff intercepted them, announcing before they could even step out, "Today's my last day of school, and Mawma's, too, and I got me a three-leg frog in the bathtub." He pounced on Geoffrey, wrestled a bit, then wound up climbing aboard for a piggy-back ride to the trailer. Pamela insisted on hugging them before she would let anybody inside.

"I hope you're not busy," Geoffrey started.

"Oh no, I'm taking the final test today, but I know it all backwards and forwards, so ain't no use in studying, which means I'm trying not to think about it, so I'm killing time dusting things that ain't dusty."

"Well, I spent all morning pretending to help Phrekka while she set up a non-profit foundation named after Sara. It's gonna buy or make copies of as many of her sketches as we can find, then have an exhibit at her gallery in Sausalito and do fund-raisers and give art scholarships for kids, plus whatever else we can think of." He glanced at Phrekka, her cue.

"Permanent *and* traveling exhibits, collectors' books, and—who knows—maybe something like a documentary or movie on the story of her life."

"We need to hire a foundation director to run it all—and we'll provide whatever advisors are needed to help—so we're looking for someone who knows computer accounting and is familiar with Sara's art, who knows many of the local people she would need to contact, somebody qualified to authenticate that each sketch is really Sara's."

Pamela's expression changed from astonishment to delight as she noticed the obviously tailor-made specifications.

Geoffrey continued, "The board of directors would draft long-term plans. That's Phrekka and me, plus Charles, who's Phrekka's friend and business partner, and Marva—"

"She runs my art corporation," Phrekka supplied, "an expert who's very well-connected in the art world."

Geoffrey explained, "So if you're interested in a three-year contract, here's the salary we're offering." He showed her the paper, then had to grab her to keep her from staggering, a major hug his reward. Phrekka got hugged, too, then Geoffrey again, so the little one decided to climb up on Geoffrey's back for another of his macho versions of a not-a-hug hug.

"There are some fringe benefits," Phrekka prodded.

"Oh yeah," Geoffrey continued. "The headquarters will be in my parents' old house—which, apparently, we're *buying* this afternoon, along with the adjoining property and pond—and we think it would be beneficial to have you nearby, so the director gets the cottage rent-free—" She squealed and grabbed him again. "—And a company vehicle."

"Your choice," Phrekka added, "but we recommend a mini-van so you can carry artwork *and* groups of rowdy little boys."

"What's this about a publicist?" Geoffrey asked.

Phrekka explained, "He's meeting us at the hotel in thirty minutes." To Pamela, "Are you available for an hour or so?"

"Honey, I got all the time you need."

Andy-Geoff's patience used up, he tugged at his mother, demanding, "What's this mean?"

She knelt and held him in front of her, her eyes glistening with excitement. "We're gonna help Geoffrey and Phrekka find Sara's sketches and show them to lots of people."

He barely had time to grin before she squeezed all the air out of him.

Geoffrey examined the back of the paper. "This is our mission statement: To honor the memory of Sara Drousseau, to share her vision with the world, and to encourage children to discover and nurture the artist within."

That made Pamela mist up, and suddenly another round of hugs ensued before they wrestled shoes onto Andy-Geoff for a trip to meet the publicist.

They found him waiting with a photographer in the suite. A thin man who towered over them, he started with several photographs of Pamela and Geoffrey holding the sketch of a happy threesome eating cotton candy at the carnival. The photographer hurried out to print and transmit the shots, leaving them discussing the stories behind Sara's *scatches* and Geoffrey's return to Laurel.

"I have a one o'clock with the local reporter for tomorrow's edition," the publicist confirmed. "So how will you avoid driving up the prices through rampant speculation?"

Phrekka suggested, "Let's advertise a flat rate for outright purchase, a lower one if they want a high-quality print to replace it, and an even lower one for those who want to keep their original but are willing to let us make a print for ourselves."

"Good," Geoffrey agreed. "I'm sure some will have sentimental value, the people who knew Sara, maybe sketches of themselves or their family members. It wouldn't honor Sara to take gifts from the people she made them for. Hey, let's make part of Pamela's job collecting notes on the story behind each one. That would make a great display, little cards next to the sketches telling their background, maybe a photograph of the subject, something that also tells the story of Sara's life."

Phrekka smiled approval, her eyes sparkling.

A call from the real-estate agent interrupted them just as they concluded their interviews, providing their new foundation phone number in time to include in the article.

They returned Pamela and Andy-Geoff with time to spare.

Pamela asked, "Can I start moving stuff to the cottage when me and Andy-Geoff get back from school?"

"You know where the keys are hidden," Geoffrey quipped.

She smiled, suggesting another round of hugs would be in order, a motion carried, seconded, and approved unanimously.

"Now," Phrekka said, "let's get something accomplished." Geoffrey could only shake his head. He thought they'd already done that much and then some.

It turns out she had a whirlwind shopping spree in mind. They started with a print shop in town, ordering business cards and letterhead and other various forms and documents. They crossed the street to an office-supply, ordering ten of these and a dozen of those, all to be delivered first thing tomorrow. Then they selected computer equipment, copier, scanner, postal meter, machinery for collation and mass-mailing, plus other items for good measure. They tried several furniture stores until they found one Phrekka liked, opening an account and authorizing for Pamela Greenstone to choose whatever she needed, the name of their favorite banker and a quick phone call earning them preferred-customer status. They followed that with a similar deal at the mini-van dealership, a pre-negotiated discount on whatever Pamela chose, the hint of a lot more business where that came from. The salesman acted like he'd be willing to throw in his first-born.

Returning to the office suite, they found Gumper Lewis and his agent waiting, the documents prepared. Phrekka checked the miscellaneous charges, then called the bank to have a draft sent over, everybody chatting while they waited. Gumper didn't need much encouragement to regale the crowd with a compendium of his various successful business exploits. Finally, the discussion turned to that ill-fated day.

"I was the one found you, remember?" Gumper asked.

Geoffrey's heart started pounding as he recalled the horrible sounds, the odor, stumbling toward his house . . . Dead birds and squirrels lay sprawled in the yard, then somebody zoomed up on a bike, dropping it to grab Geoffrey by the hand and hurry him down the path, away from danger, away from the horrible sights.

"You kept me away from the gas?" Geoffrey asked.

Gumper nodded, swallowing hard, the room quiet as everybody paused.

"Now's your chance to pay me back," Gumper said quietly. "I have a sketch Sara made for me, a big two-by-three footer. I'm standing next to my bike folding newspapers, a flat shoe on one foot and that big platform-lift on the other." He swallowed hard. "I used to be *real* self-conscious, thought I was a freak, but Sara always told me I was handsome, that my leg was just another thing that made me special. She drew me that sketch to show me." He rubbed his eyes, embarrassed by the sudden show of emotion. "I never saw myself the same way again after that," he said, looking at some far-off point within himself. Looking back to Geoffrey, he pronounced, "I'll consider the debt repaid if you make a copy of that sketch and show the whole world that Sara thought little Gumper Lewis was an all-right boy."

"She *scaught* you," Geoffrey said, nodding approval.

The draft arrived, the closing a mere formality of signatures and handshakes; then Gumper had to hurry back to Tupelo for a meeting. Everybody exchanged contact information, Gumper vowing, "I'll be donating to the foundation, and I hold sway with a lot of people up around Tupelo who'll want to help, too."

Soon everybody cleared out, leaving Geoffrey and Phrekka alone in the suite, a set of house keys on the table whispering for attention.

"I'll understand if you want to go out there by yourself first," she offered.

He shook his head. "I said last night that doing this together is what's making it so fantastic."

She nodded, obviously pleased by his choice.

"I can't believe you did all this," he said.

"I just helped you get started," she said quietly. "Where it goes now is up to you."

He nodded, and he looked at her, feeling an overwhelming sense that he would never stop trying to move closer to her, no matter how much patience that required, until the day she would fully accept him without reluctance or fear.

"A Pamela hug?" she suggested, reading his mind.

Before he could answer, she tenderly folded herself into his arms, letting him hold her briefly, another important step that he understood shouldn't be pushed too far too fast. As he released her, he watched for her reaction, relieved by the blissful serenity he found reflected in her eyes.

Everything would be all right, and then some.

He took a deep breath, chuckling and imitating her words from this morning. "*—A contractual employee—and the amount for which I invoice you remains still to be determined.* So what's the tab, Phrekka?"

She turned and fished in her purse, and for a moment it appeared she might have an invoice already typed up, but she curled whatever she found invisibly in her fist. "Eleven dollars," she pronounced.

"Huh? That's an odd figure."

"One dollar for helping you set up the foundation."

"A good deal," he agreed. "And the rest?"

She opened her hand to offer him a ten-dollar bill. "You said you wanted to borrow this 'til Friday."

CHAPTER 18

Phrekka would help Geoffrey paint new promises for the future, together choosing from the colors of possibility, refusing to let him varnish the original scarred finish of an imperfect past. She'd wielded her considerable resources this morning to surprise him, applying the first coat as one friend anticipating the best interests of another, hoping he would see the selfless wisdom in her choice.

She had arranged to purchase his early-childhood home, not so he could revere the building as a shrine, some monument to commemorate the scenery of tragedy, but rather to offer him this rare opportunity to imbue it with new purpose, to create a memorial for the spirit of a beloved sister whose greatest accomplishments have for too long languished hidden from the world. By rejecting all temptation to cling forlornly to the loss and grief it symbolized, they would affirm that life is a work in progress, that through repainting and daring to risk new veneers to the storms of circumstance and fate it becomes possible to find acceptance, to find new meaning and new relevance for what might otherwise be lost.

Geoffrey had resolved to share Sara's sketches with others, to resurrect and breathe new life into the people and impressions she'd cared enough to capture, and now this foundation would present exciting new ways to reach a growing audience of kindred souls and thus honor her with a legacy for generations to come, to learn more about her through the eyes of others than he ever could by keeping her selfishly to himself. Facing the harsh realities of his own past would necessarily be an important step, but only in the context of moving forward. That he wanted Phrekka to be a part of this proved him ready to join her in painting new layers of triumph together, in new textures and unimaginable new colors. Phrekka loved Geoffrey, and she knew in her heart that what he needed, what he wanted, what he would embrace . . . would be the constantly transcending hues of change.

"It needs a new coat of paint," she pronounced as they paused before the great porch, Geoffrey clutching a set of keys in his hand.

"New gutters, too," he agreed.

A growling Chrysler roared toward them, its tail a trailing cloud of scattering gravel and billowing dust, all manner of home furnishings jutting from its windows. It parked and sputtered so a determined mother and her boisterous little boy could join Phrekka and Geoffrey standing before the house. Andy-Geoff stopped fidgeting and stood by solemnly, perhaps sensing the gravity of what lay ahead.

Pamela whispered, "It's like I expect her to come right out that door—only, she's still eighteen, and she doesn't recognize me now that I'm older."

"She would know us, Pammy," Geoffrey insisted. "She would."

She nodded. "She'd like Phrekka, too—be good friends in no time."

Phrekka was pleased to see how much Geoffrey liked that idea, and she liked it, too.

He responded, "She would consider me very lucky to have such a friend."

Pamela smiled at Phrekka, then glanced awkwardly toward the front door. "I can go start unpacking," she offered, "—come back in a while if you'd rather have some time to yourselves."

Geoffrey sighed. "I'd rather we all do this together, now, if that's okay."

She nodded again like she'd expected that.

They stepped inside, then stood frozen, Pamela the first to explain the confusion in Geoffrey's face. "It looks so *different*."

He gazed around, surprised, relieved maybe, hard to read. "It's the same place, but it's been remodeled, and the furniture is all changed—" He took a deep breath, and his relief showed more obviously. Expecting to find the naked ghosts of his own past, he'd discovered them dressed in new finery for this reunion.

Too late for varnish, the house had already been painted over.

Pamela said, "It's been fifteen years, Geoffrey."

"It seems like everything should have stopped back then, waited for me to come back, not gone on without me."

They stood there for a full minute; then Phrekka brought them back to the present, pointing out, "We need to call in a cleaning crew." She traced a line in the dust on a table, a clear invitation for Andy-Geoff to start drawing finger pictures on all the flat surfaces.

As they walked through the house, Geoffrey and Pamela reminisced, noted familiar objects, recounted tales, rated the changes, and mourned the losses; but they punctuated their narrative with increasingly frequent remarks about potential: set up the office here, store files there, hang a Sara sketch at the center of this . . . Not content to limit their vision to fleeting glimpses of a bygone era, they searched for Sara's unique brand of phoenix, seeing the hope of new meanings and new directions bathed in the rising light of potential and renewal.

Eager to show Phrekka his bedroom, Geoffrey registered utter surprise to find it completely transformed, converted to a bathroom, the fabled dresser of the *Sweet Dreams* sketch missing, the hardwood floor of his halting first steps now tiled.

Pamela quickly led them to where Sara's room looked across the back porch toward the woods, and she froze in the doorway, surprised. "It's just like she left it," she breathed reverently.

"Almost like she's still here," Geoffrey agreed.

All stood there transfixed as if waiting for something important to happen, maybe anticipating a sign, listening for Sara's song, expecting her gentle touch, hoping to glimpse her face among the dancing motes stirred by their passing explorations. Pamela finally broke the spell, crossing quietly to the dresser, pausing for a moment, then opening the top drawer. Everybody gathered around, all visibly disappointed to find only dust undisturbed by hands that would never return.

"We should leave her room as is," Geoffrey suggested, "maybe for overnight guests or whatever, at least for now."

Pamela agreed, and Phrekka knew this would be right, protecting the heart to mitigate any risk of rejuvenating its body. They lingered for a moment longer, then moved on, closing the varnished door behind them.

The entire kitchen had been repainted, walls and ceiling, doors and cabinets and shelves, but inside the broom-closet door, Geoffrey found the only surface not covered over, the original stained finish with a series of ascending lines and notations scored by a ball-point pen:

—5 years
—4 years
—3 years
—2 years
—18 months
—12 months

Sara never lived to mark her little brother's sixth birthday, to preserve another reminder of how small he'd once been even as she celebrated how tall he'd grown. Geoffrey winced and covered his face, then swallowed hard as if tasting the bitter harvest of overwhelming loss. Without concern, Andy-Geoff suddenly positioned his back against the door, trying both to stand still and look behind himself at the same time, measuring up. This simple and innocent curiosity dispelled the tension, soliciting chuckles from Pamela and Geoffrey. The little guy, at nearly six, the age of Geoffrey's tragedy, towered a full inch taller than the boy who'd stood in this very spot some fifteen years before.

"Let's make sure we mark it on his birthday," Geoffrey suggested with a gleam in his eye, "and keep the tradition going." Another little boy would dwell here, the next generation, this passing of the torch, a new coat of acrylic in the vibrant colors of exuberant youth.

Geoffrey located the pull-down attic ladder, relating his penchant for sneaking up there against strict orders. The women waited while he and his little namesake crawled up, the beam of their ancient flashlight piercing the shroud of mystery.

"It's full of boxes," Geoffrey called down. "Most are files from the lawyer Ms.

Lewis worked for."

"That was Bill Foranower," Pamela called up. "I heard he died a few years back, probably had the records sent to Ms. Lewis for storage."

"Oh wow," he said quietly, barely audible. Then louder, he called down, "I found some of my old toys, and Sara's stuff and—and here's more of her drawings! Dozens of them!" He brought down the sketches first, followed by a half-dozen various boxes, and a fat file marked *Drousseau*. "This was in the lawyer's A-through-D carton."

Pamela started to summon her son, but Geoffrey put a hand on her arm, suggesting, "He's building a monster with my old Creep-Kit. It'll keep him busy for a while."

She smiled knowingly, calling up, "Don't get into anything else, creep-boy!"

Phrekka spread out the sketches, propping them against furniture, everybody drawn to the images captured and preserved by Sara's unique vision, rendered alive by her gentle touch, scenes now narrated alternately by the only two survivors who would know: the Casey brothers, wrestling in the grass, Ron letting little Kent win; Geoffrey helping Gumper fold newspapers, the young assistant's first job, the pride of responsibility aglow in his face; Becky Tessin eating an ice-cream cone, drips down the front of her dress, big gleaming eyes peering through Coke-bottle glasses, butterflies as pigtail barrettes; the Bibby boys, all five lined up big-to-small, a receiving line of barely restrained frenzy punctuated by a profusion of freckles; the Drousseau family—

Sara at nine or ten, Alain and Rachel full-grown, the first image of his parents.

Geoffrey stood there motionless, enthralled; then he slowly sat on the floor and moved closer, studying it, nodding in recognition. Alain looked very handsome, very much like a Frenchman in his beret, dark hair feathered over his ears, a thick mustache. Rachel showed delicate features, the softer, more feminine version of her brother Ernest, long curly tresses not quite as dark as Alain's . . .

"Mom must have been sleeping with the mailman," Geoffrey joked, reaching up to touch his own blond hair, chuckles breaking the tension.

Pamela explained, "They always said you got your hair from an ornery grandfather, that it was a good thing you didn't get his meanness, too."

Pamela and Phrekka started unpacking boxes while Geoffrey continued to study the sketches. They found mostly trinkets of no major significance, a disappointing lack of photo albums or other revealing mementos, so a stack of school yearbooks piqued Phrekka's curiosity most.

Then Pamela found Sara's diary. "Geoffrey, I'd like to go through this first—you know, in case there are personal things not meant for a little brother."

He nodded, and Phrekka could see his gratitude for this discretion, his understanding of the wisdom in her suggestion.

While Pamela started leafing through the pages, pausing here and there to read, Geoffrey tore himself away from the sketches to look through the legal file.

Phrekka opened the seventh-grade annual from Gulfport Middle School, disappointed to find Sara Drousseau listed as *Photo Not Available.* When she opened the eighth-grade book, a sheaf of thumbnail sketches fell out, scattering across the floor. She looked up and noticed Geoffrey sitting Indian-style, his face buried in his hands, papers spread around him. She moved closer to him. "Geoffrey?"

Wordlessly, he showed her his birth certificate, pointing at the registration date, nearly three weeks after his birthday. He gestured toward a court petition, the words jumping at her:

> . . . full parental rights and responsibilities for the minor child, hereafter known as *[Minor Child]* Geoffrey Drousseau, shall be granted per the Order of this Court to *[Adoptive Father]* Alain Drousseau; and *[Adoptive Mother]* Rachel Drousseau . . .

"The *Drousseaus* adopted you as an infant?!" she asked, incredulous, the proof in her hands.

Geoffrey finally looked at her, his eyes searching for understanding, his face tense. They both glanced toward Pamela, but found her staring open-mouthed at the scattered thumbnail sketches, the one on top a depiction of Sara at about the age of twelve or thirteen . . .

And very pregnant.

Geoffrey buried his face again.

Pamela, in hushed tones, recited a passage from Sara's diary, the date three days after Geoffrey's birth:

> *I guess I understand now why everybody says I'm too young to be a mother. It wouldn't be fair to him. I know this has been hard on Mom, but I'm glad Dad finally said yes to her idea. We'll move to a new town where nobody knows my secret, and they'll adopt him so he can grow up without ever knowing about my mistakes. I love Geoffrey with all my heart, so even though I have to pretend to be his big sister for the rest of my life, that's OK. It's the only way I can keep my beautiful baby boy.*

"Sara was my mom," Geoffrey breathed through his hands, a fleeting concept more real when spoken aloud, the layers stripped away to reveal a past marked indelibly in the grain. He looked into the distance, his eyes glistening with confusion.

Phrekka put her arms around him and held him close.

Pamela touched his hand, curling her fingers around his.

"Oh Sara," he breathed, "the more I learn, the less I know."

All waited expectantly, the friends of a man poised on the threshold of an uncertain future, watching him strip the successive layers of a glossed-over past, the little boy within him still searching for the unvarnished truth . . .

"If Sara was my mom, then who's my dad?"

CHAPTER 19

Like reading a story from the middle, Geoffrey found himself playing lead character in the pages of an ancient memoir, its ending a tragedy already revealed, the opening act a mystery yet to be solved.

"I want to read her diary," he said quietly, his pervading reluctance to intrude giving way to one of determination.

Pamela nodded, closing the cover and cradling the collection of Sara's private ruminations reverently. "Remember, Geoffrey," she cautioned, "Sara wanted to protect you, for people to see you just as you are, not as some story of how you come about." With that, she passed it to him, then stood and called for her son.

As Geoffrey and Phrekka rose, too, he reminded her, "In that passage you read, she expected to pretend for the rest of her life. She did, as long as she lived, and now we don't have to pretend anymore."

"She never expected to die so young . . ." Pamela looked away, lost for a second. "I just wish she'd trusted me more—"

"Don't think that," he protested. "Remember what she'd been through, how scared she must have felt. Don't judge her based on all you've experienced since then, not after all this time."

She looked up, still profoundly sad, the faint lines in her face more pronounced than ever. "You're right. You know, I think she *would* have told me by now, us grown up, you older, me with a boy of my own . . . but I wonder if she ever would have told you."

He glanced at Phrekka standing at his side, remembering the lesson she'd been trying to impart. "What's done is done," he breathed. "What matters is *not* what anybody thought might happen, but what *did* happen. She's gone now, and I've come looking for answers, so I think she would understand and want me to find the truth."

Phrekka nodded agreement, placing her hand tenderly over his heart, and she said, "Sara used the word 'mistakes,' but those don't exist anymore. She made everything right in her brief time."

"She'd be so proud to see you today," Pamela added, both women very close to him now, Andy-Geoff watching from the portal above. "Bless your heart, Geoffrey; I hope you find what you're looking for. Just remember, we're all human, and no matter what, she shore did love you, and she did right by you." She started to grow misty-eyed, but she managed to stem the tide, giving him a big hug, then one for Phrekka and another for Geoffrey.

He said, "I just hope her diary tells me who my father is."

Pamela suggested, "Knowing Sara, she loved him very much. I always wondered why she didn't want boyfriends; now it looks like she just never found another one good enough."

"I wonder if he knows what happened to me," he said, suddenly struck by the possibility he might find him and come to know him. He turned the diary over in his hands.

Pamela offered the hint of a knowing smile. "We'll be next door unpacking. Holler if you need anything." With a wordless mother's look, she summoned her son and led him out, Andy-Geoff glancing back as if to offer his support in matters too weighty for a little guy to fully comprehend.

Geoffrey and Phrekka moved to the divan in the front room. She settled in beside him, her legs curled under, head resting against his shoulder.

"You knew," he whispered.

"That you wanted me to stay?"

"Yeah."

She nodded. "And you knew I'd understand if you asked me to leave you alone."

He chuckled under his breath. "I don't think that'll *ever* happen."

He opened the diary, the two of them reading together. The first page showed a date two days after his birth, a detailed description of Sara's adorable blue-eyed, blond-haired little angel, adding:

> *I knew Dad would change his mind once he got to hold Geoffrey. He just called the lawyer and said we still hadn't decided about letting that woman have him. I'll quit school if I have to, but I won't give up my baby.*

The next page included the passage Pamela had read aloud, the decision to have her own parents adopt him. The following entries described Geoffrey's development, his bout with colic, Sara's own recovery. Then they found one written in the bold slashes of frustration and anger:

> *That county worker showed up again asking all her questions. She's mad I won't tell her who Geoffrey's father is. She figured out it's Zach 'cos he was my boyfriend. She says since he was only 14 when it happened all they'll do is get him some counseling. I know she's a liar. But it don't matter 'cos I won't say. This has already been too hard on Dad and specially Mom. I won't ever see Zach again after we move and I won't ever have another boyfriend, at least not till after Geoffrey's grown up.*

Several notes followed, confirming the adoption and their move north to Laurel.

"Zach," Geoffrey pronounced. "That narrows it down," he added with irony. Then he faded for a moment, tested the idea, and listened to the word, whispering, "Zach."

> *There's a beautiful pond in the woods here. I took Geoffrey out and we sat beside it and watched butterflies. He looked more happy than I can say in words. Dad says I draw good and I should start making pictures of him.*

A few weeks later:

> *Mom's not doing so good. She's taking so many pills now she don't know who I am. She won't hold Geoffrey anymore. I guess that's good 'cos I'm afraid she'll hurt him, but people are gonna gossip if she doesn't start acting more like a mother.*

After that, the dates showed Sara's entries coming after increasingly longer increments of time, the narratives mostly exercises in finding new words to describe her growing baby and how much she loved him. Geoffrey felt his grief rising, his frustration at knowing he could never assure her that he understands. He wanted to fling himself against that barrier between life and death even as a moth flies relentlessly at a light he can never penetrate, both responding to an innate need, neither with any hope for success. The question he most wanted to ask her started to dim in his mind, the illumination of facts not as important as the glow of affection he wanted to express, and he wished desperately for one more chance to tell her how much he loved her, to burst from the woods and find her where she'd fallen and hold her one last brief moment to tell her good-bye . . . to replay the tragedy so he could help Sara achieve Phrekka's concept of a good death as she moves toward the pure, colorless light. He swallowed hard and felt his wounds salved by Phrekka's healing presence, then turned the page . . .

> *Geoffrey looked into my eyes today and he spoke to me. He doesn't know words yet, but I could hear him. My little boy said he loves me. He said he forgives me for the secret game we have to play. Someday he'll grow up and be on his own, then he'll find somebody and fall in love, but I'll always be part of him, and he'll always be part of me.*

He lowered the book, feeling himself pulled in, floating freely yet somehow tethered by his tentative bonds with Phrekka. He realized his head rested against her shoulder, and that she held him tenderly, and he knew she would always be a part of him, too. The lyrical strains of Sara's song undulated like dancing wisps floating through the house, and for the first time he could hear snatches of words, and he felt her touching his heart as she sang, *I'll always be right here . . .*

He held Phrekka closer, but she tensed slightly, the unpracticed intimacy catching her off guard, so he eased his embrace just enough to remind her that he posed no threat. This saddened him, bumping again into that incomprehensible barrier, knowing he could never dare fling himself moth-like against this wall of smoked glass through which shined the warm light of her tenderness, this shield to deflect the harsh glare of her secrets. He resisted the urge to guess about its source, trusting and respecting that overriding reflex to protect against denizens real or imagined, understanding that people like Sara and Phrekka and even Geoffrey can love somebody even while that very feeling renders them afraid. He knew Phrekka's reticence must be rooted in some kind of fear, not of him, but of something recalled at the instant she would give herself entirely to him. He admired her tenacity in defying all that conspires to draw her away, the courage summoned each time she dares to step further into the blinding light that exposes her vulnerabilities, to risk everything in her determined devotion to Geoffrey . . . all of which proves she truly must love him, indeed.

He held this conviction closer than he dared hold her, and he knew this would sustain him forever, no matter what circumstance and fate might cast between them.

The next entry jumped five months ahead to Geoffrey's first birthday. With only a few pages remaining, it looked like the mystery about young Zach would remain unsolved. The momentarily imprudent expression of teenage love between Zach and Sara would condemn Geoffrey to remain forever the lost son of a father he would never know.

Then he found a page with only two lines:

> *Zach turned 16 today. I wonder where he is, if he ever thinks about what happened, if he wonders about his son.*

Geoffrey's second birthday marked a long description of how he'd learned to walk and talk, loved to play in the edge of the pond, and kept a pet caterpillar from whose cocoon would eventually emerge a beautiful butterfly. The next entry jumped ahead to his fourth birthday, followed by another from the autumn of that year.

> *I broke up with Jeremy today. I stayed in my bedroom and cried. I wouldn't even let Geoffrey in because he would just cry, too. I knew I shouldn't try to have a boyfriend. Will I always compare every boy with Zachary Holmes?*

"Zachary Holmes," Geoffrey said. "Now I know his name, and I have his birthdate."

"That should be enough," Phrekka said. "A good investigator . . ."

He turned to the last page, an entry with no hand-written words, just a pasted newspaper clipping dated weeks before Sara's death.

CYCLIST RECOVERS FROM COMA

Gulfport—Doctors at Gulfport Medical Center report the Gulfport teen injured in Tuesday's three-vehicle accident has emerged from his coma. Zachary Holmes, 19, suffered severe fractures to his pelvis and both legs, but is expected to recover from head trauma.

According to witnesses, Holmes was driving his motorcycle south on 34th Ave. when he struck a car driven by Charlene Watlick, 81, of Gulfport, which had turned left from 28th St. into his path. A car driven by Hardy Bledsoe, 40, also of Gulfport, skidded into both vehicles, pinning Holmes under the wreckage.

The drivers of both cars were treated and released. Watlick was issued citations for reckless driving and failure to yield.

Doctors expect to transfer Holmes to Biloxi Regional after another day of observations.

A driver's-license photo flanked the article, Zachary Holmes at about eighteen or nineteen, a boyish-looking fellow with silky blond hair feathered down below his ears, his faint mustache downy, unshaven patchy wisps on his cheeks and the underside of his chin.

Geoffrey stared dumbfounded, holding the page close as he looked at the unkempt mirror image of himself . . .

And his father looked back.

"I have his name and birthdate, and I know he lived in Gulfport fifteen years ago," Geoffrey told the private investigator over the phone. "I checked, but found no phone number currently listed in that area."

"If he gets paychecks with taxes deducted," the detective told him, "I can find him anywhere in the country. If he's still in Mississippi, I'll cross-check drivers' records, too. Address and phone number is all you want?"

He imagined walking into his father's life unannounced, the disruption it might cause, especially since the man probably has a family, with children who would be Geoffrey's . . . An illegitimate son's very existence might be a shameful secret. "Marital status and children—are those easy to find out fast?"

"If he's paying social security. I'll also look at the national registry for child support. Beyond that, I can check other sources locally once I know where he is."

"Can you do all this tonight?"

"Not without risking my contacts. It's best first thing in the morning when people are already at their computers."

"As soon as you can," Geoffrey urged him. After twenty years, every minute would seem like hours. He imagined his father languishing in the final stages of a terminal illness, wishing on his deathbed he could see his lost son . . .

And Geoffrey arrives one minute too late.

Geoffrey enjoyed watching Phrekka eat carry-out pizza, the foursome christening Pamela's new home. Phrekka began in a proper manner, using her knife and fork, watching the little one with delight until she relented and let him teach her an entirely new approach. First, he picked off all the toppings, buzzing each morsel around in the air before capturing it with a deft frog-like flick of the tongue followed by announcing, "*Ribbet-ribbet.*" Then he peeled away the cheese and stretched it taffy-like into various shapes, the final result hanging from his mouth, a misshapen, jaundiced human tongue. Tired of that, he licked off the sauce, then tore the crust into great chunks and chewed with gusto. Phrekka managed to add nuances of sophistication to the procedure, a hint of polite decorum, but she ultimately snared just as many "bugs," and her own ersatz tongue even achieved an impressive if not sensual level of artistry.

Geoffrey watched these antics, trying to ignore the visions that kept distracting him: reunion scenarios conjured from the overactive imagination of a disenfranchised son; young Zachary holding hands with Sara, the agony in his tender face as she's taken from him, his child denied a father, circumstance and fate conspiring to threaten prosecution if he acknowledges responsibility for his mistake; Sara's eyes fearing somebody will take her baby, the look of steeled determination to protect him at any cost, the relief in deception that allows her vicarious fulfillment of her natural role; the shy smiles of all boys who ever liked Sara, young suitors never imagining her secret that puts the welfare of a young child above all else; Geoffrey's future with Phrekka, together cuddling their own blond-tressed little girl and cinnamon-banged little boy . . .

He looked across the table and saw her gazing at him, and he knew that if young Zachary had felt even the slightest glimmers of the same kind of affection Geoffrey felt for Phrekka at this very moment, then his heart must surely have broken beyond repair. She smiled at him, then placed a mushroom slice on the tip of her nose, crossed her eyes, and snatched it with one practiced flick of the tongue.

"*Ribbet.*"

Everybody lingered out front for a moment, but rumors of blood feast quickly spread throughout the mosquito community, so Pamela limited her good-night hugs to one per customer. Phrekka had some kind of private communication going with Andy-Geoff, something that involved noises and tongue antics, but nobody found it appropriate to ask.

They drove back to the hotel; then Geoffrey walked Phrekka to her suite and hurried back to his own to brush his teeth and freshen up. He returned and found her gazing across the courtyard from her balcony, adorned in a long, flowing robe that sparkled like crystalline glitter. Scented candles flickered here and there, bathing the room in a soft glow, reflections of serenity shining in the wise eyes of the stranded sailfishes.

"Hi, Geoffrey," she greeted him.

He joined her there, standing close, tasting the Mississippi night air, not so humid for a change, a cool breeze stirring their hair. All at once, he felt very tired, and he yawned. She yawned almost simultaneously, then giggled at the coincidence.

"Couple of old codgers," she joked.

"You're holding up nicely," he countered, "though you *are* three months *younger* than me."

They stood there for a moment. She closed her eyes, tilted her head back, and shook out her hair, then breathed deeply. He could feel the air swirling around and through him, tickling here and there, filling him with life and siphoning tension with each warm breath. He wanted to hold her, but instead he reached and touched her hand, letting her curl her fingers around his.

"It would be too hard for me to talk about," she sighed, surprising him by boldly broaching the subject.

"I just need to know if something is *still* hurting you, and how I can stop it."

She shook her head slowly. "It's from the past," she said, gazing into the rippling waters of the pool, breeze-stirred undulations chasing each other to lap longingly at the barriers of containment. "It's my fault that I let it keep bothering me."

"No," he insisted, dumbfounded at the very idea. "How could that be *your* fault?" His anger at whatever had scared her rose in his chest, his white-knuckled hand gripping the balustrade, throat constricted, heart pounding again. "If you're not happy, we'll work on that together. But however else you feel—" He stopped, lost for words.

"How I *feel*, deep inside, is wonderful, like nothing I've experienced before, and I hope that would make you very happy. It's how I *react* that I can't control; that's what hurts you."

He shook his head vigorously. "You've never hurt me."

"Haven't I?"

"No," he insisted, his face resolute, no way to be any more clear without shouting it across the courtyard, taking out an ad, declaring it to the world . . . something he would gladly do, be there any chance it might help.

She closed her eyes and breathed deeply. "I almost did yesterday, trying to withdraw to *avoid* hurting you."

"But you didn't, and from now on we'll face everything together."

She turned toward him, then folded herself tenderly into his arms, resting her head against his shoulder, her warm breath kissing his neck. He could feel her trembling, but knew it couldn't be from him touching her, that she dared to let her feelings swirl around them both.

"Someone held me down and threatened to take me against my will, taunting me that there was nothing I could do. Well, I guess I *have* been doing something ever since, making sure I never get in that position again. Now I do want to be close, and I know in my heart you're the person I should never fear, but the part of me that still makes me act scared . . . I can't make that go away."

"Don't even try," he urged, forcing calm even while trembling with rage and wanting to lash out at whoever had done this. He knew he loved her, loved her in ways he never thought possible, and he knew that for her to stand here at this moment and let him hold her despite the panic such a simple act induced, then her love must surely have carried her past a barrier that would never again completely contain her passions.

"Why *not* try?" she asked.

"It's there for a reason. If we deny it, it'll never trust us. If we ignore it, it'll demand attention. Let's humor it, don't let it win, don't force it to lose, just prove that its job is done, and keep proving that until it gets tired of playing and goes away on its own."

"But that's not fair to you."

"Letting it win wouldn't be fair to either of us."

"What if this is as close as I can ever get, like we are at this moment?"

"Then you're giving me everything you can, and that's exactly what I want." He held her tighter, confident of her desires, knowing that right then they both needed it.

She sighed good-naturedly. "You'd stand here like this for me all night, wouldn't you?"

"Bring me an IV and a catheter; I'm going for a week."

She chuckled, looking up at him now. "It seems like whenever I'm being childish and immature, you just act like a kid with me."

"I'll bet you were the prettiest little girl in the sandbox."

"I *know* you were the handsomest little boy in the pond."

"Imagine how impressed you'd be if Sara hadn't drawn those reeds in front of me."

They both laughed awkwardly, but it felt good.

She eased out of his hug, reached up and straightened some strands of his hair, searched his eyes, and said, "I believe you."

"You better, 'cause I'm way too shy to prove it."

She snorted. "That's not what I meant!"

Smiling, he assured her, "Your loss."

She glanced inside. "The candles are burning out."

"Sounds like a metaphor for something."

"Yeah," she said wistfully, lost for a moment.

"I could pull the couch over like last night so we can watch the sky and fall asleep together— I'll try not to drool this time."

She smiled, then thought for a moment, glancing inside again. "Well . . . really, my neck was sore all day. I know this sounds stupid, but what if we propped up some pillows and climbed into the canopy bed, but agreed in advance that we would limit ourselves to holding hands?"

Actually, he liked that *very* much, but he preferred not to sound too much like a lecher by admitting it so readily. "But Phrekka," he whined, "that's a *girls'* bed."

She looked indignant. "*This* girl invited you to stay. Of course, if you'd rather go find a *boys'* bed and sleep by yourself—"

He made a rude noise. "Well, can we at least curl each other's hair and swap make-up tips?"

"I could probably learn a lot from you. What about dress code? Night gown for me . . ."

"Shorts and t-shirt for me," he offered.

Looking very pleased, she cupped his cheek, then hurried off to the bathroom to do whatever it is women do. By the time she emerged, he'd retrieved his shorts from next door and nestled into bed, a construction of pillows propped and waiting. He started, amazed by her transformation into an ethereal goddess in flowing wisps of cream chiffon, exotic, exquisite, stunning. Anticipating a platonic night beside such a vision, he almost wished she'd chosen plaid flannel and bunny slippers, soup-can hair rollers and a faceful of that green goop used by women who could never dream of achieving Phrekka's beauty.

She blew out most of the candles, leaving two flickering side-by-side in the balcony breeze, approval sparkling in the sailfishes' eyes. She hesitated, then sat on the bed, lay back, and moved close to him. He settled in and offered her his hand, which she held, curling her fingers around his.

Feeling her trembling, he whispered, "We're okay, Phrekka, I promise."

She held tighter, and after a moment, her trembling stopped. She eased her head against his shoulder, a cascade of cinnamon spilling down his chest. "I never imagined this could feel so wonderful," she whispered back, suddenly yawning again. She chuckled, "Yet I feel so tired."

"It's hard work being afraid. Now it's time to rest."

"Thank you, Geoffrey," came the whisper, barely audible.

He realized he'd grown tense, too, so he willed his body to relax . . .

The candles flickered.

The breeze played a melody.

Phrekka's fragrance swirled around and through him.

He found himself breathing with the rhythms of her body, felt the air stirring with the rise and fall of her breasts, basked in the warmth of her touch, grew mesmerized by the shimmering candle-lit highlights of cinnamon strands . . .

He recalled holding her on the balcony, feeling her breath on his neck, his hand gently caressing the delicate curve at the small of her back . . .

He felt his shorts tightening, a tingling sensation pulsing with the tempo of his heartbeat, now beating synchronously with hers. He moved his hand subtly, pretending to scratch his hip, adjusting his shorts so the unnatural fold in his body could stand straight and dwell more comfortably. He knew she sensed his arousal, could read his mind, and he felt her trembling again.

"Being so close to you just makes me feel good," he assured her, afraid his words might bring apprehension, unable to think of any ploy but honesty, unashamed that she could do this to him, that he could feel this way toward her.

Her trembling stopped, her breaths coming deeper. "I feel it, too," she whispered back.

They squeezed their hands again and lay there in the shimmering light. For a man who had devoted so much energy during his teen years to learning the ways of seducing women, he knew he would never try to lead Phrekka somewhere she wasn't ready to go. He would wait for the right time, and then they would soar to an enchanted place like neither had ever imagined, together.

As the night faded, Phrekka's breathing slowed, and her body fully relaxed, her grip on his hand easing. The candles burned out almost simultaneously, as if by intent, like they understood.

"I love you," he whispered, though she slept through his words. That didn't matter, though, because he counted on something very important as he drifted into a dreamworld of wonder and bliss . . .

She already knew.

CHAPTER 20

They drove South from Hattiesburg toward Gulfport on Highway 49, Geoffrey at the wheel, Phrekka studying the map. After a lifetime seeking the merest form of tenuous connection with her own father, she'd come to play the role of navigator, leading her friend on a quest to help him achieve what she could only dream for herself.

"It should be just past Interstate-Ten, off to the right," she said, lost for a second in her ruminations.

What an astounding concept, beyond anything Phrekka ever could have imagined, the overwhelming notion of finding her father alive by simply discovering his address and following the directions of a map. As long as she could remember, she'd wished some way existed to cross the barrier between life and death, always seeking to learn something indistinct yet important from her father, wanting his approval, desiring his assurance, longing for his affection, hoping he would fill the void in her world; yet now, even as she imagined again the reunion played out in so many childhood fantasies, she noticed for the first time one pronounced difference: she no longer needed his help to find something missing from her life, but rather she wanted to show him what she'd found. One brief chance to speak with her father would shatter every haunting image she'd conjured of him drowning in the indifferent sea of fate, and it would blunt the anguish of knowing he died fearing for the baby girl destined to seek her own place in a challenging world without him. She would seize that moment of serendipity to give him the answer which would allow him to move on to the serene void of pure, colorless light . . . *Yes, Daddy, I missed you so very much, but I did what you would have wanted: helped Charles carry on your work, devoted myself to caring for Grandmamá, pursued a passion for art, found somebody who loves me, fell in love.*

Geoffrey offered her his hand, then held tightly when she gave him hers.

"I can't imagine how you must feel," she said.

"I'm ambivalent. Just because we couldn't find records of a marriage or children doesn't mean I don't have more relatives, and knowing only that he has a job at a carton-assembly factory sure doesn't tell me much about him. Plus, I don't know if he knows what happened to my mother and me. After all, Sara had moved away five years before the train wreck, so he might not even know she died, or that I survived and was adopted. I hope my showing up will be good news, but I'm worried about being a disruption to his life, or becoming a painful reminder about what he lost."

"But how will seeing him make *you* feel?"

He allowed a slight smile, acknowledging he'd thought quite a bit about that. "There's a lot of things that come to mind. Like, I wonder how much we're alike—we must be, because that's the kind of person Sara would love; and it's a chance for me to get to know the one guy who loved Sara, for him to tell me about her in ways different than Pamela; and I want to see his reaction to me as an adult, transformed from a baby to a man, just like that—" Quieter, keeping his eyes on the road, he added, "And I want him to be proud of me. At first, I just assumed he would, but then I think about it and wonder, What do I have to be proud of? My money is from my parents' deaths; I've been fired from my job; I have no clear direction—"

"You graduated from college," she interjected, saddened to see him not realizing how much he had accomplished. "You're an honest and caring person, a good man who would make any father proud."

He glanced over, admitting sheepishly, "Actually, what I'm proudest of, what I most want him to see about me, is that I deserve somebody like you—and I *do*, Miss Churán, lest you be thinking about embarrassing me when I introduce you."

"Trophy girlfriends aside," she scoffed good-naturedly, "you made the best with what you were given, and together we're going to do a lot more. That's what's important."

"I don't know," he said, unconvinced. "I took my money and just ran away like a whiny brat, but you sacrificed your education, and left your friends behind, all to look out for your grandmother when she most needed you."

"And you just returned to Iowa to take care of Marjorie, and now you're planning to do more to honor Sara, and if you find out your birth father needs your help, you'll do the right thing for him, too."

He drove in silence for a moment, then pointed out, "It's incredible to think about them being so young and so in love, their first love, Sara's only true love, and how they achieved such a level of intimacy against all that's prudent and approved, consequences be damned, sex when it's all still a mystery."

"But sex is what made him lose her," she blurted out, surprised at such intense feelings the notion engendered. "Sex ruined everything between them. She went too far and lost it all."

He looked at her with concern. Carefully, watching her reaction, he asked, "Do you worry that sex ruins relationships?"

She shook her head. "No, but it certainly changes them—I hope for the better—and Sara's experience proves it *can* all go horribly wrong."

"Are you afraid of losing *me*?"

She felt the air rush from her lungs, a vague sense of vertigo or motion sickness. She held the door handle firmly and composed herself, thinking. Finally, she breathed, "I *do* worry about losing you, but not for becoming too intimate."

"Then why?"

"For not being *able* to."

"But we *have* been intimate."

"No, I mean—"

"I know what you mean. I'm telling you we have. We've already played together at the carnival, maybe not riding the roller coaster yet, maybe not even the Ferris wheel, but we *are* on some kind of ride—" The enthusiasm in his voice grew exuberant. "It's a wild ride, and I'm hanging on tight, and maybe someday we'll be so used to looking at the roller coaster that we just get on it without even thinking." Then quieter, he explained, "I don't want to worry about strict definitions or rely on euphemisms like 'making love,' Phrekka, because we've shared as much closeness as we can right now; that's going all the way in my book."

She liked that very much, and she settled back into her seat, amazed at his casual propensity to defuse escalating tension, to act so matter-of-fact about a concept that had preoccupied her with uncountable hours of anxiety, that he could make her feel so confident about what used to terrify her. Teasing him with a nudge-nudge, she accused, "Thinking about the coaster there for a while last night, weren't you?"

He looked over and grinned. "I stayed behind the yellow safety line, and I know to keep my arms and legs inside the car at all times."

She chuckled. "Oh, here's I-Ten; let's start looking for an address."

The speed limit dropped as they passed into a developed area, warehouses and shopping plazas, access drives entering the divided highway at numerous junctures. They spotted an address, then another, and—

"There it is!" she pronounced.

"Huh? It's a run-down hotel."

Ballbusters, it appeared to be named, surrounded by pickups with confederate flags and gun racks, motorcycles—mostly Harleys—people loitering about, long hair and beards, tattoos, redneck bikers.

"I don't know about taking you in there," he said, pulling into the lot.

"We can just play it by ear, leave quickly if it looks too outrageous."

He drove around the side where an entranceway boasted the logo of *Ballbusters Lounge*. He stopped beside two guys with cigarette papers rolling a—well, she couldn't be sure what, but they certainly had a gleam in their eyes. Lowering his window, he asked, "Do people live here?"

The man jerked his thumb toward the main entrance, so Geoffrey circled back up front and parked, asking Phrekka, "Are you sure?"

She nodded, wishing she'd dressed in jeans rather than her simple dress, maybe play the Asian redneck biker chick, studded and pierced.

They were met inside by a gruff-looking black woman, her face flat, lower lip jutting out pugnaciously. "Visited here before?" she demanded, thrusting clipboards at them before they could say no. "Who you here to see?"

"Zachary Holmes," he answered, taking the forms and handing one to Phrekka.

The woman picked up a phone and said, "Two to visit Holmes."

Geoffrey completed his just as Phrekka reached the point of answering if she was on probation or parole, and if so where, for what, and is she on visitor restriction.

That done, the woman accepted their paperwork, then gestured for them to sit along the wall where several other people waited. After a few minutes, she summoned them, pointing toward the elevator. "Third floor, across the hall. Don't go anywhere else."

They thanked her and rode up. They found the door open, a small recreation room of sorts with a billiard table and vending machines. Zachary stood alone behind the table, a mix of confusion and surprise on his haggard, gaunt face. Phrekka reached for Geoffrey's hand as he practically swayed on his feet, all three staring at each other in shock. Zach prominently featured a scar down his cheek and tattoos showing below a cigarette pack tucked under his t-shirt sleeve, but his unmistakable hair told the story, silky strands, like blond gossamer, feathered down to his shoulders, and his eyes shined of deep sapphire just like Geoffrey's, but with a depth that promised visions of hardship and misery.

"You're Sara's kid," he spat with a snarling southern twang.

"And yours, too," Geoffrey said quietly, adding, "and this is Phrekka."

"You're twenty by now," he replied, ignoring the introduction. "Can't get child support no more. Whatta you want?"

Geoffrey took a deep breath. "To meet you."

"Ain't nothin' but disappointment, shoulda stayed away. You ain't gettin' nothin' off me, and I don't want nothin' off you."

"Did you know what happened to my mother?" Geoffrey asked, all three still standing awkwardly, squaring off over a game table.

"I kept track, had to worry about her comin' after me for child support, pressing charges, whatever."

"Did you know what happened to *me*?" he asked, his voice very small.

"Newspaper said you was adopted. End of story."

Phrekka felt a lump rise in her throat, Geoffrey's grip on her hand getting tighter. After living most of his life in the shadow of a man who disapproved of him, now he'd discovered the kind of father who is, in many ways, even worse . . . one who doesn't care.

Everybody stood there.

"Is that all you wanted?" Zach asked.

Geoffrey lowered his head, then looked up, his face set, resolute. "I want to know about Sara."

Zach shook his head, clearly frustrated, this intrusion on his life not yet willing to leave him alone. He reached for something, revealing a cane in his hand, then started to come around the corner of the table, barely able to walk, practically dragging one leg, struggling to keep his balance. He stopped and leaned against the edge.

"Your motorcycle accident?" Geoffrey asked, sympathetic.

Zach looked up, surprise in his face; then he narrowed his eyes, and assumed the grizzled mien of reckoned hardship again. He nodded once. "No insurance, and that old bitch had nothin' I could sue for. Needed money bad; that's how I come to get busted and land in the joint."

"You were in prison?" he asked, surprised.

Zach snorted. "You think I'm livin' in a goddamn halfway house 'cause I want to?"

"I didn't know."

"Yeah, well, I was set up. That cop's been after me ever since they couldn't get Sara to press charges."

"She wanted to protect you."

"No, she wanted to pretend you was a love baby."

"You two weren't in love?"

"Is that what you think?" His face twisted into a malevolent grin. "Statute of limitations is run out, so ain't nothin' you can do about it now."

"Answer me."

"Listen, I spent three months kissin' up to that little bitch, playin' boyfriend, tryin' to get me some o' that sweet little snatch of hers. Bitch wouldn't give it up, so one night me and Floyd got to drinkin' and went by where she was babysittin' and pressed her a bit." He grinned, showing badly chipped front teeth.

Geoffrey squeezed Phrekka's hand hard, his face flush, his breaths fast and shallow. "You pressured her even though she didn't want to?!"

"Fuckin' bitch wouldn't give it up, so I took it."

"You raped her?!"

He grunted a guttural, humorless laugh. "You know how it is to get a whiff o' some young snatch." Gesturing toward Phrekka, he added, "Hell, you must have it bad if you're fuckin' a dirty gook—"

Geoffrey let go of her hand, curled his into a fist, his chest heaving now, beads of sweat on his forehead. Phrekka tried to quell her trembling, pushing aside her own resurrected fears of violation, concentrating on Geoffrey, Geoffrey . . .

"Yeah, Sara had a tight little pussy, but she wouldn't shut her fuckin' mouth. Floyd had to hold her down, and I had to slap her a few times so she'd quit screaming. Squalled like a baby, she did, even after I was done with her—"

Geoffrey lunged and pounded him with a punishing blow to the face.

Zach slammed to the floor and scrambled back, cowering, fear in his eyes . . . or maybe satisfaction.

Geoffrey towered over him, a barely contained explosion of smoldering fury. "She let you off because she was ashamed of being raped?" he demanded, his foot poised to kick his father in the face, his leg twitching.

Zach swallowed hard, then remained perfectly still, maybe resigned, accepting. Quieter, the braggadocio missing now, he said, "She didn't care so much about herself, you should know that. She just didn't want people to be callin' you no rape baby."

"I would've survived," Geoffrey ground out.

Zach covered his face, wiped his mouth, and glanced about nervously. "Listen, it wasn't right. I was young and drunk and stupid. I never done nothin' like that ever since, ain't hardly been able to live with it. I figured you come to kill me for it, and I didn't care—hell, maybe wanted you to—figured I'd talk it up, make it worth your while. You don't need no piece o' shit like me for a daddy."

"You screwed yourself. You had somebody like Sara, and you hurt her. You had a chance to know me, and now you've blown that."

Zach's eyes welled with tears now, and he looked more pathetic than dangerous. "I pissed away my whole life," he said.

Geoffrey stepped back, watching without offering to help as Zach struggled to pull himself up and hold on to the side of the table. Then he turned his back on his father, taking Phrekka in his arms. "I can't believe," he told her, "that I came here worried if somebody that low would be proud of me." She could feel him trembling, his cheek moist as he held it against hers.

"I am," the man said, his voice choked with contrition.

Without turning, holding her tightly, Geoffrey said, "This is Phrekka. You call her a name again, and I'll crack your head open, then shove that cane up your ass and see if *you* scream."

"I got it comin'. How-do, Phrekka. I 'pologize for what I said."

Geoffrey took a deep breath, wiped his face, looked in Phrekka's eyes, then hugged her again, reaching gingerly to wipe the tears from her cheeks. He turned again toward his father. He shook his head, perplexed. "I just don't understand. Why?"

Zach looked away, touching his face gingerly. "I knew I wasn't good enough for her, couldn't stand to let her get away, so I took something that wasn't mine so nobody else could have it."

"What could somebody like Sara possibly have liked about you?"

"Long as I live, I'll never know."

"Yeah, well, whatever it was, you need to find it again—in yourself."

"I'm doin' better than ever now," he said, drawing himself up. "I'm off parole next month, stayed clean since I been down, don't touch a drop o' drink no more, got a good job." Quieter, he admitted, "I gotta think about lookin' out for myself; I'll be an old cripple someday and ain't nobody gonna help me 'less I look out for myself."

"It isn't fair that you're still here while the one who loved me and took care of me is the one who died so young."

Zach looked surprised. "When did she die?"

"I thought you knew. There was a train wreck—"

"Yeah, but you say she's died since then?"

Geoffrey looked dumbfounded. "That's what killed her."

"No, just messed up her brain. Last time I called about her was—what, four or five months later? She was still in that state hospital up at Tupelo."

CHAPTER 21

Geoffrey nearly lost his marbles the summer of his tenth birthday.

Twenty perfect cat's-eyes in a draw-stringed chamois sack crashed to the pavement when his bicycle bounced over a bump, his newly acquired stakes for playing "funsies" and "keepsies" scattering along the roadway. He gathered them quickly, then inspected and counted each. The tally: one badly cracked, another one missing.

He tossed his damaged marble into the languid, roadside ditch stream, convinced nobody would be willing to play for such a flawed treasure; then he searched diligently for the other, so determined to find it that he risked punishment for missing supper, all to no avail.

That night, he carefully lined up the remaining eighteen beauties along a groove in his desk, then held them one at a time in front of his lamp and studied their swirls of colored glass, wondering what magical process had conjured such marvels. He pondered again where the one might have disappeared to, and he regretted discarding the other, realizing he should have kept it, if only for himself.

He rode back to the same spot the following morning and searched at length for his missing marble, finally discovering it nestled among some gravel and covered with dust, mortally fractured, a sizable shard broken away. He carefully burnished what remained of it, then plumbed the ditch's shallow depths and found the other, swishing it in the water until it sparkled and peered back at him with gratitude. That night, he studied the pair of damaged cat's-eyes in front of his lamp, feeling sorry for the one that could never again be whole, fascinated by how fate had transformed the other into something unique and grotesquely captivating, now refracting light in unusual new ways. It didn't matter that nobody else would accept these imperfect prizes, because they belonged to Geoffrey, and he would keep them for himself. He placed them in his desk drawer, thereafter palming and fingering them absently whenever important matters weighed heavily on his thoughts, letting them remain a part of his world long after he'd lost the others to childish games, their sack pressed into alternate service.

More than a decade later, in the early springtime before Geoffrey's twenty-first birthday, the marbles moved with him from Des Moines to his new apartment in Mill Valley, there to preside over a tray of paper clips on his desk . . . until the day he tossed them into his overnight bag without thinking, packing to fly home for an unexpected funeral.

He would lose a lot in his lifetime, and what little he recovered might be seriously damaged, but the option to destroy, the power to cherish, these choices would always be his, because these things, these memories, these people, they all belonged to Geoffrey Drousseau . . .

Flawed or not.

Phrekka took the wheel for the return leg of their Gulfport excursion. A pad handy for taking notes, Geoffrey called the hospital Zach had mentioned, repeating his request for information about Sara to various harried people until he finally reached an administrator willing to assist.

"I'm sorry," she said, "I don't recognize that name, and my records don't list her as a previous patient, either. Are you sure she's a state ward?—that's all we have here, you know."

"I would think so, with no living relatives to assume custody. Look, I *know* she was there about fifteen years ago; I just learned that my father used to check on her by calling a Nurse Barlucci."

"Selma Barlucci is retired now. Since my computer only shows the past ten years, you'll have to see our director for access to the archived files, but he won't be in until next week, and you'll need prior authorization. Do you have any legal standing in this matter?"

Geoffrey had never considered this. If she were still alive after all these years, he certainly couldn't claim guardianship, and the only documentation that might legitimate his association would be a diary, incomplete adoption records, a yellowed newspaper clipping, some sketches . . . "No, I guess I don't—not yet. Can you suggest where she might have been transferred, someplace I could check right away?"

"What is your interest in this patient?"

"She's my sister, but I didn't know until recently because I was adopted after the accident that killed our parents and left her—left her—"

"I'm so sorry," the woman said, more sympathetic now. "What was her condition, do you know that?"

He hesitated. "Nurse Barlucci called it 'permanent vegetative state,' a coma she would never wake from, with extensive vital-organ damage."

"Oh my. I'm afraid the news probably won't be very good," she said delicately. "People in that condition aren't likely to survive more than a few months, a year or two at most, and I can't think of any reason she'd be transferred, not with that prognosis. I'm sorry."

Geoffrey rubbed his eyes, then thanked her and disconnected, recounting the discouraging news to Phrekka. Sparked by the most unlikely of discoveries, his chances of ever finding Sara alive had flared to a bonfire of possibility and hope, only to flame out amid the discouraging embers of improbability. He felt powerless and angry, frustrated that she might still be lingering out there just beyond his grasp, yet resigned to the reluctant admission that learning she had passed quickly would be far preferable to finding out she suffered for an extended period. He decided that, if nothing else, he must verify the truth, and if that meant discovering she had perished, at least knowing *when* would tell him how close he'd come to having one last chance, even if she could never know, to hold her hand and tell her he loved her. "I need legal standing," he pronounced.

"Let's have Charles fire up the lawyer-pult," she suggested.

"The what?"

"He has a painting in his office of a medieval setting, a mob of heathens catapulting briefcase-toting lawyers at the castle wall, which is crumbling under the onslaught. Charles takes pride in keeping a formidable phalanx of attorneys prepared to take on any enemy, to help any ally."

Geoffrey liked that idea a lot, feeling the surge of confidence that comes from facing down the schoolyard bully while one's friends stand by for support and assistance. Even more, he liked how it seemed reasonable to ask Charles for help, not for something Phrekka needed, but for himself, as if all challenges now would be faced by the couple, together. "He won't mind?"

"Silly guy," she said, handing him her phone, "just hit pound-one and tell him you need a new suit of legal armor and a battalion of litigators."

He punched the buttons and said, "Hello," but before he could introduce himself, Charles had already figured out who besides Phrekka might be on this apparently private, direct line.

"Greetings, Mr. Drousseau. I trust you are looking out for our Miss Churán?"

"Yes, sir."

"Good man."

"Um, she says you have a lawyer-pult?"

He chuckled. "The royal munitioneer and several of his minions are right here in my office. I will put you on speaker-phone."

Geoffrey felt a rush of pride when Charles introduced him to the lawyers as Phrekka's close friend, further buoyed by their gushes of profound pleasure, all proclaiming downright thrill to make his acquaintance. He quickly explained the situation.

After a brief interval of sympathetic pronouncements, the attorneys engaged in rapid-fire discussion among themselves, finally concluding, "We'll have an excellent team assembled out of Jackson first thing in the morning—"

"Including people out of Tupelo," another interjected, "—just in case."

"But why a whole team?" Geoffrey asked.

"To move quickly, and in the event we need to assert your prerogative to access certain information, especially if we find her still living and you decide to pursue some form of intervention."

Charles asked, "You'll be near Miss Churán's phone when they learn something?"

For the rest of his life, he hoped . . . "Yes, yes I will." He thanked everybody, disconnecting after telling Charles that Phrekka sends her best.

"Were they helpful?" she asked.

"Watch the sky for flying lawyers; he's already flung a few."

"Good. I thought of suggesting the private investigator as an alternative, but Charles's team will have their own, and they'll certainly be more intimidating if bureaucrats prove uncooperative."

"That reminds me," he said, fishing the number from his wallet and dialing the detective. He asked him, "Can you locate the felony court information of Zachary Holmes, plus anything else that tells his personal history?"

"Conviction records and sentencing reports should cover a lot. I can do that in an hour, then keep looking if you need more."

"Good. Transmit whatever you find to our office at the Ramada." He placed the phone in the console and told Phrekka, "I'd like to stop at the hotel and check for those documents before we head out to the foundation."

"Then I'll freshen up, change clothes, maybe even shower, because we'll be out there until late, I'm sure."

"You're right; once this hits the newspaper, people will probably show up expecting to meet me."

"You may get more reporters, too, so dress the way you'd want your picture taken," she teased, smiling at his USM cap, "—just in case."

"I'm not looking forward to telling the same story over and over again."

"But the story keeps changing," she pointed out.

"And I still don't know the most important part: What ever happened to the artist?"

They rode in silence for a few minutes, Geoffrey lost in his thoughts, obsessed with needing to know if Sara survived more than a few weeks, if any part of her had remained sufficiently aware to suffer the knowledge of what happened. "Horse Creek Cemetery should know the date," he said suddenly. He called, but reached a recording that promised somebody would be in after nine the following morning. He sighed and lay his head back, closing his eyes and extending his open hand, which Phrekka took immediately, curling her fingers around his. He tried not to think about Sara . . .

"Pretty trees," Phrekka whispered after a while.

He opened his eyes and saw the sign for DeSoto National Forest. He stared into the dense thicket, thinking how it might feel to be lost in uncharted wilderness, helpless and confused, alone. Soon after, they drove through Hattiesburg, admiring the architecture they'd missed during this morning's zealous rush to find Zachary Holmes. When they passed the USM campus, Geoffrey released her hand just long enough to adjust his cap, smiling and striking a regal, varsity pose. As soon as they veered northeast toward Laurel, her phone rang, Marva calling to check in with Phrekka. Relaying messages back and forth since she was driving, Phrekka spent the next ten minutes reviewing a litany of messages, rendering business decisions, confirming social commitments, and fulfilling myriad other responsibilities, all of which served to remind Geoffrey that she lived a very busy life beyond the distraction of his own selfish personal odyssey. She must have put a lot on hold to help him pursue his quixotic quest, the scope of which seemed to grow more ambitious with each new day. A vague sense of apprehension welled deep inside him, dawning recognition that she must inevitably withdraw, at least for brief periods, in order to follow her own varied interests.

She took the phone for a moment and closed the conversation with cryptic answers to questions he couldn't hear, glancing toward him and smiling, then disconnected and said, "I need to zip back to the city for most of a day sometime very soon."

He feigned nonchalance, embarrassed to acknowledge his insecurities, perplexed by the fear that mere distance could somehow diminish the bond they'd affirmed, yet resisting the instant temptation to blurt out, "You'd take me with you, wouldn't you?!" He settled instead for dipping into the wellspring of his patience and loyalty. No wonder Melanie had fled his overbearing and insecure grasp, a result Geoffrey would avoid with Phrekka, even as a little boy must learn that when birds spread their wings and soar on the winds, that doesn't necessarily mean they have abandoned his birdhouse.

His brief bout of anxiety apparently too obvious, Phrekka interrupted his thoughts. "Geoffrey?" she asked, concern in her words and face.

"I'm sorry," he sighed. "I'm sitting here freaking out about you being away from me for a while. I'm stupid that way."

"I meant both of us would go, silly, unless you're busy here—but please don't say you're stupid, not for wanting to be close to me. If it's stupid for a boy who lost his whole family in an instant of separation to grow up apprehensive—even though that's not likely ever to happen again—then I'm stupid for freaking out when I lie beside you afraid of something awful I know you could never do."

"We sure are messed up," he pronounced, offering her a smile that she repaid with interest. He put his head back, basked in the glow of mutual empathy, and asked, "When does it go away? I mean, when will we be so confident with each other that we stop worrying?"

"I don't know," she admitted. "For me, it means changing how I react to an unreasonable fear, but yours is something we all live with, the possibility of catastrophe, of indifferent fate dealing us a harsh hand, like when I lost my father before I ever knew him. We just can't let it weigh too heavily on us, or let it interfere with enjoying what we do have. Last night," she admitted sheepishly, "I finally felt safest when I imagined the possibility of us spending our lives together, even raising a family, but then I thought about having a little boy or girl, then something horrible happening to us, and our baby being left alone and confused and helpless, relying on strangers—" Her voice broke, and she fell quiet.

He leaned close and stroked her hair while he searched her face, her eyes glistening even as they carefully watched traffic. "We can't deny ourselves what we most want just because it scares us or because we fear losing it."

"I've known people who don't seem to care about anything, and I think that's how they hedge their bets against being hurt."

"I can't be that way. I want the best, even if I have to learn to let it go someday."

She seemed to like that. "I think my father still would have wanted me, even if he'd known he could hold me in his arms for only six weeks before giving me to the world."

"And I can't imagine what kind of person I'd be if I never had the time I did with Sara."

"She touched you in many wonderful ways, taught you so much," she said, exiting toward the hotel.

"Yeah . . . she's the one who taught me how to love you."

Geoffrey found the marbles in his overnight bag while looking for toothpaste. He held them up to the light, wondering why he'd even brought them, why he still kept them, and he finally decided without any real conviction that it might be time to toss them once and for all into the next trash receptacle he passed.

He opened the bathroom tap, watched the water swirl in the sink, and tried not to dwell on his vision of Phrekka taking a shower in her own suite at this very moment, the sudsy liquid cascading in waves over her cinnamon hair, tiny droplets trickling down her exquisite body, curving circuitously around her buoyant breasts, lingering for a moment before pooling in her navel, finally bursting free only to be trapped in a thicket of soft curls, seeking release to mingle with the moisture of her delicate . . .

He tried to divert his attention, staring into the sink, reaching down absently to adjust the suddenly uncomfortable fit of his briefs; then he flashed on the explosive image of a pin-pricked over-inflated balloon, trying very hard not to imagine the intense response Phrekka might coax from him with even the slightest touch, and how that surely would exceed anything he had ever felt, the sensations, the ripples, again and again.

The water swirled impatiently, pulling him inexorably into the opening at the center.

He studied his face in the mirror, then reached up and stroked his hair, everything real again for the moment. He relished the expectation that tonight would bring another chance to lie beside Phrekka, unashamed of how he knew that would make him feel, understanding there would be limits to how he might express himself, at least for now, possibly even forever, nevertheless anticipating a most profound level of intimacy shared in the kinds of simple ways he'd never bothered to fully explore in his ignorant haste to "score."

He brushed his teeth, shaved all but his mustache, and combed his hair, then felt surprisingly young again. Deciding to change into loose-fitting slacks, he emptied his pockets, holding the marbles up to the light and studying their flawed swirls, glancing around for a wastebasket, finally shrugging and placing them with his keys.

The phone rang, the private detective calling to say he had just sent the documents. Geoffrey refilled his pockets and started toward the office suite, but then he paused in the hallway, listening for the sound of running water in Phrekka's shower, imagining how it would feel to slip in there with her—

Then he had to try *not* to imagine slipping in there with her, letting some air out of the balloon, the pin much too close to pricking.

He found some papers waiting patiently in the hopper, took them to the desk and turned on the lamp, shifting yet again to adjust his inexplicably too-tight loose-fitting pants. The marbles pressed into his leg, so he removed them, fingering them absently while he sorted through the printouts. The top sheet listed his father's convictions, the rest a narrative describing the crime and Zach's life:

Receiving stolen property over $100, 7 counts

Instant Offense(s): Zachary Holmes was arrested by Ofc. Jekkel and charged with 26 felony counts (RSP-$100) after police, acting on a tip, obtained a search warrant for 97562 Stockbridge, Apt. 126-B, and found him present where new appliances still in their original cartons were stored in a walk-in closet. The items were traced to the theft of a DeBliss Electronics delivery truck. The apartment was leased by Walt Rogers but Holmes lived there for approximately two months. Holmes admitted suspecting the items were stolen, but he claimed no other involvement, explaining he needed a place to stay while he saved for his own. He refused to cooperate with the investigation of Rogers or provide further information, declined a plea offer including probation, and demanded jury trial during which he was acquitted of nineteen charges and found guilty of seven. Holmes had no adult record to consider at sentencing, but juvenile records show a history of being a truant and a runaway. He was sentenced to seven terms of five-to-fifteen years, concurrently.

Personal History: Father unknown, mother's parental rights terminated after reports of physical and sexual abuse three weeks before his sixth birthday—

Geoffrey gasped, noting Zach had lost his family at the same age he'd lost the Drousseaus. What a contrast between the early positive impressions Sara had left him and the bad ones Zach must still carry even to this day. He continued reading:

Holmes's mother petitioned for visitation, but died of narcotic overdose before the hearing could be held. Zachary Holmes lived in seventeen foster homes over the next eleven years. He was hospitalized for three weeks requiring surgery at age twelve after an older ward held him down and burned his chest and abdomen with a hot iron. He was also hospitalized briefly after attempting suicide at age fourteen by stabbing himself in the chest with a penknife. He was ordered into alcohol rehab at age fifteen but failed to complete. He dropped out of school permanently during eleventh grade, held employment as a shipping-stocker at FranFruit in Gulfport until severely injured in a motorcycle accident at age nineteen. Hospitalized for three months, he was left substantially disabled (see attached medical statement). His employment and residential records have been sporadic ever since.

Personal Data: No outstanding warrants, no known relatives, no assets, claims alcohol consumption is down to "five or six beers a week,"

```
admits occasional marijuana use but no other il-
licit drugs, no known history of violence or ag-
gression, not a practicing homosexual, no
religious affiliation, no gang activity, no mil-
itary record, indicates remorse but exhibits an-
ger over "extortion prosecution," symptoms of
depression evident, wants "to be left alone."
```

Geoffrey sat back and rubbed his eyes, considering what Zach had finally admitted to him and Phrekka: *"I swear, Geoffrey, I don't remember nothin' from that night, just what Floyd told me the next mornin'. I couldn't live with knowin' I hurt Sara, so I tried to kill myself with a knife, but Floyd stopped me before I could do much damage. It's probably good I can't remember it, or I know I'd be dead by now. Ain't no way to fix it, so I just go on."*

Geoffrey fingered the marbles as he recalled Zach's confession, the achievement of understanding too elusive, forgiveness an incomprehensible concept, so he focused on his anger, let it flare into the licking flames of rage, and tasted blood in his mouth as his heart pounded and his mind pulsated with visions of vengeance. He pictured Zach as he'd first found him: a scarred relic of a man trying to goad him into an assault, hiding his disability so Geoffrey would attack without hesitation, begging to be punished for something he could never remember.

Geoffrey tried to imagine how it would feel to kill him, to aim a pistol and pull the trigger and be done with it, retribution for a moment of drunken insanity that changed Sara's life forever . . . but every time he tried to fire the imaginary weapon, his hand wavered. Determined, he pumped the blustering bellows of fury, then aimed again and squeezed, the marbles threatening to shatter in his palm, and at the last instant he saw a slight, fourteen-year-old boy standing before him, his shirt soaked with blood from stabbing himself in the chest, his face soaked with regret for debauching the integrity of his own heart.

The shot missed, and Geoffrey dropped the phantom gun, the marbles bouncing on the carpet below, a small hole and several radiating cracks marring his reflection in the window to his own compassion.

He buried his face in his hands, then reached for the marbles and cradled them close to his heart.

He wondered how many regrets Zachary Holmes would collect, and which of those would someday allow him the chance to make amends.

One of the marbles whispered to him, and he could hear Sara's gentle and loving voice:

Move on, Son . . . What's done is done.

Geoffrey carefully returned the flawed marbles to the protection of his pocket, then turned in time to see Phrekka coming through the door.

He tried to speak, but his jaw quivered, and his eyes blurred.

She held him in her arms, whispering, "I know, I can't make myself hate him, either."

CHAPTER 22

Just glimpsing down Bruce Trail instantly reminded Geoffrey of Ernest's post-funeral wake, a procession of cars lining both sides of the gravel roadway, the buzz of activity swirling around his family home . . . but as he and Phrekka drew closer, he noticed all the ingredients for percolating the facts and stirring up a simmering cauldron of spicy media stew: hulking TV-station broadcast vans powering roving news crews, sage reporters waxing eloquent before video cameras focused to evoke on-the-scene in-your-face immediacy, the requisite helicopter boasting a Jackson affiliate's technical capabilities with a dragonfly's-eye view, still-photographers fondling the bulging shafts of their thrusting zoom lenses, curious bystanders construing proximity as participation in a clearly historical event, a uniformed officer directing traffic in his dutiful quest to promote safety and order amid chaos . . .

Phrekka reacted instantly, reversing and turning around.

"That way," Geoffrey suggested. "Park down by the tracks."

They exited the vehicle quickly, lest anybody notice their arrival, and slipped through the woods, working their way parallel to the tracks until they found a path that cut through behind the cottage. Staying out of sight, Geoffrey called the foundation. The PR guy answered, then casually sauntered over to let them in through Pamela's back door.

"Phenomenal success," he pronounced. "TV news broke it at noon, and it's already poised to expand to the national media by tonight."

"This is nuts," Geoffrey countered.

"It took off faster than I expected," he admitted, spreading his hands, "but you *are* accomplishing your goals. More than thirty sketches have already been brought in, and several dozen more calls provided information on the whereabouts of others, not counting the cranks and crackpots, of which there are surprisingly few, by the way." He offered Geoffrey a copy of the *Laurel Leader-Call.* "The human-interest angle is a winner, and it's being stoked by the tremendous outpouring of community support, not people seeking attention, but ones who knew your family, some who even remember you, others who simply remember the tragedy."

The newspaper headline blared:

MIRACLE BOY COMES HOME

Survivor sets foundation, seeks sister's art

Two separate stories flanked the large, color photo of Geoffrey and Pamela holding the carnival sketch, with a lower-corner inset showing Sara's high-school yearbook picture. The first article focused on Geoffrey's return, the foundation, and his search for sketches. The other recounted the tragedy of some fifteen years before.

"I'm sorry, Geoffrey," Phrekka said. "I didn't mean to immerse you in something that would spiral out of control."

"No—no, this is good," he said, unfolding the paper. "I don't like being the center of attention, but right now it's our best shot at launching this thing right."

They started reading the homecoming article together, an excellent and accurate summary of recent events, right down to the foundation's mission statement and man-on-the-street quotes of hearty endorsement. It ended by exhorting people to see the back page for contact information. The tragedy article started with a brief description of the accident and its aftermath, then continued on the back page below a large photo of the wreckage with a smaller shot of a dead squirrel, plus a line-art diagram mapping the sequence of events, the last item showing the outline of a body where Sara had fallen just before where the path entered the woods, no doubt hurrying to save little Geoffrey. A mid-column photo showed Gumper Lewis from his seventh-grade school picture. Geoffrey stared at the wreckage shot, a vivid depiction of twisted rail cars, emergency vehicles, men in containment suits, a hazy cloud . . .

And he remembered.

He remembered seeing something, a fleeting glimpse showing the top of a tanker car thrust high into the air, a yellow cloud expanding in slow motion, tendrils reaching toward him like fat grasping fingers, somebody calling his name from behind, Gumper Lewis calling and grabbing him, being pulled, falling, Gumper lifting him, the paperboy's awkward uneven-legged gait as he stumbled under the boy's weight, Geoffrey scared and crying, calling out for Sara. He remembered how they finally stopped beside a road where Gumper collapsed, panting from exhaustion, pulling Geoffrey in to hold him close. Geoffrey had wiped his eyes and looked up, then saw that Gumper was crying, too, and then he heard a siren, saw flashing lights, a man coming toward them, but Gumper wouldn't let go of the boy, the stranger saying, "It's okay now, Gumper," but the paperboy was crying too hard, holding too tightly, protecting Geoffrey no matter what . . .

"Geoffrey?" Phrekka whispered, bringing him back to the present.

He looked at her, then realized he was breathing much too hard, and he whispered, "Gumper must have seen what happened, then went around the long way and risked his life to get me out."

She put her arm around his waist and held him close.

> Gumper Lewis, 12, of 7496 Dogwood Avenue, is credited with saving the life of "Miracle Boy" Geoffrey Drousseau . . .

"Oh Gumper," he breathed, "I didn't know. I sure hope they treated you like a hero." Then to Phrekka, he added, "Sara was right; his leg wasn't the only thing that made him special. She used to tell him he was an all-right boy, and he repaid her kindness by granting her last wish, what she would have wanted most in the world: protecting me."

> . . . surprised doctors by breathing on her own. She was transferred in critical condition to a state facility in Tupelo, diagnosed with permanent vegetative state and severe organ damage. One doctor who wished to remain anonymous suggested that long-term survival is extremely unlikely, that her prognosis is considered terminal.

All that followed was an abstract of other Mississippi rail disasters, then the promised box of foundation contact information, no mention of when Sara eventually died.

Geoffrey took another deep breath, then told the PR guy, "I just found out Sara wasn't my sister; she was my biological mother. She'd been raped at twelve and had her own parents adopt me before moving to Laurel so I wouldn't be scandalized growing up."

"Wow," he said. "Are you ready to reveal that?"

He considered this, unsure which way to proceed. "It seems like that would detract from our mission right now, but I do have to call her something. I guess the truth is an important part of her story, but that feels like violating her secrets. After all, she chose to share her art with people, her vision of the beauty in others, trying to *scatch* them as pure and carefree, not to reveal her own lost innocence . . . but then again, her diary said that was to protect me, and I don't need protecting anymore. I just don't know."

"You'll be asked a lot of questions today."

"Am I the front man?"

"They've been getting shots of Miss Greenstone talking about the foundation, her own fond memories of you and Sara—though not a hint about what you just said—but you're the one they've all come to see, to hear from."

"How do we do this?"

"We'll walk toward the house, you in front with me trailing behind to intervene and control things, and you'll be mobbed. What about Miss Churán?"

"Will you walk with me?" he asked her.

"Yes," she said without hesitation.

"Good," PR said, "that makes a nice image, especially for her company."

"I'm not sure I want that mentioned," she said.

"I talked to your partner earlier, and he indicated that all decisions would be left to you. He did say that announcing the donation would be good public relations, that you might choose to play it like a challenge for other companies to step up, that you might even decide to pledge more money, but he wanted me to remind you there are drawbacks to all this, especially naming the precise figure."

That seemed to surprise her. "If he thinks it's too small, I'll—"

"No, that's not it," Geoffrey interrupted, already understanding the implication. "It's *too high*. Lots of everyday people will want to pledge small amounts or volunteer to help, so trumpeting a breathtaking figure would only diminish their contributions."

PR smiled. "Precisely. You should see what's going on next door. A whole cadre of people swooped in and cleaned the house from top to bottom—three old women are over there sewing new curtains as we speak, for crissake—a local landscaping company came by earlier and mowed, the beverage store stocked the refrigerator with sodas and snacks, the hardware donated materials for the local scout troop to paint the exterior this weekend, a gallery in town offered frames and mattes—the list goes on. Miss Greenstone's so busy greeting people and recording the stories behind each sketch that her friend from the accounting program—a rather tall fellow, I must say—is in there keeping the books and doing paperwork. The whole town is thrilled to be a part of this, proud that Laurel can host something that will do so much good for so many people in the years to come."

"Geoffrey," Phrekka said, "let's not even mention the corporate donations for now. We'll play that card later when we get into high-stakes solicitation. Right now, I just want to be your friend rallying to the cause."

He smiled, agreeing. He could feel it, and it felt like being part of something very meaningful, something bigger than any one person could achieve. "Thanks, Phrekka," he whispered, his arm around her now. Then to PR, "So they'll mob us as we walk to the house; then what?"

"Climb the steps to the porch and take questions until I cut you off. There's less than an hour 'til the five-o'clock news, so I'm sure some will request a live-on-the-scene stand-up with you, which I'll coordinate, if you're up to that."

"Actually, I'm thoroughly freaked by the very idea, but it won't get easier thinking about it too much, so let's do it."

They managed to walk about twenty feet before the crowd spotted them and surged forward, cameras clicking, microphones in Geoffrey's face. He led the entourage to the porch and stood with Phrekka on one side, Pamela on the other, introducing them and the PR guy, spelling all four names. "Thank you all for coming.

We're overwhelmed by your support—but we're not surprised. The people of Laurel stand among the best, and we knew there could be no better place in the world to launch something so important, to honor Sara in a way that fires the spark of creativity in America's children."

The crowd cheered, Phrekka and Pamela both hugging him, and he felt wonderful, wishing Sara could see this, that she could know her legacy.

"The people of Laurel were heroes that tragic day; from young Gumper Lewis, who saved my life; to the Greenstones, who took me in; and the emergency personnel who risked their lives; and friends who gave from their hearts for my trust fund; and even those who simply held their loved ones close later that night, reminding each other what matters most—it's taken nearly fifteen years for me to find my way back to the people I always loved, and now we can begin to heal old wounds by working together for the common good." His voice broke, and he could feel the power of the crowd swirling around and through him, some of the women openly crying now, men wiping their eyes, teenagers thrusting their fists in the air, a few of the reporters actually moved beyond words.

And he wondered what to say next, what to say about Sara, if he should reveal her secret. Maybe she'd given so much to others and had tried so hard to find the innocence and fragile beauty in those around her because she needed to keep the dark and distressing pain for herself, to shield the people she loved from the heartache and anguish that ultimately caused her own mother to break down. The unspeakable truth too much to bear, keeping her private burden hidden had allowed people to see only her joy, not her suffering. Geoffrey couldn't be the one to violate what Sara had considered so important, not now, not ever. Her secret had become his own, and Phrekka would help him protect it, and Pamela would honor it, and the people whose lives Sara touched would know her for the images she created, for the love she *scaught* in the faces of children.

"We'll give something back to the community," he said quietly, "and nurture the fragile potential of all children so they may discover in themselves what Sara's unique vision revealed, and this will be Laurel's gift to the world, and it will be my gift to Sara, whom I'll always love, my cherished sister."

The hazy disk of a long day's weary sun hung low in the sky, casting the assembled throng of reporters in its shimmering orange glow.

Geoffrey answered myriad questions, encouraging Phrekka and Pamela to interject, then wrapped up the session with four live stand-ups for local TV affiliates. He agreed to another interview on one of the national networks in thirty minutes, so he used the time in between to meet many of those who had brought sketches or memories or both, listening to their stories, their heartfelt gestures of friendship and support buoying him in ways he never imagined. The network interview turned out to be one of his best, he liked to think, owing to feelings of goodwill lifting him beyond his performance anxiety over public speaking. The last stragglers wished him the best before hurrying home to spread the message among friends and neighbors.

Pamela introduced her classmate and friend, Dwayne, a towering but gentle fellow from Toomsuba, the developer of a precise system for tracking the foundation's donations, purchase obligations, sketch-reprint orders, and several computer-generated forms for verifying tax deductibility and other pertinent information. "I've started a database of people who want to buy copies or be informed when books of Sara's sketches become available," he added, clearly proud to be playing a part. "I should get here really early in the morning because this news coverage will no doubt bring a lot more sketches—"

"Then stay at the cottage tonight," Pamela insisted.

"Yeah, stay with us!" Andy-Geoff seconded, tugging frantically at his shirt until the big man lifted the small child and cradled him with one arm.

"Then I should make a run to my apartment and pack a bag right now."

"Can I go?" Andy-Geoff asked, announcing, "I'm going with him, Mawma," before waiting for an answer.

Geoffrey noticed the first hints of something very good to come of this for both Pamela and her son—and for the very lucky Dwayne, too, a man with a big heart and no ring on his finger. Dwayne leaned over and surprised Pamela with a kiss atop her head, then lumbered down the drive, hoisting Andy-Geoff up on his shoulders and provoking the boy's squeals of delight.

"I move that the foundation hire him," Phrekka pronounced.

"I second it," Pamela agreed.

"It's settled then," Phrekka concluded. "The board votes unanimously." Good thing Geoffrey would have said yes—had they even asked.

Pamela led them into the family room, now a temporary gallery with sketches propped here and there, some framed, others mounted, most with numbered cards attached, all portraying children of various ages. Two unmistakably depicted Pamela as a grade-schooler while another showed Zachary Holmes at about twelve or thirteen, younger and no doubt more innocent than the teen who'd drunkenly lost control of his desires. Other drawings included a little girl dressed like a school marm standing in front of a chalkboard, her features stern, the notation: *Teacher's Pet Pauline*; a couple of bib-overalled country lads wrestling in the hay, cheered on by a trio of exuberant ringside mice; two big-eyed, curly-haired little boys given the appearance of being nude, their modesty appeased by a table in the foreground; the mischievous eyes and cherub face of a young girl peeking through a mountain of suds in the bathtub, bubbles containing enchanted castles and unicorns and cute trolls floating in the air; a pouting lad having his hair cut by Mom, little brother in the background frowning in the mirror at his own jagged mop; a graceful ballerina striking a regal tip-toe pose, her waist encircled by a profusion of butterflies weaving a magical tutu; big-eared twin brothers sitting on a bench holding identical big-eared puppies . . .

Geoffrey, three or four years old, cross-eyed, watching a doodlebug on the tip of his nose . . .

Geoffrey with his shirt off, eating an ice-cream cone, more dripping on his belly than in it . . .

Geoffrey, sitting beside the pond, drawing his own sketch of two proper little grasshoppers wearing jaunty rakish caps . . .

"Wow," he said, taken by the last image. Sara had obviously drawn part of it, but the sketch on the boy's pad showed a different style, simpler and bereft of her subtle shading, nevertheless compelling in its impression, the grasshoppers' faces full of personality and life . . .

And Geoffrey remembered drawing it.

Incredulous, Phrekka pointed out, "You *both* signed it." His first name appeared in blocky, juvenile letters beside hers. "*You* drew the grasshoppers?"

Geoffrey hesitated, lost in his reverie.

"He used to spend almost as much time drawing as Sara did," Pamela answered for him. Then she told Geoffrey, "You was *really* good for such a little dab. You remember her teachin' you different styles, always saying you'd be a great artist someday, better than her?"

Vaguely . . .

"There was a whole bunch of those," she added, "where Sara drew you holding your pad and then you filled in whatever picture you wanted. I hope we find more of 'em."

"You did this when you were only *five*?" Phrekka sounded dumbfounded.

He felt a surge of discomforting sensations, unpleasant images, anxiety and tinges of outright fear. Phrekka seemed to sense this, making him feel self-conscious, so he quickly chased it all away, a glance letting her know it had passed.

"Let's rearrange these," he said, noticing how the series of depictions struck him as disrespectfully disorganized. The women stood to the side and watched patiently while he studied each sketch. He started imagining what Sara must have thought as she drew them, how they all represented children's views of their worlds, expressions of the need to explore, or the essential desire to show affection through touch, or physical mani-festations of vernal states of mind, or the blurred demarcations between reality and fantasy, or wide-eyed fascination with the minutiae of extraordinary lives. He moved the sketches around, grouping them different ways, seeking balance, continuity of theme, sequence of time, private moments in contrast to social immersion . . . and he noticed gaps that ached to be filled, considering how the sketches found in the attic might enhance the display, wondering how many more remained to be discovered, and how much of Sara's vision would forever be lost.

Phrekka and Pamela continued to watch, clearly enthralled now, exchanging glances with each other, increasingly enthusiastic as he came closer and closer to achieving his own vision . . .

"Yes!" they both blurted together, laughing at the coincidence of response.

"You must be the one to arrange the Sara exhibits," Phrekka insisted. "You have a gift, and you understand Sara's work more than anyone."

He nodded, agreeing to the assignment, not necessarily to her assessment. He would arrange Sara's legacy for her; he needed to.

"I didn't know you could draw," Phrekka persisted.

He shook his head.

"Used to follow her around with his own little pad," Pamela supplied. "Every letter she sent me had a little Geoffrey drawing on the bottom."

He shook his head again, collapsing in a chair and averting his gaze. "That's gone," he said.

"Artistry never goes away," Phrekka countered.

"I outgrew all that."

"I knew you liked graphic arts, had a flare for design and arrangement, but—"

"And that's all," he insisted, feeling trapped, wary, panicky.

"But, Geoffrey—" Pamela pressed, cut off by Phrekka shaking her head, a signal to desist.

Palpable silence hung in the air, and Geoffrey found himself wringing his hands, his stomach churning, his shoulders tense to the point of pain, and he knew Phrekka regretted pursuing the issue, that she realized too late he couldn't control the reaction it triggered, that he felt scared even if he couldn't explain why. "I just like graphic arts," he said, not sure what he meant. He looked to Phrekka, and he knew she understood that it would be okay to help *him* understand, a challenge to be faced as a couple, together.

"Graphics lets you arrange everything a certain way," she said, "—the final result turning out exactly as *you* want, not to satisfy your clients, not to please your various families, not dictated by the fateful arrangements of chance."

He looked up and saw it in her eyes, and he knew she had discovered something about him he'd long been reluctant to face. "Sara's artistry was to portray something *real*, to *scatch* the truth as she saw it in all people," he said.

She nodded. "And you looked for it in *every* kind of life, even a little doodlebug."

"I tried to be an artist like Sara, except I wanted to show others what I saw, and it was a lot of fun, but then—" He felt it again, the sensation of straddling the rift between vision and depiction, twirling faster and faster to see both directions at once, but what he glimpsed seized him violently, and all innocence drained from the world, and the image imbued him with a clarity he must never reveal to another soul, a perspective lurking dangerously below the surface of all desire to draw, agony denied by leaving pads of sketch paper forever blank.

Phrekka squeezed his hands, preventing him from spinning out of control. "Geoffrey?" she whispered, a tether.

He closed his eyes, nausea rising, heart-pounding panic, and he couldn't catch his breath, desperately wanting to call for help. "I can't—can't ever show it . . ."

"Geoffrey, what can't you show?"

He heard the hissing gas, stared through the trees, and he saw a pretty yellow cloud . . . but then Sara stumbled into the picture, gasping and sobbing, falling to the ground, vomiting on herself, and she squirmed in the dust and clawed at her own bloody eyes—

He heard a voice call his name.

"Sara!" he cried, reaching out to her.

And Gumper grabbed him from behind, turned his face away.

CHAPTER 23

Phrekka kept her eyes on Geoffrey while she listened absently on the phone, waiting for a front-desk clerk to confirm their laundry pick-up. He appeared to be in a trance, staring blankly at the mounted sailfishes in her suite, as transported from his own world as they from theirs. Finally learning an attendant would come in ten minutes, she disconnected and quickly set about gathering her clothing.

"I need your key," she told Geoffrey quietly, which he fished from his pocket and surrendered without question. She hurried to his suite and found only one decent ensemble still clean, so she laid it out with socks and underwear, then stuffed the rest in a bag and lugged it back to her place. Since neither had come to Laurel packed and prepared for an extended sojourn, she decided a whirlwind shopping trip would be in order, looking forward to the idea of dressing him time and again like some life-sized guy doll. Make that action figure . . .

Anatomically correct, to be sure.

Still he stood there, drifting rudderless, the wind gone from his sails. At least his nausea seemed to have passed, its sudden cause still a mystery to her, that brief bout of trepidation that she'd committed some unintentional faux pas yielding before her rising confidence that he would have explained and forgiven her.

"Hurry, get undressed," she said quietly.

His reverie broken, he turned with an exaggerated, "I beg your pardon?"

"I've arranged a pick-up in five minutes."

"Do you even know her name?"

"Your *laundry*, Geoffrey," she scoffed, fetching him a robe from the bathroom.

As he removed his shirt, she noticed for the first time that a few wisps of blond hair had sprouted on the otherwise smooth expanse of his chest. She turned and averted her eyes while he removed his pants, surprised with herself over how much she wanted to peek, to gaze openly and study him like she would a newly discovered sculpture by Donatello or Carpeaux. She turned back in time to see him pulling the robe around his body, a glimpse of how his tight briefs had gathered that distinctive masculinity against his lower abdomen, his unassuming navel winking acknowledgment of her admiration. "Undies, too," she said, suppressing a smile.

He peeled them from under the terry-cloth curtain, then hesitated, so she took them before considering the impropriety of such casual intimacy. She paused with awkward indecision, amazed by the power of her feelings during such a playful, non-threatening encounter. She started, then realized he was staring at her hands while she actually stroked his most personal of garments. He blushed, and she felt the flame in her own cheeks, but then he looked up and gazed at her face, and something unpracticed yet somehow exhilarating passed between them. Without forethought, she stepped toward him—

Knock knock. "Housekeeping!" came a woman's voice, breaking their spell.

She quickly stuffed his bag and delivered both to the door, thanking the attendant for this extra service, then returned to find Geoffrey staring again at the sailfishes. She stood beside him, pleased when he reached for her hand and held it affectionately.

"I'm sorry," he said, "for weirding out on you."

"It was *your* turn for a change," she said, and they both chuckled.

He sighed, still watching the wall-mounted trophies, perhaps searching for something indistinct, maybe having just discovered something inexplicable. "It's the eyes," he whispered.

Glassy orbs, frozen in time, the sailfishes' eyes peered blankly at their keepers. "You mean on the fishes?"

He shook his head slowly, then rubbed his abdomen and said, "I'm still feeling queasy."

"Why don't you lie down? Let me help take care of you." She led him to the great canopy bed where he stretched out.

"Well, it *is* almost time to watch the news," he said.

She handed him the remote control, then retrieved a nightgown from her garment bag, heading into the bathroom and closing the door. She studied her face in the mirror, then caught herself picturing Geoffrey hastening to cover his briefs, no longer the unaffected boy whose essence Sara captured while he played among the cattails so long ago. Phrekka had seen those same innocent sensibilities still thriving in Andy-Geoff as he emerged from the pond with rivulets of water running down his body, when he peeled off his soaked underpants and stood unabashedly naked before her, unashamed and unconcerned, indifferent to Phrekka's appreciation for the simple beauty embodied in this unadorned manifestation of a pristine boy. People would teach him embarrassment soon enough, just as Pamela had suggested he wear his undies to swim, and ultimately he would grow into an impetuous young man ruled by his physical urges . . .

Unless, hopefully, like Geoffrey, he might be different, too.

She sighed, then stripped to her panties and washed her face, pausing to study herself in the mirror, no longer the modest little girl, now a young woman longing to be held and touched in ways so intimate as to bring both excitement and distress.

She splashed more water onto her face, then felt it trickle along her neck and trace lines of liquid sensation down her body. Noting the silk lingerie caressing that soft mound of her pubis, she recalled studying Geoffrey's body while he talked on the phone in his apartment, then again while he slept on his childhood bed in Coon Rapids. She envisioned him as a man, coming to her naked from the pond, his flaxen hair clinging damply at the top, patchy wisps on his chest dancing in the breeze, nipples firm from the chill water cascading in rivulets down his sleek body, bare skin glistening in the late-evening sunlight. Her eyes moved cautiously lower, there to find his navel winking at her while the pristine beauty of his handsomely proportioned masculinity rested peacefully, droplets gathering tenuously at the fully exposed tip before falling in whispers to the shifting sands, his pubic tuft a precisely bordered patch of fuzz cordoned off from the smooth skin of his lower abdomen like so many stalks of golden wheat-grass planted in a tight little circle around the tinkling-cherub fountain of a private garden.

She cupped her hands under the faucet, filling them with water to caress her face and shoulders, reveling in the electric tingle of droplets curving circuitously around her breasts where they would linger a moment before collecting in her navel, eventually breaking free to soak the swatch of silk that protected the portal to her soul. Turning the tap down to a trickle, she wet her fingers and drew swirls around her nipples and along her arms, and she felt the front of her panties clinging with the growing dampness of her reckless abandon. She took a deep breath and carefully peeled them down and stepped out, the rush of moist air tickling her. She dribbled more water onto her stomach and felt the pool bursting free only to be trapped in her thicket of soft curls, seeking release to mingle . . .

And she imagined Geoffrey again, and he reached to touch her, but she shied away. He blushed, found his robe, then quickly pulled it tightly around himself, no longer unashamed and unconcerned, instead embarrassed and confused. Phrekka had taught him this, denying him the freedom to share with her even his simplest expressions of intimate love.

She touched her nipples and felt the air swirl around them, wanting so very much to reassure Geoffrey that she could stand naked before him, that she trusted his carnal desire, that she would truly embrace him as he gave the essence of his self to her . . .

But she felt afraid.

And she knew she feared not that Geoffrey had gained the dangerous potential to hurt, but that she had forever lost that uncorrupted capacity to love with the faith of an innocent child who cherishes her world.

If the little girl Phrekka cradled in her heart could trust the little boy Geoffrey carried in his, they would frolic together in the pond of their dreams, and the woman Phrekka had become could finally learn to share her own simplest expressions of intimate love.

In her mind, she looked to Geoffrey, a suggestion to remove his robe and come to her, but he waited, refusing to risk the gesture or touch that might scare her, so she dared to let her own gown fall with a whisper to the sand. His eyes swimming with expectation and delight, he cupped his hands and touched her face, releasing the first tentative tides of ecstasy that traced rivulets down her tingling body and plumbed the depths of rapture pooling between her thighs, and she felt cleansed, safe to share the sensuality of passion's liquid touch in this fantasy realm even while dangerous storms raged all around them in the real world.

She opened her eyes, found herself back in the bathroom of her suite, and saw her image naked and wet in the mirror, soaked panties clutched in her hand. She sighed, then quickly dried off. Realizing she'd need to retrieve more dry undergarments from her bag in the other room, she pulled the chiffon nightgown over her nude body.

Shutting off the tap, she noticed how, unlike touching the canvas of a storm-ravaged tent, this time the *drip-drip* she'd unleashed while testing the waters didn't seem so out of control after all.

She steeled herself, then opened the door and saw Geoffrey's face light up with wonder and awe. She glanced toward her garment bag, but the television-news theme music began, so she took a deep breath, then crossed instead to the bed and slipped in beside Geoffrey where he'd fluffed a pile of pillows, safe haven for a woman who understood where she wanted to go, unsure how she might ever arrive, yet determined to find her way.

An ebullient anchorwoman announced tonight's lead story with an over-the-shoulder collage contrasting Geoffrey's face with how he used to look photographed as a child. He flipped between channels so they could watch various incarnations of the same story unfolding on four affiliates, an impressive ensemble of footage, quotes from the afternoon press briefing, encouragement from local citizens, archival footage of the original disaster, and graphics including a montage showing several of Sara's sketches. Phrekka noticed Geoffrey looking away when shots of the train wreck appeared, his face a brief revelation of anguish quickly replaced by eye-rolling mockery as clips of his speech followed. He paused his shenanigans whenever Phrekka's image entered the picture, breathlessly demanding to know the identity of that exquisite enchantress with the delicate Asian features and penetrating eyes. She feigned not recognizing herself, admitting he showed impeccable taste in goddesses even as he showed remarkable capacity to recognize and appreciate the power imbued in fine art. Geoffrey smiled at her, but still he appeared pale and melancholy.

They lost interest when the last station brought in an expert to advise viewers how to react the next time a train derails or toxic gas leaks in their neighborhoods. The room phone rang, the PR guy calling to say several national TV news magazines wanted interviews. Geoffrey reluctantly agreed to a late-morning back-to-back schedule, then hung up and looked very sad. Phrekka moved closer, but noticed a momentary hesitation before he gathered her into an embrace. Intensely aware of his nakedness under the robe, she suddenly felt apprehensive, but her desire to comfort him during this mysterious malaise won out, the frustration with her limited range of expression overshadowed by growing confidence that with Geoffrey she would always be safe. In this, she found a sense of contentment, proof that a man's intimate touch could signal protection rather than threat.

"We're doing okay, Phrekka," he said, reading her mind.

"I wish I could make that invisible barrier melt away, the one that stops me from being even closer to you."

"There is no barrier, Phrekka."

"But . . . but it—"

"There *is* no it. By focusing on something that's not real, you lend it the illusion of substance. When we truly believe nothing will come between us, then we can move on and discover new vistas together. Sometimes that'll make one or both of us nervous, so we'll take our time, help each other, wait if necessary, but never stop exploring."

"But you can't touch me how you want because it makes me feel scared—"

"No, Phrekka, the only way I *want* to touch you is however makes you feel good. We just need time to learn, and be willing to make mistakes."

"You already make me feel good."

"And simple gestures from you, like holding my hand a few minutes ago when I was spacing out, those affect me more profoundly than I ever imagined possible."

"I wanted to help, but I still don't understand why you were upset."

He rubbed his face and looked sad. "I'm sorry," he said quietly. "That's my fault, not practicing what I preach. I remembered something back at the house, and that took me someplace really bad, and I didn't want to pull you there, too."

"But that means leaving me behind, alone, and that's when I start giving substance to that barrier I want to believe doesn't exist."

He moved closer, rested his head against her shoulders, then let her hold him and stroke his hair. "It was her eyes," he whispered. "All Sara had to do was look at me and I could see how much she loved me. She must have seen it in mine, too, because that's what she showed in that *scatch* of me standing in the pond looking back at her." She could feel him start trembling. "What I remembered today was seeing Sara after the accident," he continued, barely audible, the voice of a distraught little boy. "She'd fallen, and her clothes were ripped where she'd clawed at her herself. She looked up, trying to find me, but she couldn't see because her eyes filled with—filled with blood."

Phrekka's breath caught, myriad images conjured in her mind, nausea rising amid heart-racing panic.

He continued, his voice breaking, "She knew it was too late for her, but she needed to see that I would be okay, and to have one last chance to show me the love in her eyes."

Phrekka felt a single tear crawl down her cheek, and she tried to speak, but no words would come.

"I kept thinking about Zachary," he said, "imagining how Sara used to look at him with that same love and trust, but then I would see him hurting her, and her eyes would fill with fear, then sheer terror, and she's crying and struggling and—and—"

Phrekka held him tightly, both trembling furiously. "Shhh . . . You're here with me," she soothed, saving him from being pulled into the same feeling of violation and defeat that had scared her for so long. They managed to calm each other, basking in mutual reassurance.

"Phrekka, I—I can't imagine how she could still find so much beauty in the world after that, especially to capture the uncorrupted innocence of children, but now I see how she used some of her *scatches* to speak to people, to communicate her love for them, and that's what she showed in their eyes."

"I could tell that little boy hanging in my gallery was searching for someone, and I knew he'd found him when I saw how you looked back."

"He was there to remind me of something very important, and even though it didn't make sense at the time, what I needed was to know somebody loved me, and with one look from him I felt that, plus everything else Sara ever wanted to tell me."

"The eyes speak the truth."

He rubbed his face. "Yes, good or bad. The few times I've tried to draw faces, I could never get the eyes right. They always look afraid."

Phrekka wondered how many times he'd searched her eyes and found only the irrational fear that held her back, the person he loved scared of his very touch. "I'll never again be afraid of *you*, Geoffrey," she blurted, a declaration rising from somewhere deep inside. "Maybe of something in my own past, but not of you. Find that in *my* eyes."

He shifted to look closer, his face aglow, but his robe came loose, and she glanced down and saw the briefest flash of lavender skin and towy curls before he quickly pulled it closed, his face flushing with embarrassment. He looked so adorable that despite her sudden rush of panic, she knew the source hadn't been fear, but rather sheer excitement, washing her with the intimacy conferred by a single fleeting impression—

"I'm sorry," he blustered.

And she kissed him.

Just like that, without thinking, not realizing her intent, her heart leading her mind.

He held her so tenderly that she felt cherished, permission to be delicate and fragile and vulnerable; then he kissed her back just long enough, pausing before her anxiety could return, brushing his face with her cinnamon hair, reaching up to stroke her cheek with his finger—

And she kissed him again, a few seconds longer this time, deeper and more passionately, not so much an exploration of someplace new as further immersion, their feet already wet, wading into liquid sensations now familiar and proven safe. She did feel anxious, but he must have sensed this, because he paused just beyond the shoreline with her, caressing her with his hands, and he looked into her eyes and smiled, then settled in beside her, his head snuggled close, both floating on a cushion of understanding. She dared to steal a peek at the front of his robe, relieved to see his arousal hadn't soared higher than her vertigo would allow her to follow.

As if sharing her very thoughts, he promised, "Even those times my feelings race ahead, I'll always stay with you. Together, Phrekka, nothing between us."

She felt the tears welling in her eyes, and she let them spill without embarrassment, wanting nothing more at that moment than to be held.

He cradled her close, rocking her gently, stroking her hair, humming a melody of bliss and wonder.

"I love you, Geoffrey," she whispered.

"I know . . ." he whispered back. "I see it in your eyes."

Phrekka roused without moving, the gentle rhythm of Geoffrey's measured breaths confirming he'd finally drifted off to sleep. She wondered how long they'd lain there, swaddled in the contentment of affection. Lamps still bathed the room with their soft glow, the bedstand clock reading: *12:50 AM*. She turned to study Geoffrey, surprised to find him sprawled on his back, the front of his robe wide open, his unabashed nakedness revealed—

Her heart suddenly pounding—

Breath catching, swallowing hard, her face flush, body warm . . .

The first blush of all-too-familiar frustration made her angry with herself, then furious that a uniquely intimate moment like this would be so inexplicably marred by irrational anxiety. This vision of Geoffrey offered the purest, most exquisite image she'd ever witnessed, handsome beyond comparison, powerful and masculine, yet gentle and loving. She imagined him as the young blond-haired boy who'd learned to love and trust without question, and she could see how his innocent little peeper snail had since grown to become the center of his masculine essence, the utterly personal means of his most profound expressions of affection . . . now reserved exclusively for her. She recalled how it looked pressing outward from his shorts, contrasting that to the peaceful form now reposed in its nest of fluffy curls, and she started to feel that familiar anxiety again, but her anger quickly overshadowed it, her determination to savor this relatively safe experience stronger than her exasperation over so much nervous hesitation. She'd been following Geoffrey's suggestion to let her fears abate by simply proving them obsolete, and while the results so far proved positive, her patience with such a slow and halting process had already started to wane. She yearned to build upon the foundation of their burgeoning romance, but feared she might yet lose him because she'd failed to help support the fragile framework of their dreams.

Her apprehensions now seemed petty, considering the severity of Sara's ordeals. Geoffrey's birth-mother had endured *all* the elements of a brutal rape, loving a blond-haired teenage boy with sparkling sapphire eyes only to suffer betrayal and degradation at his hands. Sara let that agony prevent her from sharing intimacy with any other young man, her one attempt ending in failure and painful regret, yet through it all she'd discovered her own special brand of happiness, devoting herself to that fragile spark of life who would always love her back, her little boy, Geoffrey. Phrekka felt the injustice pounding in her breast, heard it echoing from the walls, even watched it rouse the marble-eyed sailfishes. Her greatest unrealized fears could never compare with the nightmares Sara had actually lived, especially the ultimate . . . losing Geoffrey.

She gazed again upon his slumbering physique, moved by his exquisite symmetry and the sheer impact of nature's artistry, and she yearned to touch him, to unleash the passions coiled in his wiry body. She dared to place her hand gently on his chest, mesmerized by his beating heart, and she moved her other hand to her own bosom, her very soul dancing to the rhythm of life. She stroked along her breasts, lightly brushing one nipple, then the other, imagining how it would feel for Geoffrey to touch her there, the tingling ripples cascading down her body.

"Geoffrey?" she whispered, massaging his chest.

"Hmm?" he mumbled, awareness dawning. He quickly reached to close his robe, but she stopped his hand, assuring him, "I hope you don't mind, but I've been peeking."

He smiled, blushing in the muted light.

She guided his hand to her cheek, caressed it, maneuvered it down to her breasts, felt him cupping one gently then moving across to stroke the other, more tingles spreading, her nipples virtually aflame. She played her fingers down his body, exhilarated by her own audacity. She tickled his soft curls, then held her breath and dared to caress his manhood, feeling his pulse fill him with excitement, impressed by the wonder of how he swelled with expectation. She helped him pull her gown strap over her shoulder, following that with the other, easing her top down, then wiggling it over her hips until she wore nothing but goose bumps, exposed for all the world to know Geoffrey would be the one. She shifted her position until she could feel him pressed against her leg, and the sudden electric shock took her breath away, yet this time it would not be fear, but rather her own anticipation, the most intense desire to discover that extraordinary place she'd never experienced, trusting Geoffrey's patience as she learned to find the way.

"Please don't let me hurt you," he whispered, his breaths deep, his engorgement breathtakingly pronounced.

"You can't, Geoffrey, so don't be dismayed if I act foolish or scared or even start to cry."

"It's okay, Phrekka," he assured her. "However you feel is okay."

She moved his hand lower, then hesitated when he touched her own soft curls, but she pressed on, guiding him to the supple rise at her center, overwhelmed by her own responsiveness, and suddenly she felt tears coursing down her cheeks with the realization that no part of her would remain separate from him now, nothing left to require protection. She kissed him, felt him gingerly stroke her sensitive contours, and she shifted to encourage further access.

He kissed her back, their hands exploring like children with fingerpaints, and he moved closer—

Then he hesitated.

"Wait," he whispered, "we're not protected—from pregnancy, I mean."

"Oh no," she sighed, passion yielding to pragmatism. "I have no birth control, never dreaming I would—that I'd want—"

"I have thingies in my overnight bag."

"But that's down the hall!"

"It's a big risk," he said, holding her tightly. "Remember, I was born as the result of a one-time encounter."

"Well—hurry then. Put your robe on."

She had him up and tangled in terry cloth so fast they had to unravel the mess and try again. He tried cinching it tightly, but that proved rather revealing of his jutting appendage, so he loosened the strap and closed the robe awkwardly with one hand. She pushed him toward the door, holding her gown to cover herself as she let him into the hallway, both giggling and *shushing* each other. "Don't get lost," she warned him.

"*You are my beacon,*" he singsonged, bowing with a flourish, then pausing to kiss her briefly.

Glancing at his mid-robe tent pole, she corrected, "I think you're the one with a towering lighthouse—now go!"

He hurried down the hallway while she peeked around the door, then realized he'd forgotten his key-card and had to trot back for it. Repeating the process, he fumbled in front of his door, dropped the card, warned her again to hush her snickers, then disappeared inside his room—for all of about three seconds, rushing out again while stuffing several packets into his pocket, a sneaky grin plastered to his face.

"Close your door, silly!" she hissed, sending him back. He caught his robe strap in the door, made faces pretending he'd caught more than terry cloth, had to wrestle with the key-card again, managed to free himself, and rushed gleefully back toward her room . . .

And she quickly closed the door in his face, locking him out.

He tapped urgently.

"Who is it?" she singsonged.

"Open up, it's the police!"

"Shhhh!" she warned. "Not so loud." She chained the door and opened it a few inches, peeking out. "Let's see some ID."

He opened his robe and pointed, positive identification, easily picked out of a line-up, so she quickly fumbled the chain off and yanked him inside.

"Let's hurry," she admonished, "—my parents will be home any minute."

"Just tell them I intend to marry you—"

They looked at each other, and she could see it in his eyes, and she knew he could see it in hers.

He took her gingerly in his arms and kissed her, his heart pounding furiously.

"Geoffrey . . ." she whispered.

"I can't believe how nervous I am," he whispered back. "This is like nothing I've ever experienced—"

"Hey, *I'm* the virgin at this party," she teased, touching his lips with her finger, exploring his mustache, then following that with her mouth.

"I'm honored," he breathed at his next opportunity, "that you never settled for less than me."

"Wait," she said, struck by a thought. "I have something." She hurried to her bag and pulled out a small box, removing an exquisite candle, explaining, "I'd planned to take this home, but . . ."

He helped her place it in a glass holder, caressing her shoulders while she lit the wick, both watching the flame flicker tentatively as it gathered its determination to burn with exuberance and flair. Geoffrey's face registered surprise, his eyes twinkling with recognition at what Phrekka had seen when she first discovered the candle, that what appeared to be swirls of sienna wax wrapped around each other all the way to the top were actually two distinct colors: pale yellow intertwined with light sepia . . . *blond embracing cinnamon.* He smiled, the guttering flame sparkling dual reflections in his glowing sapphire eyes.

She nodded slowly, then folded herself into his arms, both intertwined.

The first few droplets of melted wax mingled together in flowing liquid passion, clinging precariously at the precipice, then breaking free as one to explore unfamiliar terrain.

The young lovers stood there holding each other for a moment; then she felt him move her gently toward the great bed.

The balcony breeze blew in small gusts, the candle flame dancing patterns across the canopy.

She felt nervous anticipating Geoffrey's expressions of abiding love, but prepared to join with him as together they would climb the pinnacle of abandon that rises only from the bedrock of trust.

Yet, he didn't.

Instead, he cuddled beside her, and she felt the profound intimacy of his simple nakedness so close to her own, and that felt pure and bereft of preconception, more than a means to any end. He gently massaged her shoulders, helping her realize that she'd tensed.

"This is enough for now, Phrekka," he whispered. "Just this much is a big step for us."

"I'm nervous," she admitted, "but it's from not knowing what to expect, hoping I don't do something wrong."

He actually chuckled at that, so she poked him in the ribs, but the relief that she'd not made him uncomfortable washed over her. "Phrekka, you couldn't possibly do anything wrong. It's you I love, not some ten-step procedure. Just step one with you is phenomenal—or number seven, if you prefer—or we can just make up our own. Whatever happens is because you're helping me learn how to make you feel good and I'm helping you learn about me."

She stroked his abdomen, swirling in the reassurance of his words, and she explored lower, gently fingering his soft curls again, noticing how he rippled with excitement from the slightest brush of skin. "It seems like it would hurt, growing so big and stretched like that."

He grinned. "Well, thank you for the compliment. It *does* hurt when you're fifteen years old and sitting in a boring class wondering what some girl in the room would look like with her panties off, and your blue jeans are *way* too tight, and you're throbbing with no way to do anything about it right then. It's like cutting a tooth—hurts so much it feels good, and you just can't stop messing with it." He chuckled again, making her laugh, guiding her hand carefully to demonstrate the nuances of his erogeny, subtle cautions showing how to avoid too much too soon.

"When I was a girl—" she started, feeling herself blush, a little embarrassed about revealing her secret, yet charged with electric excitement that Geoffrey had become the one person in the world with whom she could share this. "I figured out, you know, where I was most sensitive. Sometimes at night I would, um . . ." She guided his hand, gingerly cupping two of his fingers and showing him, liquid fire flowing through her lower abdomen, pausing lest too much consume her too fast. "By the time I turned twelve, I'd become a young woman, and I discovered those little tingly feel-goods could be *really* powerful—" Geoffrey had taken over, freeing her hands to explore his body, and he surprised her with how perfectly he sensed her reactions, and how carefully he eased her to each plateau without pushing her beyond the confidence of sure footing. "Every now and then I feel good like this," she admitted, liberated by the exhilaration of unabashed confession. "I like to imagine being held, but if I ever think about one specific guy, that's when I kinda, you know, freeze up, get nervous—mmmm," she gushed, stronger waves cascading over her, breaths coming in spasms. "But—but with you—*wow*—"

He reached suddenly to slow her exuberance, his own responsivity flaring into barely contained raging fire, this she could sense, this she could feel. Breathing hard, he joshed, "Well, I wish *I* could truthfully say *every now and then*, too, but with most guys, I think, it's more like *all the damned time*—and that's still not enough to keep us from acting stupid and letting our little fellers do our thinking for us. I always found it easier just to imagine the sheer sexiness of a woman's body, but when I found myself fantasizing about somebody I liked, it always left me—I don't know how to describe it—I guess *frustrated.* It's easy to pretend some woman in a magazine or on TV is horny for you—*real* easy sometimes—but trying to pretend being in love always leaves me feeling somehow empty, like being reminded that she *doesn't* love me, and that always ruins the moment."

Forced to shift her position, she felt herself swelling more than she'd ever thought possible, literally in awe of the sheer power of Geoffrey's touch and her extraordinary need for it never to end.

He suddenly stilled her hand, and she realized that he must be as aroused as she, if that be possible. "I'm way too close," he gasped. "I want this to last forever. From what I know of women, you can, like, go on successive waves, like cross-country skiing where you race up one rise and zoom along to the next. With guys, it's more like climbing up a mountain. You have to be careful lest you fall off, because the higher you climb and the longer you make it last, the greater the view and the more intense the feeling. But when we just can't climb any higher, we suddenly soar, and gliding to the valley is fast and furious and indescribably exhilarating—but then we're all the way to the bottom again, still sensitive—and sometimes even sore from the fall—" he chuckled, "so we have to dust ourselves off and rest for a bit before we can try to climb again." He moved her hand slightly lower, and she could feel his throbbing spasms, how very close she must be to detonating the avalanche that would carry them both into oblivion.

And she heard fierce gusts blowing across the balcony, the winds of consummation swirling around the room, the heat from their bodies carried off into the night, and she felt herself slipping, and had to still his hand for a moment to let the guttering blaze subside, not wanting to achieve the ultimate transformation until they would find that place together.

"I'm not nervous anymore," he whispered, "because I believe in us."

And she felt her eyes welling with fresh tears as he held her in his arms and rocked her gently, a lifetime of anxiety washed away by her faith in Geoffrey always loving her so much that his own happiness could never exist without hers. As he wiped the droplets from her cheeks, she could see his eyes glistening, too, and she felt his body swirling around and through hers, together moved by the forces of the moon and the stars even as the tides and the winds and the rains. She realized in that moment that she would finally discover the self-understanding and inner peace she had always sought, reaching out to ignite Geoffrey's spark so they may join together to burn brightly as one amid the great conflagration that is humanity, learning the truth she would forever know, a connection she would always embrace.

She could see the candle's liquid cinnamon and blond melting into a conjoined existence of mercurial ginger . . .

The fire of anticipation reflecting from the eyes of the sailfishes . . .

And Geoffrey held her close, and she believed they would lead each other to explore realms beyond their imaginations.

She felt the tide rising, the ebb and flow of natural motion, and she knew that no matter what lingering fears conspired to pull her away, she would need only to hold on to Geoffrey, and they would be swept together wherever the currents of trust and devotion would take them.

The candle's flame flared up and consumed the entire world, and nothing existed for Phrekka Churán except Geoffrey Drousseau's sustaining love.

The sailfishes were on their own.

CHAPTER 24

Geoffrey could feel Phrekka snuggled against him, the rhythm of her gentle breaths snare-brushing a back-beat in time with his own heart's pulse, syncopation for the quiet strains of radio music dancing whorls throughout the hotel suite. He opened his eyes and squinted at the bright light as the warm, sun-drenched breeze wafted from the balcony to swath him in its morning embrace. A blue jay perched on the railing, peeking in at the young couple.

He shifted slightly to study her slumbering form, her sensual contours sculpting the drape of sheer bedsheet, a princess reposed in satin frills beneath her royal canopy. He touched her cinnamon hair, instantly transforming her from some imaginary vision into the substance of realized dreams, wishing some magical spell could allow them to remain there, side-by-side, savoring their first time, always. Still astounded by the unabashed intimacy of their night together, he found an exhilarating sense of honor and integrity in knowing he'd already pledged his devotion beforehand, that he cher-ished her so much he'd accepted the limits of her physical expressions, never imagining how their ultimate consummation would so intensely exceed his vernal teenage fantasies of falling in love. By infusing her with the power of his promise, he helped her finally rally the strength to shed that suffocating chrysalis of deeply ingrained fears and thus rise with him to the very heights of tender passion that artists and lovers throughout history have long striven to capture and evoke. That initial sensation of pristine purity might well have sustained him forever, but then she'd quickly exceeded it, both rollicking in their new-found freedom to surf the pounding waves of ecstasy. Geoffrey had eventually floated ashore to bask with her on the shifting sands of expectation . . . until she lifted him up yet again, leading him to the highest mountain, there to climb beyond the clouds in search of enchanted realms, Phrekka transformed into the proverbial wild woman who steams windows and shocks even blushing sailfishes into closing their eyes. They claimed the summit as their own, then trusted each other so much as to surrender their footing and reach for the sky, soaring together wherever they may.

He lay back and felt her hair against his cheek, willing his sore muscles to relax, pretending that nothing existed outside this room, outside their world—

Ring.

He scrabbled to answer the phone, but she roused and squeezed his arm while he spoke. "It's the PR guy," he whispered to her.

She stroked his hair and kissed him atop the head, then slipped from under the sheet and disappeared into the bathroom, an arousingly exquisite portrayal in nude which Geoffrey would never forget.

Shaken from his reverie, he confirmed his appointment for interviews two hours hence, declining variously worded offers to spend the interval in meticulous preparation. Just as he finally managed to disconnect, a knock sounded from the door. He struggled into his tangled robe and retrieved two bags from a gracious attendant, then hesitated outside the bathroom and shouted, "Clothes are here. I'll be next door for a bit."

He hurried to his own suite, unpacked the clean outfits, then raced through his morning routine and found himself obsessively combing his shock of blond, wanting to look his best for Phrekka. He returned in time to find her speaking into her personal phone while brushing her long, damp hair.

"Here he is," she said, extending the handset, then encircling his waist for a hug while he talked.

Charles's lead attorney greeted him. "We just faxed some documents your way for signature. We need them right back."

"Have you found out anything?"

"Those forms listing you as next-of-kin should gain us access to her case-file, so what we've learned so far is, um, incomplete." The man's reticence suggested anything but good news.

"What *do* you know?" Geoffrey persisted.

"Well, we confirmed that Sara *was* declared a ward of state shortly after the accident, then placed in the hospital you named. She was terminated approximately fourteen months later, but not as an institutional transfer." He hesitated, finishing, "She's not listed anywhere in the system after that."

Geoffrey closed his eyes and took a deep breath. "She finally died," he breathed, his voice betraying sadness, maybe some relief.

"I can't say that, not until we have the case-file." Then he added, quieter, "But with irreversible brain damage, that's the likely explanation. I'm sorry."

"Good news or bad, I just need to know, need to be sure," Geoffrey said. He thanked him, then disconnected and stood there holding Phrekka for a full minute. Finally, they walked together down the hallway so he could sign and fax the documents.

"At least you'll know within a day or two," she soothed.

"I can still find out sooner," he said, "by calling the cemetery."

She nodded, then thought for a second. "Would you prefer we drive out there?"

He'd not considered that, but he appreciated her forethought, liking the idea very much. "Yeah, because when I finally confirm she's buried there, I might want to walk back to the site and, well, you know. Thanks for helping me think straight right now, Phrekka."

She hugged him again. "I just wish I could do more, that I could find some way to take care of you completely."

He smiled and squeezed her hand. "Hey, that sounds like fun. You could feed me and water me, give me bubble-baths—"

"You just want me to wash your peeper," she sparred, the muting shade of their melancholy lifting to expose the light of new-found bliss.

He wagged his eyebrows, guilty as charged; bring him a confession to sign.

As they walked back toward her suite, the food-service cart arrived with breakfast. This time he let her sign the check, both amused by a very pleased waiter bowing and scraping his way toward the elevator.

"I acted with presumption," she said, "assuming you'd want to eat—"

"See? You're taking care of me already," he joshed. "Um, I might need some help washing up afterwards, though. I think my little hoo-hoo *is* feeling a bit dirty."

Her arms akimbo, she declared, "No baths right now, Geoffrey—you have a lot of interviews to give, but if you perform well, I might give you a standing ovation—later."

"Ah!—the star has found his motivation!"

They attacked the breakfast with surprisingly voracious appetites while discussing his TV appearances, a no-pressure opportunity for him to practice summarizing their foundation goals.

Afterward, they steeled themselves for the trip out to Horse Creek in search of unvarnished truth. Phrekka offered to drive, so Geoffrey sat back and closed his eyes. He felt himself pulled by rising apprehension, but this time he allowed it to carry him where it may, confident in his connection.

They found the cemetery office tended by an older woman wearing thick bi-focal glasses. She recognized him instantly. "I seen you on the news, Geoffrey," she pronounced. "Well, bless your heart."

He thanked her for such kind thoughts, then explained, "I need to confirm when Sara was buried."

"Oh yes, the Drousseau sites," she said, wrestling open a narrow file drawer and flipping through a series of 3X5 cards. Finally, she pulled one and peered at it, a puzzled expression wrinkling the contours of her time-worn face.

"That's hers?" he prodded.

"All three," she said, looking at him over the top of her glasses. "I have the dates for Alain and Rachel," she said, studying the card again as if, given enough time, new information would be revealed.

"No date for Sara?"

She took her glasses off and looked at him sadly. "I'm sorry, Geoffrey, but she was never buried here."

"Buried somewhere in a state-paid, unmarked potter's grave," Geoffrey mumbled sadly, his first acknowledgment of the subject he'd been avoiding during their drive toward Bruce Trail to meet another phalanx of media mavins.

"You can have her reinterred," Phrekka assured him, "once they crack the files and find out where she is."

"*If* I have the legal authority."

"Don't underestimate the influence of Charles's attorneys," she assured him. "We'll provide the kind of memorial ceremony she deserves."

"Finally buried with her family," he murmured, pushing aside images of a mass grave bulldozed open, a man in coveralls pointing toward a tangle of bones, *That might be part of her over there . . .*

"Think about Sara's foundation for now, Geoffrey," she prompted, reminder that a series of probing, camera-lensed inquisitors still loomed before him. "Don't let impatience mar this chance to honor her memory." She squeezed his hand, urging him to feel better.

The PR guy and Andy-Geoff greeted them as they stepped from the car. The little one tugged at Geoffrey's sleeve, pronouncing, "Come on! You gotta look! They brung bunches of pitchers!"

A platinum-blond, business-suited producer woman and droopy-jeaned, camera-shouldered shooter introduced themselves to the young couple. "Ooo!" she said, "let's get shots of you looking at the new *scatches!*"

A small entourage followed them into the house, Geoffrey pulled along by his exuberant little namesake. His disposition improved as more than a dozen neighbors and friends welcomed him, followed by the customary round of Pammy hugs and a gentle handshake from her towering friend. Geoffrey reminisced for the camera as windows to his past opened with each new sketch, easily identifying many of the faces while Pamela supplied stories about the few beyond his recognition. Discovering a drawing of Gumper flying like the wind on his bicycle, a poignant contrast to the boy's difficulty with walking, Geoffrey explained, "This is Gumper Lewis, now a successful businessman and philanthropist in the Tupelo area. He's the hero who risked his life to save mine, snatching me from the poisonous cloud and carrying me to safety. Laurel should be proud to be the home town of Gumper Lewis."

He examined several more sketches, blushing over a rather immodest depiction of himself as a toddler standing in the bathtub with a washcloth atop his head; then he found himself moved nearly to tears by one of young Sara cradling a big-eyed, blond-fringed infant to her bosom. Their eyes seemed to speak to each other, expressing immutable love, whispering to him from the page now after all this time. Sara simply looked at her little boy, and all she needed to know from him could be seen in the merest glimpse as he looked back . . .

Finally, everybody laughed at the images of Sara and Pammy shoving ice-cream cones into each other's faces, the pouting little Geoffrey standing there, arms akimbo, failing to understand why they'd just wasted so much perfectly good confection. It was the feelings engendered by those carefree memories that sustained him through several hours of grueling interviews, all of which succeeded in their intent, he liked to think, judging by the pleased reactions of producers and onlookers alike. Whenever his stamina flagged, he needed only to glance toward Phrekka, and her eyes would suffuse him with renewed purpose. She did slip away for a few minutes at one point, which he assumed to be a bathroom break, but she returned appearing quite melancholy until she noticed him looking and conjured a beatific smile to replace the frown. He remembered how difficult all this must be for her, vowing not to let her feel like he requires her constant support.

When the last shoot wrapped and the crew started to clear, Geoffrey noticed the sadness returning to Phrekka's face. As soon as they had a moment together, she whispered, "A local attorney is waiting at the airport to fly with us to Tupelo. I'm not sure what it's about, but I suspect he might have bad news."

They explained their hasty exit to Pamela, who hugged them both before distracting their visitors so the young couple could slip away.

A surprisingly solemn version of little Andy-Geoff met them at the car, clutching a child-sized cluster of tiny yellow wildflower blossoms in his fist. "You're gonna find where Sara's buried at, ain't you?" he whispered, his eyes glistening.

"I hope so," Geoffrey said.

The little boy proffered the flowers. "You should give her these. I bet she'll like 'em," he said, letting Geoffrey pick him up and hold him. Phrekka joined them, both cradling the wiry child. Geoffrey swallowed hard to fight the lump rising in his throat as he placed the heartfelt gift carefully in his shirt pocket, determined not to imagine Sara's face lest he be swept wistfully away by memories of a time long lost. Andy-Geoff squirmed free and dashed away, a mercurial flash of all-boy lightning.

They drove in silence to the airport. Peter Gomill, the attorney who handled the trust-fund lawsuit so many years before still hadn't arrived, so Geoffrey and Phrekka settled into the cabin lounge to wait. She answered a call on her cell-phone, then handed it to Geoffrey.

The lead attorney greeted him, asking, "Gomill's not there yet? Well, he's been in a meeting, so we don't know all the details, but his secretary promised to send him straight over—should be there any time now. He did the original paperwork, so he ought to be able to answer your questions."

"What paperwork? What's this about?"

"Well, it's good and bad, son. We found Sara, and she *is* still alive—" Geoffrey's heart started pounding furiously. "But I'm sorry to say she's suffering from liver failure and hasn't much time left."

"Still brain damaged?" he managed to ask, a new image of her in pain now tearing at his soul.

"Yes," the attorney said quietly. "She never recovered, and certainly can't communicate or anything like that, but she's not suffering, that they've assured me."

"Who is *they*? I thought her records ended more then a decade ago."

"Her *state* records did. It turns out she's in a private-care facility, no longer a ward of state. Gomill had sued for guardianship on behalf of his clients—and won; then they arranged to have her moved. I thought gaining direct access to her would be difficult, but all you need is permission from her surviving guardian, somebody we're trying to contact right now."

"Who? Who is it?"

"A woman in—of all places—*Iowa.* Her name's Marjorie Calhoun."

"I sued the hell out of 'em," Peter Gomill explained as the jet lifted off for a ten-minute flight into Tupelo.

Geoffrey regarded the elderly, long-nosed litigator who wore his oversized suit the way a coat hanger fills out a baggy jacket. "I know you sued for *me*, but I never saw Sara's name on anything."

"*Two* lawsuits," he explained with what Geoffrey would have to describe as a Brooklynesque southern drawl. "Once the Calhouns adopted you, I had the court grant them next-friend status so they could seek to recover the cost of your upbringing, plus to compensate you for personal trauma and the loss of your parents. Since Sara was already eighteen, she'd been declared a ward and placed in a state hospital. When Ernest went to see her, he didn't take to the kind of treatment she was getting—not anything wrong, but sixty in a ward, strapped to her bed, heavily sedated—and nobody would tell him what was being done to help her recover. He wanted her moved, but he didn't have the legal right, nor could he afford three-hundred a day like most places cost, so we got the Calhouns declared Sara's next friends, then sued to pay for lifetime private care. It took more than a year, but he finally got her out of there. He said it didn't matter if she only lived another day as long as she was comfortable, whatever it took to give her that much." Gomill leaned across as if to share a secret. "He did right by her, Geoffrey, more than most woulda done."

Geoffrey nodded, closed his eyes, and saw Ernest standing proudly at his adoptive son's graduation, the face of a man who'd made many mistakes but never wavered in trying his best to accomplish what he believed to be right.

"I expected to find her buried in some unmarked grave," Geoffrey whispered, his eyes still squeezed shut, Phrekka holding his hand.

"Oh no," Gomill said. "Ernest wouldn't have that. He pre-paid for a top-flight funeral service and interment. The card and instructions are in her file. If I remember right, she's to be laid to rest there in Laurel with her parents, the spot right beside her mama."

Geoffrey imagined Ernest standing before Rachel's grave, his hat pressed to his breast out of respect for his only sister, sadness and regret etched along deep grooves in his face. Geoffrey focused on this vision as if watching from a distance, and it seemed like Ernest could sense his presence, the old man turning to glance his way. Ernest nodded knowingly, asking for neither acceptance nor approval, then bowed his head and began to weep. Having spurned his family obligations once, he'd finally returned to fulfill them, something he would harangue his adoptive son about many times in the coming years, desperately trying to stress the importance of not repeating his mistakes, punctuating these lectures with the lashes he'd accepted as natural and necessary during his own boyhood.

Yes, Ernest had made a lot of mistakes rearing Geoffrey, but he never gave up, accepting responsibility for his sister's daughter and son . . .

His sister's daughter and *grandson.*

Geoffrey wondered if Ernest had learned the truth about Sara's "little brother," but somehow he already knew the answer. He could see it clearly, Rachel reaching out to Ernest through her haze of tranquilization, her only brother reminding her the family must fulfill its obligation to Sara's child, that Sara be given that chance even if it meant hiding the truth forever.

Some half-dozen years later, the same choice had fallen to Ernest, so he brought the scared and obstinate child to Iowa, struggling to convince him and Marjorie to accept each other; then he returned to Mississippi to ensure Sara received the best possible care . . .

Proving that he'd never stopped loving Rachel after all.

The sprawling, one-story building with various wings spider-legging from a central activities center impressed Geoffrey, especially the woodsy grounds overlooking Tulip Creek. They'd been joined by another attorney at the terminal, their group now a litigation-itchy foursome toting a pair of briefcases, locked and loaded.

They startled a polite young woman at the reception counter, the attorneys stepping forward to assert privilege when she dared suggest visitation might be restricted. Just then, a slash of sunlight announced an elderly visitor pushing her way through the front entrance, a tiny hunched-over woman hobbling toward them with the assistance of a cane.

"Selma!" the receptionist blurted. "These people say they're here to see Sara."

The old woman paused and peered up at them through thick glasses, her face registering surprise, then recognition. "You're Geoffrey," she pronounced, a gleam in her eye. "I saw you on the TV."

"This here's Selma Barlucci," the receptionist supplied. "She used to work here."

"Nurse Barlucci," Geoffrey breathed reverently. "You took care of Sara at the state hospital, too."

"Why, yes!" she said, smiling.

"So," he kidded, arms akimbo, "are you a Drousseau stalker?"

She answered with a cackling laugh. "Why, I guess I am! I was eligible to retire about the time Sara was moved, so I come here and got myself a job—until my legs started to give out a couple years back." She placed her palm on Geoffrey's chest, her eyes glistening. "They was always somethin' special about her, so I still try to come by every day or two, just to brush her hair and sit with her a spell, let her know I'm here."

Without realizing his intent, Geoffrey suddenly hugged the woman, checking his exuberance so as not to crush this fragile blossom whose loyalty to Sara bloomed through dark days and harsh storms, a hardy perennial bringing sunshine to her withered friend.

The attorneys shuffled impatiently while she explained, "My niece has been after me to move nearby to her in Memphis, but . . ." She tilted her head, studying Geoffrey sadly. "Sara don't have much time, you know."

Geoffrey nodded, words too difficult to find right then.

"I believe she knows me," Selma explained, "and I just couldn't let her be alone, not now. She ain't had nobody else except her Uncle Ernest, who calls every month to check on her. There used to be a young feller who called regular, too, until she got moved, but then I had no way to get hold of him. He couldn't hardly stand knowin' she was hurt so bad."

"Zachary," Geoffrey whispered.

Selma's face lit up. "You know him."

"He was her boyfriend when they were very young."

She shook her head, then removed her glasses and examined them. "I suppose he's moved on with his life by now."

Geoffrey bit his lip, but didn't offer to explain.

She put her glasses on again, looked surprised like she could see the world for the first time, then took one of Geoffrey's hands and studied his face. "She ain't gonna look like you remember her," she cautioned.

He swallowed hard, nodding.

"The only thing she can move is her arms. Her left one flails something fierce, has to be strapped down so it don't get broke or bruised up bad, especially when she gets agitated. Her right arm's not so bad, just kinda makes these swirling motions, real peaceful-like sometimes, kinda frantic other times. Used to be, whenever she'd see me was the only time her arms would quit movin', but these past few months since her liver's been givin' out, not even me comin' by seems to help." She hesitated, whispering, "I think she knows she's dyin'."

"You think she can see you?"

"I know she can, but since she can't turn her head or move her eyes except to blink, all she can see is whichever way she's facing."

"How do you communicate?"

"She can't understand words or nothin', just seems to sense that I'm here to take care of her."

"How does she eat?"

"She's got a tube, plus a catheter and evacuation bag. I know you've come a long way and can't wait to see her, but you need to be prepared. It's gonna break your heart."

The facility director arrived, everybody introduced around. He and the lawyers decided to argue about files and releases and other matters, so Selma motioned for Geoffrey and Phrekka to follow her, leaving the men to their blustering.

They peeked into Sara's room from the hallway. Four beds with safety rails cradled patients festooned with tubes and wires, all lying perfectly still except one: a sallow, jaundiced woman with long chestnut hair. One arm jerked violently against padded straps, the other waving gracefully as if to conduct a symphony orchestra.

Sara.

Geoffrey's breath caught, and he felt the world spinning as he desperately tried to conjure the competing images of Sara as an ebullient young woman, the little girl with the gentle smile . . .

Selma stepped into the room, moving directly in front of Sara, pausing for unmoving eyes to register. Her presence seemed to have no effect on the wild gesticulation, so Selma patted Sara's arm, then removed her own glasses and rubbed her eyes, fighting back tears and murmuring, "These past few weeks it don't seem like she even knows me anymore."

Geoffrey felt Phrekka squeezing his hand. He planted his feet firmly as if to resist some invisible force pulling him into the room, stark reality lurking just across the transom, truth too tragic to bear.

"We don't have to go in," Phrekka whispered, reading his mind, reminding him why he'd come.

Waves of guilt washed over him, shame that he would be repulsed by the woman who loved him, his secret mother.

He stepped forward, hesitated, then moved closer, his heart palpitating. He lingered at the side, away from Sara's eyes.

Her breaths sounded raspy and labored as if fighting against the intrusive tube, her eyelids fluttering for a moment with each blink, face and neck and body mere skin and bones, arms oddly muscular from more than a decade of flailing mindlessly.

Selma removed a brush from her satchel, then hesitated and stood back. "Let her see you, Geoffrey."

He moved toward the foot of the bed, steeled himself, and noticed his own arm twitching nervously. He willed himself to calm, then stepped into Sara's line of sight, gazing into her eyes . . .

And he found her.

Her arms stopped moving, her breath one long sigh before resuming its labored rhythm.

He looked even deeper into Sara's eyes, and he saw all the love she'd ever shown him, ever felt for him.

Then he remembered the wildflowers, and why Sara had liked them so much.

Reaching into his shirt pocket, he gingerly removed the child-sized cluster of tiny yellow blossoms and held them before her just like he'd done the last morning they ever spent together, when he'd watched her face light up before she gathered him into a lingering hug, when she'd thanked him and said he could run along, go play by the pond if he wanted. He'd turned on his way out and noticed something seen so many times throughout his young life, what for many people would have signaled sadness or hurt, but which for Sara always meant he'd found a way to make her happy . . .

She'd started to cry.

Geoffrey tried to push the memory aside, his own eyes blurring now, his lower lip trembling. He wiped his face, fighting to regain his composure.

Selma Barlucci gasped, breathing, "I've never seen her do that . . ."

Geoffrey glanced up, sill holding the child-sized spray of tiny yellow wildflowers, and he looked upon the vegetative, paralyzed, last vestiges of the Sara who'd traded her own childhood for the chance to share her little boy's, and he gazed into her eyes . . .

As they filled with tears, a single droplet crawling down each of her jaundiced cheeks.

Geoffrey seemed to be missing something that hovered just beyond comprehension, a fleeting intangible that kept dissolving under the glare of direct scrutiny. He squeezed Sara's hand, concluding that his uneasiness must stem from the stark reality of her brain damage, a wrenching contradiction between the Sara he'd only recently remembered and this diminished semblance of her former self.

Sara would never again offer him her gentle embrace, never speak to him and say she loves him or teach him about lightning bugs and lecture him about responsibility, unable even to manage the simplest gesture of turning her head to gaze upon the man he'd become . . . yet the person whose hand he now held did somehow comprehend that Geoffrey had come back to her, and she'd marshaled every remaining bit of capability to prove she could still feel love for him, the truth revealed in her eyes. He'd come to this scenic locale along Tulip Creek never expecting their exceptional bond to have inexplicably survived, Sara still defying the betraying relic of a body that would sustain her at most for a precious few more weeks, already surpassing by years what mere medical science could explain. Geoffrey considered how much Sara had lost, haunted by the notion that even now he continued to miss some elusive possibility created by this miraculous opportunity to make up for lost time.

He listened to Phrekka and Selma speaking quietly by the doorway, the kindhearted elderly nurse recounting her own health problems, how several small strokes had portended a threat of full aneurysm, her fear that she would become a burden on her niece in Memphis, forced to accept an invitation she knew issued from a sense of guilt and obligation.

Selma whispered, "Sara has been a good excuse, I hate to admit, for me to stay right where I am. Until you and Geoffrey came, I was all she had. I couldn't up and move away and leave her to spend her last days alone."

Geoffrey glanced over to see Phrekka tenderly stroking the woman's liver-spot-dappled arm, those beautiful almond-shaped eyes glistening with empathy and affection. He felt a lump rising in his throat as he tried to imagine Phrekka growing that old someday, how she would appear wrinkled and spotted and stooped and slow, yet still glowing with a radiant beauty appreciated by nobody more than her shriveled old geezer who'd traded blond for gray so many years before. He would cling tenaciously to life and outlive Phrekka, even if only by a minute, to remind her every day how much he adored her, sparing her the grief of losing him first . . .

Sara sighed, her eyelids fluttering, left arm still relaxed, right hand cradled in Geoffrey's.

"That sounds wonderful," Selma said wistfully. "I've never seen the Golden Gate Bridge."

"Then you *must* come visit, and stay as long as you like," Phrekka insisted.

Geoffrey rubbed the knots in his neck and decided he needed to stretch. He lay Sara's hand gently on the bed, then watched in frustration as she lifted it and started making those swirling motions, her left arm twitching and pulling against its strap.

"I want the best doctors in the world to examine her," he said quietly. "Every possible test, every therapy, anything that might help her—"

Phrekka said, "I'm sure they're limited in what they can do at this facility, Geoffrey."

"Then I'll get Mom's—Marjorie's—consent and take her somewhere else. It needs to be someplace where I can stay with her, and where you can visit, too, Selma—"

"Geoffrey," Phrekka interrupted, brightening, "Grandmamá had an entire wing of her home set up as a hospital, plus I can bring in extra equipment or specialists if needed."

"Wow," Geoffrey said, overwhelmed by the providence, not the least reluctant about accepting her selfless contribution.

Phrekka turned to Selma. "You could stay with us, have your own room or a whole suite if you like, plus we'll have the best medical care available for you, as well."

"Well, I'd hate to imagine never seeing Sara again."

"Phrekka," Geoffrey breathed, his heart palpitating with excitement, "I don't know what to say—"

"Just say *yes*, silly."

As if on cue, an attendant brought in the staff physician, a chubby, balding man in frumpy clothes with his tie knotted haphazardly. He greeted Selma fondly, squeezing her shoulders and kissing the top of her head, earning a cackle for his reward. He bowed to Phrekka, then pumped Geoffrey's hand vigorously, but he frowned after they took turns explaining their plan. "I hope you don't believe there's any way her brain damage can be reversed," he cautioned.

"Maybe something's been discovered in the years since it happened," Geoffrey argued weakly.

The physician shook his head sadly, explaining, "She was poisoned, son, by a massive dose of halogenated hydrocarbons, so bad she went into convulsions and coma within minutes. You don't recover from that kind of trauma."

Geoffrey asked him to explain, retrieving a pad and pencil from Phrekka's satchel for taking notes.

"The gas molecules attach to hemoglobin in red blood cells, blocking their ability to carry oxygen, which starves the brain and vital organs. Sara's brain activity is very limited except for a marked tendency to secrete quantities of serotonin whenever Selma sits with her, which has a calming influence on what would normally manifest as an endless series of minor seizures."

Geoffrey felt the air go out of his lungs, then held his breath a moment. "What about her liver?—at least doing something to help her survive longer."

He shook his head sadly. "Most of it was destroyed, but a small part has kept her alive by regenerating. Now she has cirrhosis, so its function has dropped to virtually zero."

"What about a transplant?"

"Look at her, son," he said gently. "She couldn't survive the anesthesia, let alone an invasive surgery or the post-operative anti-rejection regimen. No, even if a suitable donor were available, the very attempt would no doubt prove fatal."

"There's other physical debility, too?"

"Besides the atrophy of being bedridden for so long, only one kidney still functions—barely. She's been in renal failure needing dialysis three times so far this year, and the scarring in her lungs is so bad that even minor colds can put her on the respirator for weeks or longer."

"Then what *has* kept her alive so long?"

"I suspect I'll never understand. She must have a pact with God—that and I think having Selma has given her the will to hang on."

A wave of regret and guilt washed over Geoffrey, despite knowing that's not how the doctor intended his remark. He swallowed hard, checked his breathing, and managed to whisper, "Can she be moved?"

He considered this, then decided, "Assuming it's handled by professionals who understand her requirements."

Distrusting his quivering voice, Geoffrey nodded understanding.

The physician seemed to sense this, squeezing the young man's shoulder and offering, "I'm making rounds, so just have me paged if you have more questions or make any decisions." He disappeared down the hallway.

Geoffrey stood there in a daze, watching Sara's oscillating hand, and he felt Phrekka step behind him.

"Whatever you want," she whispered.

"I want her to come home with us," he could hear himself saying from another world. "—But no tests, no invasions—only whatever will make her comfortable."

"Yes," Phrekka agreed, affirming he'd decided what's best for Sara, not for himself.

"With Selma there, too," he said quietly.

The old woman answered from her seat, "You know, Geoffrey, now that she has you again, she really doesn't need me anymore."

"But she does need you," he said quietly without turning, hypnotized by the grace of Sara's hand tracing patterns in the air. "I could never fill the place she holds for you in her heart."

Phrekka turned toward the old woman. "And *you* need *her*, I think."

Selma's eyes glistened with acceptance and belonging. "Yes," she whispered, "I suppose I do."

That settled, Geoffrey looked toward Sara again, but he still felt like he'd missed something, an intangible both somehow familiar yet elusive . . .

Suddenly, he ripped the notes from Phrekka's pad and showed the blank page to Sara, then he lifted her hand so she could see him placing the pen between her fingers. She grasped it with instinctive familiarity as he positioned it atop the pad on her lap.

Phrekka and Selma gathered close to watch.

Sara's left arm quit straining, her right hand starting to move, slowly at first, then with renewed vigor.

Vertical lines, horizontal lines, sloping angles, squares and rectangles, receding perspective, stair-steps, gables . . .

Phrekka gasped. "Is it—?"

"It *is*," Geoffrey whispered, allowing himself to breathe again. "It's where we lived."

"She doesn't want to go to Sausalito," Selma declared.

Geoffrey shook his head and squeezed his eyes shut, holding the edge of the bed to regain his balance. "She wants to go home."

Geoffrey leaned on the balcony railing and looked across the night-lit courtyard, gazing into the glowing ripples of the hotel swimming pool. A young boy and girl stood poised along the edge of the deep end, anticipation reflected in their shining faces, urging each other to forsake the kiddie pool to seek the exhilaration in diving in over their heads.

He heard Phrekka finish a call, then felt her hugging him from behind, her chin on his shoulder, the steadfast outrunner come to keep him on even keel. He squeezed her hands, feeling the waves of uncertainty smoothing to the glassy calm of tranquility.

"We're all set," she whispered.

Craving details, Geoffrey couldn't help but stir up a few ripples of concern. "She'll have nurses round-the-clock?"

"Coming by every two hours to monitor, and to handle feeding and personal hygiene. That's what the consultants recommend."

"How do we get her inside?"

"They're building a ramp and checking thresholds and clearances."

"When do we go?"

"The ambulance will meet us at Tulip Creek at nine, so we should have Sara in Laurel by lunchtime."

"What did Selma decide?"

"She needs to pack and organize, so I'm to call her tomorrow afternoon to find out when to send the limo. She's really excited about it, but still worried about becoming an intrusion, so I reserved her a hotel suite—with maid service and meals—and leased her a car with driver. She'll have privacy, visit when she wants, rest if she's not feeling well, and get out to see the sights whenever she takes a notion. I offered to get a list of dance clubs in case she wants to shake her booty."

"She'd probably *break* her booty," Geoffrey chuckled, but then he resumed the interrogation. "Will the gurney—?"

"It's all handled, Geoffrey," she told him sternly, urging him to relax. "We'll take care of problems when they arise."

"I'm sorry for obsessing," he said quietly, closing his eyes. "I just wish I felt more confident that I'm doing the right thing."

"What's causing your doubts?"

He lifted his arm to accept her as she slid around beside him. "I've screwed up so many things in my life, even with the best of intentions, but Sara's too important, her time left too precious."

"Just listen to your heart."

"I want more chances to prove that I remember . . . that I love her." He sighed, glancing away. "But it feels like I'm being selfish."

She stroked his hair, then lifted his face to gaze into his eyes. "Then I hope you'll always be so selfish with me, too."

He couldn't stall the smile she was coaxing from him, so he surrendered, then reached up and caressed her cheek. "I guess I *have* done a few things right."

"See?—now your life is perfect."

"Ha—not quite, Malibu chickie. I still need to accomplish a few things—like a real career, for example, and making sure my friendship with Bill doesn't fade again. Come to think of it, I still owe him a sleep-over."

"Ooo!—randy boys in sleeping bags passing around girlie magazines, up all night swapping lies about what it must be like to *do it* with a real woman!"

He snorted, secretly struck by how the past twenty-four hours had put to shame what he once considered a respectable teenage track record. "No, Phrekka, only spooky stories about monsters and chainsaw murderers. Boys never think about sex."

"Well, then girls don't, either—and I'm sticking to that story," she added, surprising him with a rather aggressive and intimate squeeze of his booty. "Now, regarding your career, you have a *scatches* exhibit to develop, a bigger job than you might realize."

"That's right," he said, lost in the possibilities for a moment. "The foundation will provide opportunities for me to help, too . . ."

They stood there quietly until he finally sighed, deciding, "Bringing her home is the right choice, at least so she can spend her remaining days where she'd lived the happiest part of her life."

"Grandmamá considered that *very* important—helping a loved one experience a *good death*. Geoffrey, I don't know what to believe, but maybe there really are Bodhisattvas waiting to help Sara pass into nirvana. Maybe she clung to life all these years because she thought her work was unfinished, and all she needs from you is the assurance of some simple gesture like holding her hand. Then she can reach out with the other to seek the glory she's always deserved."

He felt her trembling, so he wrapped her in his arms, anchored her firmly to his world so she could reach out safely with her mind and explore realms beyond mortal comprehension. He knew they might never understand the mysteries of life and beyond, but he believed with all his heart that what matters most *can* be comprehended, and touched, and embraced, just as two people who love each other can share this moment on a balcony in the steamy Mississippi night. Their confidence in the vivid reality of their enduring bond would urge them to question even obvious assumptions, exploring every possibility, accepting that not all truths will be revealed . . . and learning to cherish all that is good.

Soon after, he found himself snuggled with Phrekka in bed, surprised that he preferred not to rush into intimate exploration, realizing he could feel just as close to her if they simply floated like this, drawn along without effort or intent, subject only to the currents of time and the cycles of life.

"I like this," she whispered, "—you know, not relying on sex as the only way we share intimacy."

"Giving ourselves time to discover other ways."

"Like feeling safe while someone I love holds me—that's just as new for me as what we tried last night. Don't get me wrong—I'm looking forward to that getting even better and more intense—"

"Like that's possible!" he blurted, rolling his eyes with self-mockery.

"Just you wait 'til I get past my nervousness," she teased.

He gazed into her sparkling eyes, stroked her hair, then kissed her gently on the cheek. "Good night, Phrekka Churán. I do love you."

He held her while she drifted into a dreamworld of wonder and bliss, savoring the balance she had brought to his life, how the slightest touch as they lay together could feel just as wonderfully exhilarating as the most passionate love-making. He recalled his insecurity when she mentioned a trip home to pursue her many interests, but now he understood there's no reason to dread their times apart, for those would remind him to cherish their every moment together just as the deepest valley contrasts the majesty of a peak, as the darkest night spreads canvas on which the sun paints its glorious rise.

He needn't mourn having lost so many years with Sara because he'd been given one precious last chance to fill her with a lifetime of love, and he'd found Phrekka to help him paint exultation over the dark stains of tragedy.

Geoffrey had discovered faith after all, devout belief that whatever their future might bring, whatever mysteries lay beyond, he and Phrekka would persevere. Together they could overcome any challenge, and whenever they yearned for spiritual revelations, they would discover the most profound yet simple truths in each other's eyes.

Geoffrey watched Sara drawing furiously on her new sketch pad in the back of the ambulance as it wended its way toward Laurel. Phrekka brushed Sara's hair, carefully affixing it on each side with jeweled butterfly barrettes, cooing how pretty she looked for the big homecoming. A stocky male nurse monitored vital signs in silence, also fascinated by Sara's relentless sketching. As she flipped back and forth between drawings, adding detail here and background there, the top pages would rest across her hand, obscuring Geoffrey's view. He'd tried positioning the pad where she could see, but she always stopped until he returned it to her lap, just below her field of vision.

"They appear to be literal renderings," he commented to Phrekka. "I've seen at least two of Nurse Barlucci, one of me alone, one with you and me holding hands, and one of Pamela as a teenager—which is how she would have last seen her. They're not interpretations of childhood or innocence like her previous work."

"Yet they're stunning," Phrekka said reverently, "—so vivid, so full of life, more real even than a photograph—"

Sara flipped again, continuing her work.

"I think that was a blank page, starting a new one," Geoffrey said, "—near as I could see."

"How does she do that—know where to draw without looking?"

"Notice how her little finger keeps brushing the edge of the page. That must be how she orients her position, seeing it in her mind. How she knows which page she's on, I can't figure. I don't think she can count, so she must envision some kind of sequence only she can fathom."

"It's all so amazing," Phrekka breathed. "It doesn't matter if they're literal or interpretations, she's still infusing them with pure artistic power."

The ambulance stopped for a security officer to move the temporary barricade blocking Bruce Trail. They drove through and approached the converted foundation headquarters. "Stop here," Geoffrey instructed when they reached the driveway. "I want her to see the house."

The driver opened the back doors while Sara's nurse pronounced her ready to move; then together they lifted her out and lowered the platform of her gurney. Pamela and Dwayne, the big man carrying Andy-Geoff on his shoulders, stood to the side where Sara wouldn't see them yet, the little one's brows scrunched in curiosity while Pamela fidgeted nervously, biting her nails. She gasped at her first sight of Sara, gauzy memories suddenly transformed to harsh reality.

Geoffrey turned the gurney so Sara could see the house. She instantly stopped drawing, her eyes wide with unabashed joy swirling in their depths. Geoffrey stepped into her view, the house at his back, motioning for Phrekka to join him. Suddenly, Sara flipped to an earlier sketch and resumed drawing.

Geoffrey leaned down for a glimpse, telling everybody, "It's the one of me and Phrekka holding hands. She's adding the house in the background."

Phrekka ventured, "Maybe these images are messages, and now she wants to show us she knows we're here."

Sara flipped to another blank page. Geoffrey crouched to observe, narrating, "It looks like a watch—no, a clock, and a dresser, a bed table— It's her room!"

"She's worried," Pamela supplied. "She's afraid we're only stopping by, doesn't know yet that she's here to stay."

Geoffrey leaned in front of Sara, touched her hand, then offered her a smile of reassurance. He walked where she could see him as the attendants rolled the gurney up the drive, onto a ramp traversing the back porch, directly inside and into her bedroom. Geoffrey thanked the driver and nurse before they left, then turned the gurney to afford Sara a view of the woods through her window. She flipped to another page and started drawing the scene, adding her own legs at the bottom, proving awareness of her circumstances even if understanding eluded her.

Always the impatient soul, Andy-Geoff demanded, "Well, when can we tell her hi?"

"Let Mama go first, hon," Pamela suggested. She hesitated nervously, then took a deep breath and stepped into the room. Sara stopped drawing, the two women's eyes locked in ethereal embrace. Pamela's filled with tears, soon mirrored by a lone streak down each of her friend's jaundiced cheeks.

Sara flipped back to an earlier sketch, Geoffrey peeking under the pages to see, announcing, "It's the one of you, Pammy. She's making you older and, um, a bit heavier . . ." Now choked with emotion, he added, "And she's putting tears in your eyes."

"Me now," Andy-Geoff announced, hesitating for an instant, then rushing to his mother and eyeing Sara curiously.

Pamela lifted him up and hugged him, both turning their faces where Sara could see.

Sara stopped drawing, her breaths coming rapidly for a moment before settling back to their natural rhythm. Andy-Geoff squirmed free and moved closer while Geoffrey hugged Pamela, drying her tears with a tissue.

"She's drawin' *me*!" the little boy announced, peering between the pages where Sara had resumed drawing. "Me and you, Mawma!"

Geoffrey stepped over to peek, carefully pulling back the top pages for a better view. Sara continued without hesitation as if she urgently needed to complete this rendering of Pamela holding her little boy, a new image that must be committed to paper so she can comprehend such an important change in the life of her best friend. Dwayne joined them as they all gathered around to watch her add the final touches. She had drawn the precise moment when Pamela lifted Andy-Geoff, each glancing at the other before turning to face their artist, unspoken assurances swirling in their eyes, the purest essence of love captured in simple lines and subtle shades.

Then Sara turned the page and started another . . .

The sketch of a glassy pool surrounded by trees, cattails and reeds, a butterfly . . .

Geoffrey looked to Phrekka, Pamela giving words to their thoughts. "She wants to see the pond."

"Her favorite place," Geoffrey agreed.

A knock interrupted them, a young, dark-haired woman introducing herself as the nurse, here to check on Sara. She ushered the group out to the living room to afford her patient some privacy.

"How can we show her the pond?" Geoffrey asked, finding problems with all of his possible solutions.

"We could carry the gurney," Dwayne offered.

"There must be an easier way," Phrekka suggested, retrieving her phone and making a call. She complimented somebody on the excellent ramp, then explained their problem and listened, finally gushing her gratitude before disconnecting. "He's on his way out to set up a track like movie crews use to dolly cameras. He'll rig it so the gurney clamps right on, easy as taking a stroll with a carriage."

Geoffrey grabbed her in an exuberant hug, then braced himself for Pammy to join in, surprised to find her already being held tenderly by Dwayne, Andy-Geoff cradled in the crook of the big man's arm.

The nurse emerged, smiling reassurance. "She's fine—just fell asleep, in fact. I know you're all excited, but let her have some rest. I'll be back in two hours."

As soon as she'd left, Geoffrey declared, "We've missed lunch—let's order some pizza."

"Yeah!" Andy-Geoff seconded.

"You got some flyers?"

"At our house," the hungry boy answered, hopping down to grab Geoffrey's hand and lead him next door.

"I'll check on Mrs. Barlucci," Phrekka called after them, "—see what time to send the limo."

After collecting various pizza coupons and trying to convince his little namesake that anchovies are what grow behind unwashed ears, Geoffrey headed back to the main house to find Phrekka waiting for him on the porch.

"Selma changed her mind about coming," she said sadly. "Last night she asked her landlady to let you know she's not feeling well, that it's okay because she's already done all she can for Sara, and that it's up to you now."

Disappointed, he said, "Well, at least when she feels better, she can come visit."

Phrekka shook her head, her eyes glistening forlornly. "The landlady checked on her again this morning and discovered— Oh, Geoffrey—" she said, folding herself into his arms. "Mrs. Barlucci died in her sleep."

A glorious evening reigned over the countryside as Geoffrey, Phrekka, and Pamela sat arrayed in lawn chairs surrounding Sara, all gazing in wonder at the enchanted setting. The pond reflected damselfly ballets and breeze-stirred hula-dancing trees undulating to the chirp-buzzing tempo of garrulous birds and amorous crickets, all swirled in the fragrances of flowers and pine pitch and rotting logs, a fairy-tale realm shimmering with vivid colors and the quiet exuberance of all life.

Geoffrey studied the detail: a delicate butterfly flitting in the hazy mist, the caterpillar grazing a curled leaf, two fuzzy bumblebees making their wildflower rounds, cattails and reeds hosting a doodlebug gathering, the tiniest birds' nest swaying in the branches . . .

"We should put a birdhouse out," Phrekka suggested, her soft voice echoing across the water and stirring the tiny yellow blossoms sprouting around the shoreline.

Geoffrey just smiled, looking forward to tackling a new project, the shelter he would build especially for Phrekka's winged friends.

Sara resumed sketching, Geoffrey peeking at her new, nearly filled pad, a collection capturing images from her life: scenes around town, people she's known, the friends and family she loves gathered around her to laugh and eat pizza while little Andy-Geoff eyes an anchovy with considerable suspicion. Sara paused, then turned to a blank page and started drawing a young teenage boy with silky blond hair: Geoffrey— No, the subject had to be Zachary, skinny and vulnerable, dressed in threadbare clothes, his eyes brimming with tears of contrition. Geoffrey would never know if she'd actually witnessed Zachary's realization of shame for hurting her, now a literal depiction captured for all time, or if she'd interpreted what she knew would be in his heart. Whatever the truth, this sketch proved she'd forgiven him, maybe even that she wanted to tell him this in her own limited way.

Geoffrey absently touched his pants pocket, feeling the small lump of two flawed marbles, and he recalled his rage as Zachary revealed the horrifying assault. Geoffrey had lashed out, beating his own father in blind retribution, thus breaking his own vow never to hurt another. Geoffrey *Calhoun*, Ernest's son after all . . .

He peeked under the top pages to watch Sara adding highlights to Zachary's hair, the first hint of where a mustache might someday grow, a small scar on his cheek, and Geoffrey felt ashamed for attacking the fragile, crippled man so wracked by guilt that he had refused to defend himself. Geoffrey's fury had driven him to make a terrible mistake, as so many people do in myriad ways, their greatest tragedies the festering wounds of squandered opportunities to learn, to make amends, to forgive.

The second-shift nurse appeared in the clearing, joining them long enough to check Sara's condition, a brief interruption to her patient's sketching. Satisfied, she disappeared back up the path just as Dwayne lumbered into sight, Andy-Geoff riding astride his shoulders, alerting everybody that dinner had arrived.

"You all go ahead," Geoffrey said. "Sara and I will stay here a bit longer, then I'll bring her up."

The big guy set Andy-Geoff down long enough to light several mosquito coils arrayed strategically around the clearing. Pamela stroked Sara's hair and kissed her cheek, then led her ersatz family toward the house.

Geoffrey whispered to Phrekka, "I've not been alone with her yet."

She hugged him, assuring, "She'll like that." She paused to adjust Sara's butterfly barrettes and kiss her forehead before heading up the path.

Geoffrey stood beside Sara and looked across the pond, the last shimmering rays of golden-orange sun refracting through the trees and melting the clouds, those billowing violet blooms dripping with the nectar of liquid sky. "It worked, Sara," he whispered, knowing she would never understand his words but hoping she could feel the rapture that filled his heart. "You said I'd be big someday, and that you wanted your *scatches* to remind me how much you loved me. After all these years, thousands of miles away, at a time when I needed you most . . . it worked. You made me remember, and you helped save me from myself." He touched her hair, gazed across the pond, rubbed his eyes, and whispered, "It worked, Sara."

The purple bruise of evening sky descended across the horizon, dissolving the ephemeral hues of iridescent cobalt that haloed the tree-line, the clearing coming alive with the fairy-village display of flickering yellow lights winking reminders through a gauze of rising mist. Sara stopped drawing, allowing the pad to close, the pencil to lie on the gurney beside her. She waved her hand tentatively, then rested it gently on her lap. He squeezed her shoulder, standing close to share the resplendent wonder of nature's magic revealed.

Geoffrey closed his eyes for a moment, and he breathed deeply, tasting the flavors of pecan ice cream and fresh-sliced watermelon; and he felt the sensations of soft cloth gently brushing his face and of warm sand squishing between his toes; and he could hear the melodies of songbirds rising in syncopation with percussing crickets and cicadas, counterpoint to the basso of bullfrogs and the cymbal-brush of snakes in the tall grass; and he floated, a wisp of all he had ever known, pulled toward the sea of flickering lights, holding tightly to his true mother, tethered to the life she had given him, buoyed by the love she had shown, filled with the ecstasy he would devote his lifetime to sharing with Phrekka.

He looked across the water, a place in the world, a point in time, the confluence of his past and future. He stroked Sara's hair, then gazed into her unmoving eyes. "You gave me two gifts, Sara," he told her quietly. "You fought to keep me, and you helped me grow up, and I'm proud of who I am because of what you gave me. Then at a time when I'd forgotten, and I didn't know how to help myself, you came back to me again with another gift, a reminder of who I am, and the encouragement I needed to pursue my dream. Now I'm trying to give you something back. Bringing you home, showing you the pond again . . . these are what I can do for you, Mom, to remind *you* that I—that I—" His voice cracked, so he swallowed hard, rubbed his eyes, and tried to explain. "Phrekka thinks you need me to help you now—to make it so you—so you can . . ."

He heard a voice whispering to him, rising and falling in familiar melody, embracing him even as distant stars began to dust sparkles across the velvet night sky.

Sara lifted her hand and waved it tentatively. He curled his fingers around hers, and for the first time, he felt her squeezing back, holding tightly as she reached out with her heart and soul . . .

Sara's song wafted among the trees, her voice rising from the glassy water, a lullaby dancing among the lightning bugs in the warm air, and she wished him a life filled with the kind of love they had always shared, the memories he would always cherish.

He wiped his eyes, leaned close, held his mother tenderly, and kissed her cheek.

She curled her fingers tighter around his.

He gazed into her eyes . . . and saw them move! She glanced toward the pond and the trees and the sky, then finally gazed back at her son. In the depths of her eyes, he saw gratitude for the last gift he would give her in this lifetime, and he felt her serenity, her acceptance of all that may come.

She closed her eyes and squeezed his hand . . .

And the world paused.

Geoffrey gathered her close to his heart.

And Sara sighed with peace and tranquility one last time as she stopped breathing.

And Geoffrey held her even as she let go, then wept as the swirling lightning bugs bid silent good-bye to the enchanted girl who had come home to die in the arms of her beloved little boy.

CHAPTER 25

Phrekka helped Geoffrey pack Sara's sketches for shipment to the gallery in Sausalito, an important transition they preferred to share with each other rather than trusting anonymous professionals.

She paused to gaze around the room, moved by the scores of new drawings, all juxtaposing in her mind with visions from the past few days: the governor and mayor paying tribute to Laurel's lost daughter at Mason Memorial's amphitheatre, satellite trucks lining the roadways, thousands bringing flowers and cards and *We Love You, Sara* banners; the private funeral-home service where Zachary hobbled painstakingly down the aisle to stand beside Geoffrey at Sara's coffin, the father faltering, his son reaching out to support him; the motorcade cortège wending through streets lined with everyday people pausing to pay their respects, old men holding hats to their breasts, children waving pink ribbons; Andy-Geoff beside the grave, standing solemnly between his mom and Dwayne, stepping forward to place a child-sized cluster of tiny yellow blossoms on the Drousseau headstone; Geoffrey separated from Phrekka when reporters and cameras swarmed around him, the panic in his eyes as he searched the crowd, the determination in his face as he pushed his way through to take her hand . . .

Geoffrey laid another sketch on the table, pausing to study it. "Each one seems to have its own power," he breathed, tilting it up to show Phrekka one of his favorites: the pre-school version of himself crouched frog-like to study a regal old toad, nose-to-nose.

Smiling to herself, she carried more packing materials to her work table. "Ah, yes . . . the power I've tried way too hard to explain. At least it made me curious about you."

He picked up the pad of Sara's final sketches, turned it over in his hands, and touched it reverently. "You're trying to unravel a mystery that you already understand better than anybody I've ever met."

"But the more I figure out, the less I seem to know."

He smiled at that, flipping through the pages, pausing to gaze in wonder at each. "So what did Sara teach you?"

"You're the one who taught me—that it doesn't matter what the artist puts into her work, but rather what the audience takes out."

He looked up, and she could see that he liked that very much. Then, with a mischievous twinkle in his eye, he added, "But the artist must put in something that inspires people to find more."

"The artist's interpretation," she said, enjoying the repartee, back where she started again.

He shrugged, gesturing at the pad. "I expect to have very intense reactions from these, too, even though they're what I call Sara's *literal period.* Before the accident, with the everyday world within her grasp, she tried to see beyond people's façades, to show the innocent child in each person's heart; then when the real world she'd always known was taken from her, she reached beyond her own tragic circumstance even though all she could show us was that she understood we'd come back for her, her way of touching us one last time for closure, what she needed before she could let go . . ." He rubbed his eyes, took a deep breath, and turned the page. He gasped, uttering, "What—?"

"What? What is it?" she demanded, her hands busy holding a box together as she taped its corners.

"It must be her last sketch—I wasn't watching just before she closed the pad. It's the pond, but she's added a shimmering image of herself, young and healthy again, her face reflecting from within the water, her hand extended."

Phrekka's breath caught. "She knew . . ." she whispered.

"Oh wow," he breathed. "I just noticed; there's faces, but you have to look carefully. They're blended into the trees, in the clouds. Oh! Here's Alain and Rachel, and Ernest, and—oh, man—" He shook his head, quietly adding, "And Selma Barlucci."

"People she loved who've passed on before her."

"Her final sketch was interpretive after all," he sighed.

"You said yourself that those are literal, Geoffrey. Maybe she really did see those people—coming to show her the way." Then quieter, she added, "Maybe they're her Bodhisattvas."

They gazed into each other's eyes, the mysteries of life and death swirling around the room to pause before each of the images Sara had captured, answers beyond mortal grasp, a world where anything is possible. "I don't recognize all the faces," he said, "but they must be people who were important to her."

"And showing you what she understood in her last moments is now her greatest work of art." She moved the box aside, crossing to put her arms around him and admire the one piece infused with more power than any she'd ever seen.

"See the faces?" he whispered, pointing out Alain and Rachel, then Ernest, Selma, a young girl beside a heavyset man, an old woman with Asian eyes—

Phrekka gasped, drawn to the image she'd held close to her heart for so many years. "It's Grandmamá," she whispered.

"Huh? Are you sure?"

She nodded, feeling her grandmother's gentle caress, inhaling the potpourri of rose petals and gardenia, the room filled with the lilting strains of her favorite Korean song.

"But how—? Sara never met her, never saw a photo—"

"Grandmamá's been watching over me, and she knows Sara is important to both of us, so she revealed herself . . ." Phrekka felt herself swept into the loving embrace that spanned time and space, the substance of living memories, of devotion made real.

"Are you okay?" he asked, putting his arms around her.

She nodded, melting into him as he held her close. She reached out and pointed toward the patch of tiny blossoms sketched along the shoreline, another face come to greet Sara, another soul watching over Phrekka and Geoffrey for all time, a handsome young man with glistening eyes . . .

And she whispered, "Take good care of Sara for us . . ."

And Phrekka's father promised he would.

CHAPTER 26

Phrekka had never felt more nervous about a social event, mired in logistics and details, yet exhilarated by the anticipation of opening their big *Scatches Exhibit*, first with an afternoon media preview, then followed by an evening black-tie benefit for Sara's foundation.

"Your young man is waiting for you at the gallery," Miss Cilla reminded her. "Shall I alert him you intend to continue fussing with your hair for the rest of the day?"

The matronly Korean housekeeper reflected in the dressing-room mirror, a teasing twinkle in the woman's eyes. Words failing her, Phrekka stood, then hurried to Miss Cilla, embracing her with a kiss on the cheek that left Grandmamá's faithful servant and friend standing there too flustered to respond while Phrekka made her escape.

Zipping down the long winding drive on her golf cart, she noticed the mid-morning sun rising above the Bay Bridge, perfect weather for Geoffrey's outdoor press conference in front of the gallery. As she eased in through the back way, the image of Charles startled her, her mentor having arrived uncustomarily early, chatting with Geoffrey.

"Excuse me, Miss Churán," called the caterer, wanting to introduce himself at the precise moment she urgently needed to join Geoffrey's conversation, when she wanted to make sure the two men impressed each other favorably. She did owe this gentleman whose company had donated a very expensive service in support of the benefit, so she steered him toward the serving table closest to Geoffrey so she could pretend admiring the ice-sculpture centerpiece while eavesdropping.

"When I lost my partner and best friend," Charles told him in that taking-care-of-business tone he always used at the juncture of important decisions, "I felt a certain obligation to ensure his daughter's well-being, but I've come to consider *her* my friend, too—"

"I'm so glad you feel that way," Geoffrey interrupted him, his voice ringing with confidence, not the least intimidated by the powerful man standing before him. "I mean, it's obvious she thinks the world of you."

"Oh, um, well—" Charles stammered, disarmed by Geoffrey's frankness, but clearly pleased.

Phrekka had to suppress a smile, nodding to the caterer in rapt approval as he proudly recited a litany of hors d'oeuvres.

"Now that she's nearly twenty-one," Geoffrey pressed on, "I sure hope you don't expect that to change."

"Oh no, of course not. Needless to say, I still feel very protective of her—"

"Good, then if I ever fail to honor her with the respect she deserves, she'll have you to kick my butt all the way back to Coon Rapids."

"I *would*, too," Charles said, chuckling, and Phrekka could hear the acceptance and approval in his voice.

Unable to resist any longer, she just had to turn and look their way, to see the image of her men standing beside each other, Charles's smile beaming with reassurance, his arm around the shoulders of a new friend, Geoffrey glancing at Phrekka and winking mischievously.

"Miss Churán?" someone called. "Your guests have arrived."

Phrekka excused herself from the caterer, winked back at Geoffrey, and turned in time to see two women being led her way.

Geoffrey gasped, his face lighting up.

"Ladies," Phrekka introduced, "this is my friend Charles, who's always been more like a father to me."

Charles gulped, obviously thrilled to hear her use those words she'd always thought might be too awkward to voice. He reached to grasp their visitors' hands as Geoffrey made the introductions.

"This is Mrs. Marloney—"

"Oh!" she gushed, "just call me Opaline."

Charles bowed gallantly.

"And this is my mother, Marjorie Calhoun."

"Indeed, madam, I am honored," Charles greeted her.

"The pleasure is mine," she replied, delighted by all the cordiality.

"You can call her Marjorie," Geoffrey continued, "but I'm the one who gets to call her *Mom*."

Mrs. Calhoun's eyes glistened with pride, and only then did Phrekka realize how uneasy all the revelations about Geoffrey's life must have made her, how left out and unsure of her role she must have felt . . . how much Geoffrey understood this and wanted her to know she would always hold a very special place in his heart.

Without warning, Geoffrey hugged his mother, then Mrs. Marloney, then his mother again, then with a what-the-heck grin he hugged Phrekka. "So what's Bill been up to?" he asked Mrs. Marloney, clearly anxious for news.

She grinned. "Why, parking the car."

"There's TV trucks blocking the streets," Bill blurted as he hurried toward them, a package under his arm, obviously enjoying all the excitement. The young men stared at each other as if deciding whether or not this scene could possibly be real; then they suddenly grabbed each other's hands for a vigorous shake that somehow turned into a back-slapping embrace.

"So did you bring me a present, or what?" Geoffrey asked, his voice cracking, eyes glistening . . . and Phrekka knew she'd succeeded in her intent with this surprise reunion.

"Phrekka said you might need this," he answered, offering the plain-wrapped package, barely suppressing a grin.

Geoffrey tore it open and found himself gazing upon the ultimate step-by-step guide for building any kind of birdhouse a handyman could want. He snorted, then warned, "I'm gonna need help."

"I figured as much," Bill sparred, rolling his eyes. "I'll be in town a few days."

"So what—how—?" Overwhelmed, Geoffrey seemed to be struggling with too many thoughts at once. "Where are you—?"

Phrekka interrupted. "The *women* and I," she started, all three now on the verge of giggling, "have reserved suites in the city for the next two nights, planning to see the sights tomorrow, followed by a girls' night out."

Mrs. Marloney added, "She's promised to show us how to shake our booties."

"And you're supposed to have a fancy place up on the hill where I can stay," Bill informed Geoffrey.

"Yeah, Phrekka's house—"

"*Boys only* through tomorrow night," Phrekka corrected. "The staff is off for two days, and Miss Cilla's coming with us girls. It seems she knows several good places for booty shaking."

Bill spread his hands, eyeing Geoffrey sheepishly. "Somehow, Phrekka found out you owe me a sleep-over."

"There he is!" shouted the uncustomarily shirt-and-tied version of Andy-Geoff as he virtually leapt into Geoffrey's arms, Pamela and Dwayne rushing too late to catch their flash of dressed-up little boy.

Another round of introductions ensued; then Pamela looked around at the *Scatches Exhibit* in awe, breathing, "This is incredible, the way you've arranged it all."

"He's worked on it all week," Phrekka explained, "and now it takes my breath away."

"Are you gonna give us a tour?" Pamela asked Geoffrey.

He shook his head, allowing a hint of smile. "No, I want Sara to speak without me adding extraneous words. I just helped give her the chance is all."

Phrekka watched their faces while they wandered among the displays, each person moved in different ways as they stood before the various pieces, and she knew Geoffrey had succeeded in his intent, the way he placed some sketches in sequence of time, grouping others by subject or mood or setting, positioning bold eye-catchers to draw attention toward smaller and simpler depictions, leading the visitors through a mélange of alternating curiosity and provocation, sadness and delight.

"You decided to study the literal sketches some more," she heard Pamela whisper to him, "before putting them on display."

He nodded, whispering back, "And the one of me standing in the pond is hanging over my desk. That one's only for family and friends . . . and for me."

She smiled and hugged him, then put her hands to her mouth, catching her breath, her eyes shining with love as they all turned to see Andy-Geoff stop tugging at his shirt-collar and tie long enough to stare in rapt attention at a depiction of his own mother, the way she looked at his age, a pretty little girl adorned in a frilly dress . . . pulling awkwardly at her stiff collar.

Phrekka felt herself floating, the emotions swirling around and through her, and suddenly Charles appeared beside her, and she folded herself into his arms.

"All I've ever wanted for you," he whispered, "is that you find your own happiness."

"I know Charles, and I love you for that."

He gestured toward where Geoffrey now stood holding Andy-Geoff in his arms. "I hoped someday you'd bring me a nice young man to train—it's a tough job, you know, looking out for you—but I'm convinced you've found a natural."

"You showed me what to look for," she whispered, feeling him holding her tighter than ever before.

"It's time!" the PR guy announced. "They're set up, press conference to start in five minutes, let's go!"

How will I know I'm in love, Grandmamá? she heard the little girl inside herself ask as the woman she'd become followed Geoffrey out to be greeted by throngs of well-wishers, reporters, crews and cameras.

Geoffrey stepped onto the dais, so handsome in his suit, his silky blond hair shimmering in the blazing light. He gestured for her to stand beside him, but she shook her head, and he seemed to understand that she wanted this moment to be for Sara.

It's like the power of art, sweet Phrekka, Grandmamá answered.

". . . Foundation will give children everywhere the chance to share the power of art . . ." she heard Geoffrey telling the world, watching him look across the faces swirling in the rising bay mist. "And to honor Sara, and her vision that allowed her to see into people's hearts . . ."

You see, child, some who love you will be like mirrors, reflecting back whatever you give them, afraid to risk venturing beyond the safety of their looking-glass worlds . . .

"We'll never decipher everything Sara tried to show us, nor could she predict everything we'll find within ourselves . . ."

Others will be like the obsidian, dark and mysterious, absorbing your light while sharing none of their own . . .

"... I used to be in graphic arts, but I couldn't keep depicting what others wanted to show, regardless of truth. What Sara has taught me, and can teach us all, is that true art reflects belief—and Sara believed all people possess something wonderful, and she believed this so much that she wanted us all to have a chance to see. Maybe you don't want Sara's art to change your life, but I know it can if you'll let it, just like she showed me how to discover a kind of love I never dreamed possible . . ."

Your true love will be like a prism, the most special one who shares the light of the world with you, in ways more beautiful that you can possibly dream . . .

Phrekka looked up to see Geoffrey gazing lovingly toward her, and at that moment the sun touched his face, its refractions in the rising mist casting a rainbow across the glorious sky.

CHAPTER 27

"Is this for me?" Sara asked, surprised and smiling.

"Uh huh," answered the little boy. "It's a present."

She opened the carefully wrapped box and found a necklace of candy hearts, and her breath caught, words failing her for a moment.

"You like it, Sara?"

She nodded, her eyes glistening. "Oh, Geoffrey, thank you. I like it very much." She carefully tied it around her neck and straightened the hearts until it met his approval; then she pulled him into a hug. "What's this for?—it's not my birthday."

"Just 'cause."

"Just 'cause you love me?"

"Uh huh."

"Oh, Geoffrey, you're going to grow up and make some young woman very happy someday."

"Nuh-uh."

"Oh yes you will. You'll fall in love with her so much that you'll even want to get married."

"Nuh-uh, I'm gonna get married to you, Sara."

"No, Geoffrey, there's a special little girl out there somewhere right now who'll make you fall in love with her."

He considered this for a moment, then said, "But I'd still love you, too."

"Of course you would—just like I'll always love you."

Geoffrey combed his hair until his scalp hurt, checking his watch for the fifteenth time in the last five minutes. Finally, the phone rang.

"We're about to wrap up," came Phrekka's good news. "I'll meet you at Ghirardelli Square in thirty minutes."

"I'll be the handsome guy with blond hair."

"The silly one," she countered.

Heavy traffic seemed to conspire against him as he wended his way to the Golden Gate Bridge and crossed, noting the late-afternoon sun searing the surface of the sea, the timing never more perfect. Entering the city, he circled eastward until he found a good place to park, carefully gathering two soft seating pads, a small box, and a large, flat package wrapped in plain brown paper. He hurried to the plaza just in time to spot Phrekka walking up, her face glowing with surprise and curiosity.

She hugged him thoroughly, then shifted her satchel so she could carry the cushions. "The annual report is wrapped up, so no more long days taking me away—at least for a while. You've been such a sweetheart."

"That's okay; I've been keeping busy," he said mischievously. "Let's go before it gets too late."

They walked down by the waterfront, working their way westward until they reached the spot where they'd sat among the rocks to admire the view during their first official date. He arranged the seat cushions and guided her into a comfortable spot, carefully setting the box and package to the side. They tentatively held hands, both giggling at their simultaneous sighs of relief, as if one simple touch could prove they'd both found where they belonged.

The sun hung low in the swirling-misted sky, weeping brilliant hues in amber and orange, the great bridge glowing with a corona that painted its towers blood red. At that moment, the sun dipped just below the roadway and, splayed through wisps of distant clouds, fanned out into a flaming peacock's tail that filled the sky and reflected across the strait, a kaleidoscope of violets and reds and yellows all washed in a gauze of translucent, shimmering orange and gold, its radiance absorbing all trace of azure from the waters as it danced forward and licked, like the lapping waves, at the rocks before them.

"I was wrong about the rocks," he said.

"You mean when I said you should remove them if this was a computer image?"

"Yeah, I argued that we needed them there to make us safe, to keep us from being pulled to the edge of the world."

"You're not afraid of being carried off into the light anymore," she breathed, not a question, but rather an intimate understanding only the two of them could share.

"Not with you."

She squeezed his hand, then rested her head on his shoulder, her cinnamon tresses kissing his cheek. "We don't need the rocks," she whispered.

They watched a lone sailing yacht disappear into the brilliance, slowly emerging scrubbed and renewed from the other side.

"I've started drawing again," he said.

She turned and looked at him, her delight shining brighter than the sky. "I've looked forward to this," she said knowingly.

"That's how I figured out the rocks didn't work."

She smiled, nodding sagely. "Imagine how much more you'll figure out."

"I learned something else, too, Phrekka, and it's that I—um, well—what I mean is—" He closed his eyes, huffed his frustration, then looked back in time to catch her thoroughly enjoying the fluster of his overwhelming feelings.

"Geoffrey, I've been trying to figure out how to ask *you*, but now *you* have to say the words first," she teased.

"Well, okay, but *don't answer yet.* I wanna know if you'll, um—if you'll marry me."

"When do I get to answer?" she asked, her eyes sparkling.

"Not 'til you see your presents." He carefully opened the small box, explaining, "I tried to buy a ring, but none seemed right, so for now I decided to start with this."

She gasped, her eyes welling with tears as he removed a delicate necklace of tiny hearts and placed it around her neck. "It's stunning—oh, I love it," she whispered.

He carefully unwrapped the paper to reveal a framed, full-color sketch. "I drew this—" His voice cracked, so he whispered, "I drew this for you, Phrekka."

Together they gazed at his heartfelt expression of love, and of truth, and of what he believed more than anything else in the world.

It depicted the scene they'd come there to witness: the great bridge, the sun splayed across the sky, the shimmering water reflecting to the edge of the world . . . all rendered now in delicate shades of pastel, a medium he'd never before attempted.

He noticed a sparkling tear crawling down Phrekka's cheek as she studied the images he'd drawn in the sky, for there floating beyond the horizon stood a little blue-eyed, blond-haired boy; and the most beautiful little girl in the world, with hazel eyes and long cinnamon hair; both given the appearance of being nude except for her delicate necklace of tiny candy hearts; the bridge's spans drawn to protect their vernal modesty, though neither seemed embarrassed to share this most natural and pristine of magical moments.

Phrekka wiped the tear from her cheek and turned to gaze at Geoffrey, whispering, "Yes," though words could never convey what he saw in her eyes.

For that's what he'd tried to *scatch*, because the little boy gazed not out toward the artist, nor the audience, nor anybody who could possibly matter more.

He was looking at the little girl . . .

And the girl looked back.

The Fresh Ink Group

Publishing
Memberships
Share & Read Free Stories, Essays, Articles
Free-Story Newsletter
Writing Contests

Books
E-books
Amazon Bookstore

Authors
Editors
Artists
Professionals
Publishing Services
Publisher Resources

Members' Websites
Members' Blogs
Social Media

www.FreshInkGroup.com

Email: info@FreshInkGroup.com

Twitter: @FreshInkGroup

Google+: Fresh Ink Group

Facebook.com/FreshInkGroup

LinkedIn: Fresh Ink Group

About.me/FreshInkGroup

www.ingramcontent.com/pod-product-compliance
Lightning Source LLC
LaVergne TN
LVHW091027080826
845145LV00002B/381
* 9 7 8 1 9 3 6 4 4 2 0 3 4 *